DARK ATHENA

A Novel

Arthur Houghton

ISBN: 1535171774
ISBN 13: 9781535171779
Library of Congress Control Number: 2016911189
Createspace Independent Publishing Platform
North Charleston, South Carolina

Front cover design by Oliver Hoover

For Peggy
who started it all,
and for Andrew and Laura

with thanks to all those
who have helped me make this story what it is

PREFACE

Dark Athena began as a week-long fictional essay, one in which I had intended to show, in a humorous way, some of the complexities facing those who deal in the art market. At the end of the week, I found that it needed a little more, some small embellishments, and that another week would allow me to fix it. Two weeks went to three, then four, and I found that the stream of writing had begun to carry me along with it, not the reverse. By the end of three months, I found myself clutching a fully developed (if not wonderfully written) book-length story about villainy in the museum world, the looting of antiquities, art fakery, and desperate escapes. It needed much attention, and so I passed it through my closest family, then through in-laws, close friends, occasional acquaintances—anyone who I thought might helpfully comment, and finally through two fine editors, Susan Heath and Benee Knauer, each of whom taught me what it meant to describe persons and places, to write dialogue, and to build and maintain an interesting narrative.

Many friends have seen and commented on *Dark Athena*. These include Richard Aherne; Frank Anderson; Chris Dewey; my brother, Peter Gates; David Hendin; Sherry Houghton; Thomas Hoving; Frank Kovacs; Lindsay Johnson; Derek Leebaert; Henry Miller-Jones; Geraldine Norman; Harry Parker; Selwa "Lucky"

Roosevelt; Paul Ruimerman; Gary Vikan; Dimitri Villard; and Terry Weiser. Melik Kaylan and Bill Waldman provided helpful suggestions about content and structure.

Finally, I wish to give special recognition, for their important comments on the narrative and for many other improvements, to my wonderful daughter-in-law, Laura McClure; to Carol J. Russo; to two friends of many years, Patricia Beard and Diana Sargent; and to Mary Lannin for her extraordinary editorial eye and generosity of spirit. All have my heartfelt thanks.

Arthur Houghton
August 2016

THE EXHUMING

It's something to die for, he thought. Nothing had ever been like this one.

Long after the moon had gone below the horizon and the early morning stars painted the sky above the Serra ridge, Cosimo Galante assessed the dark shape at the bottom of the scarred earth and glanced again at the distant glow in the eastern sky. His voice cut across the night to the two men who had backed the rig close by the excavation.

"*Tiralu fora! Annacamuni!* Get it out—move!"

One of the men lowered the boom lift and angled the heavy rubber sling toward the pit. Deep inside, another wrapped it around the shoulders of the headless figure. The sling was tightened, the winch engaged.

Galante watched as the figure rose, twisting slowly in the harness, dark soil falling from its surface as it was placed on the truck bed and covered. The man in the trench reached downward, brushed aside the earth with his hands, and with a nod hoisted the great marble head upward, onto the lip. It tilted, then turned, in his hands, white crystals glittering faintly in the predawn light. A woman's face appeared, the eyes open, a nose that fell straight from the brow, a mouth with full lips turned slightly upward at the edges.

Galante took the head and cradled it in his arms as the men came up beside him. The one in the trench, called Sergio, the last, approached.

"*È qualcosa!* It's something, isn't it, Cosimo?" he said.

"*Qualcosa.*"

Sergio shot a glance at the excavation and then turned. "You know, the Carabinieri would chase us to hell if they found out."

Galante fixed his dark eyes on the speaker. "And how would they do that, Sergio?"

"Well, they wouldn't. But…"

"But what?"

"Nothing. But this one is important, not like the other stuff. You'll do well with it, Cosimo. We should all do well with it."

Galante put down the head. "What are you saying?"

Sergio shifted his feet and looked down and then back again.

"I'm saying I should have a little more for this one."

"More?" It came out as a laugh. "You agreed before you came here what you'd get. And now you want more."

"Something. Twice. Not that much."

"And if there's no more for you?"

"Cosimo, there's a big risk here. I don't want trouble."

A man moved slightly in the background.

"What am I going to do with you, Sergio? You talk about the Carabinieri then say you want more."

"Just twice. That's not so much, is it Cosimo? Not for this."

Galante was silent for a moment and then nodded, but not at Sergio.

It was quick. A hand was held over Sergio's mouth, pulling his head backward. A blade bit deep into the ribcage, once, then twice more. The body spasmed as the life left it. In a short moment it was done. Galante stepped forward, rolling the corpse over the edge of the trench, into the deepest part of the pit where the statue had been. Dirt was kicked over the body, spades bit into the earth, and the excavation was filled.

Galante picked up the head again. The smell of fresh-turned soil entered his nostrils and a flood of images came to him of other things he had taken in the dark of night from the rich earth of the ancient city that lay beneath his feet.

But none like this. Nothing ever like this. This one is something to die for.

CHAPTER ONE

"So, Jason, what's the problem?" It was pure Kate, direct and insistent.

Jason Connor had eased the Black Shadow out of his garage in the early December morning, kicked the pedal, coasted quietly down West Channel, and then throttled up when he turned onto the coast highway. Working around the early northbound traffic with the drumming of the cycle's engine in his ears, he passed through Malibu township, then accelerated for the short run up along the shore, and turned into Chaparral Canyon and the Gabriel Museum of Art.

He waved to the gate guard, drove up into the museum's lower garage, and killed the engine. He went to a side entry, swiped his identification card across the security lock, pushed open the door, and walked across the ground-floor portico to a door that said simply "Antiquities." His own domain, his small kingdom, where just a stir of air would bring with it the complex scents of books and binders, ancient textiles, and the earth that still remained in the fissures of ancient objects, aromas mixing and competing just below the threshold of consciousness.

Around him, the museum was coming awake. Early staff arrived, first a trickle but then in groups of twos and threes. Office lights were turned on, and the windows and doors that led to the back gardens were unlocked and opened. The footfalls of the day guards echoed in the corridors as they made their first sweep of the public rooms. Voices murmured, the muffled *thunk-thunk* of circuit breakers resonated as the galleries were illuminated. Connecting doors were pushed back onto their stops and locked into place. Elevators began to hum. There was a squeak of small wheels on marble tiles, the noise of a small cart being rolled along the museum portico. And at exactly ten o'clock, the building's great bronze doors would open to the outside world and the first visitors would begin to flood in, moving around the covered portico into the high, light-filled first-floor exhibits of ancient art, ascending the stairs to the upper floors to view the museum's other collections, adding their voices to the receding echoes of the museum staff.

The ringing phone broke into his thoughts.

It's Kate. Kate Emerson. And it's Monday. Her turn.

"Roosevelt." She had picked presidents this time. His response was immediate.

"Taft."

"Truman."

They had slipped into the game months earlier at a reception that neither wanted to attend and that both were chafing to leave. He had come up to her, raised his glass and said "Knightsbridge, cabernet." He was teasing—his glass held chardonnay—but this time, instead of simply smiling, she shot back. "Ehlers, Sauvignon Blanc." It had taken a moment for him to get it. She had taken the vineyard name from the last letter of the one he'd mentioned.

"Sanford. Chardonnay," he replied.

"Domaine Drouhin. Oregon. Pinot noir."

He stood speechless, and she gave him a sly smile and turned to talk to someone else.

They had gone on from there to movies, then books, then authors and places, every Monday unless one of them was traveling.

"Truman," he repeated.

"Nixon. Gotcha." There were no other N presidents.

"OK, Kate, enough. You did that to me last week too."

She laughed.

He looked at his watch. "And you're here for the same reason I am." It was not a question.

"Of course. The boss." The boss was the museum's director, Martin Pryce. They were to see him in an hour.

"So, what do you think of it?" She didn't need to explain. *It* was the great statue that stood in the barricaded gallery off the museum's inner courtyard. *It* was the reason Pryce wanted to talk to them. Andrew Gabriel was coming that morning, and the director wanted no surprises.

"I just don't know what to think. I've told you that."

"So, what's the problem?"

"You know what the problem is. *It*"—he emphasized the word— "it's like a damned lightning bolt from a clear sky. Where the hell did it really come from?"

The sudden appearance of such an immense and extraordinary object, with almost no one knowing about it, had worried him since its arrival at the museum three weeks earlier. Almost no one? No collector, no dealer. No living scholar. He had first seen it when it had been lifted from its shipping crate in the conservation lab. The figure of the goddess Athena. But unlike any he had ever seen, with a white, crystalline marble head and hands, and a body so dark that it seemed to absorb the light. *Dark Athena*, he'd said to himself the moment he saw it, and the name had stuck.

"But what can you do?"

3

"I can try to get Martin to slow down. I need more time for the background check."

"Good luck with that. I hope he gives it to you. But Martin runs pretty fast." She paused for a moment. "But, Jason, it's good. It's real. I can tell you that myself. And you want it in the museum, don't you? Martin does. And Andrew will certainly want it."

For Andrew Gabriel, Jason knew, the museum was a lifetime dream. He had designed it, given it his most prized works of art, endowed it, and continued to provide for its financial well-being. He chaired the museum's board and headed the collections committee. He had the final decision on every purchase the museum made. He was aging, frailer, not quite as quick as he had been only a few years before, but he still ran Gabriel Assets and the constellation of transportation, financial, and power companies it controlled—with an iron hand.

"Yes, Kate, I'd really like to see it here. Who wouldn't?"

CHAPTER TWO

Across the courtyard, Martin Pryce brushed a hair from his lapel and regarded himself in his washroom mirror. The man who stared back at him was, at fifty-three, still young looking, with dark-brown hair combed back over his head, steel-gray eyes behind wire-rimmed glasses. He had carefully chosen a dark suit and a floral-pattern necktie for the day and event.

He combed his hair for the second time that morning, knotted his tie for the third, and straightened himself. He would convey absolute assurance to the old man.

Gabriel's call the previous afternoon had been short.

"I want to see this thing, Martin. We've talked about it enough on the telephone. I'm coming over there tomorrow."

The connection was broken before Pryce could respond. He put down the receiver and thought through the things he'd need to do before Gabriel arrived.

Another check of the Athena gallery, the lighting in particular, a special guard to stand outside. The verbal reports from Jason and Kate, although they wouldn't stay. Gabriel was his business. He'd talk to the old man about the statue himself.

Pryce knew Gabriel well. The man was still sharp but was increasingly preoccupied with maintaining control of the many enterprises of Gabriel Assets. He had visited the museum only half a dozen times since Pryce's appointment and left its management entirely in the director's hands. Gabriel never hesitated to call if he needed to, but his appearance at the museum was unanticipated, a disquieting surprise. He wanted no issues, certainly none now.

Jason and Kate were a small concern. Kate's technical conservation reports were virtually complete. They would support the authenticity of the statue without caveats. Jason's review was also nearly done. Pryce had talked to Jason a week earlier and knew his report would detail examples of related sculptures and cite the views of specialist scholars who had been brought to the museum to see the figure.

All agreed it was made at the end of the fifth century BC, somewhere in the Italian south. One, an archaeologist who had excavated in Italy for many years, asked with open skepticism written all over her face, how the figure had come to the museum without her knowing about it. Pryce showed her the letters the London dealer, Richard Maybank, had sent and told her he had no reason to doubt them at all. The woman had gone away stony-faced, lips compressed, without uttering a further word.

To Pryce's eye, the letters were clear, interlocking, and unquestionably authentic. They were proof positive that the figure had been in England with the family of the current Earl of Weymouth for five generations. Richard had done the right thing to send them all to the museum. Jason would fuss over them, but he'd find nothing wrong. Richard said that he accepted them unequivocally, that Weymouth's story of the statue's background was unassailable. What more was there to know?

Still, he wanted to be sure he knew exactly where Jason was going with his review. He wanted no surprises.

A switch thumped distantly as the courtyard lights were turned on, and calls sounded along the corridors as the guards began their check of the Museum's interior rooms. He glanced at his watch; it was exactly nine o'clock.

Pryce insisted that the morning ritual be carried out precisely and meticulously every day the museum was open. One of his first tasks had been to make sure the opening and closing procedures were flawless, from the moment when the day guards arrived to the end-of-day closedown, when the last visitor was gone and the gates to the entry driveway were shut tight to everyone but museum staff. The year before his arrival a visitor had been shut into the museum grounds after the driveway gate and building doors were closed. The guards had been celebrating a retirement, and the man had wandered around until he found an open rear door that allowed him into the museum's unattended main building. No damage had been done, and the confused and somewhat querulous visitor had been found and escorted out.

When Gabriel learned of the incident he uttered five words.

"Never—no more of this!" he said, and meant it. He had personally directed the immediate firing of two guards and told his new director to make certain such a thing never happened again, not ever.

At a quarter after nine, Pryce rose from his desk, clipped on his security badge, and went out into the covered portico that surrounded the central garden and gave access to the building's lower galleries. He opened a door in the temporary partition that shielded the statue from public view and stood in sheer wonder at the figure that towered above him.

Pryce had instructed the preparations staff to mount the statue on a marble base that would add another foot to its nine-foot height. He had asked for spots at the ceiling with light that would rake across the rippling surface and emphasize the dramatic interplay between the figure's dazzlingly white marble head and hands and its darker body. It was perfect for the Garretts and Havilands. And Gabriel.

Roger Garrett and Oliver Haviland were major figures on the museum's board and collections committee. Garrett headed Paramount's legal division and had majored in Art History at Princeton, and although his particular interest was the Italian mannerists, he read broadly across the field. Haviland managed one of Los Angeles' most prestigious architecture firms and painted in his spare hours. Both sought ways to demonstrate their proficiency with art, and both liked show and drama.

Pryce curried to them shamelessly. He called to ask their advice, cultivated their attention with flatteries about their knowledge, and invited them to small dinners he populated with scholars and artists that played to their sense of culture and intellect. It was all theater, what the French call *cinéma,* and it worked. Neither man had turned down a single recommended acquisition.

He expected no turndown now. The great figure stood in isolated splendor, flooded with light, a majestic presence that still had the power to hold him in awe. There would be no problem with Roger Garrett or Oliver Haviland, he knew. Or the old man.

CHAPTER THREE

Pryce opened the partition door to see Jason and Kate deep inside the gallery, two figures dwarfed by the statue.

He wanted to hear Kate first. She had come to the Gabriel from the Walters Museum three years earlier and led a tight team of bright young men and women, all of whom thought of her as their polestar and not just the head of the museum's conservation department. The director was comfortable enough with her, but he'd never been able to break through the small barriers she put up against a close friendship.

"So, what can you tell me?"

She glanced at him over her glasses, pulled at a sleeve of her cotton overcoat, and looked at a small sheaf of papers.

"Martin, we've done all the physical tests now. Soil samples, pollen analysis, SEM/EDS on the paint at the hem and on the top of the head."

"And SEM/EDS is—?"

Kate's laugh echoed in the gallery. "Oh, for heaven's sake, Martin, you're impossible! Someday I'm going to give you a full course on technique."

"Yes, yes, I know, materials analysis." It was an old game between them. "Just explain it again, please. In simple English."

"OK, fine. We use a technique that can show the elements in a paint sample. It can't prove a painted surface is ancient, but it can show it's fake if there's any modern material in it. Now, Martin, are you sure you don't what to know what the acronyms mean?"

"No, no, that's enough. But it passed the test?"

"With an A. But I wouldn't have imagined any other grade. There's old vegetal matter and root marks on *top* of the paint in a number of places. Any way you look at it, the statue is ancient.

"And the stone?"

Stone analysis could be problematic. Some years earlier the Getty further down the coast was so convinced by a technical study that showed the surface of a marble youth was ancient that they put aside reason and good judgment. The museum had to announce later to its embarrassment that its presumably ancient, magnificent, and very expensive purchase might be no more than a brilliant fake.

"We got the analysis two days ago. The head is high-quality marble from one of the Greek Islands, probably Paros. The body is Sicilian limestone, probably from one of the eastern quarries."

She glanced briefly at Jason.

"Then there are the breaks."

"What about them?"

"The statue came to us broken: you saw it in the lab. At the waist and below the knees. The breaks are all modern. There's no weathering of any kind on them, no ancient patination at all. They simply couldn't have been made in antiquity."

"And that means—?"

"It means it was broken apart when it was excavated. Or later. They're not ancient. They show none of the effects that water or soil gives marble that's been in the earth for a thousand years or so."

She glanced at the statue and then looked back at Pryce.

"It must have been roughly handled when it was taken out of the ground. It would have taken a lot of force to break it apart like that."

"And you can't tell when the breaks were made?"

"No. Nothing can, really. They could have been made any time since the statue was found in—what? The early nineteenth century?" She glanced at Jason and then at the figure before turning back to Pryce.

"There's also a scrape at the left leg. Probably caused by a digging tool. We haven't repaired the breaks. We've just given the statue enough support to put it up safely."

"But it's all consistent?"

"Yes. No question about authenticity or where it was made. The surface has pollen grains stuck to it of a type we know existed in Sicily in the fifth and fourth centuries BC. That supports the paint analysis also." She gave him a mischievous look." Then there are the eyes."

"The eyes?"

"We took a little paint off the left eye and examined it. It's calcium copper silicate. That's Egyptian Blue, Martin, the same that was used all over the ancient world to paint wood and stone.

"Painted eyes, Martin. Think of her with painted eyes. Probably blue. The ancient Greeks liked blue eyes."

Pryce smiled and turned to Jason. The curator felt the old scar at his shoulder begin to itch again.

"Martin, we've been working on two tracks, as you know. One is the nature of the figure, which is certainly an Athena. You can tell that by the ornate helmet. There's no doubt about what it was. Or that it was modeled on the original Parthenon Athena, but updated. The clinging drapery style was picked up in Greece and was used around the Mediterranean toward the end of the fourth century BC.

"But the marble head and arms and feet, different from the material of the body—they're just what you'd expect of large sculptures from Sicily and Southern Italy. When *this* figure was made, the Greeks in Italy had begun to use high-quality marble for the extremities of their cult figures. They'd work the bodies in local stone. They wouldn't have cared what was used for the body anyway, since they would have painted it, or draped it. In this case, it was painted."

A nearby elevator stopped, spilling visitors onto the portico. The sound of voices faded down the corridor.

"The other track is provenance, Martin. If we buy it—when we buy it—we'd really hate to have an issue come up over where it's been."

"But there's no problem, is there?"

Jason hesitated. "I really need a little more time. A week perhaps. Maybe two. No more."

Pryce looked up at the statue and was silent for almost a full minute. Jason wondered if he had been heard and was about to speak again when the director cut in.

"Any problems?" It was pointed.

"No. No problems. Questions."

"Questions?"

"Some."

"Tell me."

"One is how the Weymouths got hold of it. The sculpture is very local, right out of Sicily. It had to have come from there. But the fourth Weymouth never went south of Naples when he visited Italy and seems to have spent most of his time having fun in Rome and the north. And he doesn't seem to have bought antiquities much. A few unimportant Etruscan objects, small vases mostly. No one else in his family collected ancient sculpture. So, how did they get it?

"Then there's another question. Why didn't they put it up or show it anywhere? That's just *odd*. Not impossible, just odd. Who keeps a great work of art for generations and never shows it in the light of day? And keeps it stored in a *granary*, for God's sake!"

Jason paused. He wanted Pryce to understand the next point clearly.

"And finally, Martin, there's the letters Maybank says he got from Weymouth and passed on to us."

"Don't tell me there's something wrong with them."

"No, there's nothing I can see. But all the writers are dead, except for Weymouth himself. There's no one left to confirm that the statue was in England in the last century. And the letters are all photocopies. I'd really like to get hold of the originals so we can do a technical analysis of the ink."

The director held up his hand and moved it to the side, a small gesture, as if he were waving away something unpleasant.

"Jason, I really don't want to seem impatient, but we need to bring this to an end. Andrew is coming to see it today, and the museum trustees meet in two weeks. We can't prolong the investigation. Reasonable assurance that we can buy it is enough. Let's wrap it up."

Pryce waved a hand toward the figure." Look, Jason, I really don't need to tell you, but this will be the most important thing the museum's ever acquired—in fact, the most extraordinary ancient object *any* museum has acquired in the past hundred years. It will be the first thing people see as they come in the front doors. It's also the most expensive ancient work of art we've ever bought. Or that *anyone* has ever bought. I had a hell of a time getting the price down to where Andrew could manage it.

"Forty million is no joke. And the offer won't hang on for very long. Every month we delay is a month that another museum or collector may get into the deal. Maybank's almost said as much. It's time to bring this to a close. Finish up by Thursday. Can you do that?" His eyes went to Jason and then to Kate.

She nodded.

Pryce turned to leave when Jason stopped him.

"Martin, please. A week. No more than two. If we can get hold of the original letters from Weymouth—"

"I need it Thursday. Thursday latest."

Jason thought of asking again, then stopped. He tried to swallow, but his mouth was dry and he could not.

"OK, Martin. I'll give you what I have. Thursday."

Kate's eyes followed Pryce to the gallery door but now came back to Jason.

"What's biting him?"

"Who knows? Gabriel's visit, probably. Others on the board. Maybe some problem with Weymouth. Or Maybank. But it's still odd."

"What's odd?"

"All the things I mentioned, and the other that I can't."

"And that's what?"

"He's done all the negotiations with Maybank. Normally, that's my job. There are lots of reasons to slow this down, even just for a few weeks. He really doesn't need to have it all done right away. His remarks about another museum getting into it don't make sense. It's on consignment here, and it's not going to run away."

He threw a glance in the direction of the exit door, and his eyes took on an absent look.

"There's some puzzle here. Part of it is missing. I'd like to find it."

CHAPTER FOUR

What's his problem?

Even now, after working with Jason for three years, Pryce still had no clear grasp of the man. He was complex, at times clear and specific, at others dark and impenetrable. When he had been appointed director of the Gabriel, Pryce had carefully read through the files on each of the museum's curators. Jason's stood out as unusual, and he had given it particularly close attention.

Jason, he read, had come to the museum a year earlier as a newly minted PhD out of Harvard's art history department, and had been appointed associate curator of antiquities. That was unusual in itself. Curators always started at the lowest assistant level before they advanced to associate. And junior curators were younger, generally in their twenties. But Jason was thirty-nine when he had joined the Gabriel's staff, having turned to scholarship after a first career in Washington. In the Department of State, his resume read. He had been assigned to the American Embassies in Paris, Bucharest, Cairo, and Beirut. He spoke French and Arabic.

Pryce had asked both Andrew Gabriel and Edward Barovsky about Jason. He spoke to the old man first. Gabriel told him that four years earlier Barovsky, who headed the museum's antiquities department, said he needed a full associate curator, not just a new assistant. Barovsky was nearing his own retirement, he said, and needed a successor. He had raised his bushy eyebrows at the museum's founder and said he did not want just another bright young academic with no clue whatsoever about the antiquities market or how to behave with dealers and major collectors. He wanted someone with real world experience.

"Savvy," he had told Gabriel. "Whoever it is, they have to be savvy. I don't see a lot of that, but there must be someone, somewhere, who has it. And a *collector*, Andrew. We're a collecting museum. That's what you want, isn't it? Most of the young curators I see have none of the killer instinct that makes a great collection. They'd rather study an object than get it. No balls."

Barovsky had reminded Gabriel that antiquities were not the same as other art. "They're not like European paintings or modern sculpture or anything like that, Andrew. They're different."

Antiquities, the curator explained, were bought and sold in a shadowy world where discretion reigned and knowing less than more about where an object came from was sometimes the better part of virtue. But not always. When to be silent and when to demand more information was a matter of experience and judgment.

"Now, Andrew, you can't get that in some guy fresh out of a university, believe me. Buying antiquities needs special care. A subtle mind, someone who's prepared to disbelieve, who knows about the kind of lies they'll be told. We can do ourselves a lot of good by finding someone who knows how the market works. There must be someone out there who understands these things."

Gabriel had agreed. "What else could I do?" he asked Pryce. "I don't know a damn thing about antiquities or where they come from or how. I just know what I like and want to see in the museum.

Edward knew what he wanted. So I told him, 'All right, go get your guy. But he'd better be damned good!'"

After a long search, Gabriel said, Barovsky was pointed toward Jason Connor. Connor was on the verge of completing his PhD and was said to be an able scholar. He knew people in New York, Washington, and Europe. He was at ease with people of different backgrounds. And because he was himself a collector of ancient engraved stones, he knew many of the dealers who sold antiquities. And they knew him. In their small circuit, Barovsky had reported, Jason was known as smart and relentless.

Gabriel repeated the word with a small smile. "Relentless. I still have some of that myself."

Pryce thought about the old man's remarks and started his own slow, methodical search to learn more about the younger man. He found that Jason had entered Harvard directly from Washington, where he had begun his professional life. In the Foreign Service, his résumé said. So Pryce called a few friends at Harvard. They all thought highly of the young scholar, but one mentioned a story that had circulated around, that "Foreign Service" meant the service of another government agency. Jason, the story went, was a former intelligence officer, a case officer in the language of the trade. A spy.

One evening, when the visitors had left and the sunlight had gone and the sweet, pungent scent of eucalyptus flooded the museum's open spaces and the junior staff had left, Pryce had sat with Barovsky in the Gabriel's courtyard between the two fountains that framed the small interior garden and listened as the curator told of his first meeting with Jason.

Barovsky said he had taken Jason to dinner in New York, and at the end of a conversation that covered everything but ancient art, he had been so impressed that he offered the younger man a job on the spot. Jason had given him a thoughtful look.

"Andrew Gabriel runs the museum, doesn't he?" he asked.

"Well, yes."

"And he passes on everything that goes on there, doesn't he? I mean, not just appointments but acquisitions, exhibitions, displays of material? Everything?"

"Yes."

"Then I want to meet him. Before I can answer you."

Barovsky had been taken aback by this young scholar who wanted to meet one of the most powerful men in the United States. He had started to say that meeting Gabriel would be difficult, but Jason had continued before he could speak.

"And I don't want to meet him in his office. In some other setting, something more informal."

"You want to tell *Andrew Gabriel* where and how he's to meet you?" Barovsky had replied. "Who's interviewing whom?"

"To be fair, I'm interviewing him," Jason said. "If Gabriel wants me, he should want me to look him over too. And to answer the question you're about to ask, I'd make the same request of anyone."

Barovsky told Pryce he had not known whether to be pleased or dismayed. He had returned to the museum and reported the conversation to Gabriel. The old man had chuckled. "Now that's someone I want to meet! Tell him I'll see him next week. Send him a ticket, put him up for a couple of nights, waltz him around the museum, then both of you meet me at Torino on Friday." Café Torino, in the center of Beverly Hills, was Gabriel's preferred restaurant. They held a table for him every Friday noon.

For reasons that Barovsky later said he could only dimly understand, the two men—one older, the other very much younger, one with extraordinary power, the other an almost unknown, one self-made from scratch, the other with "establishment" written into him from the beginning—got along.

Barovsky had watched as the old man's wariness of the young scholar fell away. Jason had asked question after question, prodding

Gabriel about his vision for the museum and what he was prepared to do to make it truly great. And Barovsky was floored when Jason had told a silenced Gabriel that he wanted to be with a museum that had not only an outstanding collection but one that could be a center of scholarship in the arts, a gem of a place from which almost any visitor would emerge with a sense of uplift about art as the highest material expression of the human spirit.

Barovsky found himself listening with a mild sense of awe as the unknown young man told the museum's founder and chairman what his vision of his own museum should be. In the end Gabriel's answers seemed to satisfy the younger man. Over dessert, when Gabriel repeated Barovsky's invitation, Jason had accepted.

In the gathering dusk of the courtyard, Pryce asked Barovsky about Jason's past. He had heard, he said quietly, that Jason's former career might not have been with the State Department.

"Edward, what's that about? Do you know?"

Barovsky had shrugged. "Look, Martin, when I first heard the story I really just dismissed it. I mean, who cares? A spy in the museum? Laughable, that's what I thought. But you know, the more I thought about it, the more it interested me. No harm, I thought, it wouldn't do any harm to have someone who knows how to operate in a shadow world. And, Martin, that's what the antiquities business is—a shadow world where truth and untruth aren't so clear, and where sometimes you have to deal with people who are crooks and smugglers, real criminals, and who will lie to you all the time if you let them."

Barovsky paused and looked at Pryce, who had a slightly glazed look in his eyes. "You know what I mean, Martin?"

Pryce said, a little drily, that yes, of course he knew.

The older man went on. He said that while he knew nothing of espionage except for the novels he had read, and while he had no real idea whether the story about Jason was fact or fiction, the idea of a former spy in his own department had given him a small ripple of excitement.

"But Jason's always denied the stories, hasn't he?" Pryce asked.

"Oh sure. He says he was a diplomat. He'll go into tedious detail about his embassy assignments in Europe and the Middle East and the country desks he's served on. Sometimes he'll make a bad joke about not wanting to tell anyone about his clandestine past, because he'd then have to shoot the person who asked."

"So why did he leave?"

"Jason says—says—that after fourteen years, government service just didn't hold his attention. He wanted something else. He says he was bitten by the idea of becoming an archaeologist. A dirt archaeologist, a scholar. And that led him into ancient art at Harvard, then here."

"Do you believe that?"

"Yes, I guess so. I don't know. It makes sense. He's difficult to fathom. Affable on the surface. Something else underneath."

"Deceptive?"

"No, I wouldn't say that. He looks like the old-school Eastern type, all manners and polish, you know what I mean. But I've seen him with dealers who've tried to put something over on him. He played them, not the reverse. You wouldn't know it by looking at him, but he's not someone to fool around with. And he has the other thing I like to see."

"What's that?"

"He's got a sort of relentless curiosity. I've seen it drive him."

The director thought for a moment. "Where's the problem? There must be one, somewhere in the man?"

"He's one of those people who believes in moral abstractions, you know, right and wrong, the values thing. Tends to see the world in contrast, not much in between. And he's not so tolerant, Martin, particularly if he thinks someone's crossed him. And stubborn. When he gets into something, he won't give it up. Unforgiving and stubborn. Those are faults, I guess. But they don't take away from his work. He does really good work, Martin."

Pryce knew the rest. By the end of his first year at the Gabriel, Jason was regarded as a major asset to the antiquities department and by his second year a coming star. He had the respect of the Gabriel's staff and strong relationships with the curators of other museums and with scholars and collectors. His own relationship with Jason was good, he thought.

Then one day, Barovsky had died, suddenly, with a chicken bone in his throat. Pryce wondered at the time whether there was more he should try to find out about Jason, but quelled his misgivings and told Gabriel he could think of no one better to assume Barovsky's position. Jason was confirmed as chief curator of antiquities two months later.

But the director's misgivings were never fully stilled. Adding to his unease, Jason had financial means and an independent-mindedness that set him apart from most museum curators. It made him a hard target for dealers who hoped to compromise him with small favors, or large ones.

One day at lunch, in the company of Pryce and other members of the museum staff, Jason had told the story of a visit he'd had from two dealers, Iranians out of London who had come to see him with a large portfolio of beautiful color prints of a collection of ancient glass, a great deal of it, good material and very expensive. The curator had asked how much they wanted, and they'd said it would be $6 million dollars—and added that thirty percent would be Jason's, if he could persuade the museum to buy the collection.

"You told them no, of course?" The question had come from one of the younger assistants.

Jason's smile reached the eyes. "In a way. I thanked them for coming to see me. I could see them smell a deal. Then I asked if they remembered the security guards in the museum court. They seemed a little confused by the question." He paused.

"Go on, go on!" It was from an associate in the decorative arts department.

Jason said he'd told the dealers that if they mentioned a bribe one more time, just once, he would have the two largest, most muscular guards he could find take them by their arms and legs, frog-march them to the big bronze doors, and throw them down the steps and out onto the driveway. He told them in detail what it would mean to their Savile Row suits and carefully cared-for complexions to skid along the driveway's gravel surface. The two men had almost run out of the museum, clutching their portfolio.

"And, of course," he said, "they came back, the next month, this time with photographs of Sassanian gilt silver. But no personal offer."

"Came back?" one of his listeners asked.

"Of course. They're businessmen. The Gabriel's business. So they came back."

Jason had told the story with a smile. Some of those at the table must have wondered, Pryce thought later, what they would have done if they had been offered almost $2 million to push through an acquisition.

Who is Jason Connor? Pryce wished he had the answer. The statue was too important for him not to know what the man was thinking.

CHAPTER FIVE

Pryce found his attention wandering at the senior staff meeting. When he returned to his office, Patricia Waller, his assistant of three years, said he'd had a call.

"Richard Maybank."

"Call him back and tell him I'll talk to him later today."

Maybank could wait until he'd met with Gabriel. And that would be in a few minutes.

The director picked up a recent copy of *The Art Newspaper,* running quickly through the pages for articles about forgeries and dealer chicaneries and the most recent foreign country allegations about works of art they believed to have been looted. It had all become a huge legal morass, tarring many of the larger collecting museums, generating a continuous stream of scandalous stories about mismanagement and outright theft. But none of it had touched the Gabriel. Not yet.

Waller put her head through his door.

"Dr. Pryce, the front gate's called. They say Mr. Gabriel is on his way up."

Pryce exited his office and descended the museum's external stairs. As he reached the road-level entryway, he could see Gabriel's deep-blue Mercedes approaching. The car swept slowly up the driveway winding through the museum's gardens, turned along the entryway curve and came to a halt beside the director.

Walter Jackson, Andrew Gabriel's driver of more than thirty years, opened the vehicle's right rear door. Gabriel, wearing a carefully tailored seersucker suit cut to make him seem taller than he was, with a midnight blue shirt and signature bowtie, stepped out, cane in hand, still spry in his early eighties. Dick Carrington, all verticals from his tall frame to his pinstripe suit to his blue-on-white shirt, with a demeanor that reminded Pryce of Edgar Allen Poe, emerged from the front. Ellen Finch, a heavyset woman of indeterminate middle age, with short blond hair and glasses through which she peered suspiciously, struggled to get out of the rear, her mouth working a silent curse as she did. Carrington had been Gabriel's personal assistant long before Pryce had come to the museum. Finch dealt with the museum's legal issues. She kept problems as far from the door of Gabriel Assets as she could and often seemed disapproving of the array of thorny and uncomfortable matters Pryce put on her desk.

Gabriel and Carrington were inseparable, but the purchase of the statue was Finch's business. He had been talking to her for weeks about a final contract for the statue that could be signed immediately after the museum's board had approved it. She had asked why there was such a big rush for "this item," when it normally took several months for a contract to be finalized. Pryce had had to use all his persuasive powers to get her to finish it up. The week before, he had almost exploded on the telephone when Finch had maddeningly picked at some meaningless stipulation she wanted in the document. He'd bitten his tongue and had reminded her in steely tones that this "item," as she insisted on calling it, would be the most important acquisition the Gabriel had ever made.

"Martin." Gabriel held out his hand.

"Andrew." Short, diminished further by age, the museum's founder was still a commanding figure, and Pryce still had difficulty knowing when to address him by his first name.

At the top of the stairway, the older man stopped and turned. "So, Martin, tell me about this statue you're so excited about."

Gabriel was playing with him. Pryce had never known the old man to have a memory lapse. He had discussed the statue over the telephone more than half a dozen times and had sent him a set of large color prints, along with a full description of the object and details about its price and terms of offer. Gabriel acknowledged getting these but said nothing about either the object or the money.

The old man's silence didn't mean there was a problem, Pryce knew. A negative would have been conveyed to him immediately. And Gabriel had taken up his invitation to see the statue at the earliest moment, which meant as soon as could be arranged.

With Gabriel, cane in hand, pushing ahead, the small group passed into the central courtyard and entered the first of the museum's antiquities galleries. It was already filling with visitors—individuals, couples, others in groups that clustered around docents who tried to explain what they were being shown. Most knew little or nothing about ancient history and had few reference points to the museum's antiquities collection. Even a common object such as a decorative Roman fibula, a metal clasp to pin garments, had no modern function and most people needed help understanding what they were seeing.

Nodding to a nearby guard, the director opened the door to the closed-off gallery where the statue stood, put his hand on Gabriel's back, and gently nudged him forward. He could hear the old man's intake of breath. Gabriel took a step, then another, until he was directly beneath the great statue, looking up at the figure's face as it stared into the remote distance behind him. He turned.

"My God, Martin. This is *something*." Gabriel's voice echoed in the vaulted gallery. It's bigger than I realized. Much bigger."

Pryce congratulated himself once more on his choice of the foot-high mount that made the statue seem colossal.

"Tell me again how it got here."

"I was in London in August, Andrew. Richard Maybank called and asked when I'd be there and said he had something he wanted me to see. He seemed quite secretive, so I dropped by, and he took me directly to a storehouse in Battersea, and there it was. Maybank said he hadn't shown it to anyone else and asked if we were interested. The statue was really amazing, even lying down in pieces. I knew we'd had to have it if we could get it."

Gabriel stopped him. "The price, Martin. Tell me again about your discussion of the price."

"Maybank wasn't coy about it. He wanted fifty million for it. Fifty million! I was stunned, Andrew. When we went back to his office, I said we couldn't buy it, and probably no one could. Fifty million was higher than anyone had paid for an antiquity of any kind. I said I couldn't even dream of telling you. I said I didn't know if you'd be interested in it at half that amount. So I let him think about it and went back to my hotel. The next day he asked me to come by again."

"And you went?" Gabriel knew the answer. He had been through it all before.

"Of course not, Andrew. I wanted him to think it over a little more. I said I was going to the country for the weekend, and I could try to stop by on Monday. I didn't sound too enthusiastic."

Gabriel visibly enjoyed the story. The offer, the false departure. The *deal!*

"Go on, Martin!"

"Well I took my time and called Monday and said I had an important luncheon engagement, and I might not be able to come by until late that afternoon, and that I had to leave the following morning. That must have killed him."

"Yes! Then?"

"So I had a nice lunch by myself, took in the Tate, and went to see him much later, just as he was about to close. He was in a state. He thought I'd disappeared, gone back to the hotel, and he'd lost his last chance at us! We finished it up in five minutes. He said forty-five, and I said that was also impossible, and finally he said forty. I told him I could probably take that number to you, but it would take a hell of a lot of convincing to get you to agree."

"God that's such an interesting account, Martin. You certainly knew how to handle him."

Was there irony in the old man's voice? Pryce thought about it for a moment and then shrugged. There was no need for him to respond.

Gabriel's eyes went up to the statue that loomed above him.

"Athena. I understand there are many Athenas, Martin. Except for the size, what makes this one different, or special?"

Pryce had spent days immersing himself in the statue's background. He'd be discussing it with the museum's board, and he wanted his presentation to be flawless. He had taken special pains to have detailed answers to questions of exactly the kind Gabriel had just asked.

"You know the story of the goddess's birth, springing from Zeus's forehead, fully armed. Athena became a guide and protector to Odysseus, Heracles, Perseus, even to the Greeks themselves. They put up temples to her everywhere. They sometimes called her "Virgin Athena," *Athena Parthenos,* and the name was given to the Parthenon statue, the most famous one ever created."

Pryce stopped to let the Gabriel absorb what he had been saying.

"And is this Athena like the Parthenon's?"

"It's smaller of course—the Parthenon figure was almost sixty feet high. But the sculptor of *this* Athena was certainly looking over his shoulder at it.

"And look at the drapery, Andrew! See how it hugs her body. And here," Pryce said, his finger on the center of the figure's body. "Her navel!"

The old man reached out to touch the figure, his eyes glittering. "So, is it Greek, then? Or Italian? It was found in Italy, wasn't it?"

"There wasn't a Greece or Italy when it was made. Those are names we give those countries today. The ancient Greeks called themselves Hellenes, or Athenians, or Thebans, but never Greeks. In fact, the word 'Greek' comes from the name of a small tribe that migrated to southern Italy from the Greek mainland. The word went into Latin, and English from there. The statue is Greek, nothing else. But from Italy."

Gabriel gave Pryce a long look.

"So, how did Maybank get it?"

Pryce had told the story to the old man weeks ago but knew he wanted to hear it again.

"It isn't Maybank's. It's the current earl's—that's Frederick Weymouth. Maybank is his agent. He told me that Frederick Weymouth is virtually penniless and wanted him to find a buyer for it. Weymouth told him the statue's been out of sight since it was brought to England by the fourth earl in the 1830s."

"How's that possible?" Gabriel's sharp blue eyes focused on the director.

It was a new question, one the old man hadn't asked before. Pryce considered his next words carefully.

"It *is* possible, Andrew. The fourth earl bought huge numbers of objects during his visits to the Continent when he traveled there. Everything—paintings, furniture, decorative objects, antiquities. And it all went into the family home, Brigham House in Dorset, except for a few items that were sent to the London house. Maybank says the Weymouths could never find a place in the house to put it, so they stored it in a granary. Some of them seem to have thought it a monstrosity anyway—the dark body may have put them off. It's nothing like the beautiful white Parthenon marbles that Elgin brought back and that the English are used to. It was certainly kept out of sight."

"But they showed it?" Gabriel pressed.

"Only to a handful of people. A few close family friends who wouldn't talk about it to anyone else. And a few scholars who were sworn to silence. The Weymouths didn't want to be bothered about it."

The voices of museum visitors echoed distantly in the galleries.

"And the letters, Martin. Tell me again about the documents Maybank sent you."

"We have copies of letters the scholars wrote after they'd seen the statue. The first is from the end of the nineteenth century, one from the 1920s, and others from the 1950s onward. They support Weymouth's account that the object was in Brigham House for more than a hundred years. The history of the statue from the fourth earl on is pretty well known."

"And the letters are good? They're not a pack of lies?"

Why is he asking the question?

"They're good. As far as we can tell."

"Martin, I've had too many problems with good things coming from bad people who cover them up with bad documents and lie about them. I don't want a problem here."

"Of course not, Andrew. Jason's onto it. He'll have the background check done at the end of the week."

"Let me be clear, Martin. I want no problems with this object. I don't need them. At all." Gabriel's voice was emphatic. He looked up again at the statue and then fastened his eyes on the director.

"And the price is right? It's not too high?"

There was something in the old man's look that Pryce could not interpret. Money perhaps. Gabriel was always concerned about money.

"Andrew, there's nothing like it. If we don't get it, someone else will."

"OK, Martin. It's magnificent. Let's get it. I'll talk to the others on the board. But get it."

Gabriel, with Carrington and Finch in tow, headed for the gallery door. As he left, he turned back to look one more time at the statue, then at Pryce, and shook his head. Pryce followed a few feet behind.

Pryce closed his office door, sat down, adjusted his chair, picked up a pen, and tapped it lightly on his chin for a moment. He lifted the telephone receiver, entered a number, and waited as he heard the characteristic double buzz of the London exchange.

"Yes?" Richard Maybank's voice came over the line.

"It's done, Richard. It's fine. Gabriel came this morning. He wants it."

"And there's no problem?"

"None. It's a done deal. I told him how we fought like dogs over the price. We just need to finish up the paperwork here, but that's my concern, not yours."

"The document check's done?"

"Not yet. Jason is taking his time with it. You know how he is. I've told him to end it by Thursday. He'll pack it in then."

"No problems there?"

"None. Don't worry, Richard. There'll be no problems." Pryce hung up.

At the moment Pryce put down the receiver, Jason was picking up his own. He keyed a number and heard the long, high, intermittent tone of the telephone ring at the other end, in Zurich.

"Leo," he said, when the voice answered. "Leo, you remember the signature we talked about last week. Could you scan it? I need it now. Tomorrow if possible. Not later than Wednesday."

The soft accented voice on the other end asked the question he knew was coming.

"No, not yet, Leo. I'll tell you all about it in a few weeks or so. Be patient. And thanks. I'm in your debt again, old friend."

He cradled the telephone and stared for a moment at a photograph that hung on the opposite wall, the image of an older man with an impish smile on his face seated next to a stiff-looking woman in the museum's courtyard. Edward Barovsky, with his secretary of many years, Amelia Mumford, who in minutes would be settling herself into her chair just outside his own office.

Maybe it's fine. I'm probably just chafing. It's fine.

CHAPTER SIX

"Kate, are you busy?"

"Yes. No. What's up?"

"Can we talk? Somewhere out of the office."

"Sure. Where?"

"Meet at the elevators? We can go from there."

"Twenty minutes."

She was surprised. He was never this urgent. She replaced the receiver and put away the tool she had been using to remove a smear of chalk on a small Greek cup. Carefully resting it on its base, she removed her surgical gloves, washed her hands in one of the laboratory's sinks, and smoothed her hair backward and retied it behind her head.

She debated whether she should wear her lab coat and then took it off. She glanced at the cup, considered asking an assistant to work on it, but decided she wanted to do that herself and put it away and went to tell an associate she would be out for a while. She did not say she would be seeing Jason.

What made me do that? Jason couldn't care less if we're seen in the galleries with visitors and staff poking about. Why would it matter? Or would it?

She decided not to look at the question too closely. Perhaps she simply didn't want to give her staff something to feed on. The museum community was tight, an echo chamber that generated and magnified every rumor. She and Jason were professional associates, comfortable in each other's company. The light sparring they engaged in amused her.

It was sufficient, she thought. Jason was attractive enough, particularly his unsettling blue-gray eyes that held one's attention. A thin diagonal line ran through the right eyebrow, an old scar from an accident, he'd once told her. Sometimes, not often, he would stop what he was saying and take on a distant look and the moment would pass and he would resume from the same point he left off. It wasn't something she felt she could ask about, and she'd never done so.

Still, he was clever, not like so many others on the museum staff who seemed to have had their humor trained out of them. A few months earlier, he had brought a young dealer into the conservation lab to show a new and very complicated piece of equipment, something he said could expose a fake. It wasn't true, but the dealer got the message: don't screw with me, don't try to sell me fakes. The man had left the museum in a state of mild shock, and Jason had laughed at his own story. Soon she and the rest of her staff had started laughing too. It took minutes to quiet things down. Work seemed to lighten up when he was around, and she wondered whether she should invite him by more often.

Once, not long after she had come to the Gabriel, Kate had a dream that involved a figure, a man who she knew later had to be Jason. It had taken her a week to suppress the memory. She had never mentioned it to him, of course, and she'd gone about her work as if it had never occurred. And he never seemed especially taken with her at all, or with anyone else at the Gabriel. It was sufficient that they were colleagues, close colleagues, she thought. She had enough to do as it was and had no desire to stir the echoes of her own past.

He was waiting by the elevators, with a different jacket, still slightly worn, much like the one he'd had on at their meeting with Martin the day before. He could buy a closetful of clothes, but he had some slightly perverse idea about using things up and wearing them out. It was a small affectation that was part of his offbeat manner, and it mildly amused her.

The look in his eyes was not amusing.

He motioned with his hand. "Let's go outside. It's quieter."

They went down the museum's main western corridor and then, outside, started up the pathway to the south garden, the more luxuriant of the museum's two landscaped hillsides.

The Gabriel gardens were a grand conceit. Covering well over a hundred acres, they blanketed the sides of the shallow ravine in which the museum was built, reaching upward to a high northern hillside that held a small, pristine meadow bisected by a stream that ran downward to the sea.

Andrew Gabriel had spared no expense here, taking his cue from gardens created during California's exuberant golden age of horticulture in the early twentieth century, but he had added his own accent, collecting the truly exotic, including nearly ten thousand varieties of plants, many of which existed nowhere else in North America.

Great trees framed the periphery of the grounds and were interspersed throughout the lower slopes, where glades opened out under the southern California sun. Ferns of every shade of green thrived in shaded nooks beside spread-leaved, dark-green cycads that rose above them. Succulents were everywhere, clusters of century plants with white interiors on their blue-gray sawtooth leaves;

larger agaves, green and blue with thick white-bordered leaves, standing singly or in small groups; great sisals with hard spear-like tips, blue-green with light yellow borders and sharp jagged edges, a jungle of spiny plants of every type and form.

They came to a lily pond, a secret garden in itself, enlivened only by the small freshet that fed into it and a waterfall that led the stream away toward the lower slopes. They sat on a wooden bench and watched two fat, spotted koi, both black and orange on white, swimming lazily around the edge before submerging with a swirl of dark water behind them.

The silence lasted for more than a minute before she spoke.

"So, Jason, what's the problem? I seem to be asking you the same question a lot these days."

"Yesterday. Martin. I've never seen him so obsessed with an acquisition."

"But it's a major event, isn't it, Jason? This huge, nine-foot goddess! It will be just stunning to anyone coming into the museum. And no museum has anything like this. You must see his point."

"Yes, sure. But he's never been so abrupt about a purchase. He's given us time to complete the physical and background checks. But now he wants them stopped short. It's not his way, and it's odd. You must have seen it too."

She watched a koi rise to the water's surface, suck air, then disappear.

"Odd? You know, Jason, I don't know him as well as you do. Do you think he's being pressed by Gabriel?"

"Maybe, but not about the statue. Gabriel hadn't seen it until he walked into the museum yesterday. I just don't see him pushing Martin to get it without looking at it first—and it's Martin who's pushing. Every time I see him he seems to find a new reason to move the acquisition through quickly. He seems to forget his own sense of caution. And I want him to be cautious about the statue. I am."

"Oh? Why?"

"The documents Maybank sent. Letters to the Weymouths, or from them. Except for the last, one from the current Weymouth, all were written by people who've been long dead."

"But that's not a negative, is it?"

"No, not in itself. But I'd really like to check them further, have an analysis done on the ink and paper to be sure they're good and not faked."

"Faked? Really?" She turned and looked carefully at him. "You're not imagining problems?"

He smiled at the question. "No, there really may be a problem."

He paused for a moment. *She's never been with the people I've seen, and she's got no idea what they could do.*

"Think about it, Kate. If the background is faked, then when did she appear? If not in the nineteenth century when Weymouth is supposed to have bought it, then when? This *thing*," he went on, "this huge and wonderful object, is going to get the attention of every museum, every scholar, everyone with any interest in museums and antiquities.

"It'll certainly get the attention of the Italians. They'll raise a huge stink if they think for a moment that it was taken out of Italy recently. They'll do everything they can to find out where it came from and when, and they'll squeeze everyone they think was involved."

The light played across her face and he thought, again, that her nose was a little too long and that it didn't make any difference at all. Her small imperfections added up to a sum that was different and interesting. The fit worked.

He came back to earth. "Let's say we buy it. And then let's say that two weeks later, or two years, or ten, someone, some Italian runner—one of the men who got it to Rome or out of the country—stands up and says, '*Bene*—Sure! I know where it came from. And how it got out! And who did it!' The Italians will claim it immediately—and with that kind of evidence, they would probably have the claim sustained by a US court."

He shook his head slightly, only a small movement. A single koi sucked air, almost at their feet, and then disappeared into the silted depths.

"If that happens, it's no longer a wonderful statue in the Gabriel. It's become a huge problem. And it raises a huge question of what we should have known. What do we say about our own background check? That it was thorough? That we were really diligent?"

Kate thought for a moment and then turned back to him. "What are you saying? That you think Martin wants to avoid knowing the statue's background. Deliberately?" But isn't that preposterous? Why would he do something so stupid? What would he want?"

"I don't know what he wants. He appears convinced the background check is complete enough as it is, and the decision should now be the board's, and Gabriel's. He seems to have total faith that the seller—Weymouth? Maybank?—has given us perfectly good and acceptable information and that we should put any reservations aside and buy it, no further questions.

"And you don't think so?"

"What I think is that going down that road would not be very smart. And the matter isn't theoretical. I don't know for certain if there's a problem. Yet. But there may be. If anything turns up that makes any one of the documents wrong, then they're all wrong. The damned thing is, Martin must know this."

"But if you're right, and you tell Martin he can't have it—or that he has to tell Gabriel that he can't have it now and they have to wait to find out if it's buyable—he'll be furious."

"At what? The documents? The offer? Maybank?" Jason paused. "Me?" He smiled at the idea.

"Maybe you. You're the messenger."

"So, what should I do? What choice do I have? Martin *needs* to know." He found himself searching for the right words.

"I don't really understand it. He must realize that knowing isn't the problem. Deciding not to know isn't a solution."

"'Know the truth and the truth shall make you free?'" She was quoting the biblical words written at the entrance to CIA headquarters in Virginia.

"Come on, Kate, don't play with me. Not on this. I don't have a choice. Martin doesn't either."

"Don't you think Martin understands that? He's not an idiot, Jason."

"I don't know what he understands. Maybe he just hasn't thought it through. Look at the consequences. Loss of the statue. Loss of reputation for the museum. Damage, maybe irreparable damage, to his own reputation. And if the Italians think he was willfully complicit in the acquisition, they could try to extradite him. They put one of the Getty's curators on trial for doing essentially that."

"Would that work?"

"I don't think it would get that far. A federal prosecutor could get him indicted and probably convicted first, of theft and conspiracy. It's been done before.

"Jail. Think about it. What does he think he's doing?"

It was not a question.

As they walked along the winding garden pathway, they could see on the slopes of the hill further to the east the outlines of the conservatory, a museum piece in itself. A white-painted domed metal frame structure built in the 1880s to adorn the gardens of a Massachusetts textile magnate, the conservatory had been personally selected by Gabriel to hold his more exotic plant specimens.

The conservatory contained one of the most stunning displays of tropical forest plants Jason had ever seen. It held a surprisingly complete selection of carnivorous plants—flytraps, pitcher plants, bladderworts, flypaper plants that trapped their insect prey with sticky droplets, corkscrew plants that seduced bugs into long tunnels leading into their interiors, where they were dissolved. The methods varied, but the outcome was always the same: death by suffocation for their hapless victims.

There was a story that when Gabriel was a young mining engineer in the Amazon he had run out of food and ate worms and insects until he had stumbled on a river tribe. The insect-eating plants, the story went, had become a metaphor for that desperate moment of the old man's life.

There was more to that hillside than the Conservatory. A narrow pathway wound downward from the building toward a high promontory of land between the trees, a small open spot overlooking a sheer drop of fifty feet, where a single wooden bench faced outward toward the waters of the Pacific.

On late summer evenings, long after the visitors had left, Gabriel himself would occasionally come to this spot in the gardens and watch the sun set. He had done so for almost a decade, since Norah, his wife and life partner of almost fifty years, died after a long, losing fight with lymphoma. Gabriel had put the bench on the same ground where the two of them had often sat since they were very young, and marked it with a small plaque that said simply, "Norah. Light of my life. I miss you."

Beneath that there was a very small letter, a curving A in Andrew Gabriel's own hand.

They started down the back pathway toward the rear of the museum.

"This may go nowhere. Maybe you're right—I'm imagining a problem that's not there. I hope so; I want the Gabriel to have the statue. It's just, well—let's get it the right way so we can keep it."

"When will you know?"

"Tomorrow. The next day. I have a few lines out. I need to pull them in."

"Let me know?"

"I will. I really shouldn't vent at you like this. But you know, I can't talk about it to anyone else in the museum. I hope you can hold it to yourself."

"Be serious, Jason. I don't have to say you can trust me. Of course you can. But Martin's not the only one who's wound up. You are too. Be careful where you go with this. I don't understand what's on Martin's mind either. But I'd hate to see him upset with you."

She put her hand on Jason's arm. "I don't like where this is heading. You shouldn't either. Be careful."

Her thoughts began to spiral.

I should be careful. Jason was swimming in a fast current. She was in the shallows, but she could feel the tug of deeper water at her feet.

CHAPTER SEVEN

When Pryce's appointment to the Gabriel was announced, Jason set about learning as much as he could about the man. He checked all the open sources and then, making sure he left no trace of his interest, began a careful search for information through former colleagues and friends, some, indirectly, who would never know it was he who wanted the information. It was delicate, subtle work, and it took time to develop the right sources.

One of his Washington friends who was versed in the quiet collection of information and who had too little to do in his retirement had posed, unasked, as a journalist seeking information on Pryce's early life in Detroit. Jason told his friend that he would never have countenanced the act if he had known about it. He chastised the man for the deceit, then promptly asked to know what he had discovered.

He learned that Pryce was the eldest of five children born to devoutly Catholic parents with strong conservative values set down and enforced by a domineering father. Norman Pryce was a driven man who had risen through the ranks of automotive workers to become a plant manager with General Motors. He told his children that he expected great things of them and pushed each to get the best education they could. He was thrilled when Martin rose to the top of his high school class and won a scholarship to the University of Michigan.

The young Martin, prodded by his father and his own growing ambitions, worked hard to earn what he could. He took summer work as soon as Michigan's labor laws allowed and had held odd jobs throughout his adolescence. In his first college year, he delivered laundry and told no one about it. And in the summer of his second, he took the first vacation of his life, a three-week bicycle trip along the Rhine and into France.

"Then what happened?" Jason asked his former colleague. Where did he go?"

"Don't have the faintest idea. Would you like me to get someone in Europe to do a run on it? It'll cost a little, but I'd be glad to handle it."

"No," Jason had replied, emphatically.

From all the evidence, the young Martin's European trip was a turning point in his life.

Jason could imagine what had happened, since it had also happened to him during his own first visit to Europe. The young Martin must have been enthralled by the magnificent art and architecture that was to be seen in every city and town and overcome by sights, sounds, and smells of a totally different culture. Jason remembered the first time he had bitten into a fresh brioche at a café next to the Esmeralda, in full view of Notre Dame across a break in the Seine, and knifed open the bound pages of a book he had just bought and thought he had gone to a distant heaven. Something like that must have happened to Martin, he thought.

From another source, he learned that one of Martin's neighbors said that the young man's bicycle trip had caused his parents intense anguish. Norman Pryce wanted his son to go into business, where the money was. But after his first sight of Europe, the younger Pryce began to take courses in fine arts. At the end of his senior year at Michigan, he told his father he intended to go into the graduate program of New York University's Institute of Fine Arts. He added that he had secured a day job that would help pay his tuition.

Norman Pryce had been apoplectic at the news. "Art is for sissies!" he declared. "You're not one of those, are you?" But words failed to move his son. There was nothing the elder Pryce could do.

According to a very talkative scholar who was close to Pryce and who wanted to pour all his thoughts into the ear of Jason's faux-journalist friend, the young Pryce learned very quickly, and he knew how to work very hard. But he also seemed to be nagged by a deeper uncertainty, about what was not clear.

"I can't really say what it was all about," Pryce's scholar friend had said. "Something to do with his father, you know, and Martin's not matching up to his old man's ambitions. But then there was the other thing, about always being on the outside. He wanted to be inside, you see? Inside the country clubs, inside the gates of the people he really just loathed, you know, the ones who are very rich and take long vacations on the Costa Smeralda or wherever.

"He was really bitter about it," the friend said. "But look at Martin now!"

Look at Martin now. His life had been an immense success. He had built a reputation as a scholar, teacher, connoisseur, author, curator, and, finally, museum director. He had written countless articles on medieval art and history and had even headed a small team of archaeologists working at the Crusader fortress of Kerak in the hills of central Jordan. In a brilliant display of erudition, he debunked the Ephesus Shroud and was invited to give a series of talks that appeared on *Nova*. *Time Magazine* called him the Carl

Sagan of medievalists and named him as one of the one hundred most influential people of the year.

When Jason was reminded of the Ephesus Shroud, he telephoned Gerald Robertson. Robertson had been director of the Met when Jason had first befriended him six years earlier. He was a fount of wisdom about museums, and Jason had come to depend on his experience and good judgment. He told stories, amazing stories, and had a repertory of tales that became more vivid and dramatic with each year that passed. He would know all about the shroud, and something about Pryce.

"You want to know about the Ephesus Shroud? It was a real *coup*. You've been to Ephesus, no? Then you may remember the stone hut up in the hills behind the ruins of the ancient city. The 'Virgin Mary's House'—it's in the guidebooks. The local legends say Jesus's mother spent her last days there. When she died, she was wrapped in a shroud and put in a coffin, and when the coffin was opened again by St. Thomas, who wanted to see her a last time— you know, Doubting Thomas—her body had disappeared! Only the shroud was left.

"That's the legend, anyway. And of course a shroud was found. With a faint ghost of a woman's image on it! And it's been worshipped ever since. For centuries."

"The Shroud of Turin, but with an image of the Virgin?"

"Exactly. A little creepier, though. The figure's eyes are open and appear to follow you around the room."

Jason tried to visualize it, but the image seemed almost comedic. "So what did Martin do?"

"The shroud was church property, and Martin had to persuade the Patriarch of Constantinople to have it examined. That was a story in itself. The Patriarch was particularly difficult, since if Mary's image was real, destructive testing of any kind could be considered sacrilege. Martin told him that testing would be done at Oxford and that it wouldn't be destructive—nothing of real substance would be removed. Even if it was found that the shroud had nothing to do with the Virgin Mary, it would have no effect on those who still believed the stone hut was her house. The faithful would still come, he said. But there was no response from the Patriarch."

Robertson paused for effect. "Then he applied the kicker."

"What are you talking about?"

"You know, Jason, the kick in the ass, the thing that gets someone to see the light and do something they'd never have done otherwise."

"And what was that?"

"It was brilliant. After working over the Patriarch for months, Pryce got an interested friend—one of those very rich people he'd cultivated—to make a donation to the Patriarch's renovation fund. A big one. It was really funny. Until then, the old guy didn't know he had a renovation fund."

"And then?" Jason prodded.

"The old Patriarch gave in, of course. A few fibers were sent off to Oxford. And the shroud turned out to be a twelfth-century painting with most of the pigment gone. Something that was probably taken to Ephesus during one of the earlier Crusades."

Robertson had ended the story, and there was a moment of silence between the two men before he spoke again.

"You're interested in Martin, aren't you?"

"Yes."

"Good luck. I know him. I mean, I've met him. But I don't think anyone knows him. There's something I can't put my finger on there. He's restless, dissatisfied somehow—wants some kind of recognition he can't seem to get. A parental thing, maybe. Needs some kind of assurance they didn't give him, perhaps."

There was a pause before he spoke again.

"But Jason, he's not all ambition and ability. He's got a sentimental side too. Got two daughters, but then there's a third child, almost a member of his family."

"What's that about?"

"I don't know much. Martin doesn't talk about it, but I heard the story last year from someone who worked with him pretty closely. He's putting a girl from a really poor family through a private school in the east."

"Why would he do that?"

"The kid's mother. Seems to have taken care of his own children when they were growing up, for years. It was a way of thanking her, paying her back."

Jason hesitated before asking the next question. "Is there anything else behind the story?"

"If I can guess what you're thinking, don't go there. His wife wanted him to do it. I'm sure you know Frances. She worked on him to help the girl.

Martin, Jason later thought, a legend, hugely successful, a model for young museum directors. Close to his wife. Kind, generous. And dissatisfied.

Why? About money?

He thought about it for a few moments, then decided that couldn't be it.

Martin was well paid. At the Gabriel he had the salary equivalent of a CEO of a small company, with a hefty budget for travel, entertainment, a house paid for by the museum, and with enough to put his daughters through college without needing scholarship money. He was at the top.

What more did Martin want? Something less tangible, something he wasn't given when he was younger? Approval from a deceased, overbearing father? Something else?

What had Martin's scholar friend said? About a young man who could never be accepted by the people he loathed?

Jason thought about it but found no answer.

CHAPTER EIGHT

H e decided not to close his office door. The most private discussions, those one did not want anyone to think were other than innocent, should be held in plain view, with the door open.

Keep the voice low, let the background noise shield the conversation. Make it appear normal. It was a simple deception he had learned long ago and helped avoid the interest of Amelia Mumford.

Mumford had been passed on to Jason after Edward Barovsky's death. A woman in later age who inevitably put her hair in a bun and wore long, front-button flower-print dresses. She had no social life that he knew of but took an unnatural interest in the personal lives of the department staff. To the curator's amusement and slight discomfort, she seemed to have developed a crush on him. She also sat immediately outside his office door and took in everything around her. It was harmless, mostly, but something he needed to remember if he wanted privacy.

Gerald Robertson was often difficult to reach, but he was on the telephone after the second ring. He was ebullient, as always. Jason pictured him on the other end of the line, tall, lean, probably wearing stone-washed jeans of the type he'd adopted when he left the East for an unquiet retirement in Pasadena, with a collarless long-sleeved shirt, straw-soled sandals, no socks, the picture of someone from somewhere else trying to look local.

"Gerald, what are you doing for dinner? Say tonight?"

"Tonight's good. But what's this about? Are you OK? You sound as though you're in a rush about something."

Jason decided not to answer the question. "I'll tell you tonight. Meet around seven? And you make the reservations. Someplace without a lot of noise. And put on something decent."

Robertson laughed. "Good! Ritz Carlton, here in Pasadena. Dining room. Nice. Pricey. Bring your platinum card. But it's quiet. You'll like it. *I'll* like it!"

Ebullient, he thought. The man reminded Jason of the remark once made by a foreign ambassador to Washington about Theodore Roosevelt: "You must remember," the ambassador had told an acquaintance, "the President is only about six."

Jason exited the museum drive and headed south toward Malibu, his thoughts drifting toward his older friend.

Robertson was the only child of a surgeon father and a socialite mother who atoned for her patrician birth by crusading for the homeless by day while giving luminary-studded soirées by night. At the beginning of his second year at Princeton, someone had told him of a gut course, Fine Arts One, a survey of art "from the caveman to Corbusier," that would add polish but needed little effort. He took it on, and as he told Jason, it took him over. He changed the premed major his father hoped he would pursue to art history and never looked back.

He completed his PhD at Princeton and, at the age of twenty-six, was hired by Boston's Museum of Fine Arts. Three years later was taken on by the Met as an associate. In six years he was the European paintings department's full curator. When he was offered the directorship of the de Young Museum in San Francisco two years later, he took it.

The de Young led to the Kimbell in Fort Worth and, almost inevitably, back to the Met. Twelve years later, at fifty-five, full of energy and with friends across the country, he decided he had done quite enough and wanted to write a book. After many departure lunches and dinners, he picked up and left for a fellowship at Princeton that allowed him to write, teach, and travel. That lasted only three years.

One day he told Jason what happened.

"I couldn't live there, really, those damned eastern winters, and I wanted to try a little writing, a novel, not academic stuff anyway, so I found a place up here in Pasadena and wrote. I've got one book out and another in print."

Robertson was still writing and still enjoying life in southern California, but Jason wanted to know less about what he was doing and more about what he thought. The former director knew about museums, a great deal about museums, and about issues of provenance and fakery.

The Shadow was wrong for the Ritz, so he took his old Jaguar. He had bought it at an automobile auction two years before, rebuilt the engine and electrical system, reupholstered it in leather, and painted it in British Racing Green, a conceit that only another Jaguar owner would appreciate. He loved listening to the car's big engine hum for long minutes at a time when traffic allowed.

He found his way to the Ritz Carlton, entered the dining room, and saw Robertson waiting for him at a window table. The room was only partially filled, widely spaced tables served by formally dressed waiters who moved about silently or hovered in the background.

Robertson poured an expensive Echezeaux into Jason's glass. Over the years the two men had gamed each other with good wines whenever they had dinner together, and this evening was no exception. It would be Robertson's turn to take Jason out the next time, and the favor would be repaid.

"So. Jason. What's this about? You usually give me a week's notice, but here you are, same day. And you want a quiet restaurant. Unlike you. And how is the Gabriel?"

"I'm not certain. That's why I wanted to talk to you. Sooner than later."

"Uh-hmm. Let's order, then talk."

The two men went through the formula that marked their discussions whenever they met, chatting idly about small matters until the main course was over.

"Now," said Robertson. He sat back in his chair, folded his hands in his lap, and arched his eyebrows. "What?"

Jason leaned forward and lowered his voice.

"Gerald, there's something odd going on. You know Martin, and you certainly know me. We have a major work of ancient art under consideration, a statue, and it's to be decided on at the next board meeting in a couple of weeks. Martin is in a state of nerves about it, more than I remember him ever being about anything. That's one thing. Then there's another, which is the letters we got from the seller, through a dealer. They're supposed to prove where it's been. Except for the current owner, none of the writers are living, and no one else has heard about it before now. Technical analysis of the letters might help, but Martin wants to go ahead without that."

"What's the statue?"

"An Athena. A huge one. Almost certainly from Sicily. Originally."

"Good?"

"Perfectly good. Can't be modern."

Robertson sat back for a moment. When he spoke again, he had a thoughtful look on his face.

"You've got several matters to think about. Let's take Martin first. Any number of things could make him anxious. There may be a problem with the museum you don't know about. He may be having difficulties with the board. Maybe it was Gabriel's arrival on his doorstep. Anything. Including the statue you're talking about."

He stopped talking for a moment, then continued in a lower voice.

"Leave it alone, Jason. Fussing about Martin won't get you anything but trouble."

The dining room had emptied. Only two couples remained. Robertson looked around, found a waiter, signaled for a coffee, and then went on.

"So, let's talk about the statue. You say it's big, and it's probably very expensive. Big, expensive works of art create big, complicated problems. Problems of authenticity, problems of current ownership, problems of provenance. Only ten, twenty years ago an antiquity could be bought by anyone, home free, if it was in a country that allowed its sale. England, Germany, Switzerland, the United States, wherever—even though you *knew* it had been illegally excavated.

"But now, if the provenance of an object isn't clear for the past thirty or forty years, a museum generally won't get it. In fact, they can't even take it as a *donation*. It's an orphan—legal, sure, but unwanted.

"They've really shot themselves in the foot on that one."

"Shot—what do you mean?"

"For God's sake—do you have any idea how much great art can't find a home in a museum? How many of these *orphans* there are? And what that means for them over time? Even excluding small things, there must be more than a million—maybe a lot more. And over time, many will deteriorate or be damaged or lost. It's a wretched way to take care of our own past. And, damn it, we—our own museums—did it to ourselves."

Robertson's eyes returned to Jason. "But of course you know all this, don't you? So let's get back to your statue. And the letters. You sound as if you don't like them."

"I don't know what to think. I don't have enough information. I don't have the envelopes to check, and I don't have the time to test the ink or paper. And there's the damned silence."

"Silence?"

"No mention by anyone else about this huge statue that's suddenly appeared. Someone else on the circuit—some other art dealer, some living person—should have heard *something* about it. But there's been nothing. Not a whisper."

The older man sat back in his chair, silent for a minute, and then gave a short laugh.

"Ah," he finally said, "I see the problem. I'd be concerned too. Faked documents aren't a new thing. I've seen them going back to the early nineteen hundreds. But they began to reappear in the 1960s, not so many at first, but then in bigger numbers in the seventies and eighties."

Robertson paused to take a last sip. "Faked documents are everywhere. So you have to be careful. If your letters are wrong—if they're fake—what does it say? Maybe a lot. The only reason to fake documents is to give a false history where there's no past history or to cover a history that the seller doesn't want known.

"With your big statue, Jason, I think you have to presume the last interpretation is the most likely. To be clear: if the letters are fake, the statue is probably recently out of the ground. Now that's a presumption, as I say, but any other one would be foolish. If anyone stepped forward with credible evidence that the statue was recently excavated—looted, in a word—the museum would look stupid for having bought it."

He set his glass on the table. "But its goes way beyond that. If it could be shown that a museum official—say a curator or a director—was involved in buying the statue *knowing* that it had been taken from Italy illegally, I don't have to tell you what that would mean. Dismissal from the museum. Possibly prosecution, even jail. Why the hell would anyone want to do that?"

"But I don't think that's the case here. Martin seems to believe the story the dealer's given him. He thinks the letters are good. He just wants to go ahead and get the thing."

"And you want to—what? Slow it down? Find out the truth?"

"Find out the truth. And protect the museum. That's what I'm supposed to do."

Robertson thought for a moment before he looked at Jason again.

"You may have a loyalty problem. Not really yours, but Martin's. If you pursue the documents, then you may find yourself running up against him. He may think you're disloyal. You'll need to be careful. But I see your point."

"Which is?"

"Deciding to simply ignore an object's provenance isn't a solution. It's a pathway to disaster."

Robertson was saying the same thing Jason had said to Kate that morning, in almost exactly the same words.

The cars arrived, one after the other. Robertson's was the first, and as he got in, he rolled down his window.

"You know, Jason, there's something about this that's not right. I don't know what it is. But I think you should take care with it. I've seen some things just turn bad, almost as if there's some sort of curse about them. I'm not saying that's the case here. Just take care of yourself."

Robertson waved as he drove off into the night.

The evening was late, but Jason took a slightly longer route home that ended with a snaking drive along Sunset and then a descent along a series of back streets until he reached his darkened house.

Thanks, Gerald. Talk my ear off and leave with a remark like that.

He turned out the garage lights, entered the house, went up the stairs to his bedroom, peeled off his clothes, and fell into a troubled sleep. Very early in the morning, long before dawn, he awoke and thought of his friend, an older man who had nothing between him and God.

Concern yourself with the statue. That's what he said, didn't he? Leave Martin alone. It's the statue that counts. And take care of yourself. What the hell did he mean by that?

CHAPTER NINE

The rain was falling in torrents, a cold rain off the Pacific that flooded down the escarpment edging the coast highway, carrying with it soil and loose rock that settled on the side of the road.

Jason exited Sunset at the coast, glancing briefly at the early morning traffic at Gladstone's restaurant, and then turned north, the wipers of the Jaguar banging all the way to Malibu and the museum beyond. The morning was entirely open, no appointments, and he wanted to shut himself in for an uninterrupted examination of the material Maybank had sent with the Athena—the examination Martin said he wanted by Thursday.

He had looked at Maybank's papers more than half a dozen times. All were letters, seven photocopied on European standard A4 paper, one on Richard Maybank's office stationery. Several were quite short, while others almost filled the page. They had puzzled him when he had first seen them three weeks earlier, and he had not been able to still his unease about them. And today, he needed to go back to basic analysis, the kind he once did routinely. But there was a vast difference between then and now. Once, he had almost limitless technical and human resources to call on. Not today. And not here. His staff could assist, but the success or failure of judgment lay on his shoulders alone.

He asked Amelia Mumford to hold his calls and shut the office door. He opened the Athena dossier and spilled the letters onto the desk.

There were eight, and Jason spread them out in chronological order. He had looked at them repeatedly but now wanted to capture, fully and finally, the essential information on each—who had generated or signed a document, what it said, what it meant, and the status of the author—and imbed it in memory for his discussion with Pryce the following day.

The first letter was a stiff note from the fourth Earl of Weymouth to his wife, written from Rome. It was dated 1832.

"My Dear Wife," it began—Jason could picture the earl, likely a portly fellow with muttonchops who cared not a whit about his wife. He let his eyes run through the scrawled handwriting until he came to the words that stood out: "...and on this trip I have bought many things that I am having sent back to Brigham House, including something quite large, a marble that will astound our visitors..."

But it doesn't mean a damn thing, he thought. Could be the Athena—or just a stone relief. In the nineteenth century, virtually every stone was a "marble."

The second letter was from a certain Reginald Fortescue, a Weymouth relative who had visited Brigham House in 1898. It was a thank-you note to the sixth earl following a weekend of what must have been extremely energetic grouse shooting. In his letter, which mentioned his thrill at having bagged "twenty brace" in a single afternoon, Fortescue referred to a "wonderful large statue lying down in the granary."

"My dear Weymouth," Fortescue had written, "you must bring it out and put it up! Imagine the effect in your entrance hall!"

Fortescue's effusiveness about the "statue in the granary" carried nothing about what statue was meant, not a word.

There wasn't anything there either. Fortescue could mean the Athena. Or something else. But why the tantalizing hint, with nothing clear? Fortescue's indifference? Or was it chum on the waters, a subtle lure? Was he being too convoluted here? He had been over it all before, perhaps too many times.

The third letter was more promising. The letterhead showed the signature of a certain Professor Weston Gates, writing from King's College, Oxford, where Gates taught. It was dated October 1925.

Gates's letter mentioned a statue. It urged the then eighth Earl of Weymouth, who Gates referred to as "My Dear Philip," to "have it put together properly, so that the world can see it in all its beauty."

Jesus! Beauty? What was the man thinking of? The Athena? What's beautiful about it? Colossal—staggering, maybe. Not beautiful. And dark, with a dark shadow that seemed to come from inside. Or was Gates referring to the Athena at all?

He extended his finger and touched the signature. It was smudged, almost beyond recognition.

Too bad. Or too convenient?

Jason peered at the fourth document. It was penned by a Professor Ernst Langlotz to the ninth Earl of Weymouth and was dated September 1952.

Langlotz was writing from Bonn, where he taught Greek and Roman Art at the Friedrich-Wilhelms University. During a visit to England, he had evidently learned of a large statue in the possession of the Weymouth family—by Gates?—and had obtained an invitation to visit Brigham House.

Langlotz's letter, typed on personal letterhead stationery, was specific.

"What an amazing figure!" Langlotz wrote. "It is the largest imaginable. The great body of the goddess is wonderful in itself, but the head, which I believe is of purest Greek Island marble, is a miracle in its own right. Of course it is from *Magna Graecia*. I would be honored if your lordship might allow me the privilege of publishing this piece, which is something for the interest of all scholarship." The language was stilted but clear. So was his signature.

Langlotz was a figure. He had died years earlier, in 1978, but he was widely known to scholars and collectors alike. Jason had read several of his remarkable articles on the sculpture of the Greek colonies of southern Italy—the *Magna Graecia* mentioned in his letter. He'd have had no doubt about what he'd seen, certainly—but, now, the curator could not care less about what the scholar thought. What he cared about was Langlotz's signature on the fourth letter and the friends he had made who were still alive today and who could verify it. Leo, to whom Jason had spoken two days earlier, was one.

Leo had studied and taught in Berlin before he was dismissed from his job by the Nazis, who arrested him a few years later. Somehow he had survived the horrors of the death camps. After the war he found a teaching appointment at the University of Zurich and in time had started a successful business buying and selling coins, first by himself and later for one of the great Swiss banks that lined the Bahnhofstrasse. As the market for ancient objects had grown, Leo expanded the business to include antiquities, getting to know suppliers from Italy, Greece, and Turkey, many of whom worked out of small shops in Munich, just a short train ride from Zurich.

Jason had met Leo more than twenty years earlier, and since then their lives had become interwoven at many levels. They attended conferences together, gave dinners for each other, even traveled together for two weeks into eastern Turkey.

Leo had known Ernst Langlotz, of course. When Jason called to ask if he could find something with Langlotz's signature on it, Leo had said yes immediately. He did not ask why.

Langlotz's letter, with his clear signature, was essential. The others could be thrown away. This is the one that had to stand.

Letters five and six linked. The fifth was from a London art dealer, Arthur Tanner, who appeared to know of the Weymouth family's declining fortunes. Tanner had written Robert Weymouth, the ninth earl, then in his eightieth year, to ask if he might consider selling "the statue" that he understood the earl to own.

Robert had written a firm no to the dealer in a testy letter that said he did not want to be bothered again. Tanner died soon afterward. So had Robert Weymouth. There was nothing in the exchange between the two that indicated that the statue that Tanner and Robert had mentioned had anything to do with the one that stood in the gallery across the Gabriel's courtyard. There were countless statues in every English country house, and Brigham House had its share.

Is there anything in these *things*, anything that can help? There's nothing there about an Athena at all.

The last two letters were an exchange between the current tenth earl and Richard Maybank, stating the earl's interest in selling a statue "that has been in my family for many generations, head, arms, and body, but only at the right price," and Maybank's reply that he would be pleased to act as intermediary. The letters were both dated September of the current year—three months earlier. And then there was the original of the letter of offer Maybank had sent Pryce, confirming the offer of the statue to the museum for $40 million. Jason looked at it for a moment and then put it under the others.

He wanted a place to think things through, undisturbed. The Gabriel's restaurant would have few visitors at this still early midmorning hour, he knew, and he started out the department's door and turned in that direction, Amelia Mumford's eyes following him to the corridor. He bought a coffee and sat at a corner table.

What do we really know? What makes sense here? Or is it all nonsense? He tried to lay out the facts that he had, then stand back to see if there was a pattern he was missing. The letters seemed to hold together if he believed they referred to the Athena, but every time he thought about them they fell apart.

Why are they only photocopies? Maybank says the Weymouths want to hold onto the originals. And why don't we have photocopies of the envelopes? They've been lost, Maybank says. But that means we can't check the postmarks. Who's around to verify that the statue was with the Weymouths for even the past thirty years? Maybe Weymouths staff, or friends. But it would screw it up if I called them. And it would sure as hell screw me up with Martin.

He went through the list of letters and who had written them, ticking these off on his right hand until he ran out of fingers: Fourth Weymouth: *dead*. Fortescue: *dead*. Gates: *dead*. Langlotz: *dead*. Tanner: *dead*. The ninth earl, Robert Weymouth: *dead*.

Maybank and Frederick Weymouth were alive, but Maybank was a self-interested source, the seller with every reason to deceive. At one level, Maybank's gallery was entirely reputable. Jason could not recall any time Maybank had sought to sell anything but the best material. But the man was known to be ruthless in his business practices. He would have no qualms about making up a story that would help sell the Athena, or anything else.

But Weymouth?

Jason spent a long afternoon doing an exhaustive search on Frederick Weymouth. He gave special attention to the Weymouth family background in the online versions of Burke's and Debrett's great works on English peerage. From both, the chronology of the fourth and later earls was consistent with the dates of the photocopied letters and with the fact that Brigham House, the family home, had been until recently the property of the Weymouths since the sixteenth century. Debrett briefly noted that Frederick Weymouth had moved to London in the early 1980s and had gifted Brigham House to the National Trust in 1995.

Not with the statue, surely? So what did he do with it?

Trawling through the Internet for any mention of the reasons for Frederick Weymouth's move or any mention of the statue yielded nothing, not a clue. The letter of offer to Maybank said nothing whatever. In fact, the tenth earl's note was only a single sentence long. Maybank had probably written it himself.

And why would the Weymouths not have shown it for a hundred and fifty years? And keep it in a granary at Brigham House?

Brigham House. It was a lead.

Both Burke and Debrett said that Brigham House was a classic design by Robert Adam, one of England's greatest nineteenth-century architects. That took him to the museum's library, where he found a copy of Eileen Harris's *Country Houses of Robert Adam*. Harris had described the house and early construction and gave exterior views of the main building taken from the archives of *Country Life*. And she had included a color plate of a late eighteenth-century painting that showed the house and outbuildings, including the granary.

Yet they kept the statue out of sight in a granary for more than a century and a half? Why would they do that?

He could think of no good answer. He wanted to talk to Frederick Weymouth, to ask him directly about the statue, but he knew that would not have been smart at all. If he tried to see Weymouth, he would be going behind Martin's back. He'd be saying he thought Maybank was lying and that Martin had made a mistake in believing him.

Martin would be furious. If he were Martin, he'd be furious too. He wondered for a moment if he could ask Martin to tell Maybank they needed to see Weymouth and get the questions resolved. But that would have the same effect, to paint Maybank as a liar.

There was something else that had been at the edge of his thoughts, just out of reach, pushed far behind while he was looking at the letters, and it eluded him for a moment. Then he got it.

The breaks in the sculpture. They pointed somewhere, but where? Kate said the statue was broken as it was being taken out of the ground. But does that make any sense? Could it have been broken to move it in smaller pieces, make it easier to ship out of Italy?

There was an acid taste in his mouth. The whole thing stank. Maybe a verified Langlotz signature could save it. But if the signature was faked, if it was wrong, they would have to stop. And ask a lot more questions.

He was about to go back to the office when his department associate, Cynthia Greenwalt, appeared.

"Why are you looking so sour, Jason? No sun?" Cynthia knew he loved the southern California sunlight and teased him about the dark look he tended to take on when it had disappeared.

"Puzzling."

"Athena?" She turned her head slightly. It was a mannerism that appeared when she wanted to emphasize a point, or a question.

"Yes." They knew each other well, often lapsing into single-word shorthand.

"The provenance documents?"

"Yes."

"Problem?"

He didn't want to suggest a problem, not to Cynthia. Not to anyone, not yet.

"Maybe. I can't tell. There's nothing to either prove or disprove them, either way."

"But Martin wants this all wrapped up Thursday?" He had told Cynthia about his last meeting with Pryce.

"That's right."

"And if there's nothing demonstrably wrong with the letters?" She was probing.

He shrugged. "Then there's nothing demonstrably wrong with the letters. Even if that doesn't make them right."

"Jason, I hope there's not a problem. It's such an amazing object."

She fell silent for a moment.

"Martin wants this done really fast, doesn't he? You must feel as if he's put a gun to your head."

"No, not quite." He let the thought linger and smiled at her, and she picked up on it immediately.

"*What?* When did that happen?"

"Some time ago." His smile broadened. "I'd be happy to tell you about it, but you've heard the stories about me. I'd have to shoot you then."

She took on a pained look at his too-often-told joke. "OK, Jason, enough. Let's button this up and get some lunch. I want to tell you about a nice discovery I made in the storeroom. Or maybe not so nice."

He gave in and followed her to the restaurant line, ordering a chicken salad and a Rio Mar beer—inevitable at the museum: the Rio Mar brewery, named for his years on the Amazon, was one of Andrew Gabriel's wholly owned companies.

When they were seated, he looked at her with a slight smile. "So, what's the discovery?"

"The Nessos relief. The one Barovsky bought years ago."

Jason knew it. A lovely work in Asia Minor marble, Roman, beginning of the third century AD, a panel carved in high relief showing Hercules shooting an arrow into the centaur Nessos, who was trying to carry off his wife. The panel had been in the storeroom since its acquisition four years earlier and was waiting for a moment when it could be exhibited.

"Yes?"

Now Cynthia had a smile on her face. The curator knew she was about to spring something on him.

"Well, it seems to mate with other panels of a known sarcophagus."

"Oh, nice. And you've found out where they are?"

"Yes. They're all in Turkey. Antalya. The museum there mounted them up last summer. I just got their catalog. All the panels of the sarcophagus are in place. Except one. Ours. The fit is perfect."

"For God's sake," he said. There was nothing to do but tell the Turkish government that the Gabriel had the panel and would send it to the Antalya Museum right away. Museums did not steal from other museums.

"Thanks, Cynthia. I'm always happy to know these things." He thought he must have looked as though he had just taken a bite out of a lemon.

He pushed the statue out of his mind for the rest of the afternoon and at the end of the day was surprised that he had been able to do so. But at least he had a clear course ahead. He would have to lay out to Martin his misgivings, all of them. The director surely would want to know of any problems with it.

I'll tell him the photocopies aren't good enough. Maybank has to send the originals of the letters. And the envelopes, any remaining envelopes. That will help. Martin won't want to risk the museum's reputation or his own on a purchase that might be stolen.

It was late and he had friends to see for dinner. He was about to turn off his desktop when he noticed an incoming message from Leo. Tomorrow, he thought, I haven't time now. But he pulled up the message and the attachment and printed both and then rose and stretched and left for the garage. Tomorrow would be good enough.

CHAPTER TEN

Jason awoke to the drumming of rain on his roof. The early morning weather report was grim. The El Niño-strengthened Pacific storm that had slammed onto the coast the day before was the worst in years, dumping six inches of water in twenty-four hours, closing the airport, leaving the Santa Barbara area awash under nine inches in a single day, flooding people out of mobile-home parks, shattering tree limbs, and overflowing storm channels across the Los Angeles basin.

The announcer said the coast highway was closed below Malibu, where a mudslide had dumped rocks and dirt over a large section of the roadway. Access to the Gabriel would be cut off, Jason knew, probably through the rest of the day. He would have to take the long back drive to the museum on Interstate 405 and the Ventura Freeway, a detour that would add an hour or more to his travel time. The report said the rain would continue into the morning.

He considered waiting until the roads were clear, but that would delay his meeting with Pryce. He wanted to get that over and done with as soon as he could. Martin would also have to use the same back roadways to get to the museum, and Jason wondered if the director would go to his office at all.

I'd better call, he thought, and reached for the telephone the same moment it rang.

Pryce was brusque. "Jason, we seem to be flooded out. If the coast highway is cleared by noon I'll go into the museum. But I want to know where you are with the letters sooner than that. So let's meet here, at my house. At eleven. Can you do that?"

"Of course. I don't have the Athena file with me, Martin, but I can tell you where I am."

"I'll call Kate. And Jason—"

"Yes?"

"You've good news, I hope."

Jason felt his jaw clench.

"Martin—" But before he could say more, the line had gone dead.

What did he need to resolve his concerns? The question nagged at him on the drive to Pryce's house. He'd at least have to see both Maybank and Weymouth. Get the originals of the photocopied letters. That would take three days, perhaps four. Was there enough time for that before the board met? Could the acquisition be put off?

He felt a ripple of unease. About what? His meeting with Pryce? The Athena? That something would turn up to make the statue unbuyable? All of those? He was far into a labyrinth, with no Ariadne's thread to guide him out.

He came to the cul-de-sac at the end of Hanley and eased in behind Pryce's Suburban and Kate's aging Volvo. Frances Pryce's car was gone, which meant that only the three of them would be present. He strode to the door, shook the water off his jacket, entered, and walked down a corridor, pausing for a moment to admire a set of portrait drawings that hung on the corridor wall. Pryce collected modestly but with a good eye and hung art he had carefully selected over the years.

He heard voices in the small study and found Kate, looking small in an enormous wing chair, with Pryce standing above her.

The director waved him to a sofa.

"Jason, come on in, join us," he said, a smile on his face if not in his voice. "Kate says she's finished her report on the Athena. The statue's consistent, well preserved, no question about authenticity." He turned to Kate.

"Anything else?"

"That's about it. We can't be sure the head was intended for this statue, but the cutting at the body's neckline is very close to the size you'd need for the inserted neck. The head was probably intended for *this* body." Kate's verbal reports tended to be brief and clinical, and this was no different.

"So, Jason, what do you have?"

The curator hesitated, glanced at Kate, and then turned to fully face Pryce. "I'm afraid we may have a problem with the documents."

The words hung in the air. Pryce's eyes were blank, his face expressionless. The rain continued to fall in sheets, pelting the panes of the French doors that exited onto the garden.

Pryce's voice, when he spoke, was even. "What do you mean?"

"The letters Maybank gave us are just incomplete. They may cause us a problem unless we can find something to verify them. I haven't been able to do that yet."

"What more do you want?"

"Something that shows that any of the critical letters that were written before Frederick Weymouth obtained the statue—any of them—are authentic. And that they refer to *this* statue and not some other object."

The director remained standing but did not respond. Jason began to feel as if he were swimming upstream. *This isn't going the way it should. Why doesn't Martin get it? The problem's so clear.*

He went on, more cautiously.

"Look, Martin, the whole pack of documents is peculiar. Some are smudged. We have no envelopes, which means we have no postmarks that could date the letters. All the writers are dead except for the current earl. Then we have this story that the statue was put in a granary—by a gentleman farmer who never farmed! And left just lying there, not seen by almost anyone for more than a hundred and fifty years. That just doesn't make much sense."

"Is that all?"

"Not quite. It gets worse. We've been told that the fourth earl bought the statue during a visit to Italy. The statue has to be from Sicily. The stone and the pollen grains can't come from anywhere else. But we know the fourth Weymouth never went south of Naples. It's really difficult to believe that this huge figure was carted to Naples just to show an English nobleman on a grand tour."

"What are you saying?"

"What I'm saying, Martin, is that the history we've been given doesn't really hang together. There's nothing that clearly supports Maybank's or Frederick Weymouth's claim about the statue's origin."

Pryce looked out the window and then at Jason. Kate seemed to have disappeared into the upholstery of her chair.

"So, if you can't establish a positive, you're presuming a negative about the Athena's provenance. Is that it?"

"No, not at all. Just that there's nothing positive. That's all. We have this story with nothing to back it up."

"Jason, the absence of evidence—"

"—isn't evidence of absence. I agree. Still, it just looks wrong. If anyone outside the museum saw the letters, they'd think the same thing. It really seems risky to go ahead and get the statue without some positive proof, anything really, that makes it clear it wasn't dug up last year."

"Are you saying the documents are wrong?" Pryce's voice had risen slightly.

"No, I didn't say that. I can't say that."

"Do you think we're being set up somehow, Jason? That someone is trying to damage us by selling us the statue with faked documentation?"

Jason was surprised by the anger in Pryce's voice. What the hell is that about? Does Martin want to know what I think, or is he saying something else?

"No, that wouldn't make any sense at all. But I think we have to ask some hard questions, at least to the point when we're satisfied there's nothing that can come back to bite us."

"What exactly do you want?" Pryce's tone was sharp, barely civil.

"I'd like to talk to Frederick Weymouth, and any members of his family or staff who may know about the statue." He stopped for a moment, uncertain how to proceed. What is the man's problem? What had Robertson said? That Pryce had many things on his mind, and they may have overwhelmed his judgment? But that doesn't make sense. He's as sharp as I've ever seen him, not someone distracted by problems.

"And, Martin, I'd like to be sure the critical letter, the one by Langlotz, is authentic. In fact—"

The director interrupted. "End it."

"I'm sorry?"

"End it. It's time to end it, Jason. Stop the investigation. This has gone on long enough."

Jason sat, dumbstruck. Not knowing what to say, he said nothing.

"Stop the investigation," Pryce repeated. His face was stony. "Stop it. The board meets in two weeks. I have to put a full written report in their hands before then. It's the decision meeting for the Athena. We can't go on and on. I'm sorry. It's time to let go. Let go of the investigation."

The words were peremptory. And final.

Jason had been about to mention Leo, but the discussion—indeed, all discussion—had been ended.

He thought about asking Pryce to explain and then stress the reasons for keeping the review open. But he knew he'd be asking for something he wouldn't get.

"Do you *really* want me to do that, Martin?"

"I do. Stop it. Now."

The meeting was over.

Jason felt his face burning as he left the house. He heard the door open again and turned as Kate came up to him. "Jesus, that was really brutal. I've never seen anything like it. He was wrong to treat you that way. I'm so sorry. Are you OK?"

He could think of nothing to say. He was in a quiet rage and he wanted to be alone.

"Can I call you later?"

"Yes, sure. Give me a few hours. I need to get into the open air, do some thinking." He seated himself in the Jaguar, started the engine, rolled down his window, looked at Kate as if he were about to speak, turned his eyes back to Pryce's doorway for a moment, and drove off into the rain.

Inside, Pryce remained standing, then walked to the French doors. The rain was beginning to slacken. He would make the long drive along the back road to the museum after all. The unpleasant thought came to him that the statue's story had too many loose ends to it. He shouldn't be having this much difficulty keeping them raveled up. But he'd dealt with Jason, and Jason would end his search. That would take care of it.

CHAPTER ELEVEN

Jason drove into the gloom of the early afternoon and headed down Sunset toward the coast in a state of simmering anger.

What happened back there? That was supposed to be a simple meeting. Martin should have delayed the acquisition. But he wouldn't hear of it.

He came to the highway and turned north toward Malibu. The rain had become a slow drizzle, but the roadway was passable. As he reached the Topanga cutoff, he came to an orange sign that said the highway further north was closed. A police cruiser was stationed next to the sign, and a uniformed officer was directing traffic to a detour. He would have to go inland, or go back.

He spun the wheel, exiting onto the two-lane canyon road that curved up through a notch in the hills, toward the small communities of Fernwood and Topanga before it crested and started to wind down toward the San Fernando Valley.

He hadn't been there for years, and as he geared down and drove between the increasingly sheer slopes of gravel cliffs, he wondered again how the houses in the canyon, surrounded though they were by great cities that sprawled in every direction, had managed to retain an untouched look. The buildings, mostly wood, some with stone chimneys, were small and sometimes barely visible behind a stand of eucalyptus but often just blending in with the oak, pine, and chaparral that covered the canyon floor.

Something went wrong at the meeting. Could I have said anything that would convince him? Was he listening at all?

A leftward bend around a massive overhanging cliff opened up to a roadway that ran between a set of low buildings framing both sides of the canyon. The rain had stopped. There were touches of blue in the breaks between the clouds. He pulled the Jaguar onto an open shoulder and parked and then hoisted himself out and walked up into the town.

He felt as though he had entered another world, where people escaping the chaos of the city had settled and built houses and a few stores and a schoolhouse and raised children and painted or wrote and sold crafts to passers-by to make enough money to pay for the next week of their lives. The buildings all seemed to be from the same era, the 1960s or a bit later. There was a general store and a handful of artisans' shops to his left, and on the opposite side of the road, a post office and a store that sold herbal medicines and advertised a therapy pool in the rear: "bathing suits optional." An acupuncture clinic seemed to have been added as an afterthought.

Did I screw it up? Make a mistake?

He passed a small store that sold Christian and Buddhist booklets. Years before, he recalled, a group of dedicated nudists had settled in one of Topanga's side canyons with a name the "Elysium Institute" or some such, that evoked a vision of communal bliss and sexual freedom. They called themselves the "hundredth monkey" and believed they could be a catalyst that would spread their new-age views across the country. The experiment did not last long. When they were made unexpectedly bourgeois by the money from the sale of their property, they packed up and moved on.

Topanga was dilapidated but reassuring in its own way. The memory of his discussion with the director continued to flood his thoughts. No. I didn't make a mistake. I gave a fair presentation. Something else happened. What? Martin had cornered him. Forced him on the defensive, demanded he not carry the document investigation further, and then forced him to silence. So what am I supposed to do? Be quiet and do nothing? That's exactly what he wants me to do.

He turned back and heard the cry of a gull just above his head. It was a sound he knew well from the summers he had spent as a boy on a rocky island off the Connecticut shore, when he had walked among the driftwood and eel grasses and dried kelp and watched the gulls nesting among the rounded stones. Like the one above, there was always one that would cry out at him in surprise and affront with the unanswerable questions: Who are you? Why are you here?

He pointed the car toward the road down to the Pacific shore, turned a corner, turned another, and as he did a dove rose out of the roadway immediately ahead and barely escaped being hit. He saw a quick flash of feathers from the corner of his eye, then it was gone. He braked and downshifted, slowing the Jaguar further.

Steady down, Jason, slow down.

As the sky lightened, a cold, hard determination began to take hold. An idea formed and fed upon itself.

Where do I begin to unravel this? London? Morgantina?

The thought had washed away his anger. He glanced in the mirror as he turned onto the coast road and saw for an instant his own face and, somewhat to his surprise, the hint of a smile.

CHAPTER TWELVE

As Jason drove down the Topanga road, Martin Pryce was arriving at the Gabriel museum. The garage held only a few dozen cars. With the highway flooded, most of the staff had remained at home, and there were almost no visitors. He had no outside appointments and would have no interruptions. No staff demands and, best, no insistent patrons or board members needing attention.

He knew a lot about museum board members. Some very bright ones were deeply interested in the collections, but many were happy just to associate themselves with museums and would pay for the pleasure—collectors, corporate executives, and, here, film people. But he knew they all had avarices and vanities that could be turned into financial support and, sometimes, priceless donations for the museums he served.

As a young curator, Pryce treated all of them with respect, always being helpful where he could and taking care to never seem smarter than they thought they were themselves.

He had also learned from them. From the educated and well-spoken, he learned new vocabulary and syntax; from the cultivated he learned poise; from the powerful he learned the uses of authority. And from the very rich, he learned that for some people, money had no importance at all. In time, he migrated naturally into the halls of the barons of society with whom he now associated, every week, if not every day.

But he could never match them. He had no grand house, no collection of great art, no second or third homes on vacation islands, no stable of thoroughbreds he could run at Belmont or Saratoga. He could never take an entire restaurant to entertain his friends or charter a fully staffed yacht that would take him and Frances and ten or a dozen guests to the Turkish coast. He could never charter a Lear for a ski weekend in the high Sierras. He was forever pressing his nose up against the country club window, always looking in, never belonging.

That had all changed on the day he had gone to Richard Maybank's Jermyn Street gallery, when the antiquities dealer had taken him to see a "wonderful great statue" that he said the Gabriel should have.

The museum café was vacant except for Jose Montoya, who gave him a coffee and made change. Montoya lived on the grounds and did double duty as assistant to the restaurant's cooks. But today there were no cooks, and Montoya was proudly, if temporarily, the restaurant's manager, chef, and cashier, absolute ruler of his very small kingdom.

Pryce walked slowly along the corridor, saying a few words to each of the few security guards he met. He passed the rooms with Roman statuary and ancient bronzes, then around toward the museum's exhibit of Greek sculpture and vases. These were Jason's galleries, but none of them would hold the Athena.

No, he thought, the statue will be the show-stealer from the beginning. He'd put it just inside the entrance to the museum, an awe-inspiring figure that would take the breath away from everyone who entered, just as it had done to the old man.

He came to Jason's office and started to walk past, but noticed the door was slightly open. Inside, the lights were off and no one was present. As he turned to leave, a sheet of paper in the department's printer caught his eye. He picked it up idly.

The words on the sheet, written in a neat scholarly hand, leapt out at him.

Mit freundlichen Grüßen. Ernst Langlotz.

With best wishes. Ernst Langlotz.

The signature was bold and clear on the paper.

Pryce put the sheet back in the printer tray. Less than a minute later he was in his own office, jabbing at his telephone. When Elspeth Clark came on the line, he said he wanted to speak to Gabriel.

"*Now*," he said. "I don't care what he's doing."

She put him through right away.

"Andrew, I need to talk to you about a small matter at the museum. Today, if possible."

"This is a bad day, Martin. Lawyers and accountants all day long. Can't it wait until Monday?"

"Sooner, Andrew, if you can. And not on the telephone."

Gabriel hesitated. "All right, then. Tonight. Dinner. Café Torino. I'll get a small room."

Torino was filled and noisy every evening, but the food and service were beyond compare, and it was among the few places the old man would go. A private room would allow them to talk quietly. It would be no problem for the old man to get one. Torino always treated him very well.

Gabriel completed his thought.

"Later. Say eight. But I really want to know what the hell this is all about."

CHAPTER THIRTEEN

Six thousand miles to the east, Cosimo Galante was having an urgent conversation of his own.

"Pisano! When the fuck did this happen? This morning? *Merda.* Who did this?"

The man on the other end of the line spoke briefly.

"And is he talking? That little toad better not say a fucking word if he knows what's good for him."

Galante's face was flushed. The veins stood out on his forehead. His voice had risen to a shout.

"So what do I do? Wait until the fat toad starts talking? Do I have to come up there and fix it?" Galante hated Rome, everything about it. And the people, all assholes he thought. The moment they knew he was Sicilian—and how could they not, with his accent and dark skin?—they treated him like some kind of insect.

"No, you idiot! I don't mean find him a fucking lawyer! I mean *fix* it. And I'm not going to explain that."

More words from the other end.

"So you want me to wait. You know, if that little prick starts talking, he's going to talk about all of us. You too."

The voice at the other end continued and then stopped.

"All right then. Not now. But stay on it. If I hear one word, just one fucking word, that he's talking, I'm going to have him fixed. *Subito.* Right away."

He slammed down the telephone.

"*Merda,*" he said to the empty room. He felt like strangling someone. If Pisano talks, the Carabinieri will be all over Morgantina—*my* Morgantina!—probing and digging, looking for an excavation. *His* excavation. And they'll find it. And find Sergio.

Merda! Maybe it's time to get out of the business. But Pisano first. The little toad was totally spineless. He'd probably have to fix it after all.

CHAPTER FOURTEEN

T he telephone was ringing as Jason walked in the door of his
house. His rage had abated, but his patience was near an end.
He thought of not answering but then picked up the receiver.

"Jason?" Kate had never called him at home, and he was
surprised.

"Jason, I'm going to get dinner, but would you like to come over
for dessert, perhaps a movie?"

"What?" Jason had been to Kate's apartment a few times when
she'd had people over for drinks, usually in numbers. He wasn't
sure he understood.

"It's simple. I don't want to cook tonight, so no food—and we
don't have to talk about the museum or Martin or the statue. In
fact, I'd rather not. And you don't have to say a thing. Just come
over, see a movie with me, and call it a day. And Jason—"

"Yes?"

"You'll want to know what this is about, so I'll tell you. I'd really
like company at the end of this horrible day, and I can't think of
anyone else who would understand. But—" She paused.

"But what?" Jason felt like he had been reduced to monosyllables.

"You don't have to say a thing. I mean it." Was there laughter in her voice? By the time he had thought of a response she had already hung up.

He went out onto the kitchen porch. The telephone rang again.

"Jason, look, if you're busy or just don't want to, it's fine; it's really no problem."

He found his voice. "I'll be there, Kate. Thanks."

He put down the receiver.

A movie. Then home. That's fine. But his thoughts were beyond the evening.

End it, Martin had said.

Martin meant put an end to Jason's examination of the documents. But behind those there was a trail that led to some greater truth, and the documents were just a marker on that path. To where? London and Morgantina. He'd go to both.

He knew London—but Morgantina? Why would he want to see Morgantina? To discover something that he couldn't anywhere else? Or because he'd never be satisfied if he didn't see the place?

In the end it really didn't matter. It was all the same and he couldn't let it go.

CHAPTER FIFTEEN

C afé Torino was a watering hole for the young and rich, the old and rich, and everyone else as long as they could pay the premium markup that went on the bill.

Still, as all those who had been there knew, Torino *delivered*. It offered outstanding cuisine, ambience to the eyebrows, and waiters who were the best that Hollywood's acting studios could provide, all of them assiduously working on their next audition, even as their day jobs required them to serve food and drink to the luminaries of the entertainment industry.

A suavely dark and well-dressed Augusto—no one knew his last name—oversaw the reservations hostess, politely greeted Torino's regular clientele as they entered, and carefully assessed where everyone should be placed, whether they wanted visibility or discretion or just needed to be put somewhere out of the way. Once in the main dining room, guests would either be seated or asked to stop at the bar, where they would wait for long minutes for a desired table to be cleared. Special clients, those who merited Torino's most careful attention, would be taken immediately to an open table or ushered to one of the restaurant's private rooms on the second floor. It was all part of the brilliant design of Franco Baldissaro, Torino's owner, who had established the model for his most successful restaurant in Washington before taking it to Beverly Hills. Baldissaro's showmanship was as much a part of the entertainment business as the clients he served.

When Pryce said he was there as Andrew Gabriel's guest, Augusto snapped his fingers at a hovering assistant and issued a quiet instruction. The assistant took Pryce's coat and motioned the director to follow him up the stairs to the first small dining room at the top.

The older man was already seated. "Martin, come enjoy the oysters."

Gabriel loved seafood. He had already downed half a dozen bluepoints, flown in from the east, where they bred more easily than in the cold waters of the Pacific.

"A drink, Martin? A nice wine?"

Pryce decided Pellegrino would be enough. This was a business discussion, not a social event.

When they had ordered and their waiter had left the room, Gabriel leaned over the table. "So, Martin, what's this about? Why the urgent meeting?"

"The statue. And Jason Connor."

"What's the problem?"

"Connor's got a bug about the statue. He just won't give up the background investigation."

"Really? What does he want?"

A perplexed look came across Pryce's face. "Frankly, Andrew, I don't know. You've heard the stories of his earlier work in the government. State Department? CIA? Who knows? Whoever he worked for, he now seems to see something suspicious underneath every chair. He says there may be a problem. He can't let go of it."

Gabriel's eyes steadied on the museum director. "*Is* there a problem?"

"None, Andrew. Not one. I've been involved with the statue for the past four months, since Maybank showed it to me in London, and I should know. But Jason's dug his feet in. He wants the museum to drop it, I think, just not buy it, and he seems to be using the background check as a way to scuttle it."

"Why would he do that?"

"I've got no idea. But he appears to want the statue to be seen as a huge mistake, something that the museum shouldn't buy. He even suggested the idea of a setup. Then there's the other thing."

The older man held up his hand and gave his full attention to Pryce.

"Stop, Martin. Setup? What setup?"

"He thinks someone's out to get the museum, and that they're using the Athena to do so. A stalking horse that will blacken our reputation."

Pryce was on delicate ground. He wanted Gabriel concerned but not alarmed.

"Have you ever heard of such a thing?"

"Never. Ridiculously high asking prices, sure. Fakery, certainly. But deliberately trying to bring disrepute to a museum? With a great work of art? It's unbelievable."

It had taken Pryce time to prepare for this moment, but now it was here. He lowered his voice and went on.

"But, you know, it's consistent with his background."

Gabriel had half-finished his turbot, but he put down his fork and knife and peered at the director with unblinking blue eyes.

"For God's sake, Martin, what does that mean?"

"Angleton." Pryce said the name in a barely audible voice, almost a whisper. In the long minute that followed, he took another bite of salmon.

"Angleton?" Gabriel had an empty look for a minute, but Pryce could see a small light turn on in the back of the old man's mind.

"James Jesus Angleton. Head of the CIA's counterintelligence staff. One of their brightest people—but someone who'd been made an utter fool of by the Soviets. You'll remember, Andrew, they were able to penetrate British intelligence, and maybe ours too. Kim Philby, Guy Burgess, Donald McLean. You must have heard of Philby."

"Yes." Gabriel had now also lowered his voice.

"Angleton never forgave himself. And never forgot. He went on a relentless hunt for Soviet agents inside the Agency. Moles. He became obsessed with the idea that they'd been penetrated. He went on a witch hunt that destroyed the careers of a lot of people and almost destroyed the organization. He died in the late eighties, but he left the place riddled with uncertainty and paranoia."

Gabriel had stopped eating entirely. He carefully put his fork down and placed his hands on either side of his dish.

"What's that to do with Connor?"

"Andrew, if he was in the CIA in fact, he may really think that someone is out to get the museum. Using the Athena. I mean, that's just preposterous, but he may really believe it."

The older man fell silent, lost in thought for a moment. He seemed to have grown smaller in his chair. Finally he looked up at Pryce.

"And what's the other thing?"

"Andrew, it's no secret that Jason has his sights on my job. Not now or next year, but at some time in the future. But if I can be seen to make some terrible mistake, that wouldn't bother him a bit."

Gabriel's eyes went around the small dining room. The waiters had gone and there was no one, other than Pryce, to hear his next words.

"And you're absolutely sure the statue is no mistake?"

"None. It's as good as you can get. It will be the centerpiece for the museum, the first great work of art people will see when they walk in. There's nothing like it, anywhere. Every other one like it, in every museum or private collection, will pale by comparison, Andrew. We mustn't lose it."

He watched as Gabriel's mind turned over. "It will become a monument, Andrew. If we get it, it will take the name of the museum itself. Your name. Just imagine it, Andrew: the Gabriel Athena."

The Gabriel Athena. Pryce could see something move behind the old man's eyes.

"Connor. You're really saying he's been blinded by his own ambition? I always thought he was pretty straight."

"Andrew, he either sees a conspiracy about the statue that makes no sense, or he wants to cause a failure that he can lay at my door. Either way, we'll lose it."

Pryce had led the old man to a choice that was as stark as it was unavoidable. Gabriel would have to go against his trusted director and lose the statue or dismiss the curator and have the colossal statue—the Gabriel Athena!—in the museum.

The older man slowly swirled the wine in his glass, then fastened his eyes on the director. "Can we fire him? With no noise?" Gabriel detested public exposure.

"I wish there were some other way, but we'll have to. And, no, I don't think there'll be any noise. Everything about him says he'd never go public about leaving, although I'd want to find a reason to hang it on. Also, he signed a non-disclosure agreement when he came to the museum, and that should keep him still. Our friends at the Getty have been doing that for years. Successfully. Do you remember the curator they hung out to dry a few years ago? She didn't make a peep."

"What happened?"

"You must remember the event. The Italians charged her with conspiracy to loot antiquities from Italy. They put her on trial in

Rome. The Getty paid for her legal costs. And she didn't say a thing, just stood there and took it. Even though their director and board approved every single one of her recommendations."

Pryce looked straight at the old man. "And not one of them stepped forward to take responsibility."

Gabriel took another sip of wine. "Money. Would paying him money help? We could keep him on salary for a year or so to keep him quiet."

Money was Gabriel's solution for a lot of problems. It often worked. He had fired people in the past, people with a lot of potentially damaging inside information and had made certain they did not talk by making it worth their while not to utter a word.

"Money wouldn't work. Connor doesn't need it. He'd know we wanted to buy his silence. We'd be waving a red flag in front of a bull. No, Andrew, standard severance pay is enough. Make it appear normal."

The older man thought for a moment.

"All right. Get rid of him if you really think we have to. But Martin, make the problem go away. I do *not* want a problem from the museum.

"Make it go away," he repeated. His voice was higher pitched now, almost querulous.

He stood up and reached for his cane. The conversation was over. The two men collected their coats and went out into the fresh evening air.

Walter Jackson opened the rear door of the waiting Mercedes. Gabriel stood still beside the car for a moment and turned back to the director.

"Martin, I want you to know how grateful I am for this talk. There are so many people who want to take advantage of me."

Gabriel turned his sharp blue eyes on Pryce with a small smile that seemed to have a sardonic twist.

"Who can I trust, really?"

In that moment Andrew Gabriel seemed to have become a little smaller and more tired than Pryce had ever seen him.

Jackson handed the older man inside the car, started the engine, and drove into the night. Pryce gave his ticket stub to the restaurant valet and watched the departing car until it turned and disappeared around a far corner. His breath condensed into a small cloud, and he pulled his coat more tightly around his shoulders.

Not bad, he thought. That wasn't bad at all. And the Athena's a hell of a thing for the museum to get. And perfectly good. There can't be any argument about its background. That's what Richard said, and I've no reason to doubt him.

CHAPTER SIXTEEN

The man who stood in Kate's doorway smiled, but the smile was thin, and there was a dark look in his eyes.

"Good lord, Jason, you do look grim!"

"It's not been a great day."

"White's OK, isn't it?" She didn't need a reply; he'd had white wine at museum receptions as long as she had known him. She returned with filled glasses to see him looking at the photographs on the wall near her front window.

"Maybe we should forget about the movie. I don't think either of us could get through it. Not after the scene this morning. I don't even begin to know what to say about it."

She waved him to the sofa and took a chair next to it, leaving a small barrier of space. A small gas flame burned in a corner fireplace.

"So let's just talk. About anything."

He thought for a moment, holding his glass in both hands.

"Kate, I'm at a bit of a loss. We've worked together for—what, four years? But the other day at the garden pool I realized I don't really know you at all. I don't even know why you came to the Gabriel. You could have gone to any of a half dozen other museums. Didn't Toledo want you? Or Minneapolis?"

Kate laughed. "That's not small talk! But, you know, it's not so complicated. Sunlight and opportunity. Southern California sunlight three hundred days a year. It does something for me. And, of course, the Gabriel. Almost every day I can work on new objects. There's so much interesting material there that's really never been touched. It's a huge challenge.

"And then, because it's the Gabriel, every now and then something comes along at the museum or outside that needs some new solution, something really innovative and exciting. Designing exactly the right base for something as big as the Athena so it isn't shattered by an earthquake—that's certainly one."

"You didn't want to stay at the Walters" It was more a question than a statement, and she hesitated before answering.

"The Walters was fine—actually really wonderful. But I really wanted to leave Baltimore. I'm sure you know that. Staying was painful. I needed to get out, and it was time to do something else."

She took a deep breath and gathered herself.

"There was a man. Eric. A very lovely, wonderful man. Eric was an economist at Hopkins, and we'd met at a reception at the Walters and simply fallen in love. I lived with Eric for the better part of a year. Then he went to Africa, Togo, to do some sort of work with their government. The assignment wasn't that long, a little more than a month, but when he came back, he looked awful. He saw a specialist and was told it was some form of disease that was untreatable. He said they'd try to find something that would work. There was some hope for a while."

She looked away, eyes distant, the memories coming back to her.

"But they couldn't, and it took Eric almost two years to die. Two years. There were days, even weeks, when he felt better, almost normal, and we could go out and see people and do things normal people do. But the disease was eating his brain away all the time. There wasn't a damned thing I could do except try to make his end easier. I stayed with him, fed him, dressed him. I hired a day nurse for the times I couldn't be with him."

Her voice wavered, breaking slightly. "Then, finally, he became comatose and went into the hospital, and two weeks later he was gone."

"You don't have to go on."

Her eyes came back to him.

"I do. Jason, you asked, and I'm trying to tell you something you need to know about me. The whole thing was unbearable. I was devastated, just torn apart by it. I could barely focus on my work. I felt that I'd come to the end of my life in Baltimore.

"That was when the Gabriel advertised the conservatorship position. It took me about three minutes to decide it was what I wanted to do. And they said yes, come on, and I said yes. So that's why I'm here."

She felt exposed and uncomfortable and on the verge of tears she did not want him to see. She rose and straightened herself and busied herself at the fireplace.

Jason sensed her embarrassment and turned the conversation.

"So what do you do, outside the museum? I know you're a photographer, but I don't know your work."

"Those are some of the things I do," she said, nodding at the framed pictures on the wall. "There are others. I'm a good photographer, at least that's what I've been told. I seem to touch people with it, and it was so *unexpected* when I had my first show and found that people really liked what I did. One man came up to me afterward and said that I'd made it possible for him to see things in a way he'd not done before. That was such an incredible thrill."

She brightened. "And they sold! Not a lot, three or four, but right away. That was just great. It's really wonderful to have a gallery want to show my work now. Someday, if you're interested, I'd be happy to show you some other things I've done. I have an entire room back there." She nodded toward the rear of the apartment. "An entire room with photographs from the first year I started to take them. And it's all a mess. I never seem to have time to put them in order."

She pulled her hair back and retied it and turned to him again.

"You know, I had a reason to tell you about Eric. I don't talk about him much. It's still pretty painful. But I wanted you to know what he meant to me and why I'm the way I am now. I haven't met anyone who's interested me since I came to California. Maybe I will. But every time I think about caring for someone, I know I can't go through that again."

She pulled herself together. "Jesus, I'm sorry. I don't do that often. Let's talk about something else. You maybe? Tell me something about yourself—what do you want? Where are you going?"

"I really love what I do, Kate. I've got the best of all worlds, in a great museum with some event or challenge coming up all the time. I have friends, inside the Gabriel and throughout the museum world. I can indulge my small fantasies, say, collecting art or racing cars or whatever. I've been happy here. Until now."

"What does that mean?"

"I was on the point of resigning this morning. With no idea, not the faintest, of what that would mean. Even though it would probably destroy any further museum career I could have."

"Are you serious, Jason? That would be a disaster. Why would you ruin your life?"

"You don't understand. If I really had a fundamental disagreement with Martin, I'm not sure I'd have a choice. I should be ready to resign, for that. I've done it once. I don't want to do it again, but I will if I feel I have to."

"You resigned? Because of a disagreement? When did that happen?"

91

"Almost ten years ago, when I was in the foreign service."

"Foreign service?"

He understood the question.

"CIA. Clandestine service."

"That's a long time ago. If you resigned now, what would you do?"

"I'd do what I did then. Find something that's satisfying and maybe important—and that I could do well. And then I'd go ahead with it."

She glanced at the white hairline scar that ran through his eyebrow and then looked into his eyes.

"Do you miss what you were doing? Would you ever go back to it?"

"No. I can't see doing that again. It's a young man's game. A lot of people can do what I was doing. And why would they want me? Besides, there are too many other interesting things to do. Museum curation would be gone. Something else, certainly."

"And your friends, what about them?"

"Hold on to them. Make new ones. But maybe you're asking another question. There's really no one who I'm so close to here that would make it difficult for me to go somewhere else."

The thought surprised her. *No one who'd make a difference, you mean.*

What did she know about him though? That he'd been married, but his wife had not moved with him to California and they had divorced within a year of his taking the Gabriel appointment. He turned up at museum functions, but never in company. He was pleasant enough with the younger women at the museum. He could be unexpectedly funny, sometimes with an edge, but she'd blunted that with the word-association game, and they played that now together for a few minutes every week.

The year before he had appeared in a social column with an aging former actress, a woman who was said to be charming and witty and had a long repertoire of lesser films and occasional male admirers. Younger men, older women, she had thought at the time. Anything's possible. For a few days she had wondered what it would be like but couldn't visualize a younger man who would interest her.

And what's become of his actress friend?

She felt exposed, needing to hear something, anything that would tell her more about him than she already knew.

"Jason, you said you really don't know me, and that's true, but it's the same with me, about you. What should I know about you? I know you were married once, but you came out to the Gabriel alone."

He shifted in his chair, uncomfortable at the question, and let a minute pass.

"Well, when Barovsky made his pitch about my doing something challenging and new and in a great museum, I decided I couldn't say no. Susan had already told me she wanted to leave. The steam had gone out of our marriage, she said, and she wanted more to life than following me and never having anything for herself, never having the chance to have something of her own. She'd been an editor at *Vogue* when we met. She loved working, and there was no chance for her to do anything like that when we were abroad.

"Actually, she couldn't do a thing. Embassy wives can't take jobs in foreign countries, except for the handful who teach at American schools. There was nothing I could do.

"By the time I was finishing graduate study our lives had begun to disintegrate. One day she said we should think of ending it. I thought I wanted to go on with it, but then I realized I didn't want to put it back together either.

"It wasn't that difficult. We had no children and nothing to fight over. We had just taken different trajectories. It was sad. We'd hoped for so much, and it had all disappeared."

Awkward, she thought. It's awkward for us both to go back over this stuff. Let's get onto something else.

"But you're not really alone, are you, Jason? I mean, you go out with people. I've seen you with some of them in the galleries. And women—you like women, don't you?" She arched an eyebrow. "You should have heard the talk at the museum when you appeared in that social column with the actress!"

The question amused him, and he gave a low laugh.

"I bet there was!"

At least he's out of the gloom, she thought.

He rose. His glass was empty and he was tired, drained after the tumultuous day. He wanted to go home.

"I really have to leave, Kate. Good night. Thanks. That was—" He searched for a word. "Unexpected."

He's vulnerable. My God, he's really vulnerable. The look lasted for an instant and was gone. He took her hand for a moment and then turned and started out into the night to find his car.

"Jason—wait."

He turned.

"What *are* you going to do?"

"I don't know yet. Something."

"Something?"

There was no response.

"You don't like being pushed, do you?"

"No. But that's not all of it."

"What then?"

"I don't like not knowing. In fact, it bothers the hell out of me."

CHAPTER SEVENTEEN

The drenching rains of the past two days had stopped. The morning weather report said the white fog that blanketed Los Angeles' west side and covered the coastal communities would dissipate before noon.

The coast highway had heavy traffic in both directions. When Jason arrived, the garage was half-filled with the cars of staff and arriving museum docents, several of whom waved at him as he passed into the Gabriel's basement.

Not much time, he thought. He entered his outer office and stopped at Amelia Mumford's desk to ask her to hold his calls.

Her answer was automatic. "Of course. And Dr. Connor, there's a document for you. I put it on your desk."

He had put the message from Leo out of his mind since the day before, but as he rounded his desk he saw the single page with no marking except for a few words in German and a signature.

Mit freundlichen Grüßen. Ernst Langlotz.

He did not allow himself to think beyond his next act. He opened his safe, pulled out a file marked simply, "Athena," and extracted the fourth letter, the one written by Langlotz thanking the ninth Earl of Weymouth for allowing him to see the statue.

He placed the letter on the desk and Leo's message by its side. He stared at both for a moment, stood up, walked to the window, then walked back to his desk and, still standing, looked at them again.

The signatures were totally different.

He punched the director's four-digit extension number into his telephone. Patricia Waller answered.

"Patricia, when does Martin have a moment this morning? Only a moment, it won't take long."

As Jason entered Pryce's office, he felt a calm settling over him for the first time in days. It was his meeting, and he knew where to take it and how to make it go there. It was all about deception. Dust in the eyes.

Pryce was at the window, looking out into the Gabriel's gardens. He turned as Jason came through the door. "Jason," he said. "Please sit down."

The curator continued to stand. "Thanks, but this will take only a few minutes. I've done a lot of thinking since our meeting yesterday. When I left I must have seemed upset. I shouldn't have been, and I wanted to tell you."

"It wasn't an easy meeting, Jason. I'm glad you accepted my decision."

Jason shook his head slightly. *I didn't accept it. I said nothing at all.*

"Martin, that's not the reason I'm here. Frankly, I feel burned out. It's not just the hours, but the Athena matter has taken the oxygen out of all the other things I need to do. I'd like to take some leave, if that's OK with you. For eight or ten days, beginning Monday. Cynthia has all the material you'll need for the board presentation." *No need to mention the signatures. The matter's ended.*

Pryce was surprised. *What's this about?* Take leave? He's exhausted? Really? Still, he'll be gone, and I can brief the acquisition committee. I'll give them Kate's conservation report and write Jason's endorsement myself. I'll just tell them there are no known negatives. That will do it. If Jason's away for ten days, he'll be a bystander at the board meeting. Whoever sent him that damned signature, it doesn't matter anymore. What could I have done with it anyway? Destroy it? He'd know immediately.

Now he wants leave. That makes it much easier. The statue will be bought. The day after the board's approved, I'll have the Gabriel's bank wire the money to Richard's Cayman Islands account.

"Jason, by all means. I fully understand. I hope you get the rest you need and come back refreshed."

As the door closed behind the curator, a thought came rippling up again into Pryce's mind. Is he really that exhausted? If he's not, what's the point of taking leave? But it doesn't matter. He'll be out of here in a month.

He shrugged and turned back to the papers on his desk.

Jason told Cynthia Greenwalt he would be away from the museum for the next week or two and that she'd be acting department head in his absence. She raised an eyebrow.

"Where are you going?"

"I need to take care of a few family things on the East Coast, and then I'll be back in Los Angeles for a few days, probably." He had no intention of telling Cynthia where he would be. Others would ask her, and the entire museum would know within a day. He couldn't even tell her that he felt burnt out, as he'd done with Martin. She'd know it wasn't true and would wonder why he'd say so.

"You have everything you need for Martin's meeting with the board. If you need to reach me, use e-mail."

"And the documents? The letters Maybank sent? What about them?"

"Martin's handling those now."

Cynthia gave him a sharp look and left. When she had gone, he picked up the telephone. Gerald Robertson answered immediately.

"Gerald, about our conversation Tuesday night. The Athena's documents are bad. Confirmed bad. One of the letters is forged, and it kills them all. I didn't have a chance to tell Martin that. We had a discussion—at least it started as a discussion—then he cut me off and told me not to go further. I almost resigned on the spot, but I didn't want to give him the satisfaction."

"He stopped you? Really just stopped you?"

"Yes. The board, he said. He needed all the document checks to come to an end right away."

"Now, that's just odd."

"Sure. Of course. And wrong."

"So what're you going to do?"

"Find out why. I think I know where to begin. Sicily. Then probably London."

Robertson was silent for a moment. When he spoke again, his words came out very carefully.

"Are you sure you want to do this? When Martin finds out— and he will find out—he'll have your head. You won't have to resign. He'll have every right to fire you."

"So, what are my choices here, Gerald? What am I supposed to do? We went over this Tuesday. When we talked then, Martin's decision not to ask more questions just seemed very risky. But now I *know* the letters are faked. So I know something's wrong, and I'm not just guessing about it. What am I supposed to do?"

"What do you *want* to do?"

"I want to know if it's only the letters that are bad, or if the statue itself has a bad history. A modern one, right out of the ground. The problem is, I just don't know enough. If I did, I could at least have something to sort out."

"Occam's Razor?"

"Of course. The simplest solution is the one likely to be right. I don't have enough information to make assumptions about the Athena. Even simple ones."

"That's all?"

"Of course not. There's the other thing. Martin. What's he trying to do? If there's a game here, I can't see it yet."

Robertson thought for a moment before replying "You know, I may have been wrong the other evening. About Martin. I told you to forget about him, find out about the statue. Maybe both are the problem. But Jason, do you have a plan?"

"I'll go to Morgantina first, I think. It's a big site in the interior of Sicily—you must know about it. It's been excavated, but it's still the likeliest place the statue came from. Morgantina means a flight from Rome to Catania and back, and a day, perhaps two, in Aidone or Enna. That's a lot of time, and I don't know that it would tell me much, but I keep coming back to the place as a key."

Robertson took a moment to collect his thoughts. "If you really think it comes from Morgantina, you should go. But you should talk to Ettinger first. You've met him, haven't you?"

"Yes. Once, at a conference. I wasn't much taken by him."

Gerhard Ettinger had been the principal archaeologist at Morgantina for more than fifteen years. In his sixties, he held a senior professorship in Princeton's Classics Department. He had taught dozens of the best excavators in the United States, and more dozens of German scholars in an earlier age when he had been at Saarbrucken. He was brilliant but difficult, and was given a wide berth by other scholars. He was also the bane of collectors and collecting museums, for which he held special animosity.

"Gerhard is what he is, Jason, and he won't change. But he runs the Morgantina site, and if you want to learn a thing about it, you'll have to put up with him. I'll call and let him know you want to see him. He tends to be irritable, and he's got no patience with museum people. He thinks we're all thieves. We get along, so he'll listen to me. You should see him. It'll be worth your while.

"And another thing. Are you really interested in document fakery, or just the letters that came with the statue?"

"I'm interested."

"You should be. If you go to London, there's someone you'll want to see there. Anna Estaing. She's at the Courtauld, and she's the best on document forensics that I know. I'll call her and let her know you may be there."

As Jason hung up, an upset Kate Emerson came through the door.

"What's this about your leaving?"

"I'm not leaving, Kate; I'm taking leave. I need time to myself and unwind some things."

"This is pretty sudden. You might have mentioned it to me last night."

"It hadn't occurred to me last night." He hoped she wouldn't see through the small lie.

"It's the meeting we had with Martin, then?"

"Partly. The other part is this." He pointed at the page with Ernst Langlotz's signature. "I told him this morning that I wanted time off."

Kate regarded him for a moment. "Jason, what are you doing?"

"I'll be traveling." He lowered his voice to a level he knew would not be audible outside the room and nodded toward the open door: *Amelia Mumford.*

"Sicily. London." He continued, as softly as he could. "I haven't told anyone else."

"You're still on the chase, aren't you?" Kate's voice fell further. "Yes."

"Is that smart? Martin's told you not to go on with it."

"I know."

"What's the point? What are you trying to do?"

"Something's wrong. I don't know what it is. But I want to find out. I have a few ideas how."

"You can't give it up, can you? Martin will have your job if he finds out."

Gerald's words, Jason thought. "I know."

A long silence hung in the air.

"Good luck," she said finally. "I don't really know what you're doing, but I think I understand it."

The thought that he might be dismissed from the Gabriel, go somewhere else, came back to her.

Goddamn it. And we've only just begun to talk to each other.

Then another thought hit her.

"Jason, could your poking about upset someone? There's no risk, is there?"

He thought for a moment. "I can't see it. I mean, what are people going to do? Avoid my questions, probably. But do something about me? There'd be no point to it."

"I hope you find what you're looking for, Jason. Call me when you're back. Call me when you're there, wherever you are, if you want to."

"Yes."

"Please."

"Yes. I will."

Kate came over to him, put her hands on his shoulders, and kissed him on the cheek.

"Godspeed, Jason. Be careful. Travel safely." Her voice was almost a whisper.

She hugged him briefly. They turned to see Amelia Mumford standing in the doorway with her mouth in an almost perfect O of surprise.

CHAPTER EIGHTEEN

One call, he thought. It has to work.

In Washington, true authority meant how many calls it took to reach whoever you needed to talk to. If one didn't know the person one was calling, it took at least two. If three, one was pretty low on the political pecking order.

More than three, and I shouldn't be making the call, he thought. But I need one, just one.

When Jason was on the White House staff, he could often get anyone he wanted with a single call. He would start with a simple, "This is Jason Connor, National Security Council, is this Mr./ Ms.—?" With the agencies he dealt with, the response was always immediate. There was a standing joke on the staff that you could get the Secretary of Defense more quickly than you could your own dentist.

He couldn't do that now, he knew, but he had held on to the close friendships he had made and still attended the annual dinners of former NSC staff members that brought together many of his former colleagues. He sent year-end cards to a few. Jack Harmon was one of them.

The telephone rang once at the other end. A secretary answered. "Colonel Harmon's office" only, no more. The protocol was always terse.

He identified himself, said he wanted to speak with Colonel Harmon, and added that he was a personal friend. In less than a minute, Jack Harmon, Colonel, United States Marine Corps and Assistant Deputy National Security Advisor to the President of the United States, came on the line.

"Jason. To what do I owe the pleasure?"

He could visualize Harmon, a short, wiry man with a military haircut who wore civilian clothes in his NSC job, with piles of documents to his left side, two telephones immediately to his right, his secretary just outside the door to his cramped underground office in the West Wing, and a small stack of telephone messages to his side. Unless he was in a meeting, Harmon always picked up when Jason called.

Years earlier, when Jason had been detailed to the NSC's Middle East office, Harmon was a Marine Corps major dealing with weapons transfers in the office of political-military affairs. The two men had been required to work closely with each other. They were not required to become friends, but they did.

Jason had gone on to get his PhD at Harvard, and Harmon had cycled out of White House service for a battalion command at Camp Lejeune, then two tours in Iraq and a year at the National War College, and in time was promoted to full colonel. In a highly unusual move, he was selected to return to the White House as the senior military assistant in the office of the President's National Security Advisor.

Harmon had been a busy man when Jason had worked with him. He was a busier man today, and Jason made his request short.

"Jack, I need an NSC contact who can put me in touch with the right office in our Rome embassy. I'm going to Italy, and I'll want advice when I get there. I need to talk to someone who knows something about the criminal smuggling networks that work the illegal antiquities traffic."

Harmon did not ask why Jason was asking.

"I'll have someone get back to you. Probably the Justice Department person here. That's Marty Jacobson. If he can't help directly, he'll know someone who can. That OK?"

"Exactly OK. Thanks, Jack. I can't think how I can repay the favor."

"No favor. You wouldn't have called if it wasn't important. Tell me about it someday. And take care of yourself."

Someone else who wants me to take care of myself, he reflected as he put down the receiver. In twenty minutes, Amelia buzzed and said that a Mr. Jacobson was on the telephone.

"From Washington," she added. Amelia was the only person he had ever met who could convey the impression of an arched eyebrow with a tone of voice. He picked up the receiver again.

"Dr. Connor? Marty Jacobson. Jack Harmon said you had a problem and needed some help."

"Not a problem, just advice, and it probably needs to come from someone in our Rome embassy. I need a name and an introduction."

"What kind of advice?"

"On Italian criminal groups that deal in illegal antiquities."

Jacobson was quiet for a moment before he spoke. "I don't know about this myself. But I'll call Justice and ask them to give me a name, and then get back to you."

"Thanks, that's all I need."

"Jack thinks highly of you, and if you want advice, I'm sure that won't be a problem. But that's probably it. We can't offer help officially. But you know that."

"I know that. Advice is enough. Thanks."

Jacobson called ten minutes later.

"When you get to Rome, call Pete Mancini at the embassy. He's FBI, their SAC, Special Agent in Charge, of the legal attaché's office there. He follows Italian criminal groups, the ones we've a special interest in. He works closely with the Italian prosecutor's office and knows everyone. I've spoken to him, and he'd be pleased to see you. He says you're going to have to watch your tail, and hopes that if you find out anything useful you'll let him know. He also wants me to tell you that he can't give any official assistance and—"

"Yes, I know, he can only give advice. But that's what I need. Thanks for your help."

The first step, he thought.

CHAPTER NINETEEN

Jason's Saturday was all business. At home, out of the museum, away from Pryce, and out of earshot of Amelia Mumford. He made flight reservations to New York, New York to Rome, round-trip Rome to Catania, Rome to London, then back to Los Angeles. He would need two or three days in Rome and London, and an overnight stay in Aidone.

He telephoned his older sister, Angela, and told her he would be in New York the following evening and asked if they could have dinner together. Angela said yes immediately. Her husband, Harry, couldn't join them, she said. He was in Topeka working on a silo contract for the commodities firm that employed him.

Robertson called at nine to say he had spoken to Ettinger. The scholar could meet with Jason Monday morning.

"I told Gerhard you wanted to meet him, Jason, and he remembered you from a talk you gave at an Archaeological Institute meeting a couple of years ago."

"And he'll see me?"

"He's not enthusiastic. At all. He thinks museum people don't listen very well and mostly want to pick his brain about objects from Morgantina and not about the site's history. But I told him you're interested in solving an archaeological puzzle—that's true, isn't it?—and that you intend to visit Morgantina in a few days. So he's put his reservations aside and hopes you'll sit still and listen to a few things he has to say. He's recovering from stomach surgery. He'll be testy, but don't take it personally."

"I'll try to sit still."

He turned to the most immediate untended matter. How carefully would he need to cover his tracks, going and coming? Who did he want *not* to know his plans?

Martin, of course. Who else? Gabriel? No, not Gabriel. Gabriel would have no interest in what he did. So then, Martin. Let's start with him. What would Martin already know of my plans?

Nothing from me. He hadn't told Martin where he was going or what he'd be doing. He'd told Cynthia that he'd be in Los Angeles and also the East Coast, and she'd probably mention that to Martin at some point. But he hadn't said he'd be traveling to Europe. Amelia only knew he'd be away from the museum for the next eight or ten days.

That left Kate. She knew everything—his suspicions, his rage, his intention to pursue the Athena matter to Rome and London. Would she tell Martin? Not voluntarily. But if Martin asks her directly? Would she lie? He thought about it for a moment. Maybe not lie. Maybe give him an answer to another question, an evasion.

Should I ask her to cover for me? No, don't touch it. That would be forcing her to make a choice between me and her own sense of honesty.

So, could Martin track him down? Maybe, if he gets the wind up and knows I've left the country and decides I'm trying to unravel the statue's background. If he's really determined, he'd start with the places where I normally stay. The museum had the records of his past travel, and Martin could find out where he'd been.

I won't go there, then.

In fact, he'd need a plan for the trip that would allow him to avoid visibility. That meant not changing his telephone message, not staying in his usual hotels, not going to restaurants he had been to before, not traveling by the expected means, and not seeing any of the people he usually met with while on business for the museum. It meant leaving false trails, mentioning his onward travel plans to hotel concierges and then not following them, making reservations for travel by train but then taking a bus or a car.

He had done all that once, years earlier, when security was an unconscious part of everyday life. But all of the small tricks of tradecraft weren't necessary now. This wasn't the shadow world where paranoia was normal and logic inverted. There'd be no furtive passing of documents in the predawn hours, no hurried secret meetings, no caches of papers or computer drives, no elaborate surveillance checks, no pseudonyms or cover story that might be blown away, no agonizing disappearances of one's own agents, no heart-thumping pursuits or evasions with the terror of arrest and interrogation at the end. That was all long in the past. Now, he needed only to avoid notice by one man. His training had kicked in to help.

And it was exhilarating.

Where should he stay? He made a reservation at the Wales in New York, on Ninety-Second Street and Madison. He then called and booked a single night at the Raphael, in Rome. From there, he'd make reservations only one day in advance.

And Morgantina? He could make it up when he got there. It was December, full winter. There would be many choices.

He went online and looked up Aidone. A typical Italian hill town, he discovered. He could visualize tile roofs and narrow cobbled streets and a small trattoria, and if none of that existed in fact, the hotels in the larger towns to the west, Piazza Armerina or Enna, would have no surprises and the cuisine would be better.

What else?

Cell phones. The one he normally took when he traveled belonged to the museum. Better take my own. Calls from my own phone can't be traced. Not by Martin, anyway.

There was one more matter he needed to take care of, and just before eleven he swung into the museum's entrance driveway. Inside his inner office, he pulled out the Athena file, extracted the curatorial report, the letter copies that Maybank had sent, and the single sheet with Ernst Langlotz's critical signature. In the silence of his office, it took him less than ten minutes to copy the documents, put them in a clasp envelope, address it to himself at home, and affix enough stamps to satisfy the postal service. He made a second set to take with him.

As he exited his office, he took a long look at the galleries that surrounded the courtyard—*his* galleries, *his* rooms, the ones that held the heads of Roman rulers and patrician men and women, the mounted vases, the cases of ancient jewelry, the decorated sarcophagi recovered from unknown tombs in some distant necropolis, all passed from hand to hand until they had come to rest here. Behind these things were once-living people whose sculptured faces had laughed and wept, whose lips had drunk the watered wine from these same vessels, who had adorned their hair and ears and fingers with gold and precious stones, and who, at the end of their days, had been interred in marble carved with scenes of myth and heroism. He had, sometimes, tried to think of them as they must have been. Not ghosts of the imagination but living human beings. He had never quite succeeded, and the figures he tried to summon up remained shadowy and evanescent, like wind on water. It was not something that bothered him greatly, and he had most often simply shrugged and gone on with what he had been doing.

On his way home, Jason took the envelope with the photocopied letters, dropped it at the post office on Albright, left instructions to hold his mail until he called for it, and was at his house before one thirty.

He called the Princeton number Robertson had given him. Gerhard Ettinger answered right away. Jason introduced himself, said that he would be traveling the following day, Sunday. Would Ettinger confirm their meeting Monday at ten? He could hear the scholar eating something, chips perhaps, and his tone was abrupt.

"Dr. Connor, Gerald says I should see you, but I told him I don't know why I should do that. I don't see museum people normally, unless they're from museums that don't collect artifacts. But he says you have an archaeological problem of some kind, about Morgantina. And that you listen as much as you talk. And he's an old and dear friend. So I'll see you Monday."

Jason was about to reply when he realized he was holding a dead telephone. Ettinger had hung up on him.

He changed into running pants and a sweater, and in the chill air of the early evening twilight, he ran from his house on Sumac up to Sunset, then east toward Brentwood before turning back.

Running cleared his mind, gave him a sense of physical direction and release, and he tried to do five miles a day if he could. He returned in the full dark, and when he had finished dinner, picked up de Berniere's *Birds Without Wings* and then on an impulse went to his address book and punched Kate's number into his phone.

At the end of four rings, her voice came on the line asking the caller to leave a message when the tone sounded.

"Kate, I'm sorry I missed you. I'll be in touch when I can." It was all he wanted to say.

He cradled the receiver and started packing.

CHAPTER TWENTY

The Sunday morning United flight put Jason into Kennedy a little after five in the afternoon. He was at the Wales before seven.

The Wales was a small three-plus star hotel, far less costly than the Peninsula or other establishments where the Gabriel's expense account would have allowed him to stay. The hotel had been slowly deteriorating into the nineties, but it was bought by new owners who renovated it and gave it a faux but effective old world charm and a certain sense of comfort.

Jason had spent days at the Wales during his graduate school years. The hotel was only a short walk from the Metropolitan Museum, where he had done much of his research, and they knew and took care of him well. But the Wales was right for another reason. No one at the museum could connect him to the hotel.

He checked in and walked for a cold but satisfying twenty minutes down Madison to take a corner table at the Carlyle. In minutes Angela bustled in, a woman of generous girth with bright, new blond hair cut to the shoulder, wearing coral-red lipstick and with a smile that lit up the room. The surface of her full-length sheared beaver coat caught the light and shimmered as she was ushered to her chair.

Angela Connor Klein had been an ardent cultural heritage supporter long before Jason had become engaged with archaeology. She still devoted most of her time to the protection of historic sites around the world. When her husband, Harry, could join her, and sometimes not, she took long trips to Europe and Asia with the World Monuments Fund and other groups to which year after year the two of them were very generous.

"Jason! God, it's good to see you. And do you look good! Why hasn't one of those California women snapped you up?" She laughed, her voice carrying across the room, and hugged him as he rose. Several diners stopped eating and looked around to find the cause of the disturbance.

Five years older than Jason, Angela was her brother's mirror-image. Where she was direct, loud, and impetuous, Jason was more indirect, quiet, much better at impulse control. They had been brought up by their single mother, and Angela knew Jason like a favorite, well-read book. She thought of herself as the caretaker sibling and, whether it was needed or not, had kept a watchful eye on her younger brother long into his adulthood.

"Harry would be here, Jason—you know he'd really like to be with us—but he's in Kansas. Jesus! Kansas! And he won't be back until tomorrow night. We're celebrating our twenty-fifth anniversary then; didn't you know?" Her laughter sounded through the small room.

"How do you do it?"

"Oh, I tell Harry once a week that he has to be my love-slave. Then I tell him how." She laughed again, loudly, and Jason looked around to see how many others had heard her remark.

"So, Jason, why are you here? I only see you every six months now."

"I'm off to Europe for a week or so. Rome, Sicily, London, then back to LA."

"Buying things again?"

"Not this time. I'm trying to find out about something we'd like to buy. Where it came from. Whether another country might be able to claim it. You know, the provenance thing. I've talked to you about it before. But this one is complicated."

"It's always complicated. That's why you like doing this. If it weren't complicated, you wouldn't be interested."

"I don't know, Angela. I have this lingering affection for a simple life that I've never seemed able to live." It was a remark she had heard often, part of the game they played with each other.

"Rubbish. That's just an outrageous lie, Jason. You had a horrible childhood. I escaped it because I went off to school and college and Harry came along and married me, and you've never gotten over it and you've been running off and doing things to compensate ever since. Complicated things. First it was the Agency, now the art world, antiquities, the part of it that's gotten all these other people into trouble. You love it."

Angela had known about Jason's CIA employment since the day he was inducted. She had never asked him what he did and knew he couldn't say a thing. When he told her he had been hired by the Gabriel Museum, she began to read about the antiquities trade and took up her caretaking again, often sending, with a large yellow Post-it note attached, whatever news item might appear about a dealer or collector who had an object that had to be confiscated and sent back to a country that claimed it. Over the years, they amounted to a small blizzard.

"Stop pretending you don't enjoy your complex life, Jason! You know you love it." She was about to give another loud laugh, but then looked around and decided not to.

"I don't recall my childhood as horrible. In fact, I thought it was fun, and the parts that weren't fun built character."

"It was horrible," Angela insisted. "Phyllis was an alcoholic. You've just walled it off, made a nice compartment for it, a place to put the bad memories and then forget them.

"Phyllis—" Phyllis Connor, their theatrical mother, insisted that her children use her first name. "Phyllis treated you like her only child and never let you out of her sight. 'You always want to leave me, why are you leaving me?'" Angela held her hands out in a gesture of abject supplication, her voice dripping with misery. Her mimicry was perfect, and it was Jason's turn to laugh.

"Those summers we spent on Nether Dumpling Island. She wouldn't let you go into town, and you had to fish and read most of the day to amuse yourself! What a control freak. She meddled with everyone!"

"So I read. And fished. And so I'm literate and patient. And full of character. Do you have a problem with that?" He was mocking her lightly, and she knew it.

Angela turned the conversation.

"You said Sicily, Jason. And you want to find out where an antiquity came from? One that may have been stolen? Is that safe? Isn't the Mafia into antiquities smuggling?"

"Antiquities are smuggled out of everywhere in Italy. This isn't a new thing. You know that."

"But is it *safe*? Or do you think you have some kind of special immunity because you were in the CIA? Or that you're so smart you can't get into trouble?"

"That doesn't give anyone immunity. And I'm out of it. For ten years. I've probably forgotten more than I learned."

His sister shook her head slightly. "I don't like it. Don't get in over your head, Jason. Not that you've ever paid attention to me!" She gave him a thoughtful look and lowered her voice.

"So, why *did* you leave the CIA? If you can say anything about it."

He hesitated. There's no reason not to tell her now. He took a moment to look around the room. There was no one near enough to hear them.

"Imad Mughniyah. And Judith Christensen."

"Imad who?" She pronounced the name as he had, *ee-MAD*.

"Imad Mughniyah. The most wanted terrorist of all, before Bin Laden took the title away from him. He'd bombed the American embassy in Beirut in 1983, hijacked TWA flight 847 in 1985, and had a hand in multiple kidnappings and killings—the list goes on and on. We wanted him any way we could get him—dead, alive, it didn't matter. When our embassy was blown up, Mughniyah became target number one for us.

"My boss, Venner—that's Emmitt Venner, the Beirut Station Chief when I was there—was obsessed with the idea of killing Mughniyah. And then something happened that made him think he'd finally gotten his chance."

Jason stopped speaking and his eyes took on a distant look.

"Beirut had calmed down by then. The place smelled of refuse, and the streets were filled with rubble, but the civil war was over, the mass killings had stopped, the shelling had ended. But it was still a magnet for journalists. One of them was an American woman who'd married a Shiite Lebanese she'd met at the American University in the seventies. Judith Christensen. She'd had odd jobs, became a stringer for the *Globe*, divorced her husband, then came back to the United States and went on full salary for *Time*. She convinced her editor that even though the TWA hijacking and embassy bombing were years in the past, Mughniyah was still a major story and that her Shiite contacts might allow her to get to him, interview him, tell his side of the story."

Jason shifted in his chair and took another moment to collect his thoughts.

"One day she told someone, privately, very quietly, that she'd made contact with someone close to Mughniyah who'd said yes, Mughniyah would see her. She left for Lebanon two days later. We learned of it pretty quickly and then picked her up—followed her—when she arrived in Beirut.

115

"We had a long discussion among ourselves about Christensen. Would she be able to meet Mughniyah? Could we track her some way, know where she was going, trace her right into Mughniyah's living room?

Jason's eyes focused on a spot just above and far beyond Angela's right shoulder before they returned to Angela.

"It started as a simple technical discussion—mostly about whether we could follow where she went to see Mughniyah. But then our technical guys told us that if someone could find out what shoes she'd be wearing when she met Mughniyah and get hold of them for a few minutes, we could cobble in a GPS device that we could interrogate. They said it could give us her location to within a few feet.

"And it went from there. If we can find out where Mughniyah is, how do we kill him? We'd have to do it when Christensen was there, since we knew he'd move immediately after he'd spoken to Christensen. We thought maybe we could put a bullet into him through a window.

"But if his security people made Christensen remove her things—her bag and her shoes, say—the device would be in a different room, maybe on a different floor. It was clear we wouldn't be able to get him unless we used enough force to destroy the entire building."

Angela's mouth had dropped open slightly. "So what did you do?"

"Venner wanted to know what we had that could do the job. Something that could do that—take down the whole building."

He stopped and thought for a moment, searching for words that would describe what happened. He took another drink from his glass and looked at his sister again.

"The entire conversation began to revolve around getting Mughniyah. If we could do it, then how would we do it? And somewhere in it, I asked the wrong question."

"Wrong question?"

"I asked what would happen to Christensen. It stopped the conversation for a minute. All of us knew the answer. If we took out Mughniyah, we'd take out everyone in the building. Christensen included.

"It was the wrong question. I knew it the moment I asked. The conversation stopped, and everyone else in the room gave me this odd look, as if I'd said something unforgivable. Venner told the others to leave the room and told me to stay behind. He was furious, cold and furious. He asked me if I was trying screw up the operation. I don't recall what I said, or started to say. Whatever it was, he slammed his hand down and said our only concern was taking out Mughniyah; nothing else counted. I said that the operation he was planning meant killing an American citizen, a totally innocent person. Along with a lot of others.

"Venner said we were at war with Mughniyah, and that whatever few deaths might be involved in getting him, they'd be justified. He'd been stationed in Tel Aviv, and he'd learned from the Israelis, who couldn't care less about killing others to get at someone they wanted dead. He expected me to support the operation and be quiet. And forget the consequences. If killing Mughniyah stopped him from killing other Americans, the death of one American was worth the price."

"Jesus, Jason! What did you do?" Angela had a stunned look on her face.

"I left and went out for a long walk, and when I came back I told Venner that I intended to resign, and I did. I was choppered out of Beirut to Cyprus the following day. Three days later I walked out of the Agency."

It took Angela a full half-minute to regain her voice.

"Jesus. We do these things?"

He nodded.

"We did. Not often, but we did. I don't think we do that now."

"And you resigned on principle."

He thought for a moment.

"No, I wouldn't call it that. I don't have a problem with killing Mughniyah or anyone like him. I'd have no hesitation about that at all. I just thought it was dead wrong to kill an American who happened to be in the way. I didn't want any part of it."

Angela sat quietly, considering what she had heard.

"What happened to the operation? To Mughniyah?"

"It didn't go off. I heard later, after I was out, that Christensen stayed in her hotel for days waiting to hear from the man. But nothing happened. He must have gotten wind of something. Decided it was a bad idea and ran out on it. That's why he survived so long."

"So long? He's dead?"

"He was blown up in Beirut six or seven years ago. No one took credit. Mossad did it, probably, or another Palestinian faction out to settle scores. Maybe we did it. I don't know."

"And Christensen? What's become of her?"

"She's in Washington. Moved on from *Time.* Teaches at Georgetown. Arab studies, I think. Probably with the same pair of shoes, minus the transmitter, if we ever put it in. We'd have made a huge effort to get it back." He smiled. "Or at least not let it fall into the hands of a real shoe repairman."

"And Venner?"

"The dumb fuck's still there, somewhere in Clandestine Services. I don't hear about him, and I don't ask."

CHAPTER TWENTY-ONE

The short ride on the branch line from Princeton Junction to the main campus of the university gave Jason time to think through his meeting with Ettinger.

Could a large sculpture really be taken from Morgantina? How? Aren't there supposed to be guards at the site, or at least a watchman? Would it really be possible for someone to just come in and take it away? Could one identify the findspot—could *Ettinger* identify it?

Beyond that, he thought, he'd just have to listen.

McCormick Hall was a classic example of late nineteenth-century neo-Gothic masonry, a three-story brick and stone structure that housed Princeton's art museum and the university's department of art and archaeology. Jason was directed to a ground floor office off a small courtyard that had a fountain with Roman mosaic decoration.

Gerhard Ettinger was waiting for him as he walked in.

"Dr. Connor. Please sit."

A wave of the hand. No handshake, no pleasantries. Jason took a chair and looked around at a chaotic scene of disorganized shelves and bookcases and an overloaded desk with papers in precarious location, seemingly about to fall to the floor. The director of the Morgantina excavations, a small, severe-looking man somewhere in his seventies, with short hair and a shorter beard framing his face, peered at Jason from above his reading glasses.

"Gerald says I should talk to you." The remark was a question with a missing *why*: Why are you here?

"I'm planning a visit to Morgantina. Gerald thought I should talk to you before I go."

"And why are you doing that, please?" The manner was formal, the words with a trace of accent.

"There's an object on the market that may be from Morgantina, or nearby, and I have no idea when it appeared. I decided I should see the place for myself."

"An object?"

"A statue. Said to be from a European collection, bought more than a hundred years ago."

"Then what does it have to do with me?"

"The statue may not have been bought long ago. It may be recent. I've no way to know. There's nothing to show that it's an old find. That doesn't necessarily mean it's been dug up recently, but if it's been excavated in the last few months or years, someone should know about it, or at least have heard of it. You?"

The scholar stared at Jason for a long minute.

"I haven't heard of such a thing. But you know, in Sicily anything is possible. Except for the months when we are at the site and can protect it, looting goes on all the time. It's a source of income to the local farmers. They come in to take whatever they can out of the tombs. And for something important, anything at all, the *capo zona*—that's the local boss, the one who runs everything in the region—gets into it right away. It goes on, year after year."

"But if something very big had been taken out, you'd have heard of it, wouldn't you?"

Ettinger scratched his nose and considered the question for a moment.

"Maybe not. It depends how it was done. If at night, quickly, and if very few people are involved, the Carabinieri, or an outsider like me, wouldn't know until much later. Maybe not at all. And if it was big, it would probably have been broken apart on the spot, or somewhere off-site, whatever the thieves thought necessary to reduce its visibility and make it easier to ship."

Broken apart. A small, cold finger ran up Jason's spine.

"The place has no guard?"

"It has a guard. Mostly to stop tourists from picking over the site. But it's pretty sure he's the *capo's* man.

"And the police have no control?"

"They don't try very hard. Or they don't have the resources, it's all the same thing. There are too many sites, too many looters, not enough money. Sometimes afterward they have some luck."

"What does that mean?"

"The Carabinieri may learn of a shipment going through the land borders, or Italian customs may stop a runner at the airport and then squeeze him for information on his network. Or the prosecutor's office in Rome may get another country, say Switzerland, to allow them to raid a dealer's office and get hold of his files. Like Medici."

Ettinger gave a sharp look. "You've heard of him, haven't you?"

Everyone in the business knew Giacomo Medici. Before he had been convicted by the Rome court and jailed, Medici had been the single most important channel of Italian antiquities to Europe and the United States. He had a small and nondescript gallery in Geneva's old city, window-dressing for his business, and a very much larger storeroom at Geneva's free port. Jason had seen it.

"I've heard of Medici," he said, his voice flat.

The archaeologist looked out the window toward a church spire, barely visible above the trees, and then turned back to Jason.

"The Carabinieri have gotten lucky recently, I've heard. A few months ago they picked up a major dealer in Rome. They're saying they may put him away for years. He may be talking to them now."

"Major?"

"Maybe the biggest. He's had his fingers into Morgantina for years. His name is Pisano. But that really won't help any of us much."

"Why is that?"

"A dealer would have nothing to do with the site. That's the *capo zona's* business. Whoever he is, he'd still control the place. It would take him almost no time to put together another connection to get things out. Unless the *capo* is arrested by the Carabinieri—and that's not likely, since no one would dare turn him in. They'd be too terrified to do that. Even if they did, another *capo* would appear almost immediately. The trade is too lucrative to be unattended to.

"No. The only way to stop it is to close down the market. If the market isn't shut totally—unless the collectors stop collecting, the museums stop buying—the looting will continue. Not just at Morgantina, but all over Italy. All over the Mediterranean. Everywhere."

Jason decided not to respond.

Ettinger gave a thin smile. "Dr. Connor, do you have the faintest idea why I do what I do? What archaeologists are supposed to do? Have you ever excavated a thing in your life?"

The questions came quickly, one after the other, in a voice that dripped with irony, giving Jason no chance to respond.

"What we are *supposed* to do is discover the nature of man's past. If we don't know where we've been, can we really know where we are? Now, there are some things we can't prevent. Acts of nature, floods, rises of the ocean, the corrosion of metal in acid or saline soil. We can't stop that. But there are others we can try to stop—sometimes. Like the thieves who search for everything of value that can be taken away and sold.

"And, of course, those who feed money into the market to pay the thieves!"

Jason shifted in his chair. He was not just being preached to, he was being pilloried. Gerald said the man needed to be listened to. It was the price of the meeting.

"So. What can we do to end this looting? Close down the market! Stop the collecting." The archaeologist's voice rose. He had taken off his glasses and jabbed them at Jason as he spoke, pacing the length of the room behind his desk.

"And, how does one do that? Sanction the collectors, put the big ones on trial. Take away from the museums what they have bought unless it can be proven—*proven!*—that their purchases are truly clean, that they've been out of the ground for decades or more!"

"And that's going to stop it?"

"Of course not. The thieves are going to find some way to give them pedigrees! I have to tell you, Dr. Connor, I know them too well. And Italy, where art and technology come together so brilliantly, is where it is going to happen. There are forgers hard at work in Rome, Milan, even as we speak, making new art old. What will possibly stop them from turning their hands to making old documents out of nothing."

He thinks I'm an agent of organized thievery. Or is he just delivering the same lecture he gives everyone?

He'd had enough. Ettinger was old and arrogant, someone who had pursued a straight, bright pathway in a life that had taken him from one honor to another, always in the same field, always advancing in the same direction. There was nothing that could change his mind about what was right or abate his single-minded fervor. He stood on one side of a line, and anyone who stood on the other side was wrong. It was really insufferable.

On the train back to New York, Jason wondered if he had learned anything at all from Ettinger.

He had. A major dealer had been arrested. The man might have something to say about Morgantina and a large statue.

Pisano. Just how do I get to see this Pisano?

CHAPTER TWENTY-TWO

"So, what did he say?" Robertson's call had come only minutes after Jason had returned to the Wales. "How was it?"

"Preachy. Jesus, he's preachy."

"That's my Gerhard! Bet you thought he was an old fart. A lot of people do. But what did you learn?"

"He said a big statue *could* have been stolen out from under his nose, and the police, without their knowing about it. And he said there's a Roman dealer who the police have got hold of and who they hope will talk to them. Fellow called Pisano. I didn't get his first name."

"*Pisano!*" Robertson's voice rose. "Now, there's a name!"

"Know him?"

"No, not *know*. But heard of him since the sixties, I think. You know, it wasn't my area, Roman antiquities, but even the people who did Renaissance in Italy knew of him."

"Major?"

"Almost everything went through him. Vases, sculpture, gold jewelry, whatever—everything. He had a hammerlock on Cerveteri and the other Etruscan sites. In the seventies he partnered up with Medici. But Jason, you say he's talking?" Robertson sounded surprised.

"Ettinger says he may."

There was a pause before the older man responded.

"Not healthy for him, maybe."

"Singing, trying to get himself off, or out. Italy's not Sicily, Gerald. There are different rules, I'd think."

"Depending, Jason, depending. It's a really tight place. Disciplined, very tight. Not like other places. Lebanon, say, when it was mostly open. Or Turkey."

It was the first time Jason had heard Robertson mention Lebanon.

"Lebanon was open?"

"It was, before it closed down. During their civil war."

Jason knew all about Lebanon's civil war. He had been in Beirut while it was going on. He waited.

"But Jason, the business there has changed, and it changed again, then it went back to what had been going on before—getting stuff out to another country, then on from there. I don't stay current with the business now, but I've friends who do. They tell me it's like it was in the sixties and early seventies all over again, when anything could be bought or sold and stuff just flooded into the place, then went out again.

"And no fakes! Who needed to sell fakes, there was so much real stuff being marketed around?" Jason heard a chuckle, and imagined a smile on the older man's face. He could sense a story about to unwind. He looked at his watch, then sat on the bed.

"When were you there?"

"Mid-sixties, off and on, for three months, a bit more. But you must know the objects! A lot of it. Roman. The Met was offered a really amazing set of silver vessels, bowls with interior decorations, all brilliantly done, cast then chased and gilded, amazing stuff. The owner, an Armenian fellow named Dikran said it had been in his family for a generation. And no one believed him, not me, not the curatorial department. So I tripped over to Beirut for a few days and met him and then decided to stay on for a few more days to talk to people who knew the antiquities circuit—the dealers, and collectors—people I'd heard of and who should have heard of the silver, somehow."

"Who did you see?" The words came out very quietly.

"Pharaon, Henri Pharaon. Heard of him?"

Pharaon! Of course it would be Pharaon. There wasn't any other major collector in Beirut, no one at all. More than twenty years later, the memory of the wasted figure on his deathbed and a promise he had extracted from Jason was still fresh.

"Yes. Go on."

"I didn't have enough time. And Beirut was fun, really wild. I was between wives, and they had these parties where you didn't sit down to dinner until midnight! So I went back. Four times in three months. And went over into Syria twice." A laugh. "That was crazy. A really crazy place."

"Go on."

"Nuts. The Damascus dealers were all these young Christian guys, and they had a network of diggers and sellers around the country. One of them, Freddy Ibrahim, called me at the hotel and said he'd heard I was interested in antiquities, and did I want to come with him to see Qaysoon? I'd heard of the fellow when I was in Beirut. Qaysoon controlled everything that came out of northern Syria. I said sure. So he picked me up in a long black Mercedes and put me in front with the driver and off we went, into the night!"

Jason glanced at his watch. He'd give Gerald a few more minutes before he had to check out. He put his feet on the bed.

"Off we went. It got dark, really dark, no cars on the road. And we rounded a bend, and there was a checkpoint in front of us, a military checkpoint with guys in uniform and automatic weapons, Kalashnikovs, whatever they were, pointed at us. Freddy said something to them and the driver—the driver who'd had his hand on a newspaper or something—got us through, and everyone relaxed.

"And Jesus, I realized there was a fucking gun under the newspaper, a short-barrel thing, maybe an Uzi, and we'd almost had a shootout. Can you imagine?"

Jason didn't think his friend could tell an Uzi from a broomstick, but the story was real, Qaysoon was real, and he had met Freddy Ibrahim in Paris, a blown-out Freddy who'd been beaten too often by Syrian security police who hadn't been paid off properly.

"Imagine what? The shootout?"

"No! The headlines! *'Met Director Shot While Escaping Syrian Security Forces!'* Holy shit! And that's not the end of it—"

Jason put his feet back on the floor.

"Gerald, we've got to pick this up when I get back. Rain check for now. Next time we talk, I'll say 'Syrian desert,' and you can take it from there."

"OK, but Jason, it's a great story!"

"Sure. When I get back. But Gerald, before I go—the silver. Go back to the silver. Was the Lebanese fellow's story real? What did you find out? "

"I didn't find out as much as I should have, I suppose. The Dikran guy said the silver had been put away by his father in hatboxes for years. Even showed me the backroom closet where he said they'd been kept. I couldn't get anything else out of him. But I sure found out a lot about the antiquities market in Beirut. And Syria. A lot."

"You bought it? The guy's story held up?"

"I didn't say that. I just couldn't put a hole in it. I couldn't find a reason not to buy. So we did."

The older man had come to the end of his story. Jason thought for a minute.

"Gerald, we couldn't do that now. Someone would have my hide even for thinking about it."

"I know. Jesus, don't I know! But we had different rules then."

CHAPTER TWENTY-THREE

The Rafael's location was unexcelled. The Piazza Navona, always full of life, was a few steps around the corner, and many of Rome's greatest works of art were only a short walk away.

Jason checked in and called the American embassy. The switchboard routed his call to the legal attaché's office, which put him through to Mancini's secretary. He mentioned his name, and after a short delay, she told him that Mancini wanted to see him sooner than later, and asked if a noon appointment would work for him.

Still underslept from his flight, he set out on the clear bright December morning to visit the two masterpieces of architecture and decoration he admired most, the Pantheon and the Church of Saint Ignatius, separated in time by fourteen hundred years. Each was only five minutes from his hotel and in the same general direction, and he reached the Pantheon a little after ten.

To Jason, the Pantheon not only represented the brilliance of its grand architect, Hadrian, but also a direct, six hundred year backward link to Alexander the Great. The building's interior, with the oculus in the center of the soaring dome and the coffers spilling downward in ever-increasing size, was pure Hadrianesque. But it was the brickwork, particularly the buttressing round arches imbedded in the walls, that continued to fascinate him. Before Alexander, no such arch form existed in the West—not in Italy, nor anywhere outside Mesopotamia. Alexander's engineers returned to Macedonia from Babylon knowing how to fashion round arches, and their knowledge then flowed westward into Roman and all later European architecture.

From the Pantheon, he walked through side streets to reach the seventeenth-century church of St. Ignatius, whose interior was the grand design of Andrea Pozzo. When money ran out before the church dome could be built, the Jesuits asked Pozzo for an illusion, and Pozzo gave them the most magnificent illusion they had ever seen. He painted a false dome over the altar, then painted over that soaring architecture a sky filled with figures of saints and angels flying outward into space while colossal figures tumbled downward, desperately trying to save themselves by grasping onto clouds that billowed around them.

For long moments he sat in an empty pew, mouth slightly open, gaping upward, caught in Pozzo's dreamlike depiction of God, Jesus, and Ignatius floating in the center of the composition. A grand illusion, he thought, meant to inspire, not to deceive.

Leaving the church, he decided to walk to the American embassy. He crossed the Corso and started up toward the Via Veneto and then, on an impulse, stopped and glanced at a store window. It was an old habit, come back to him now, and of course he saw no one behind him in the window's reflection.

The American embassy in Rome, like American embassies everywhere, has a triple layer of security. Jason arrived at the gates ten minutes early to ensure he made his appointment on time.

Two armed Italian police wearing dark uniforms and Kevlar vests, with cuffs tucked inside their boots, inspected his passport and waved him through the gates to a small interior court that then led to a separate security area on his right. There he was ushered through a metal detector and found himself facing a guardhouse with an armored glass window manned by an Italian security guard and a US Marine sergeant in white peaked cap and dress blues with ribbons. Both men had sidearms, but Jason knew they had other weapons within reach, M-16s, fragmentation grenades, probably a shotgun or two. With reason, Jason thought. If there were ever an assault on the embassy, the guard post would be hit first.

The marine eyed him suspiciously through the glass, and he pushed his passport through a slot beneath the window. He waited as the sergeant checked his name on a list and then picked up a telephone and spoke, listened, and then hung up.

He was instructed to surrender his cell phone and was led through a heavy steel door to a waiting room painted a dull off-white. Black-framed pictures of the president of the United States, the vice president, and the secretary of state decorated one wall; photographs of the ambassador and deputy chief of mission were on the other.

Jason wondered if a decorator had been hired to make all American embassy interiors as screamingly dreary as this one. Before he could reach a conclusion, a young man entered, introduced himself as Pete Mancini's assistant, Leonard Johnson, and asked Jason to accompany him to the legal attaché's office.

Mancini was short and energetic, somewhere in his forties, with dark hair, dark eyes and a brush moustache. His jacket hung over his chair behind a desk that held papers neatly arranged in three rows. He was on the telephone, speaking in rapid Italian that Jason could not follow, but glanced up as Jason entered and motioned toward a sofa near the window. When he had finished with the telephone, he came around his desk to shake hands.

"You have high level friends in Washington, Dr. Connor. I hardly know Marty Jacobson, and it was a surprise to get a call from him. But he said you were favorably known at the NSC and needed some advice. The legal attaché's office doesn't get many unofficial visitors, as you can imagine. None who are introduced by the White House, anyway. So this is a bit unusual. Now, tell me how I can be of service."

Johnson pulled out a pad of paper to record the conversation. Standard procedure. There was always a notetaker when one met someone outside the government.

"Jacobson's told you I'm with the Gabriel Museum in California. I'm trying to find out whether a major object we've been offered may have come recently from Sicily—that is, if it was excavated and exported illegally. I've nothing to show that it was, or wasn't. But if it was found recently, it had to have gone through one of the trafficking networks here. I hoped you might know something about them."

As he spoke, Jason noticed a small semicircular indentation above the bridge of Mancini's nose, just inside his right eyebrow, a recoil scar from a rifle with a scope sight. Must've done that when he was a kid, Jason thought. No one properly trained would make that mistake.

"Not much, really. We deal mostly with the Italians on criminal activities that involve Americans, or cases in the US criminal justice system. We've a particular interest in gangs and criminal networks that run between Italy and the United States."

Mancini thought for a moment.

"Antiquities is a bit off subject. The major dealers here and in the US seem to stay clear of things that would really catch our attention—like drugs or weapons smuggling, or money laundering through US banks. We should probably know more, I guess, but there's too much to do that's of more immediate concern. Is there anything in particular you want to know about?"

"I don't really need to know about all the networks or people involved. My interest is pretty narrow. I'm told that a major dealer was picked up recently and is being held and interrogated. Raffaele Pisano. He may have information that would be helpful to me."

"Pisano?" Mancini turned to his assistant. "Wasn't there something about him in the news about a week ago, Leonard?"

"No idea."

"Tell you what." Mancini picked his words. "I'll call the police and ask about Pisano. If there's an American connection, they'd probably want to tell me about him. If there's no connection, they may not."

He gave Jason an appraising look. "Can you give me some help here, Dr. Connor? Why would an American want to talk with Pisano? I may need a little leverage with the police."

Jason searched for something, some wedge that would work.

"You can tell them Pisano could be an important link to the US market. If he can identify an object that may belong to Italy, if he decides to talk to me about it, that could help the Italian government get it back. Will that help?"

Mancini nodded. "That's good. It may be enough. But you know, the police probably won't let you talk to him directly. He's probably got a lawyer, but you might be able to work that out through him though. I'll find out and get back to you this afternoon. That OK?"

"Sure, fine, thank you."

The meeting was over. Mancini went back behind his desk. Johnson went out with Jason. Just before he picked up his cell phone at the embassy guardhouse, Johnson touched his arm.

"Dr. Connor, I do the background work for Pete on Sicily, the Sicilian Mafia, their linkages to LCN—La Cosa Nostra—in the US, and anything that involves Sicilians and Italians that touches on US government concerns."

"Yes?" Jason said. Where was this going?

"I have a couple of things I'd like to pass on to you. One is, if you find out anything that would be of interest to us, please call Pete, or me, and let us know."

"And the other?"

"There can't be a lot of American tourists in the Sicilian hills in December. People will want to know who you are and why you're there. Everything about you. There's a saying in Sicily that if you fart in Siragusa, they'll know about it in Palermo. Things can get pretty rough there; I don't have to tell you. People kill each other the way they exterminate rodents. Whatever you're looking for, don't go too far with it. It's not worth it."

Johnson's smile was ironic.

"Dr. Connor, this isn't just friendly advice. It's about us too. Your friends in Washington wouldn't be amused if something happened to you. Self-interest, Dr. Connor. I'm sure you can understand that."

Jason spent the rest of the afternoon revisiting the Villa Borghese. When the guards ushered the visitors out as the museum closed, night had fallen, but he decided to take the long walk down through the Borghese Gardens to the small baroque church of Santa Maria del Popolo, then back to the Condotti and up the Spanish Steps to the elegant Hassler. He was given a single table on the roof without delay. He spent the next two hours enjoying himself with a good Lacrima Christi, a fine dinner, and an unequaled view of the city.

He had packed and was preparing to leave the Raphael when the room telephone rang.

"Dr. Connor? Pete Mancini. I may have something for you. The police are still holding Pisano, and he seems to be talking. They have a lot of material to work with. Photographs seized from a gallery in Geneva that have his name on them. A few clients. Some objects from a warehouse at the Geneva free zone. Also, a scrap of paper that diagrams out his principal clients and suppliers. Clients in the UK, Switzerland, and a dealer, a small one, in

Chicago. Suppliers in Cerveteri, Taranto, and also Sicily. Aidone in particular. That's next to Morgantina, isn't it?"

"Yes, right next to it."

"The police say the diagram is very specific. It has the names of people in some sort of hierarchical order, with lines connecting several of them. They call it a *cordata*—that's a word used for a group of mountaineers who are roped together. But here, they mean a criminal network. Since it includes an American, the police will let me see it in the next day or so."

"How do I see Pisano?"

"You'll need to talk to his lawyer, a guy called Gaetano Frescobaldi. He's in the phone book and the hotel should be able to get him for you, no problem."

Jason picked up a small pad by the telephone. At the top, he wrote *Pisano* and the name of the attorney. "And what about Pisano's suppliers? Is there any one of them I should know about?"

"I have the name of one I probably shouldn't pass on, and I normally wouldn't, even to you but for Jacobson's introduction. And maybe because you can tell us something when you get back to Rome. His name is Cosimo Galante, and he lives in Aidone. I don't know anything about him, but from the little I've been told, he's a very bad number. You don't want to have anything to do with him. He's someone to stay away from."

Cosimo Galante. Jason underlined the name twice.

CHAPTER TWENTY-FOUR

The arrival hall of Catania's Fontanarossa airport was filled with passengers talking and jostling each other as they were greeted by friends and waited for the carousels to deliver their baggage. Jason had just picked up his overnight bag with one hand and was trying to transfer his cell phone to an inner pocket with the other when the accident occurred. Two men rushed to embrace a young woman who had arrived on his flight, jarring him and spilling the cell phone from his hand. He watched it fall to the marble floor and shatter. The men apologized profusely, helped him pick up the pieces, then left as quickly as they had come.

He looked at the broken screen and weighed the futility of even trying to turn it on. He'd need a cell phone, for Rome and London, even before he returned to Los Angeles. He spent several minutes trying to find a telecom office at the terminal, but there was none.

Do I need one in Aidone? Probably not, he thought. The hotel phone should be enough.

The Europcar rental desk had an economy Alfa Romeo available for the two days Jason would need it. The rental agent, a dark-haired, bespectacled young man who looked as though he had only recently finished high school, pulled out a map of Sicily and spread it out on the counter. Tracing the road to Aidone with his finger, he looked up at Jason.

"There aren't a lot of visitors now, *Signor* Connor, and the drive won't be a problem, unless there's a lot of rain or fog in the hills."

"Rain?" Outside the terminal doors the bright sunlit afternoon was slowly sinking into twilight.

"Not here in Catania, but in the mountains there is fog. Much fog. It comes in the night. It's gone by noon. Drive carefully if you get into it."

The drive was short, a little less than three hours, and Jason arrived at Aidone's central square before six. He stopped to ask directions to the predictably named Hotel Morgantina, was directed to the Piazza Filippo Cordova, and drove past a bronze statue of a man in a nineteenth-century greatcoat with one foot forward and his right arm outthrust, the index finger pointing at the sky, evidently the prominent Aidonese who the Piazza commemorated. A few yards further on, a sign pointed toward the hotel.

The Morgantina had been renovated only ten years earlier. It had a warm interior with a bar and adjoining restaurant on the main floor, was decorated with houseplants and modern tapestries on the stone walls, and exuded a certain confidence that came from having no competition. The desk clerk, a man of middle years with dark, watery eyes and a receding chin, took him up two flights of stairs to a clean, white-painted room with a light-blue ceiling, a shower, two beds, a desk, and an oversized television placed on a bureau.

He washed and descended to the bar. A local white wine, any one that was recommended, would do. A younger couple, Italian, probably Aidonesi he thought, sat in the corner holding hands and talking in quiet voices. Near the bar three men with open-neck shirts and jackets were just rising from their table. None of them looked at him, but he knew they had registered his presence.

He watched them walk out, one, short, muscled, with a round face and hair cut to the scalp; the second, tall with an awkward shuffle; the third, thin with long, delicate hands. As he left the room, the third man turned and for the briefest moment glanced at him directly and then disappeared in the direction of the hotel's front door.

CHAPTER TWENTY-FIVE

The bed was hard and Jason passed a restless night. He went down to the ground floor to take breakfast in the hotel's small dining room. When he returned to his room he repacked his bag for the return trip to Catania. Minutes later, inching his Alfa through the darkened streets, he came to the road the hotel clerk had said would lead to the top of the *Serra* ridge and to Morgantina.

"You'll have to go to the top of the town, then across a ravine," the man had said. "You can't miss it. But, *Signor,* you can't get in, I think. The excavations are closed. No one goes there in December." The raised eyebrows conveyed the unspoken question: Why do you want to go *there?*

He could not answer that himself. The chance of finding out something, anything, about the Athena was almost nil. It was his own driving curiosity, and Gerald Robertson's urging that had brought him here, and he couldn't tell which of the two was the stronger.

Or was it something else? What was he trying to prove? That the museum shouldn't buy the statue? That Martin was wrong?

Mounting up to the *Serra* ridge, he passed tilled fields bathed in the fog, then an olive orchard to his left, and then a long line of low, excavated stone structures. He stopped at a low gatehouse, got out of the car, and looked around. The air was bone-cold, the fog an enclosing hand. Somewhere high above a turboprop cut across the sky, no more than the distant whine of its jet beneath the low, insistent drone of propellers. The gate to the excavations was closed and locked, as the hotel clerk had warned. A low perimeter fence receded into the fog toward his right.

Was there another way to get in? He walked along the fence and in a few moments saw a stave that had been pulled aside—for someone else's entry? He looked to his side and rear to see if there was anyone else present, but there was nothing except the dim outlines of ancient walls and trenches. He stepped over the fence and found himself standing inside an avenue with the ruins of buildings running along each side.

He tried to make sense out of what he saw. The ancient market place, a theater, and council hall, all were there. Once, when he neared the fence again, the mist drifting around him, he thought he saw a figure standing motionless in a nearby field, watching him. He waved, but the fog came between them, and he was unable to see if there was a sign in return.

Close to the center of the ruins, he came to a wide flight of stone steps that led up toward a flat area. For what? He could not know. Perhaps here he was in Athena's sacred place, her sanctuary, where her temple and statue would have stood. Instinctively his glance went upward, and he tried to visualize what she must have looked like through the eyes of those who had made her.

A sound came to him from a distance—a voice, a call, that was joined by another, equally far. There seemed a shifting of the fog around him, a stirring of echoes, and for a moment he imagined that he saw people, a multitude, a flow of spirits, men and women, common folk and courtiers, kings and priests, who swelled into a tide of worshippers come to stand at the goddess's feet.

Then it was gone, the illusion shimmering into the surrounding mist.

He descended the steps and walked slowly through the ancient streets until he came to the fence again, and when he found the broken stave, stepped across it and went out onto the main road for a long minute. He looked first back toward Aidone, then in the opposite direction, toward the *Serra's* high point, the *Citadella,* but even though the fog had begun to lift, there was no view at all.

He turned back to the gate and saw a man standing beside his car, a farmer by his appearance.

"Good morning. Can I help you?" Jason had asked the question in English. He could have spoken Italian, the little he remembered, but he wanted to know if the man could understand him.

The man shifted his feet slightly.

"*Inglese? Americano?*"

"*Americano.*"

"*Com ci fai qui?*"

The words and accent were unfamiliar. Sicilian, probably. But Jason understood: *Why are you here?*

"*Mi dispiace, non capisco l'italiano*—I'm sorry, I don't understand Italian." It was right out of a phrasebook.

"*E' stato agli scavi.*"

Something about the excavations. Probably that I've been inside. Why deny it?

"*Si, in il scavi.*" Jason wished his rudimentary Italian was better.

"*Non ha paeso niente?*"

Something about taking something. He would say no, but why was the man so interested? He was a farmer, not a guard. There was a farmhouse across the road, he remembered. He probably just walked over here when he saw me.

"*Niente, nessuno cosa.*"

"*Si ferma molto?*"

"*Non capisco.*"

In fact, he understood the question, about how long he would be there. But the questioning made him uneasy, and he wanted to end it.

He's too curious. And I don't owe him answers.

He opened the car door. "I have to go," he said in English. "Good bye."

There was no response.

Unfriendly sort, he thought. He put the car in reverse, turned, and headed out onto the road to Aidone.

The man watched him leave, then took a cell phone out of his pocket and punched in a number.

CHAPTER TWENTY-SIX

What happened back there? Why did I come? Why am I here? He had spent the better part of two days getting to Morgantina to find something, anything, that could help unravel the thread of the statue. Two air flights, a long drive up from Catania and back. A hard bed and sleepless night. A cold walk in a cold fog. And the odd interrogation by the farmer at the excavation site.

He'd come up with nothing. No new lead, no good ideas. He was frustrated and irritated with himself. Robertson had urged him to come to Morgantina, but it was the statue and his own excitement of the chase that had caused him to follow the trail into the hills of Sicily. Now, with the night fog lifting, he felt he had been pursuing a chimera, a fantasy.

What did I expect? That I'd find a trough in the ground at Morgantina with an imprint of the statue's body? That the missing hand would just be lying there waiting for me to stumble on it? Wake up, Jason. It doesn't work that way.

The loss of his cell phone made him uneasy. He needed to call Pisano's attorney now, to set up a meeting for tomorrow—or that evening, if he could. In an earlier time he would have rejected out-right the use of the hotel telephone. But who cares now? Martin? He wouldn't have the faintest idea. The Italian police? What's the point? Someone here?

He tried to think of a reason a call to Rome might interest someone in Aidone but could not. He had told no one except Mancini and Johnson that he would be here and had spoken to no one in Aidone about the reason for his visit. No one except the farmer, but what could be made of that?

What had Mancini said about the man in Aidone, Cosimo Galante, the very bad one? "Stay away from him."

So, I've done that. No contact. And I'm leaving in a few minutes anyway. Let's not get too paranoid about this.

He quieted his thoughts, picked up the receiver in his room, and made two calls in succession. The first, with the help of a Rome information operator, was to Gaetano Frescobaldi. A secre-tary answered in Italian, then switched to perfect English. He gave his name, there was a pause, and finally a man's voice came on the line, accented but clear and understandable.

"This is Frescobaldi. How may I help you?"

Jason introduced himself and came immediately to the point.

"I've heard you represent Raffaele Pisano. I understand Mr. Pisano knows a lot about the antiquities business. I'd very much like to talk to him."

There was a long pause, and Jason wondered if the man at the other end had hung up.

"Mr. Connor, you know that my client is in prison?"

"Yes. It's been in the news."

"What do you want to talk to him about? Why would he want to see you?" Frescobaldi's voice dripped with skepticism.

"About an object he may know about. A statue, a big one. I'd prefer to talk to you about it personally. Can we meet, maybe this evening? I'll be returning to Rome from Catania this afternoon."

"You're in *Sicily*? What are you doing there?"

"It's the reason I want to talk to your client."

There was another pause at the other end, and Jason could hear Frescobaldi talking to his secretary. The attorney came back on the line.

"This evening. Say, seven. Maybe I can talk to my client before then. Do not be too optimistic. He will want to know why he should talk to you."

"I'll be at your office at seven."

His second call was to the Raphael to confirm a booking for the next two nights. He had just put down the receiver when the telephone rang.

It was Mancini, who anticipated Jason's question. "You're really not hard to find. There's only one hotel in Aidone. But look, I wanted to let you know we've heard from the police that there's some kind of tussle going on between the chief prosecutor and the people in the culture ministry. It may not help you, or it may."

"What's it about? I'm going to see Pisano's lawyer tonight."

"The Carabinieri want to nail Pisano, that's for sure. The prosecutor wants him in jail. Period. But the culture ministry wants to recover anything they can that Pisano knows about. You may have a little leverage there."

"Leverage?"

"Yes. If you knew something that might help Pisano. Something, say, that might have come from Morgantina that he could verify, and that the Italian government could get back. He'd have something to help his case with the prosecutor. And there's another thing, maybe important."

Jason waited.

"They showed me the *cordata*. That's the network I told you about. A diagram with names all over it, lots of them. It has the word 'museums.' That's not you, is it?"

Mancini's question sounded offhand, but it had a hook.

"Can't be. We do our best to buy clean. We're pretty successful at it."

"Um, yes," Mancini sounded doubtful. "And in any case there's someone between the word 'museums' and Pisano's own name."

"Who's that?"

"Fellow called Maybank. Richard Maybank. I haven't heard of him myself. Maybe you have."

Jason felt a small thrill of excitement run up his spine.

"Yes," he said. "Yes, I think I have."

He drove down through the winding road to the Catania airport. As he left Aidone, the morning fog was lifting and the sun appeared, making the Sicilian hillsides with fields and vineyards and orchards and small tile-roofed farmhouses tucked under cypresses or oak trees brilliant in the early afternoon. He checked his mirror once as he left the town, and twice more as he descended, but there was nothing in sight behind him, no distant glint of a following car.

Nothing. No one gives a damn. Why would they?

As he passed down through the hill towns and hamlets toward the coast, he felt his irritation dissipating like the morning fog. For a few moments he felt a vague sense of peace, but it did not settle. By the time he had reached the coast his unease had returned. Had he missed something back in the tumbled hills? If so, he could not think what.

A few minutes after Jason's car had disappeared in the direction of the Catania road, a man entered the hotel and asked the desk clerk for a record of the calls made by *il Americano.*

The clerk nodded and without hesitation gave the questioner the three numbers in Rome. He added that there had been a call to the American, from someone who spoke Italian with an American accent, and that the call had lasted for six minutes.

Outside the hotel, the man used his cell phone to call a number that bypassed the central switchboard of Aidone's small police office. He spoke quickly then hung up and waited for the return call. When it came, his reaction was immediate.

"The call was from *where?* The American embassy? Jesus."

He closed the phone and started down the street at a run.

CHAPTER TWENTY-SEVEN

I n the middle of an otherwise quiet Thursday afternoon, Cosimo
Galante went into a seething rage.

"*Merda!*" The veins in his forehead stood out, the breath hissed
between his teeth.

"What the fuck is going on? Who *is* this American who comes
to Aidone and goes into the *scavi* and walks up and down the road
and then calls Pisano's lawyer? What the fuck kind of business does
he have with Piso—Pisano, anyway?" Galante stuttered when he
was excited, and he was very excited now. He had thrown back the
chair behind his desk and was striding back and forth across his office floor, dark face furrowed by a deepening frown, his right hand
pointing at the two men sitting on the sofa by the window while
the man who had told Galante of Jason's telephone calls drew back
toward the door.

"I am a good man who does good business, goddamn it. In
Aidone, in Piazza Armerina. In Catania. There are no problems—none. And then that idiot Pisano is arrested! Now this *fututu Americanu*—this fucking American—comes and walks all over

my place. And calls this Frescobaldi. And then someone from the American embassy calls him. What's going on here?"

Filled with a sense of unjustifiable injury, Galante spat out the words.

"*E' 'a mê casa chista. 'A mê.* This is *my* place. *Mine!* Who does he think he is? What the fuck's he doing, this Connor?"

No one spoke.

Galante topped pacing. His arms fell to his side. He pulled himself together, then threw his right hand out, and pointed to a young man on the sofa who had pulled a gray woolen cap over his forehead to avoid his eyes.

"All right. Let's get moving on this. Tonio, take that fucking cap off and get someone—get Filipo—and go find out who this Connor is. I want to know who he's seeing, what he's doing, where he's staying. He's going to Rome, so put some decent clothes on, now, and then get on his flight.

"And call me. No one else. Call me when you have something, anything! I want to know what's going on here."

"*Fututu Americanu!*" Galante said again, under his breath.

CHAPTER TWENTY-EIGHT

Jason opened the folding doors of the ancient elevator and peered at the plaque on the inside of the wooden cage that read "Schindler 1923."

If the damn thing's taken passengers this long, it can probably take one more, he thought. He pressed the sixth floor button and waited as the device jerked and slowly rose, creaking and rattling upward until it finally stopped, shaking slightly. When he exited through the elaborate wrought iron gate, a dim light turned on above his head.

He walked to the entry on his left and peered at a small, engraved brass plate above a doorbell button that faintly read *G. Frescobaldi Avocato*. He pushed the button and when the door swung open he found himself looking at a young woman with dark eyes, her hair pulled back behind her head and bound with a tortoise-shell clip. She had the palest skin he had ever seen, almost ivory, and the way she held her mouth emanated sexuality.

"Mr. Connor? Please come in. Mr. Frescobaldi is waiting to see you."

The young woman spoke in distractingly perfect English, the As flat and Rs fully pronounced in the American manner, with an accent reminiscent of one of New York's Long Island suburbs. He had difficulty tearing his eyes away from her as he entered the foyer, then the main office, and stood while she went into an inner room. He could hear her say a few words, a voice answered, there was the squeak of a chair. The young woman emerged, followed by a rotund man in his fifties wearing a dark double-breasted suit with a small ribbon at the lapel. The man's glasses were very thick; his eyes, magnified, filled the lenses.

Gaetano Frescobaldi smiled and held out his hand.

"Mr. Connor?"

Raffaele Pisano's attorney took the curator by the hand, pulled him into the inner office, and waved him to a sofa. He seated himself on an adjacent chair, asked the young woman to bring coffee, and peered at Jason for a moment.

"Yes, you're Connor. The museum website shows your photo. And your biography."

A careful man. But if he's defending Pisano and who knows who else, he should be.

"And you want to see Mr. Pisano? May I ask why?"

"We have an object at the Gabriel, an important ancient statue your client may know something about. I'd like to know if he does."

Frescobaldi continued to look at him with unwavering large eyes. "And why should he want to talk to you?"

"The statue. It could help him."

"And why would that be?"

"If the object belongs to Italy, and if Mr. Pisano can identify it, and if my museum then decides to return it, and we do that because Mr. Pisano's information was important—" Jason opened his hands, palms outward, and let the sentence trail off.

The attorney completed the thought. "Then it may help his case? Are you saying your museum would be willing to send such an important object back to Italy?"

"It would. If the Italian government had a clear case."

We damn well would, Jason thought. If they had a clear case.

Frescobaldi gave him an appraising look.

"You know, Mr. Connor, I have advised Mr. Pisano to say nothing to anyone." He looked at Jason, waiting for a reaction. When there was none, he added, "But he doesn't listen to me."

It was Jason's turn to stare. "What do you mean?"

"He doesn't take my advice. He is talking to the police. He has given long depositions. He has named names. He wants to seem like an innocent person. A victim of others, someone who has come by his knowledge as if he had nothing to do with it."

The attorney held up his hands as if to say, What can I do with him? He went on.

"Anyway, I spoke to him this morning, and he said, 'Sure, why not? Let me talk to the museum man.' He is—how would you say it? Pissed off." The word came out *peezed*. "Really angry at some of the people he's dealt with outside of Italy. He says he's made many of them very rich and he thinks they've left him to the Carabinieri— you know, thrown him to the wolves. Maybe that has something to do with it. He's very, you know, *furioso!*

"So, Mr. Connor, I have made an appointment with the prison police for us to see him tomorrow morning. They know I will be bringing someone to visit, an American. I told them that you're important to my client's defense. I had some difficulty convincing them at first. They told me they have some kind of evidence that connects Mr. Pisano to American museums."

The attorney paused and arched his brow. "But they don't know which museums. They have no names. When I said you were with a big American museum, they agreed. They wouldn't have said yes otherwise."

Frescobaldi stopped talking for a moment but then went on.

"Now, Mr. Connor, you will meet me here at nine, before the traffic picks up, and we will be at the prison before ten. Also, you understand that I will be with you. As his attorney. And to help translate. Pisano's English is not so good."

As Jason left the office he waved at the young woman with the ivory skin, found the outer door, got into the ancient elevator that groaned and shook as it descended to the ground floor, and exited the building into the evening dark.

CHAPTER TWENTY-NINE

It was still early, and Jason saw no reason to return to the hotel immediately. He walked up the Via Condotti to the Piazza di Spagna, then turned left to pass the intersection of the Via Vittoria and Via Albert. *Not Alberti,* he thought; the Romans had made a concession to nineteenth-century England on this small street.

He came to the Via Margutta with its patent pretension. Formerly filled with stables and small workshops, the Margutta once had the charm of an antique backwater, away from the city's crowded center streets. And then it was discovered. Rome's new *glitterati,* movie people, fashion designers, writers, and artists who could afford the rent began to populate the street. High-end couturiers, designer shoe stores, and art galleries of every type moved in. The Margutta became an exhibition gallery of Rome's most expensive offerings, of everything from antiquity to the present day.

To Jason, the Margutta unashamedly flaunted Italy's sheer virtuosity in marrying art and technique, in making and selling to trendy decorators and dealers beautiful objects of antique style. To unwary visitors, the Margutta also offered beautiful objects of the same style, masquerading as real antiques.

High art and great fakery at the same time. Or was it fakery at all?

He passed a window, brightly lit, that contained a small sculpture of a nude youth, almost certainly of Carrara marble, broken at the arms, legs and head but showing a lovely, lithe body without blemishes or marks of any kind, with a beautifully rendered torso, sensuously detailed nipples, and a penis carved to the finest detail. It was a brilliant work, but utterly impossible as the ancient Roman object that it appeared to be to the untutored eye. Too lush, too beautiful, with all its significant parts undamaged.

But if everyone knows what it really is, a pretty object for the hallway of a house or apartment, but modern in every way, is it fake? Of course not, he thought. But if it's sold as real, then later sold as ancient, what would it be then? A fraud. But not a fake.

The Margutta was filled with possibilities, not just marble sculptures but paintings and frescoes and beautiful wooden objects, all made with the expectation that at some time, someone would buy, believing, wanting to believe, that what they bought was an original.

Can art represent two opposite truths at the same time—the bad and false on one hand, the good and real on the other? Can bad be made good? And does it really matter?

Jeffrey Waldman had once asked the same question. Jeffrey was a young American scholar, a lecturer at London University, with a special interest in engraved gems and other small objects. He knew virtually all of London's antiquities dealers, as well as many of those who were closer to the sources, in Italy or Turkey or the Levant or further to the east, mostly younger men of nondescript appearance who made the pilgrimage to London to sell to eager buyers.

Jason had met Jeffrey long before he had come to the Gabriel. They had run into each other two years earlier in a dark corner of Grays Mews, a haven for merchants of the antique and exotic. At the north end of Mayfair and a short walk from Claridge's, Grays was close to the bottom of the great art emporium that London had become, and Jeffrey loved to inspect the continuing flow of new material that appeared there.

That day, he and Jeffrey had talked over a sandwich lunch. Jeffrey had pulled a small terracotta figurine from a bag by his side, an Aphrodite, fully nude with both hands clasped behind her head, pointed breasts outthrust, a narrow waist leading to the gentle swell of her pubis. It was an object that would charm whoever handled it. And rubbish, Jason knew, a total fake.

"But this is modern, Jeffrey, a forgery. It's not ancient. You must know that. Whoever you got it from must know it too."

"I know it. The dealer I got it from knows it—and he knows who made it. But what he says is that it *may* be real."

"That's absurd."

"He doesn't think so. He says that it *looks* real. And someone who thinks it's real will buy it. And believe in it, and show his friends, and they will all believe it's real. And if everyone, or almost everyone, thinks it's real, then who's to say it's not?"

"That's just ridiculous."

"I guess I'd have to agree. But the guy's from the eastern Mediterranean, and that's what he says. They think a little different there. You've got to admit his argument has a certain metaphysical appeal."

"Not metaphysics, Jeffrey. Sophistry. And the thing's yellow mud, Jeffrey, just yellow mud."

It was a line from Chesterton. They had tossed it between themselves at an earlier time, and Jeffrey completed it with a smile.

"All is gold that glitters, for the glitter is the gold."

They had both laughed and had gone in different directions, Jeffrey sliding back into Grays and Jason, bemused, going on to meet a dealer near the Connaught.

Jeffrey's Aphrodite was yellow mud, he thought, made to be seen as real and true, as good as gold. Did it really matter that it posed as something it was not, if it pleased the unknowing buyer? He had shaken his head in disbelief at the thought, but the conversation had remained with him ever since.

In the dark world of antiquities, fakes and frauds were everywhere. Two years earlier, he had unwittingly helped a faker. He had been in Munich and had gone to see Edip, a former Turkish runner who owned a small gallery at the eastern end of the Maximiliansplatz. Edip sold statuary, bronzes, coins, anything he could. He spoke little English, but his German was fluent, and his Greek had improved since his daughter's engagement to an Athens dealer, a known conduit of fake antiquities into the European market.

Edip had greeted Jason and had gone to a safe and pulled out a beautiful baked clay figure, a griffin with painted wings folded by its side, intact, with no breaks.

Brilliant workmanship, lovely color, Jason thought. And fake.

He had felt a twinge of compassion. He had known Edip for years, and the dealer had been generous in showing him everything he had. He knew the man had been open and honest with him. Surely Edip didn't know that the beautiful object he held in his hand was a forgery.

Should I tell him about it, or let it pass? He decided to tell.

The dealer gave Jason a long look and asked how he knew the griffin was wrong. And Jason had explained, pointing out the details of the faker's work, from the too-cute lion's face to the awkward paws, to the too-fresh paint on the wings and the shiny traces of shellac.

When he turned to look at other objects in the gallery, he heard Edip pick up the telephone and call someone, and speak in German, with Greek phrases laced into the conversation. The dealer then told his listener why the griffin was bad. Detail by detail, exactly as Jason had told him. His voice rose and fell, not always audible, but what he was saying as clear as daylight. He was instructing his listener how to make better fakes.

Jason left Edip's gallery feeling unsettled and a little foolish. Edip's Greek source could now make something that some unwary purchaser would be tricked into buying. He could have confronted Edip, but what good would it have done? The dealer would have smiled and apologized. And continued. In Edip's universe Jason was no more than the latest person to come by.

At the end of the Margutta, he came to a jewelry shop and saw in the window a pin, a scarab of deep blue faience framed in gold.

Modern or old? When he went inside and the pin was placed in his hand, he turned it over and could see that the glazed surface, almost hidden within the gold frame, was slightly broken, the faience glaze oxidized.

It was both. The setting was modern, the scarab ancient, one of the thousands of such objects that had been taken out of Egypt's tombs over centuries of pillaging and that had circulated from collector to jeweler to collector and back, never important enough to go into a museum but always something interesting to those with an eye for small beauty.

Ancient and modern at the same time. Another ambiguity. The price was reasonable, and he bought it immediately.

He returned to the Raphael, his thoughts filled with the glitter of the Margutta. He did not look back and failed to notice the figure that followed.

CHAPTER THIRTY

As Jason reminisced about fakery and metaphysics on the Margutta, Martin Pryce sat in his office in a state of mounting unease about his curator of antiquities. He'd put Jason out of his mind for most of the week, but the stiff conversation at his house kept coming back to him. And Jason was gone, somewhere, out of sight. Where?

He had asked Cynthia about Jason that morning, an off-handed question at the end of a discussion on a new exhibit.

Cynthia had told him that Jason was here, in California, and maybe the East Coast. Is that really where he went?

He could call Jason at home, of course, but what was the point? There was nothing to talk about. After all, he was going to fire the man after the board meeting.

Pryce's day had not been improved by the unexpected arrival that morning of Roger Garrett. Garrett sat on the Gabriel board's collections committee, and while his special interest was post-Renaissance Italian paintings, he said he had come to see the Athena. His first words to Pryce were unsettling.

"Andrew said I should look at it. He said he'd never seen anything like it." The attorney smiled thinly and looked at the director with dark, humorless eyes.

The fact that Garrett had rearranged his busy schedule at Paramount to come to the museum meant that Gabriel must have leaned on him to do so.

Was there a problem? Was the old man getting cold feet?

If Garrett were one of the lesser board members, that would be one matter, but the man was smart, educated in art and the art market, and took a special interest in the museum's acquisitions. He was also subtle and deceptively quiet, someone to be wary of.

"Of course, Roger. I hoped you'd come by. The Athena's in a special room, just down the corridor. Is there anything else you'd like to see?"

"Just the statue, Martin. That's all I came for."

"Fine, let's go." What else could he say? Just the Athena? Pryce felt a small hand close around his heart.

When they came to the closed gallery and Pryce had thrown on the lights, the attorney stood but said nothing at all. He regarded at the statue for a moment, then cast his eyes up at the high spotlights before bringing them back at the figure. He circled around it until he came to the front again. Garret was tall, more than six feet, but the dark body of the statue towered above him. Pryce decided to let the other man speak first.

"I see what Andrew was talking about."

More silence. The director knotted his fingers behind his back, waiting.

"Andrew says there's nothing else like it."

"Yes, that's right. The Getty had a big statue, once, but not as large or as imposing. Nothing like this one."

Pryce shifted his feet and crossed his arms in front of him.

"Where did it come from, Martin?" The words were spoken almost as a passing thought. In Pryce's experience, Garret never had only a passing thought.

"From a London dealer, Richard Maybank. Acting for a member of the Weymouth family who's asked him to sell it. It's been in the family since the early nineteenth century."

"And you know that?"

Pryce looked at Garrett as steadily as he could. *Why is he asking? Where is this going?*

"We do. Maybank's sent us a set of letters that seem pretty clear that a very large statue was in the Weymouth's country house for five generations. It could only be this one."

"And no one's heard of anything like it on the market? There's no chance of it having come out of the ground recently?"

"The market's been absolutely silent, Richard. We'd certainly have heard something about it if it had appeared in the normal places. But there's been nothing, not a word. Maybank showed it to us first. No other dealer has seen it."

"And silence on the market means what?"

"It supports Maybank's claim that the statue's been out of sight with the Weymouths for as long as they say it has."

A thin film of perspiration formed on Pryce's brow. It was unexpectedly hot, and he stepped away from the circle of light that surrounded the statue.

"I hope you're right, Martin. It would be really embarrassing if someone wanted it back. The Italians, for example." The attorney's dark eyes locked with Pryce's for the briefest moment before his eyes went back to the statue. "But Andrew's right. It's amazing. I think we ought to get it."

Afterward, in the quiet of his office, Pryce took a long breath and exhaled. He went over to a cabinet and poured a short glass half full of scotch. It was barely noon. He normally had a drink only when he was working very late, but he needed one now.

He felt as though a bullet had just passed by his head.

At least Roger didn't ask about Jason.

And where the hell *is* Jason, anyway?

CHAPTER THIRTY-ONE

Frescobaldi was silent as he drove through central Rome toward the Tiber, and Jason spent the time trying to think through the meeting he was about to have with a man who had once been the most important antiquities dealer in Italy.

Will he talk? Will he tell the truth? Will he have any reason to answer my questions at all? If Pisano was resistant, he'd fail. But Frescobaldi said he wanted to talk. What does that mean?

He needed a simple interrogation plan. But interrogation plans needed information and inducements, and he had almost none. Nothing on Pisano, no clue as to what the dealer might want, only a partially formed idea of what he could offer the man. There could be no hostile questioning with psychological breakdown and confession as the goal. The standard techniques of even non-coercive interrogation—skillful reasoning, patience, small concessions—needed time to work, days or weeks, and that was impossible.

Understanding and sympathy, he finally decided. Show Pisano that what I want he wants also, give him reason to trust me. Let him talk, help him feel important. And give him a deal, offer him something he needs. Reduced charges. If he talks, and if the prosecutor agrees. That's a lot of ifs. Not much to go with.

They crossed the Ponte Sisto Bridge, and Frescobaldi turned the car left toward the *Regina Coeli* prison.

The *Carcere di Regina Coeli* has been Rome's principal men's prison since the middle of the nineteenth century. It was once a convent, founded two hundred years earlier by the Barberini family after their return to Italy following long years in exile. Lying between the Janiculum hill and the Tiber, the prison occupies a rectangular area more than four hundred feet on its longest side. Its walls embrace a group of parallel, five-story cellblocks that face the river, and a large cruciform cellblock deeper inside. High-windowed buildings define the prison's periphery. When the *Regina Coeli* is full, as it is normally, it can hold more than three thousand prisoners.

Frescobaldi found a parking space three blocks away, and the two men walked through the enclave of shops and restaurants that had grown up around the prison over the years, arriving at the main, western entry gate a few minutes before ten. They went directly to a guardhouse encased in armored glass. Jason turned over his passport and Frescobaldi his identity card, and each was given a green visitor's badge. In a few minutes, they were escorted to one of the interview rooms set aside for inmates to meet visitors with special access. In the distant background, voices sounded, metal doors opened and closed, footsteps moved along the hallways. A faint, complex odor of cooking oil and disinfectant seemed to suffuse the air.

The room was small and had only a table and four chairs, all bolted to the floor. A guard asked them to take a seat and then departed. In ten minutes they heard a noise, the door opened, and a man wearing a single-piece short-sleeved orange uniform entered the room. The guard shut the door behind him as he left.

Rafaele Pisano was short, with brown hair cut close to the head and neck and dark eyes that reflected the wall lights of the room. Deep furrows ran down his forehead between the eyes. He had muscled forearms, large shoulders, strong hands with short fingers, and a presence that in an earlier time must have exuded confidence and command. Three weeks in the *Regina Coeli* had not been kind. The man who stood before them appeared diminished and uncertain. He stood and looked at his visitors, nodded to the attorney, and then came over to Jason.

"Good morning," Pisano said in accented English, clasping Jason's hand, and repeated himself in Italian.

Frescobaldi and Jason sat on two hard-backed chairs. The attorney took out a small pad of paper and turned to the curator. "Mr. Pisano wants me to translate," he said. "He asks why you want to see him. I told him yesterday, but he wants to hear it from you."

Jason took on a half-smile. "Mr. Pisano, you don't know me, but I've heard of you, even in the United States. You're quite famous in certain places. But that's not why I'm here.

"I'm with the Gabriel Museum in California. We've been offered an ancient statue. It must have come from Sicily originally, or maybe southern Italy. We've been told it's been in a family collection for more than a hundred years. But it may be more recent, and I'd like to know when it appeared. You may be able to help."

The curator waited to allow Frescobaldi to finish writing and translate.

Pisano turned to face Jason. He spoke slowly, with a short delay after every two or three sentences to allow Frescobaldi to put them into English.

"Mr. Connor, I'm not so happy to talk to people who want to know these things. Tell me how my talking to *you* about this—this statue—will help me."

"If you know nothing about it, it won't help at all. But if you know of it, if you can give me a clear description of it, wherever you may have seen it, that should be good enough for Italy to be able to get it back."

Jason paused. "The prosecutor will know of this talk we're having. We'll make certain he does. He'll know that whatever you've told me was done voluntarily. Will that work for you?"

Frescobaldi had been scribbling notes as Jason spoke. He took a long minute to translate.

Pisano frowned slightly, and his eyes held Jason's.

"You know, there is a risk here, Mr. Connor. Telling stories to the police doesn't win friends. A week ago a man was killed here for saying things he shouldn't have. Maybe I shouldn't know this statue at all."

The attorney scribbled. A fly buzzed in a corner. Voices sounded distantly. Frescobaldi had fallen silent. Jason waited.

Pisano shifted in his chair, then looked at Jason. "OK, Mr. Connor. What is it? What's this statue you're so interested in?"

"It's a figure of a woman. With a head of white marble, different from the body. And very tall. Almost three meters."

That's enough. It should be enough. He'll have to provide the rest.

Pisano stared at Jason. Silence filled the room.

"Mr. Connor, does the statue have drapery, drapery like the ripples of a waterfall?"

"It does."

"Would this *very big* statue have been broken? Into four parts?" Pisano said the words *very big* in Italian, then in English.

"It would."

The dealer's frown had disappeared. A slight smile tugged at his mouth.

"Would there be a scrape at the left leg, as if a shovel had cut into it as it was being dug up?"

"There would."

"Then it seems we are talking about the same thing, are we not?"

Jason nodded.

"It seems so."

It was certainly so.

In time, Pisano spoke again.

"So, is that it? Is there anything else?"

Jason's breath caught for a moment.

"Yes, if you can. You were paid for it, weren't you? But maybe that's not important now."

Pisano's smile vanished.

"Not important!" His voice rose. "Let me tell you, Mr. Connor, I have made many people very rich. Rich is important! And the person who bought it and who is selling it to you wants to be very, very rich. I know this."

The words came quickly and Frescobaldi stopped writing for a moment and held up his hand. *"Adagio, Rafaele, adagio!"*

The dealer regarded the attorney, then Jason, for a long minute.

"I know this man very well, Mr. Connor. And you should know what we did with this big statue, this big, very expensive statue, the one I had sent to this man in London, this Maybank. I told this Maybank he could show it but he could not sell it until I agreed. And he showed it to his first client—your museum! And your director said he wanted it. And then I came to London and stayed there for four days. Four days in that place, eating bad English food and talking with this Maybank about this statue, and how much he'd pay me. I told him I wanted half, only half, of what he got from his client. Your museum."

Pisano's words had begun to trip over themselves, and again Frescobaldi told him to slow down.

"And so I could know what this Maybank was doing, I stayed there until he wrote to your director and confirmed that the price would be twenty million. And I was in his office when the DHL people came and took the letter away."

"For the ten million he will get for your statue, Mr. Connor, this Maybank, he will be very rich. Very." Pisano's face darkened as he made the point.

Jason sat rooted to his chair.

Holy Christ! Did I hear him correctly?

"Twenty million? You said twenty million?"

"Venti milione di dollari." Pisano said again. Frescobaldi looked at Jason. He did not need to translate.

"One more question. When were you with Maybank? September?"

"No, Mr. Connor. August. A cold, wet English August. Four days, with bad food. *Agusto!*"

No translation was needed here either.

Jason sat, his mind racing.

Maybank wrote and asked twenty million dollars for the Athena. In August. That was a false letter, for Pisano's benefit. But he'd already worked out the deal with Martin, and Martin must have laughed at the letter and thrown it away. Then Maybank wrote a second letter, in September. The one that's in the museum's file, the one Martin showed Gabriel and me, offering the statue for forty million.

And Martin's in the middle. For what? Martin will have cleaned up beyond belief. If Pisano's not lying. But he's not. He knows the statue. The size, the drapery, the breaks are all the same as the Athena. His discussion with Maybank fits exactly. No, there's no lie here.

The dealer spoke again.

"Is there anything else you want, Mr. Connor? Is this enough for you?"

The figure in the orange uniform who sat at the table was pleading but too proud to ask the obvious question.

Jason stood and looked down at Pisano for a moment, then smiled.

"It's enough. The museum can't buy the statue. I will let them know what you've said. And Mr. Frescobaldi—" He turned to the attorney. "Mr. Frescobaldi will want to have a talk with the prosecutor, quite soon I think. And I imagine we'll want to be in touch with the prosecutor also, and start to unwind this matter. That should help you. I hope so."

I really do hope this will help you, Rafaele Pisano.

Pisano knocked on the door, and there was a stirring in the corridor. As the guard opened it, he turned back to Jason.

"But Mr. Connor?" Pisano's words were in English. "The statue. It is something, is it not? *Qualcosa!*" He smiled.

"Yes, Mr. Pisano. It's something." He took the dealer's hand and shook it with both his own. "Thank you. And good luck."

Jason had intended only to show Pisano enough sympathy to learn what he needed to know. He was surprised to find that, at the end of this short half-hour, he felt it.

He was exhausted. The answer he wanted and did not want had fallen into his hands.

Now what the hell was he to do with it?

CHAPTER THIRTY-TWO

As Jason ended his meeting with Pisano, a man across the street from the gates of the *Regina Coeli* pulled the gray cap down across his forehead and punched the single key on his cell phone that connected with a number in Sicily. He kept his voice low when the call went through.

"Tonio, Cosimo. I'm outside the prison. Frescobaldi is inside. He has the American with him."

The connection was good and clear. The voice that came shouting down the line from Aidone was loud, and Tonio had to hold the instrument away from his ear.

"*Si*, Cosimo. *Si. Si.*" There was nothing else to say.

"Rome? You're coming to Rome?"

Rome! Cosimo Galante almost never left Sicily. Now the man's coming to Rome! *Merda!* There must be a catastrophe to bring him here.

In the spring and summer, few places are more pleasant than the open roof terrace of the Raphael, where at lunch one can sit and see the spired domes of Rome's thousand churches rise above the city. In the winter the terrace is enclosed and pleasant enough. There were few hotel guests, and Jason could go over Pisano's stunning remark undisturbed.

Twenty million. And the Gabriel Museum is about to pay forty! Who gets the difference? Martin! Or Maybank and Martin together, with a scam on the London side. Maybank's first letter to Martin with the twenty million dollar figure was for Pisano's benefit, but Maybank could also show it to Inland Revenue. The British tax people would never know what he had pocketed. And if he split with Martin, that would leave fifteen for Martin. Fifteen million dollars.

The past four months fell into place. Martin's meeting with Maybank in London in August, their trip to Maybank's warehouse, the discussion that must have taken place between the two. And Martin's insistence on negotiating the deal himself.

Martin had set up both Kate and him to support the acquisition with positive reports. Kate delivered up her endorsement, exactly as Martin wanted. And Martin had insisted on terminating Jason's own document review. Now only his suspicion of the letters stood between Martin and his fifteen million. No wonder he was furious at Jason's insistence on checking further.

Of course, Martin wouldn't have cared a fig if the provenance unraveled in ten years. He'd be gone with the money. He'd retire after years of distinguished service and appear to head toward the kind of quiet, honorable life that retired museum directors led, writing scholarly books or lecturing at a local college.

But that's not good enough for Martin. He's ensuring his future forever with this one deal. Buying his little villa at Antibes or wherever and still collecting retirement pay, living like a king and laughing up his sleeve at the grand joke he'd put over on the Gabriel.

The more Jason thought about it, the more effort it took to still his sense of outrage. He finished a dessert that was as tasteless to him as it was unmemorable, went to his room, watched with a distracted eye a rerun of *Madame Bovary* with a startlingly lovely young Jennifer Jones as the tormented Emma, then turned out the light and slept badly.

When he visited the Raphael's small business center he found an e-mail message from Cynthia Greenwalt, sent the previous day. After giving small news of the antiquities department, she chatted in some detail about the forthcoming renovation of the Greek vase gallery and added:

"Martin dropped by this morning and asked after you. I told him I thought you were still in Los Angeles, or on the East Coast visiting relatives, but I hadn't heard from you and couldn't really say. I couldn't tell him more than that anyway, could I? He didn't seem particularly concerned, just curious. And Kate stopped in to talk about the spots of bronze disease that she's found on one of the Roman vessels in the storeroom and asked me to say hello when I next wrote you. Amelia was really quite short-tempered with her when she came in, for no reason I can think of."

Martin almost never just drops by, Jason thought. He's concerned, all right.

At Da Vinci Airport he saw an indistinct motion, a movement in the corner of his eye. A face in the exit hall that appeared, then turned away, no more. It eluded him, and then he caught it: the tall man he had seen at the hotel bar in Aidone. But the face in the airport belonged to someone who was shorter and younger. A coincidence.

At the Telecom Italia counter, as he was about to turn in the replacement cell phone he had rented, Jason decided to make a final call to Mancini.

Mancini cut in before he could start.

"What the hell did you do down there? In Sicily?

"What are you talking about?"

"The police say there's some huge row that's been kicked up in Aidone because of an American. Is that you? Who did you see there?"

Jason thought for a moment.

"No one. Really. I didn't meet with anyone; I didn't talk with anyone. Except for a few minutes with a farmer."

"The police seem to have a source there somewhere, and they say some American's involved, which is why they mentioned it to me. Of course they could be wrong. In Italy, 'American' could also mean Canadian or English or Australian, depending where you are."

Mancini paused. "Did you see anyone else who might be American? Or English?"

"No, no one."

As he was boarding his flight, the face of the man he had seen in the airport crowd came back to him.

What's this? Who in Aidone would be interested in me?

Jason thought back to his stay in the town. He had spoken to no one.

Martin? Could Martin be in this somewhere?

But Martin had no idea where he was, so that wasn't right. Still, someone now seemed to think he was a problem, perhaps even a big problem.

Who? And would they follow me to London? Back to Los Angeles?

That doesn't make sense. The American consulate wouldn't issue a visa to a Sicilian without references and the full array of paperwork. And that would take weeks, if it could be done at all.

Then he remembered. Italian citizens don't need visas to travel to the United States. The requirement had been dropped years ago.

He stopped and fished in his pocket and found the scrap of paper he had written on two days earlier, when Mancini had given him the name of the man to avoid in Aidone. He found it, looked at it for a moment, then tore it into small fragments and threw them away.

In the back of his mind, a distant bell began ringing.

CHAPTER THIRTY-THREE

Maybank, Jason thought.

Richard Maybank was key to the faked letters he'd sent with the statue. The Langlotz letter was faked, the other letters were a total fabrication, a lie from beginning to end, straight out of someone's imagination. Maybank's, certainly.

That put a dark enough cloud over the acquisition. But Pisano's story kills it. Pisano can't be doubted. His description of the statue was exact, down to the breaks and the scarred surface. There could be no question about the match. The Weymouth documents were created not to fill a long gap in the record, but to cover the statue's trail from Morgantina, through Pisano, to Maybank. The Gabriel could not buy it now. The Italian government would expect to get it back.

But if Maybank's documents smelled, the Gabriel's director stank. If it worked as Martin wanted, he'd be made rich with the museum's money.

There was no other possible explanation for Martin's behavior. But believing Pisano was one thing, convincing someone else was another.

Would the story stand up? Martin would call Pisano a liar who'd say anything to get his sentence reduced. He could point an accusatory finger at Jason for wanting to blacken his reputation. Jason would be made the goat, his motives and integrity suspect. His dismissal would be inevitable and immediate.

He needed something solid that could verify Pisano's story. He could only get that from Maybank himself.

He took his bags off the Terminal 5 carousel, picked up a phone from one of the cellular service stores near the exit, and made two calls. The first was to the Stafford to confirm his reservations. The second went to Anna Estaing, Robertson's friend at the Courtauld. Estaing said Gerald had called her and told her Jason would be in London. Sunday dinner would be fine, she said. The Ritz, just around the corner from the Stafford, would also be fine. She spoke softly, with a faint accent.

Jason had no appointments through Sunday afternoon. That gave him two days to visit places outside London. He rented a car and began thinking of a slow drive in the country. He ran through the possibilities, places that could give him some uplift on a cold December weekend.

Medieval castles, he thought. He'd seen his share of them in France and Germany, and even in Syria at an earlier time, when he had taken a few precious days to visit the fabled Krak des Chevaliers, an enormous structure that loomed over the Homs plain and could be seen more than forty miles away on a clear day. But all the great castles he had seen were late, most completed in the eleventh and twelfth centuries, and he wanted to see something earlier. There were several great monuments in the south, he knew, remnants of a past when Rome had imposed its imperial design on the land by military conquest.

So then castles, and maybe big churches. He exited Heathrow and headed to Chertsey and the M3 road that would take him to the south. He would find a place to stay in Winchester, revisit the great cathedral there in the morning, and then head to the sea, toward Southampton and Bournemouth, perhaps even Dorchester.

He put his finger next to Dorchester on the map the rental car agency had given him and saw just to the east the town of Weymouth.

Weymouth. Brigham House would be somewhere nearby.

Could he see it? Frederick Weymouth wouldn't be there, of course. The house and lands were National Trust property now, and Weymouth had abandoned it years ago to live in London.

But what's the point? Sure, Brigham House was the Weymouth estate, and that's where they were supposed to have kept the statue. But the whole provenance is a fake. Even Weymouth is likely a put-up, someone who doesn't have the foggiest idea what it even looks like. Maybank probably paid him to sign onto the scheme.

Still, since he'd be nearby, why not go see Brigham House? The building was one of Robert Adam's best and should be interesting.

It was almost seven by the time he came to the outskirts of Winchester. He took the first exit he could find off the M3 and in a few minutes passed a large Victorian house that advertised rooms for the night or week, He made a U-turn into the driveway. It had a name, Giffard House. It was pleasant looking, slightly run down, a walk to the cathedral, and it appealed to him immediately. He went in to take a room for the night.

The following morning, he left his car and walked into Winchester to admire the façade of the second largest of England's great cathedrals. With a long day ahead of him, he took time in the vaulted interior only to stop at Jane Austen's tomb in an aisle off the nave before heading back to the hotel to pick up his bags.

He took the back road southward to Romsey and then the A31 to Ringwood. He passed Bournemouth, reached Dorchester, and circled the city to see in the distance an enormous mound that loomed above the surrounding fields. Maiden Castle named, he recalled, not for a woman but corrupted from a pre-Celtic word for a great hill.

Jason found the site fenced but with an open entry gate. He walked in unobstructed and paced the site from one end to the other, admiring the great concentric earthworks that surrounded the hill on which the fortress had once stood and that, at the ancient entrance, snaked back and forth to funnel would-be attackers into winding narrow ravines where the site's defenders could assail them with spears and arrows. Originally a Celtic stronghold, the fortress hill had been besieged in the first century by Vespasian, then a general in the service of the emperor Claudius, more than twenty years before he himself was made emperor of Rome.

But Maiden Castle had nothing Roman about it. The Celtic earth walls were over ten feet high in some places and still dominated the site, while the stonework that Vespasian had left was small in comparison, vestigial and transient.

How unlike the Romans, he thought. Other Roman settlements had started as army camps and were built outward to become great cities. Maiden Castle was nothing like them, and he was surprised that here, only a few miles in from the English coast, the rigid traditions of Roman architecture and urban form had been overwhelmed by those of a more ancient period.

None of it, the cathedral in Winchester, his long walk through Maiden Castle, had taken his mind off Maybank. Maybank was the nut he had to crack.

How could he do that? Maybank was not as anxious and compliant as Pisano. He was shrewd, probably as versed as Jason in subterfuge and deceit. He also had a reputation for violence. A few years earlier, another London dealer had sought an arrangement with one of Maybank's Turkish suppliers. The dealer had been found beaten senseless in his own gallery. Nothing had been taken and no other damage had been done. The Metropolitan Police found nothing that pointed to the perpetrators, but no one in the community of London art dealers doubted that it was Maybank's way of sending a message.

Jason knew he would have to tread very carefully. The moment he saw Maybank and mentioned Pisano, Maybank would call Martin.

There was no other way. But he'd have only one shot at the man. It had to work.

CHAPTER THIRTY-FOUR

Gaetano Frescobaldi was on the verge of leaving his office to find lunch. It was after one o'clock. He had been forced to put in extra time because of the half-day the American had taken away from him. He was hungry and wanted to close down. On Saturdays he worked alone, and the building was usually quiet, so he was surprised when he heard noises at the bottom of the elevator shaft and then heard the elevator rise and stop at his floor. His bell rang, and when he unlocked and opened his door, he found himself facing two dark-jacketed men.

Not Italian, he thought. Sicilian.

The shorter, more heavily muscled of the two asked if he were *Signor Frescobaldi*.

"I am."

"*Signor* Frescobaldi, we would like to talk to you. Only a few minutes."

"What about?"

"In your office, please. It is difficult to explain here on the landing."

It was not a request. A *frisson* of uncertainty ran through him. He turned back to his door and motioned his visitors to come inside.

The attorney seated the two men in his inner office and took a chair.

"How may I be of help?" he asked. The men had still not identified themselves.

"Mr. Frescobaldi, you are Raffaele Pisano's attorney, aren't you?"

"Yes."

"And you recently took a visitor to meet with Mr. Pisano, no? An American?"

"Yes. Yesterday."

"We would like to know what you talked about."

"I can't—" Frescobaldi began, but then stopped and eyed his visitors more carefully. The shorter man, the one who spoke to him, leaned forward in his chair, and the lawyer had the sudden and uncomfortable thought that the man would not take no for an answer. He could think of nothing in yesterday's meeting that would be damaging to Pisano, and these men seemed more interested in the American than his client.

"The American is with a museum. He wanted to know if a particular statue had passed through Mr. Pisano's hands."

"And Pisano said what?"

"He knew the statue."

"And told the American?"

"Yes."

"And what will the American do with that information?"

"He'll probably take it back to the museum and tell his people, and they will decide to buy or not to buy, depending on what he says."

"And if they don't buy it, what will happen?"

"They will send it back to the dealer who sent it to them, I think. A man in London."

"Is that all they'll do?" The questioner waited. "And will they discuss it with anyone else? For example, the Carabinieri?"

The Sicilian measured the expression on Frescobaldi's face.

The attorney wanted to get up and leave but knew he would be able to take no more than two steps. He stared at the man in front of him.

"The American said something like that. It wasn't clear. He was offering a way for my client to get a reduced sentence."

The man who was speaking fell silent, but Frescobaldi could sense a venomous rage just beneath the surface.

The two men stood up.

"Mr. Frescobaldi, you understand this is a conversation that did not take place?"

"Yes."

"And you understand that if you tell anyone, we will know about it?" There was total menace in the man's voice.

"Yes." Frescobaldi was rigid in his chair.

"Goodbye, then. *Buona giornata.* Have a nice day."

The two men left. As they exited onto the Corso, a third man detached himself from the wall next to the building entrance and joined them. Galante had made certain that no one would come in to bother him during his discussion with Pisano's attorney.

The attorney finally rose and stood for a short time, shaking uncontrollably. In a few minutes, he collected himself, closed and locked the outer door, went down in the elevator, walked out onto the Condotti, and turned toward the Corso. He had lost his interest in lunch and wanted only to go home. He passed, unnoticing, by store windows bright with Christmas colors, restaurants filled with happy Saturday afternoon diners, and pedestrians with shopping bags in their hands enjoying the bright winter day. The tremors stopped only when he was halfway to his apartment. For the first time in his life Gaetano Frescobaldi had looked into the gates of hell.

CHAPTER THIRTY-FIVE

Jason drove into Weymouth center in search of directions to Brigham House. The largest hotel he could find, the Prince Regent on the town's esplanade, had what he wanted, a rack of brochures on sights and activities in Weymouth and the surrounding area. One, with the title *Country Houses of Dorset*, showed Brigham House as a visitor attraction.

He took the brochure and another on the local villages of Weymouth and sat down in the hotel lounge to read them. It took him a minute to realize he was going to learn nothing about Brigham House that Eileen Harris's book had not already told him. The place was only briefly described, and the postage-stamp size photograph of the front of the main building was almost useless. The brochure's map was small and virtually unreadable.

Why would the Weymouths give their family home to the National Trust? Death duties, he thought. Frederick Weymouth had probably been unable to pay them when his father had died. Along with countless hundreds of other country houses, castles, hunting preserves, and lodges, along with vast areas of undeveloped land, Brigham House then became the property of the English people.

He went to the hotel desk to ask directions. The clerk, an earnest young man with a nervous tic in his right eye, said he would have to go through the village of West Lulworth toward East Lulworth and would then find Brigham House on his right just after he passed a smaller road leading to Bovington and Wool.

Four miles past West Lulworth, Jason found a sign to the Weymouth estate and turned into a gravel road. He drove up a low rise and then, on the other side, saw in the distance a stand of oaks that framed a stately two-story structure and a number of outbuildings, with the Channel in the distance, gray in the afternoon light. The entry road ran straight as an arrow between two rows of oaks and ended in a circular drive in front of a staircase that led upward to two double entrance doors.

He came awake. Brigham House. Much bigger than I thought. Harris's book didn't do it justice. A sign at the entry said the estate was a property of the National Trust, and that the house was open Tuesday through Sunday. He was in luck.

He drove to the small parking area near the old stable and walked back to the main entry. Mounting a large elliptical staircase that rose from the driveway, he found himself in a foyer and walked inside the main entry hall. An older woman with glasses and white hair tied behind her head, clutching a heavy wool sweater tightly around her, collected two pounds and gave him a receipt and a folded brochure.

Jason stood to the side for a moment and read.

Brigham House, the brochure said, was named for the owners of the property. It had been a modest sixteenth-century country house of mixed timber, stone, and brick construction, but in 1725, two years before his death, George I had repaid a large loan made to him by Richard Brigham by making Richard an earl and granting him properties that would provide him and his descendants with substantial income. With his new wealth, Richard, first Earl of Weymouth, had engaged Robert Adam to build a large and comfortable house overlooking the sea.

Jason went outside the main building, admiring the proportions and overall unity of the structure, with its two stories, high-peaked roof surmounted by eight chimneys, the grand external staircase, and the entry hall with its classical pediment. It was the fourth earl, the brochure noted, who added wings to hold guests and staff and outlying buildings, including a granary and stables. A solarium was added to these in the nineteenth century.

The fourth earl, Jason thought, with a flash of sardonic humor. The man who made the purchase that never took place.

Inside the main house again, he stopped to view two large salons, a great dining hall, and a kitchen that was a somewhat worn example of what was available in England more than forty years earlier. The furniture was all of a period, the 1930s, the chairs and sofas recovered some time later, probably after the War. The National Trust did not seem to have enough money to maintain the place in good repair or prevent the inevitable deterioration of fabric and wood. It was a sad story, Jason thought, one that was the same for many of England's great estates.

He decided to look at the great house from the outside again and descended the exterior stairs, then circled around the east wing toward the sea. As he rounded the house and came to the stables he met a figure wearing overalls and a cap, grunting heavily as he pitched hay into a cart. The farmhand shot a glance at him and continued tossing his hay. Jason tried to catch the man's attention.

"Excuse me—could you tell me where the solarium is?"

The man put down the fork, wiped his nose on the back of his hand, contemplated Jason for a moment, and pointed in the direction of a glass-paneled structure further toward the sea.

"Over there."

"And the granary?"

The question brought a longer pause as the man considered the question. His eyes crinkled at the corner, and he gave a thin smile. "Hain't bin no granary for almost two hundred years, guvner."

"What?"

"No. Burned down, it did. Ah—'round eighteen-twenty that was. My great-great-granddad helped fight the fire."

Jason barely managed to get back to the car park before he began to laugh.

The damned granary! The whole story's been made up. Maybank's taken it from the same brochure I've been reading. Or Harris's coffee-table book on Adam's country houses, the same one that's in the Gabriel's library.

The arrogant fool didn't even take the time to come to Brigham House and check it out for himself! But Maybank is no fool. He's smart as hell. At the top, put there with a killer instinct. Ruthless. He'll probably do anything to succeed. But arrogant. Believes he's bulletproof.

Needs something. What? Fears what?

Maybank was dangerous. He'd have to be very careful with the man.

CHAPTER THIRTY-SIX

"*Ucapisci?* Do you understand?"

Saturday evenings in Rome are a time for relaxation, for dinner with friends or family, for a movie or reading, or for doing nothing at all.

This Saturday evening, however, five men were engaged only in business. Cosimo Galante and the two who had come with him from Aidone had been joined by two others. The one named Armanno was very large, with hair cut very short, wide-set eyes and broad, flat features that had caused the crueler of his schoolmates to call him names behind his back, but only once. The other was smaller and younger, with dark hair swept back from the forehead in Cosimo's manner. Both wore full suits and monogrammed white shirts open at the collar. Unlike Galante, who wore only slacks and a knitted shirt, they appeared no different from any of the urban Roman businessmen who surrounded them in the restaurant on the Via Sistina.

After making certain there was no one nearby, the men lapsed into dialect in low voices.

"'*U capisci chiddu che nuàutri vulemu, Armanno?* Do you understand what we want?" Galante said again, speaking to the man with the flattened face.

"Yes. You want us to take care of Pisano. In the prison."

"Soon. *Subito.* Not later than Monday."

"And you want us to visit Pisano's client in London. This Maybank. And take care of him also."

"Yes, that's the second part. Both have to be done. One is not enough. But an accident, yes? It has to look like an accident."

"Anything else?"

"There's another, an American, in California. You may have to send someone there to see him. Someone who won't be noticed, maybe who has been there before and who's English is good. Someone who knows the place and can go there without a problem. Not like me. You have people like this?"

"Of course. What do you take us for? And when will you tell us about this American?"

"After the London job's done."

The larger man sat for a moment, with an unreadable expression on his face.

"This will be expensive."

"Tell me."

"A quarter of a million euros. For both Pisano and the Maybank person."

Galante sat speechless.

"And another half million for the American. It's more difficult there. I don't like to screw around in America."

"And you expect me to pay that now?" Galante was on the verge of exploding, but contained himself.

"You'll need to pay the quarter million no later than Monday morning. I'll give you the details of the account. That will take care of Pisano and the Englishman. Then, if you want us to do the

American job, I'll want a quarter million on deposit. You can pay the balance when it's done."

Fucking Italians, Galante thought. These men are pigs, robbers. Not honest businessmen like him. He vaguely considered ways they might have a terrible accident. But that wouldn't work. He needed Pisano and Maybank taken care of, and maybe the American. And he'd probably need them again.

He nodded.

The five men finished their drinks and walked out into the night.

CHAPTER THIRTY-SEVEN

Sunday turned rainy with sleet. Jason left Weymouth in the early morning and took a long, slow drive, first northward to Oxford, then back for a late lunch at Cliveden, the great Italianate manor house, built on the early 1850s by the extraordinary Charles Barry for the Duke of Sutherland, a work of art in itself. He returned the rental car at Heathrow and took a cab into London and checked into the Stafford. On an alley in Saint James's, the Stafford was comfortable and gave easy access to the galleries in the West End. It was also safe from discovery by Martin and had the added advantage of being only a short walk to Richard Maybank's gallery on Jermyn and Duke Streets.

He had made a reservation for seven and was in the Ritz lobby five minutes early. A woman wrapped in a Burberry entered, folded her umbrella, and came over with a smile and her hand extended. He rose.

"Dr. Connor? You look like Gerald's description."

Anna Estaing was somewhere in her later fifties, Jason guessed. He saw a long face, dark hair, eyes a little too closely set, a simple plaid suit with a gold pin near the collar, no other jewelry. She carried herself with a natural grace and spoke with a very faint French accent, pronouncing Robertson's given name as *Zherald.*

Displaced nobility, he thought, remembering Gerald's comment that a cousin of Estaing's had been president of France thirty years earlier.

There was only a handful of other diners in the hotel's ornate restaurant, and Estaing and Jason were given a quiet table next to a window. When they had ordered, she looked at him appraisingly.

"So, Gerald says you are on some kind of quest. Something about an ancient sculpture. He didn't say much, and he said you'd explain. He thought I might be interested in a document matter of some kind."

He took ten minutes to give her the background of the dark statue that had appeared with a dealer and the trail that led toward Morgantina, not toward a noble English family.

"Even though that's what the documents we have indicate. They're all bad, however. One of them has a signature that's wrong. That makes all the others wrong."

Estaing had put down her fork and listened quietly as he spoke.

"Dr. Estaing—Anna, if I may—Gerald says you're a document person. He says I could learn something from you about document fakery."

"Well, I guess I *am* a document person. Fifteen years at the Conservation Institute, then eight at the Courtauld, all with prints, drawings, paper, inks. I was lucky. They've got the best analytical equipment that exists and the best research staff one could want." She smiled as she spoke. She had served at two of the most renowned art institutions in the world.

"Yes, Dr. Connor, I know a bit about document faking. There is a lot of it, more and more. It gets increasingly sophisticated every year. But most of the fakers have been tripped up. They've usually done it to themselves."

"How's that?"

She took a bite of prawn and looked at him, and he found himself staring at the attractive woman in front of him with her long nose and close-set eyes.

"Something, usually some obvious thing, does it. Signatures that don't match the originals, like yours. Letterheads that were never used, postmarks that were put into use only after a letter's mailing date. Paper that was made by the wrong paper mill or had the wrong watermark. The wrong type of ink. Made-up references to people who lived somewhere else, or that can't be verified by tax rolls or civil documents. Still, even when there seems to be something wrong, the evidence is not always so clear. Sometimes it can be quite ambiguous."

"Ambiguous? How would that happen?"

"I'll give you an example. Do you remember the Vinland Map? The one at Yale that caused such a stir when its discovery was revealed in the nineteen sixties?"

"You're telling me it's a fake?" Jason was startled. The map had stunned historians by showing that part of the North American continent had been charted more than four hundred years before the voyages of Columbus. He had always thought it authentic.

"Many of us think so. There are concerns about the content of the map. The uncanny accuracy of Greenland as an island—now, how would a fifteenth-century mapmaker know that? And the appearance of word forms that were not in common use in the 1430s when it's supposed to have been made. Then, the ink shows traces of anatase—that's a titanium compound—which appears in paints only after nineteen twenty or so, not before."

A small smile played on her lips as she talked, a slight upward turning of her mouth.

"So, Dr. Connor—Jason?—that should be conclusive about its being a fake, yes? But it's not. Radiocarbon tests show that the parchment is from the period when the map is said to have been drawn. The titanium could have been the result of contamination. Someday we'll know for certain. But not today."

Estaing paused, thought for a moment, and then continued.

"If it's a fake, it's a devilishly clever one. It shows what could be done fifty years ago. And it could be done again today. But, you know, all it really takes to make good document forgeries is the necessary talent, time for the faker to get the necessary paper, ink, whatever, the raw materials that would allow a master forgery to be made. And money. It starts with money and ends with money, enough to pay the forger his fee and then to pay him enough afterward to keep his mouth shut."

Jason thought for a moment.

"Is there no way that a fake document can be disproved?"

"There is. Analysis of the paper with the right equipment and with comparative material from the period the document is supposed to have been created. Or analysis of the ink to show if it has any traces of cesium or strontium."

"Isotopic analysis?"

"Exactly. Cesium and strontium isotopes are products of the atom bombs that were dropped on Japan or were detonated in the air before atmospheric testing was stopped. They don't occur in nature. Anything that contains them—paint, ink, binding glue, whatever—has to date to 1945 or later. But the analysis is delicate and very expensive. Not every collector or museum can afford it."

She sat back in her chair for a moment and looked around the room. A waiter headed toward them, but she waved him off and returned to the curator.

"Of course there's the other thing. The fraud behind the forgery behind the fake. The third level of illusion."

"Third level?"

Estaing had lost her smile.

"The deepest deception, the inside job. The one you least expect—that you're totally unprepared for."

Jason stared at her.

"What are you talking about?"

"Start with the museum. Can you be sure your museum's files aren't contaminated?"

"Contaminated? How's that possible?"

"You've probably allowed some nice scholar to look at the files on your objects? For research purposes?"

"Yes. Please go on."

"Who's to know that they're not—ah, working for someone else? A dealer, say? And that they've not inserted faked or altered documents in the file to create a false history for an object? Leave a trail for others who'd then accept its authenticity—or its provenance?"

Jason thought for a moment, then shook his head.

"Please. They couldn't do that, really. I know everything we've bought, every file we have, the acquisition history of every piece. I'd know in a second if there'd been a false insertion."

"But your successor would not, would they?"

He did not respond. No response was possible.

Estaing knew she had his full attention.

"Then there's the second possibility. The one that involves the laboratory, the really reputable lab that you send an object to for analysis, the one with the expensive equipment that your museum doesn't have. How do you know the lab's really working for you?"

Her smile had returned and for a moment he wondered whether she was playing with him, but when he saw her eyes, he knew she was in dead earnest.

"Who else would they be working for?"

"Think about it. What would it take to pay off an analyst to fake a lab report? Or have it doctored up by a supervisor?"

He regarded her for a long moment.

"You're saying it's just money, then? It's all about money?" He realized his voice had begun to sound brittle.

"No, of course not. But it just takes one or two people. One or two lab analysts, or a lab technician and a supervisor, to certify that a forged document is real. And if the money is good enough, an unscrupulous seller of a fake object, a dealer most likely, would have in their hands the opportunity to corrupt the laboratory's report."

Jason sat, stunned. "Has that happened?"

"I don't have any idea whether it's happened or not. But I am absolutely certain that it's only a matter of time before it does."

Her voice trailed off. He sensed that she had peered into a dark well and found only reason to despair.

They rose, and at the hotel entrance, Estaing extended her hand.

"Thank you for dinner. And for the conversation. There aren't many people who are so interested in what I do. I wish you luck with your statue." She was about to leave but turned and looked at him again.

"Please, when you come back to London again, I hope you'll call. I'm sure there are nicer things to talk about." She smiled, pulled the Burberry around her, and went through the great revolving door, out into the night.

On his short walk back to the Stafford, something Estaing had said caught and held his attention. The third level of illusion. It was straight out of one of the training manuals he'd been taught from years ago. With the will and money and technical skills and no mistakes, one could not be stopped.

In the early morning hours the thought finally left him and he dropped into a fitful sleep.

CHAPTER THIRTY-EIGHT

At a corner table of the Stafford's small breakfast room, Jason gamed through his meeting with Maybank. He had to get the dealer to acknowledge that he'd bought the statue from Pisano and faked the letters. That wouldn't be easy. Maybank would be defensive, even hostile. Could he get the man to talk, say something that would confirm what Pisano had told him?

He could, he thought. The man's arrogant. I should be able to get him to take himself down. He'll feel—what? Probably as if he'd been kicked in the teeth. He'd deny a connection between Pisano and the statue. He'll be outraged—or seem to be outraged. It was all the same. And fearful of the loss of the sale, and the threat of exposure. He'd have to turn Maybank's anger and confusion, find a way he'd implicate himself.

Jason had the advantage of surprise. His unexpected visit, the turn of the conversation toward the statue, the faked letters, Pisano. He'd be leading the conversation with Maybank following, not knowing where it was going and not wanting to say or do anything that might damage the Athena sale, or worse. The dealer would want a quick solution that would get rid of the problem. Could Jason show him one? His visit to Brigham House and the vanished granary had given him a key to unmasking the man, but would it work?

A small sense of pleasure ran through him. It was the kind of entrapment strategy that he'd used once before. It exhilarated him then, and he looked forward to it now. Game on.

A. Richard Maybank Gallery of Ancient Art. By Appointment Only. The sign on the door was written in discreet gold letters.

Jason rang the bell, and a loud chime sounded inside. A few moments later, a young man he recognized as Maybank's assistant opened the door. The dealer was at the gallery's rear, hunched over a small object with a magnifying glass in his hand.

Maybank looked up. His eyebrows rose slightly.

"Jason, Jason Connor. What a surprise!"

The man who stood before him had the appearance of an overgrown elf, with a pointed nose, overly large ears, and narrow-set eyes. But Jason knew that Maybank's eye for an object's quality and value, his innate shrewdness, his polished demeanor, and impeccable dress mirrored what he had become, the most prestigious and successful ancient art dealer in London, and arguably anywhere.

A. Richard Maybank—the A. meant nothing, having been added only for show—stood up, buttoned his blazer, straightened his tie, pushed his handkerchief a little deeper into his chest pocket, and reached out to shake the curator's hand.

"Jason! How good to see you! You didn't tell me you'd be coming to London."

"It's a last-minute trip. I arrived only last night."

"So, then, what are you up to? Have you come to London to see things I haven't heard of yet?" Maybank was always interested in his competition.

"Not really. I came to see you."

The dealer blinked. He shot a glance at his assistant and motioned Jason into an inner room. There was a desk with a telephone and computer screen at one end, with wing chairs to the side. It was less an office than a small gallery, displaying some of the finest ancient art Maybank could get his hands on, a showcase of his best and most expensive. Each object was remarkable in some way, and each was the finest in its category in quality and condition. Jason had seen several on his last visit, but others were new to him.

Behind the desk, running the length of the wall and almost three feet in height, a marble frieze showed men with helmets, swords, shields, and capes battling centaurs, creatures that were part man, part horse, striking their enemies with staffs and trampling them beneath their hooves. The frieze must have come from the mausoleum of a ruler or a nobleman somewhere in Turkey, Jason knew. He recognized the majestic scene immediately, a representation of struggling men and centaurs. It was one of violence and beauty in the same composition, a metaphor for the never-ending battle between civilization and what was right on one hand, barbarism and evil on the other.

The frieze was as brilliant an exhibition of sculptural art as Jason had ever seen, with spotlights above creating a dramatic rhythm of light and shadow across the deeply carved panel. Jason turned and saw an amphora against the wall that showed the single figure of a youth playing a flute. He knew he was looking at one of the handful of known works by one of the greatest vase artists of all, a man known only as the Berlin Painter because of a vase by his hand in Germany. But all the artist's coveted works were in museums, except this one.

Six or seven other objects were placed around the room. All were the best available on the market, each separately lit with recessed ceiling lights, a magnificent display of Maybank's ancient treasures. There was a story, probably apocryphal—or was it real?—about a collector who had seen, in this same room, objects so marvelous that he had fallen to his knees, begging for the opportunity to buy just one of them.

"Now, tell me what's going on," Maybank asked when they had settled into the chairs to either side of his great desk.

"Richard, it's the business of the Athena. It's just about the only thing on our plate, and it's certainly the most important. It's consumed huge amounts of time and energy at the Gabriel. Martin must have told you he's asked me to review its provenance."

"And?"

"And there's a problem. But I'm sure you're aware of that."

"What problem? What do you mean?" Maybank's voice dropped.

"The documents don't check out. The signatures are wrong. Langlotz's signature is faked."

"How do you know that?"

"I had a friend send an example of Langlotz's real signature." He smiled. "And the Weymouth granary where the statue was supposed to have been stored burned to the ground twenty years before it was supposed to have been purchased."

The dealer stared at him.

"And how the hell do you know *that*?"

"I spent an hour at Brigham House on Saturday. Lovely place. But no granary."

A few seconds passed before Maybank spoke.

"Just what the hell are you trying to do, Jason?"

"Richard, I am trying to do what I am supposed to do. Keep the Gabriel clear of problems."

"Jason, there's no problem with the Athena. If the letters are defective, that's got nothing to do with the statue." Maybank's voice was flat, his eyes like winter.

"Richard, it has everything to do with the statue. Anyone who knew the documents are faked would have to ask why, and then where it came from, and whether it's a recent find, right out of the ground. The Italians would be on it right away. You know as well as

I do that they'd demand it be sent back to them if they thought it had been stolen from them."

"Jason, let me ask again, what are you trying to do?" Maybank's voice had taken on an edge. "The statue is perfectly genuine. It's the most important object I've ever handled. It's also the most important thing the Gabriel has ever been offered. I won't tell you the documents are the best things in the world. But they're good enough for the Gabriel to buy it. No one will look at them that closely, including the Italians."

Jason held Maybank's eye as the dealer tried to calm himself.

"Except for one thing. Raffaele Pisano."

Maybank looked as if he had been struck in the face.

"Pisano! What does he have to do with anything?"

"Pisano's in prison. I'm sure you know that. And he's been talking. To the prosecutor in Rome." Jason paused. "And to me."

Maybank stood up, his voice rising. "You saw Pisano! What the hell did you do that for? What are you trying to do, Jason? Screw me? Screw the Gabriel? What's with you? What's the point?"

It was perfect.

"Richard, you're not listening. I'm trying to protect the museum. If I hadn't seen Pisano, the Gabriel would be totally at risk of a lawsuit by Italy."

Maybank took a moment to calm himself. He pushed back the shock of hair that had fallen over his forehead and leveled his eyes at Jason.

"What did Pisano say?"

"Enough. He knows the statue, Richard. He *handled* the statue. He said as much when I saw him."

The dealer rose abruptly, strode to the other side of his desk and took a pack of cigarettes out of his drawer. Jason had never seen the man smoke, and it was a small shock to see him do so now.

"Jason, do you really understand what you're doing? Do you have any idea where your little investigation is going? You're so damned convinced that the Athena's provenance is what's really important."

The dealer spun on his heel and jabbed at the curator with his right hand.

"Let me tell you what's important, Jason. In thirty years, what will really matter is what the Gabriel has, not how it got it. It's a great work of art that will grace the museum's galleries for years. In the hands of another country or museum, Jason, it could well be buried and never be seen for what it is."

The dealer took a deep breath and pointed to a bust of Augustus that stood on a pedestal.

"You tell me, where should this go? Back to Italy? This one came from an Italian family. They legally owned it. Then they sent it to me, with no export permission, and when they did that, they committed a crime under Italian law. Now, let's say the Italians found out about it and asked for it back, and got it. What would they do with it? Put it in the basement of one of their damned museums. You've seen that happen before."

A look of desperation crossed the dealer's face. He paced, searching for the right words.

"You know, Jason, it's just outrageous that you should be so concerned about some problem with provenance. I'm surprised that we're even having this conversation. I thought I knew you."

Maybank stubbed out his cigarette and took out another from the pack on his desk.

"And you take no risks in this. I'm the one who takes the risks. If I make a mistake and buy a fake, it's my mistake, and I have to pay for it. If I find things in another country and the local police decide I'm a problem, then *I'm* the one at risk. Not you. Not the Gabriel. Not any client who buys from me.

"That's why you buy from me, Jason. That's why every good collector of ancient art comes to me, or to someone who does what I do. Because I protect them. I make sure the object is authentic, and that there are no problems, not from anyone. And all they need to know is that they've bought something that's interesting, or beautiful, and genuine.

"Jason, if the documents aren't right, that's for you to know. No one else. Not even Martin. Why should you want to bother him with it? Damn it, man, get the Athena, forget the letters. Get it for the Gabriel and for the tens of thousands of people who'll see it and learn from it and benefit from it being there. What other purpose is there to a museum? In a hundred years no one will remember, or give a damn how it got there."

Maybank sat down again and took a long drag from the cigarette that was now almost a stub.

He's cornered, Jason knew. He needs a solution. Give it to him.

Maybank stubbed out the cigarette and looked directly at Jason's eyes.

"You know, there can be something in this for you."

The dealer had opened the door himself.

"Richard, thank you. But I understand you've already made that offer. To Martin."

Maybank stared, then exploded.

"God *damn* it, Jason! Why do you care about who gets something to put this amazing statue into your damned museum? Martin, me, whoever! You can be part of it too. Both of you, together. I'll make it worthwhile for you to say yes, I promise you."

Later, after he had told Maybank the small lie that he would have to think about it and had left the gallery, Jason realized how easy it had been.

Damned arrogant idiot, he thought. Of course, he'll be on the phone before Martin's had breakfast. But Martin, you son of a bitch, he's said everything I needed to hear.

CHAPTER THIRTY-NINE

When the gallery door closed, Maybank made a single call to an overseas number. He identified himself, asked a question, and with the answer, said only, "Have him call me. And tell him it's urgent."

He made no further calls and took none. Shortly before one, he crossed Jermyn Street to Wilton's, where he requested a corner table only for himself and told the waiter not to interrupt him unless he asked for assistance. Gustav, Wilton's maître d'hôtel, observed to himself that London's premier dealer in ancient art seemed unusually withdrawn.

At exactly three o'clock, Maybank told his assistant to go out and have a coffee for half an hour, closed and locked the outer door to the gallery, turned the small sign in the window from "Open" to "Closed," went into his office, and sat down heavily.

Fucking Connor. A catastrophe about to happen. *Someone* needs to stop him, now. Martin won't do it. Can't. No guts. But he'll point his finger at me if I don't get him into it. Take it slowly though. Don't push too hard. Draw him into it. You've done this before. Martin should be easy. But take it slowly.

He picked up the receiver and punched in a Los Angeles number. Pryce picked up the telephone on the second ring.

"Martin, this is Richard. Did you know Jason Connor's here?"

"Jason? No!"

"Yes. We've just had a pretty rough talk. About the statue."

"Hold on—" Maybank heard Pryce slam a door.

"What are you talking about, Richard? Jason took leave last week. He said he'd be with relatives on the East Coast. He didn't say a thing about going to Europe. If I'd known, I'd have stopped it. What's happened?"

"He's been in Rome. And the hell all over the place here. He's figured out the letters are bad and that the statue isn't the Weymouths."

"But Richard, that's not true, is it? It can't be true. I mean, you told me the letters were perfectly good. You gave me this story when you sent them."

"Martin, just shut up a moment and listen, won't you? It's worse than that. He knows about the deal. Our deal."

"How the hell did he find that out?"

"He got it from a dealer in Rome. You don't know him. The guy's in prison and seems to want to say anything to save himself from a long sentence."

"Jesus, Richard, how did that happen? How did a dealer in Rome—"

"Martin, let me finish. I can take care of the dealer. But that's not the problem. It's Connor. He knows enough to really screw us. Both of us. And I don't think he'll do a deal with us."

"What deal? What did you say to him?"

"I offered him part of our arrangement."

"You *what*? Richard, that's the stupidest fucking thing you could do. You must have known he wouldn't take it." Pryce felt his heart hammering. "And you told him about us? Both of us?"

"Martin, listen to me—"

"Both of us! You really told him that? You're an idiot, Richard!" His voice carried full force through the study door, causing Frances Pryce to spill her coffee.

"Martin, calm down. And shut up for a second and listen to me. This thing is about to fall apart. Unless we do something about him."

There was no response for almost half a minute.

"Do? What do you want done? I could fire him, but it won't be enough. He's gone too far, and he won't give it up. I know the man. Firing him isn't going to make a bit of difference."

There was another long pause. When Maybank spoke again, his voice was low, comforting.

"Martin, we can solve this. If we stay together."

There was no response.

"*Stay together*, Martin. You understand, don't you?"

"Yes. Of course. But what are you saying?"

"Are you close to Connor? Are you—friends?"

"We're not close. We've no relationship outside of work." Pryce was about to continue but stopped. "Where are you going with this, Richard?" The director felt a sweat break out on his forehead. He reached for his chair and sat down.

"I need to be a little circumspect here, Martin. Now, think of the possibilities. Particularly knowing what Connor knows. And what he's going to do. To both of us."

There was no reply.

"And the choices. Someone might say we really don't have many of those. Do you understand?"

There was a long silence. When he answered, Pryce spoke in a voice so faint it was barely audible. "What are you suggesting?"

"Martin, I don't want to get specific on the phone. Just think about what I've said. And I really need an answer now. We haven't got much time. Connor's probably still in London, but he's going back there to see you, right away. Or he'll tell someone else about the deal. Who knows what he'll do?"

Fuck! Pryce thought. A few minutes ago he had been about to have a quiet breakfast, with a busy day at the Gabriel ahead of him. The Athena matter was done, ready to go forward to the board for decision. Now everything was unraveling. No, worse: it was about to be blown up completely. And he would be implicated. Disgraced. Fired. Would the old man let it go, then? Maybe not. Could he face prison? The thought caught him like a blow to the head.

And now Richard wants Jason stopped. Killed. He hadn't said so, but he'd been crystal clear. And he wants me to agree, right away.

"Richard, we're going too fast. I don't know about this—"

"Look, this isn't just a deal gone bad. It's way beyond that. And we really need to do something about it. Now." There was a hard urgency to the dealer's voice. "Martin, we're both in this together. We need to stay together. Think of what I said. And then think where we'll be next week if he's left to run free. Now, can you think of a reason why that should be allowed to happen?"

A cold silence descended between the two men.

"Martin?"

Pryce heard his own voice as if it came from a great distance. "No, Richard."

"No what? *Say* it."

"No. I can't think of a reason."

There was silence again for another minute before Maybank spoke.

"OK then. I just want to be sure you understand. Once we go down this road, we can't go back. The first step leads to the last. Once this starts, there's no stopping it. You can see that, can't you?"

There was no response.

"Do you understand what I'm saying, Martin?" Maybank stressed the words. He was about to ask again when the director spoke.

"Yes." The word came out of Pryce as a whisper, no more than an exhalation of breath.

The dealer's response was immediate.

"Good. Now look, Martin, I can make this simple. You don't need to do anything. I can handle the matter from my end."

"How?"

"Don't ask. But it will cost us a bit. A lot, I imagine. I'll get to work on it now."

It took Pryce a moment to realize he was holding on to a dead line.

This is crazy, he thought. He felt as though a noose had been slipped around his neck. Kill Jason? A small wave of horror swept over him.

No time. Maybank knew he would have to work fast. Connor was a bomb about to explode. He had all the information he needed to stop the sale of the statue, and bring the police down on Pryce's head—and on his, too.

He reached for his Rolodex to look for a coded number he had not used for more than a year. He made the call very short.

"Ah, Bagger, I wonder if we could have a chat. This afternoon. Somewhere quiet. Four would be good."

CHAPTER FORTY

At *Regina Coeli*, the inmates go to lunch at one o'clock, and the prison guards start the second of their three daily cell checks at quarter past one. The guards check each cell for prisoners too sick to attend lunch or report to the clinic, and if time permits, they check bedding, books, toilets, or other places where prisoners might hide forbidden items: drugs or knives or metal implements that could be turned into tools. Escape from the prison is difficult, but there had been two breakouts in the past twenty years. The prison's chief warden, a man with a certain ambition and a highly developed sense of self-protection, was determined that it would not happen during his tenure.

At exactly one-twenty on this particular Monday afternoon, a guard came to cell A459 and found its inmate lying still on the floor. He unlocked the barred door and saw immediately that the figure was not breathing. By his side was a small bottle, overturned, spilling out onto the floor tiles.

The guard would later state in his written report that Rafaele Pisano was in his cell, by himself and unobserved, after the last inmate check at nine that morning, and that he must have taken his life sometime between nine and one. The guard was unable to say how Pisano got hold of poison, but as he and his fellow guards knew, at *Regina Coeli* many things are possible.

The chief warden immediately ordered an investigation of Pisano's death. He then quietly telephoned an acquaintance at *Corriere della Sera* to tell him of the unhappy event. It was always better if one broke bad news to the press oneself.

Richard Maybank's afternoon meeting with Bagger—an adopted name, he assumed—took no more than fifteen minutes. Bagger had long avoided problems by remaining remote from his clients, who knew very little about him except that he was highly recommended for certain types of work. He had been in his particular business too many years to want protracted meetings with clients, some of whom did not clearly understand that it was not very intelligent for either of them to be seen together.

Bagger had given very specific instructions to Maybank about where and how they should meet and what route he should take. In the mid-afternoon, the antiquities dealer left his office, walked the six blocks to the Green Park station, took the Piccadilly line west to Earl's Court, and after changing to an eastbound train on the Circle line, got off at the Embankment and waited at the station entrance.

With a sense of irritation and mounting impatience, Maybank watched London's rush-hour traffic push through the streets, with cars, buses, and weaving bicycle messengers that seemed to be everywhere. He had developed a particular distaste for bicycle riders the year before when one had hit his Mercedes broadside, somersaulting over his hood and skidding along the sidewalk. The repair had cost him more than a thousand guineas.

The undistinguished, somewhat disheveled young man who had, from a distance, followed the dealer from his office to Green Park and made certain no one else had taken an interest in him, came up, touched his elbow, and motioned to him to follow. In a few minutes the two men came to a small coffee shop off John Adam Street.

The man Maybank knew as Bagger was sitting at a rear table. A slight figure with glasses and the demeanor of an accountant, he was dressed in a dark jacket and a light shirt, more stylish than he had been at their last meeting. The seated man waved Maybank to a chair.

"Nice to see you, Mr. Maybank. What can I do for you today?"

"Bagger, I have a certain issue. With two people. Not here—one's in Italy."

"An issue, Mr. Maybank? What d'you want done about it?"

Maybank's eyes went around the room and then turned back and lowered his voice. "Removed. I want it taken care of. You told me once you could do that."

The other man pulled out a small pocket knife, started cleaning his nails, and then turned his eyes on Maybank with an impenetrable look.

"An' where is this fellow you want—removed?"

"Rome. In prison. You can do that, can't you?"

"Don't know. Maybe. Depends on who we can get to 'elp us in Rome. They needs to know what to do, see, and where, and when we want it done. When d'you want it done?"

"Now, right away. As soon as you can." Bagger returned to cleaning his nails, a habit that Maybank thought revolting the first time they had met.

"An' the other one, Mr. Maybank? Where's the other one? In Rome too?"

"No, he's in the States, in California. Works at a museum near Los Angeles. One of the curators there." Maybank hesitated. "Name's Connor, Jason Connor."

"Also right away, Mr. Maybank?" The other man arched his dark eyebrows.

"Also right away."

Bagger thought for a minute, got up, went into the street and made two calls from his cell phone. When he came back to the table, he sat down and looked at the dealer.

"See, Mr. Maybank, this is something new for you. Different from what you've asked for before. It's not the same as orderin' up a bit of the rough for a bloke. This job needs specialists, Mr. Maybank. Now, if you want to do something in London, we do it ourselves. Outside, like in Rome, we'll need to use one of our affiliates. Globalization, Mr. Maybank. We're a modern organization, y'know?"

Bagger ran the tip of his knife under another nail and thought for a minute.

"This is the modern world, Mr. Maybank, and the job gets done better by the folks who know the ground and speak the language. It's local knowledge that does it. We don't want to send in people who'll make some stupid mistake."

The dealer began to relax as he watched Bagger think through the problem. Obviously the man knew what he was doing.

"But I think we'll want to send one of our London men there too, an' they can work together." Bagger stopped and looked at Maybank directly. "Now, Mr. Maybank, you want all this done right away, is that right?"

"Can you do it?"

"We can. But you understand the quicker you want it, the more it'll cost. Just let me know what you want."

When the dealer heard the price, he felt as though he had been kicked in the stomach. Recovering slightly, he could only bring himself to say four words.

"All right. Do it."

As he left the coffee shop he felt ill, as if he had swallowed something large and leaden that now sat unmoving in the depth of his gut. Something had gone very wrong. Too many people had gotten involved in the damned statue. And he no longer had control of the situation.

But Bagger will do the job, he thought, and it'll be done, over. And no one will know.

As Maybank and Bagger were concluding their discussion, the late afternoon Alitalia flight from Rome was arriving at Heathrow. On it were two men in their early thirties, well-dressed, indistinguishable from any of the other male passengers in business class. When the plane reached the gate, they got off separately and passed, also separately, through UK Immigration with no more than the usual questions about their length of stay and the purpose of their visit. Each man told the immigration inspector that he was in London to finalize a business matter and would be staying at a center city hotel for no more than three nights. The name of the hotel was different in each case.

Each man had his passport stamped and was passed through without delay. The one who wore a camel-hair overcoat over a dark suit and an elaborate multicolored necktie went directly to the taxi stand. The second, with a tailored black overcoat buttoned up to the neck, spent a few minutes changing currency, then another few minutes at a coffee stand before finding a taxi to London.

There was nothing to suggest that either had any connection to the other. Or that both had any connection to the man in Rome, the one named Armanno, who had sent them.

CHAPTER FORTY-ONE

On Tuesday morning the small ripple of doubt that had been building in Jason's mind for the past week built into a wave.

Am I heading down a rathole? Do I go back to the museum, see Gabriel and point an accusing finger at Martin, and when he asks where I got my facts from, then what? Say that I spoke to a criminal who wants to get his sentence reduced? Who'd believe me? It would be my word against Martin's. He'd not only deny it, he'd fire me, then probably take me to court for defamation.

There's no one who'd back me up—and no one who'd want to. Maybe Kate.

Kate. A dark thought welled up from a corner of his mind. Could Martin have gotten to her?

He fell to earth.

Come on, that's just preposterous. Get out of it. A conspiracy was nonsense, wasn't it?

Jason knew all about paranoia. There was a time when he had lived it, almost every day, when it was normal. Not now.

He checked his messages before leaving the Stafford. There was another from Cynthia, who had written the previous afternoon before the museum closed. Unlike her note of Friday, department business was a second matter. Martin Pryce was at the top of her list.

"Jason, Martin's asked me twice if I know where you are, first after the staff meeting Monday morning and then again when we ran into each other in the galleries. He seemed upset about something. It was such an unusual thing, not like him at all. And at the staff meeting, he seemed unfocused and all of us could see his attention was somewhere else. You know, at the end of our sessions he normally asks if there's anything that's not covered in the agenda. But this time, he didn't do that and cut the meeting short.

"You always read your messages and I thought of staying behind and asking him why he didn't get in touch with you by e-mail himself. But he was acting so odd, as though he didn't want you to know he was interested. Anyway, I don't know what's behind it, and I didn't ask. I don't think I'd have gotten a straight answer from him anyway. Maybe he's sick?"

Jason also had a message from Kate, who said she had been chatting with Cynthia about museum matters, and that they had been talking about him.

"Your ears should be burning, Jason. She thinks the world of you and worries about you. She wondered where you are and what you're doing. Since she hadn't heard from you about your trip, I thought I shouldn't mention it myself, so I didn't say anything about it.

"We also talked about Martin. He was really very distracted at the meeting today. Something's gnawing at him, but I have no idea what, and Cynthia can't figure it out either. And he's not the only one who seems a bit weird recently. I ran into Amelia twice in the past two days, and she was pretty stiff with me, more so than usual. I wonder what's upset her?"

Kate's ending was more personal and direct than Cynthia's.

"Jason, where are you? When are you coming back? I miss talking to you. Safe return."

Both messages had been sent to his Gabriel address through the museum's servers. Any response through his own Gabriel account would do the same. If Pryce became suspicious, he could ask the museum's tech administrator to pull up any messages Jason had sent or received.

Kate's note, like Cynthia's, gave no indication she knew where he was or what he was doing, and even a suspicious Martin Pryce would have difficulty reading much into it out of the ordinary small talk that went on between colleagues. But if Jason replied to her through the museum's e-mail system with anything more than a neutral message, and if Martin picked it up, he'd be quick to infer a relationship between the two.

Am I being paranoid about this too? Not paranoid, he thought. Maybank would have told Pryce about the meeting the day before. The director would be in a panic, unpredictable, almost certainly irate, and likely to lash out at Kate if he thought she knew where he was and what he'd been doing.

Could he write and not bring her into Martin's sights?

Maybe. He went onto the web and downloaded an application that he had not used for years, one that would separate the identification and routing of his message, disguise his IP address, encrypt it, randomly circuit it through a global network of relays, then decrypt it at the exit node so that it would be in clear text when it arrived. He would need a caption that Kate could recognize immediately and stop her from trashing the message.

"Koi," he wrote. She'd understand it right away.

"Kate, please do *not* discuss this with anyone, but I'm returning today on a flight that should get to Los Angeles before five. If we could have dinner tonight, later, so that I can unpack and change, it would give us a chance to talk. There's a lot going on, and I'd very much like to see you. I hope dinner works for you. I'll call when I've landed."

Is that neutral enough? It had better be. She'll figure out fast enough why I'm not responding through my museum account.

He pushed the send button on his e-mail screen, deleted the special network application, turned off the Stafford's computer, and went to the front desk to pay his bill.

The trip to Heathrow Terminal 3 and the American Airlines check-in counter took only thirty-five minutes against the inbound flow of London traffic. He pulled out the business card Frescobaldi had given him in Rome and punched in the attorney's number.

I can tell him, at least, that I've been able to confirm what Pisano told us.

Frescobaldi answered immediately.

"Pronto?"

"Mr. Frescobaldi, this is Jason Connor—"

"Connor!" It was an expletive. "Dr. Connor do you know what you've done?"

Jason was unprepared for the question.

"What are you talking about?"

"Rafaele Pisano was killed yesterday!"

"What? How?"

"Si. Poisoned. Dead! The police say it was suicide. But this is not possible!"

"I don't understand."

"Listen to me, Dr. Connor. We saw Pisano—when, Friday?— and he is in a good mood, he wants to talk. He wants to get out of prison, not stay, and you told him you would help. So he tells you everything. Then, three days later, he is dead—a *suicide?*"

Jason started to respond, but Frescobaldi continued to speak, his voice rising and his words running over each other.

"Dr. Connor, I should not tell you what I am about to say, but you're in the middle of this somehow. Start with Friday. We saw Pisano Friday, yes? Then, Saturday morning, I am visited by two men. Bad men. Who ask me questions about your meeting with Pisano. Do you not see the connection?"

"How would they have known we were going to see Pisano? What are you saying?"

"They followed you, Dr. Connor! And you brought them to me. And to Pisano. Or to someone who could get to Pisano. It's all the same." Frescobaldi's voice broke. "Dr. Connor, where were you just before you met Pisano?"

"Rome. Then Sicily."

The hair on the back of Jason's neck began to rise. What had Mancini told him? About a big row at Morgantina? He knew what the attorney was going to say.

"The men, Dr. Connor. The two men who came to see me. They were from Sicily."

CHAPTER FORTY-TWO

Richard Maybank was having a bad morning.

Robert, his assistant, had called, sick with the flu. He said he would be late. Maybank had said not to worry, business was slow and Robert didn't need to come in that day. He could take care of everything himself. The door chime was working, he could let people in himself, and he didn't need help in the office.

The next call was unexpected. His private line rang. When he picked it up, he heard a voice that he recognized immediately.

"Mr. Maybank. You know who this is."

"Yes?"

"Mr. Maybank, you need a cup of coffee, an' there's a nice little place off Duke of York." It wasn't a request.

"Now?"

"You'd be right, Mr. Maybank. Now."

The caller hung up.

Bagger! Bagger never asked to see him immediately. And, whenever they had met, Maybank had had to take an indirect and convoluted path to see the man. But now he was across the street!

The dealer turned the sign on the gallery door to closed, exited onto Jermyn Street, and walked the short distance to the coffee shop. The man was waiting at a rear table, stirring sugar into a cup in front of him. Maybank sat down on the opposite side of the table.

"What the hell's this about?"

"Mr. Maybank. I've received a communication from my people in Rome."

The nearest person was two tables away, and the speaker kept his voice low.

"Yes?"

"They say they've just heard that Mr. Pisano was eliminated yesterday."

"*What?*"

"Yes. He was. Before we were able to take care of him. It seems 'e has other friends. A coincidence, Mr. Maybank?"

Bagger took a long look at the dealer.

"Is there more I should know, Mr. Maybank? I don't like complications."

Maybank thought for a moment.

"Bagger, it makes sense that someone would want him out of the way if he's been talking a lot. And I guess he has. That's the only thing I can think of."

"That's all very neat, Mr. Maybank. Too neat. I don't like coincidences."

The man sitting across the table took a drink of coffee and looked out the window. When they came back to the dealer, his eyes were cold as ice.

"Are we going to find any complications in the States, Mr. Maybank?"

"I can't imagine any."

"If there are any, any at all, I'll be pulling my man out right away."

"But you'll go ahead?"

"For now. I got your deposit this morning. It's non-refundable, like I said. Y'understand?"

"I understand. When then?"

"Soon. But when is my business. Wouldn't make sense for me to talk about it much, would it now?"

The man rose from his seat.

"I think we've 'ad enough coffee for now, Mr. Maybank, don't you? I'll be in touch when it's done."

The message was unmistakable: *no further contact.*

The man named Bagger threw some coins on the table, walked out onto Jermyn Street, turned the corner, and disappeared in the direction of the pedestrian crowds on Piccadilly.

Maybank returned to his gallery, unlocked the door, and went into his office. He made calls to clients in Germany and Switzerland to let them know of newly arrived objects that might interest them and spoke to a new supplier in Kiev about a find of Scythian gold fresh out of an untouched burial mound in the Ukraine.

The dealer went to lunch at one. Wilton's again, for the ice-cold oysters and Dover sole menu, and he was back in his office before two. The door chimed minutes after he had returned.

The two men he let in seemed out of place. Both young, in their thirties, athletic looking, with dark hair and eyes and dark complexions. They wore tailored overcoats, one camel-hair tan, the other black, buttoned up to the neck. Nicely dressed, he thought, not like some of the people who dropped in off the street. They nodded to him, glanced at the objects on the gallery shelves, but did not appear to take much interest in them.

Italians, he thought. Maybe Spanish. Not buyers. Sellers?

He turned away almost everyone who came in to offer him things. If they really wanted to sell something, they generally wanted more than it was worth. Or they could be shills for one of his competitors—or, who knows, maybe even a plant for the Customs service. He had to be careful with everyone. His regular sources, the ones he trusted, knew what to do. They knew how to get things out, and took their own risks.

But these were different, he thought. From Italy, no question. Maybe they wanted to replace Pisano?

Just the knowledge that Pisano was facing a long prison term would motivate someone to try to take his business away. It was not like England. Here, no one could take his business. There was no one in his league, not one, and the other antiquities dealers, many of them Iranian or Lebanese or some such, had neither his client list nor his business skills. And none would try to take his business away; he'd made sure of that.

But Italy was different. Italy was really cutthroat.

It made no difference to him at all, none. Business was business. He walked across the gallery toward the visitors.

"How may I be of help?"

The man in the lighter colored overcoat turned to him. "Mr. Maybank?"

"Yes? I'm Richard Maybank."

"Mr. Maybank, we would like to talk to you about a business matter."

The man's English was good, Maybank thought. The *A* came out flat, as an American might pronounce it.

Yes, Italians. Sellers. Wanting to take Pisano's place.

Maybank cocked an eyebrow and looked closely at his visitors.

"Gentlemen," he said, "won't you come into my office? We can talk there more privately."

The two men smiled at the dealer and followed him to the back of the gallery.

Half an hour later and a mile away from Jermyn Street, in the recesses of a small restaurant in Holborn, Giuliano Clemente, the man in the light tan overcoat spoke quietly into his cell phone.

"It's done."

"Any problem?"

"No problem. Fell in his office. Broke his neck."

"Send Enrico back today. Book yourself to Los Angeles. Our client wants us to finish the work in America. You've got the Los Angeles information? And the arrangements to meet the Chicago guy?"

"Yes."

"Call if you have a problem."

"Of course."

Armanno disliked long or explicit telephone conversations. There was no need for further discussion.

Clemente went to buy a business-class ticket for a flight to Los Angeles leaving the following morning, with a return to Rome four days later, on Sunday.

That should do it, he thought. If the matter goes quickly, maybe I'll have time to drive down to La Jolla after all.

Ten years earlier, he had attended the University of California at San Diego and had trained in business management. When he had returned to Italy, however, he found that his special talents paid him better than any Italian commercial firm could ever do. But he looked forward to returning to Southern California whenever he could, even though his current work kept him quite busy elsewhere.

Martin Pryce had also had a bad morning. It was only just after nine thirty, but the day ahead was filled with multiple appointments of little interest.

In fact, the director's interest in anything had vanished since his conversation with Richard Maybank. He had barely made it through Monday at the office and had had to take two Advils in the afternoon to cut a headache that would not go away. He'd been a damn fool, he thought, blinded by anxiety. Richard had forced him to agree to have Pisano killed. *And* Jason.

Absolutely idiotic, he thought. Killing Pisano is one thing. Pisano knew he was in a risky business and had been an ass to talk about it.

But Jason. That's crazy, just wrong. The police would get involved, and who knows what they'd find? It was one thing to have Jason accuse him of fixing the Athena sale. But with Pisano dead, who could confirm it? Not Richard. No, Richard's too smart, and he can't be shaken, can he?

Now that idiot wants Jason killed. He didn't use the word, but that's what he wants. Pisano's dead. That's enough. I'll stop this Jason thing right now.

He told Patricia Waller to hold his calls, then shut his door and keyed the number for Maybank's gallery. It was a little before six in the evening London time. No matter, he thought. Richard will still be there.

A man's voice came on the line.

"May I help you?" The tone was measured. Pryce did not recognize the speaker.

"Yes, I'd like to talk to Mr. Maybank."

"May I ask who's calling?"

"Martin Pryce. I'm director at the Gabriel Museum of Art in California."

There was a pause at the other end.

"Ah, Mr. Pryce, this is Inspector Taney, London Metropolitan police. I'm sorry to tell you that Mr. Maybank is dead.

"Dead? What do you mean *dead*? What happened?"

"He seems to have tripped on a carpet and broken his neck. We think sometime in the middle of this afternoon."

The director sat down heavily in his chair.

"I see," he said.

He put down the receiver.

Oh Jesus.

Richard. Dead. Tripped and broke his neck? But that doesn't make sense. People don't just trip and break their necks. And two days after Pisano killed himself? That just doesn't happen.

He tried to think of a connection between the two deaths but came up with nothing.

What does this do to the sale? End it? What had Richard told him about his family, his possible heirs? Or lawyers?

Richard's attorney! Whoever he is, I'll need to talk to him, work something out.

And Jason? Pisano's dead and Richard's dead, and whatever Jason thinks he knows, it's of no use to him. He wouldn't dare make an allegation against me without some evidence, and he doesn't have it.

Pryce's apprehension had begun to evaporate when another thought struck him.

Richard was arranging to have Jason killed. Did he do that? Before he died?

CHAPTER FORTY-THREE

The distant alarm that had sounded in Rome had now become an insistent ringing. There were too many coincidences. The farmer's interrogation at Morgantina, the face at the Rome airport, Frescobaldi's visit by the Sicilians. And, now Pisano's death.

Not his death, Jason thought. His murder. Maybank was killed to stop him from talking. His own meeting with Pisano had caused it. What had Frescobaldi said? *You're in the middle of this.*

He'd missed it. He had been so focused on the statue, the faked documents, and the stunning revelation of Pryce's involvement that he'd not seen the signs that someone else had an interest in him. Galante, Morgantina's *capo*, was not at all like Martin Pryce or Richard Maybank but someone who was cold-blooded and murderous and felt he had to protect himself. Would Galante come after him in the United States? He would, Jason thought. I would, if I were him. But the man wouldn't come himself. He'd send someone else.

Jason's American flight leveled off at cruising altitude and the seatbelt sign was turned off. He looked around at the passengers nearest to him, then went slowly to the rear of the aircraft and returned to his seat. There was no one who appeared to be Italian or even Mediterranean among them, only returning American couples, some with small children, members of a soccer team, Scots from their accents, two English businessmen busily talking to each other and comparing spreadsheets on their laptops. Three seats to the rear a somewhat older woman with a pleasant face wearing a dark sweater and Ferragamo scarf glanced up and smiled, but she was the only person who seemed to take notice of him at all.

Not this flight, he thought. It's too soon. But they won't wait long.

Who would they send? Not one of Galante's Sicilian thugs, but someone who could blend in, pass without notice in a crowd, seem like anyone else. Probably more than one. Professionals, people who knew how to get around without calling attention to themselves. That's how I'd do it, anyway.

He couldn't stop them. A professional could penetrate any defense he might set up, and they'd succeed unless he could disappear entirely. But even if he could do that, it wasn't a choice at all.

What should he do then? What *could* he do? Talk to the police? Would they believe him? And what could *they* do? Should he tell Andrew Gabriel? The first thing the old man would do would be to call Martin, so that would be a dead end. He needed a better idea. He'd have to destroy the reason for their going after him, and that meant the statue. It all came back to the Athena. The men would come to silence him, soon probably. If he could show the statue was stolen, they wouldn't need to do that. It should end it.

He'd have to take care of Martin first. That meant exposure—of the statue's origin and then of Martin himself. Uncover the background of the Athena, make clear that it had been stolen and moved through Maybank to the Gabriel, with fake documents.

Could he entrap Martin as he'd done with Maybank, get him to admit what he'd done? That would be much more difficult. But if he could do that, the other problem would go away. There'd be no further reason for Galante, or whoever he sends, to continue.

At least Martin's not dangerous. Martin would want to stop me, not kill me. Even if he did, he wouldn't have the faintest idea where to begin.

CHAPTER FORTY-FOUR

Jason's flight to Los Angeles arrived a few minutes early. He checked through immigration and called Kate. She was just about to leave the museum.

"You're back. Wonderful. And yes, of course let's have dinner tonight. I'll pick you up."

He suggested the Great Enterprise. The Santa Monica restaurant was pure cinema and served some of the best seafood in the area, Alaskan crab legs and Atlantic lobster at the top of the list and skate, once thought of as trash fish, prepared at the level of high culinary art. As they entered, the long bar on the left was full and noisy. Beyond, they could see the blur of cooks laboring in frenzied activity in front of fiery ovens. The wait was short. They were taken to one of the high booths against the wall and each ordered a house Chardonnay.

"OK, Jason, give, please. Where did you go? What happened?"

He took her through his talk with Ettinger, then with Mancini in Rome, and his visit to Morgantina, his return to Rome, and finally the meeting with Maybank in London. When he came to Maybank, Kate had stopped eating.

"That's an incredible story. Maybank told you? How did you get him to admit that? Why would he let that slip?"

"A little stupidity, maybe. Smart people can be stupid at times. Plus some fear. He needs to sell the statue desperately. My guess is he's got huge expenses and needs money, a lot of money, to hold on to his suppliers. Even with the faked-up provenance, he's not certain who'd buy it. I can't think of a collector who'd be able to buy it, and there aren't a lot of museums around that can put up ten or twenty million. The Gabriel is his best shot. He must have pitched Martin when he came by the gallery in August. And hooked him with a fifteen million dollar inducement. He got that right."

"Fear?"

"Fear. I played him."

"Played how?"

"When I told Maybank that I knew not only about the forged letters but also his deal with Martin, he became furious. And scared. Losing the Athena sale would be bad enough, but the thought of being exposed and disgraced and having his business closed down, with prosecution and even imprisonment as a real possibility, drove him wild. It worked."

"And the stupidity part?"

"Trying to bribe me, to stop me from blowing up the deal. The only solution he could think of was to cut me in. It wouldn't surprise me if he's done that with a few other museum people and thought it would work again."

She picked at the remains of the salmon in front of her and looked up.

"But he had to admit Martin's part of it, didn't he? Did you ever ask yourself what you'd do if you couldn't get him to do that?"

"I did. If I'd come back with only the story of the statue's bad provenance, with nothing on Martin but Pisano's accusation of a deal, it wouldn't have been worth anything. Martin would have me thrown out of the museum. For starters." His eyes went to the other diners and then came back to her. "It was close. I was worried Maybank wouldn't say a thing about Martin. But he did."

Around them the restaurant was in motion, arriving diners replacing those who had finished, the light from the center fires rising and falling as oven doors were opened and shut. Kate watched the frenetic activity in the kitchen for a moment and turned back to him.

"Jason, Martin knows he's got a huge problem with you. He was distracted at the staff meeting yesterday. I told you that in my message. Today he was mostly out of his office, as if he didn't want to see anyone. He must've had a brutal conversation with Maybank about the statue. And you. In fact, he must be absolutely terrified about you now. Maybank too. They've got to be in a panic about what you might do. I'd think they'd both want you to just disappear. But they can't do that, can they?"

She held his eyes. "*Can* they?"

He was silent for a moment. He had asked himself the same question. "Not Martin. I mean, think about it. This is *Martin* we're talking about, not some movie hitman. What would he do? Run me off the coast highway into the Pacific? Burn down my house with me in it? That's just bizarre. This is today, twenty-first century America, not some third-world country where people routinely kill each other."

Not Martin, anyway, he thought.

"Is that it, Jason? Is there anything more? Or is that the end of the story?"

He wished she hadn't asked the question.

"Not yet. I haven't brought you up to today."

"What happened today?"

"I called Pisano's lawyer. This morning, from London. He told me Pisano was found in his prison cell yesterday, dead."

"*What?* Who'd do that?" The room suddenly felt cold.

She had to prompt him. "Jason?"

"Someone in Sicily. I may have stirred up something when I went there. It's possible they killed Pisano so he couldn't testify. Or simply because he'd talked too much."

"Who'd do that?" She repeated.

"The *capo* at Morgantina, maybe. The man who controls the place and runs the stuff out. His name's Galante. The embassy told me about him."

"And would it stop there? Would this man want to silence someone else? Maybank? You?" Her voice had taken on a sharper tone.

"He'd have to feel really threatened to want to do something about Maybank, but Maybank's in London. This guy's a local Sicilian from Aidone. I don't know how far he could reach."

He knew exactly how far Galante could reach. Why was he having trouble telling her?

"You're saying he wouldn't want to get to you? Or are you saying he couldn't? Because you're here, in California? In the United States?"

He shifted in his chair, uncomfortable at her questions. Finally, he looked at her directly.

"He could."

God in heaven. Kate let the unspoken thought rest a moment, and then cleared her throat.

"Jason, can we change the subject? I'll get back to the man at Morgantina, but there's something I need to ask you."

He nodded.

"Do you have any idea where you want to go with this?"

She saw he had no idea what she was talking about.

"This. Us. Something's changed, Jason. We've been closer for what, two weeks? Not just talking about Martin and the statue and museum business. It's become more personal, and I've begun to think about it every day. You may see it too.

"I missed you when you were gone, Jason, and it worries me." She paused. "I don't want to get into something that leaves me hurt again. Actually I'm not sure I want to get into something at all."

Her eyes were directly on his.

"Am I interested in you? Is that what you mean?"

"Something like that. Are you interested enough so that I don't feel like—oh, I don't know." She groped for the right words and felt herself begin to color slightly. "You know, the other night, just before you left, we really talked to each other. It was the first time I've done that with a man since Eric died. And then, when you were going out my door, I had this sudden moment when I wanted you to stay. I haven't felt that way about anyone in a long time."

She glanced around her and then turned back to him.

"You must know what I'm saying. It's not that complicated, really. I'm not looking for a relationship. I do care what happens to you." She left out the unspoken *but*, hoping he would pick it up.

Quite suddenly, he leaned forward and took both of her hands in his.

"Kate, if you think I have a clear idea of what I want, I don't. I guess I was looking for something when we talked in the gardens. I was knotted up about the statue and needed a little understanding, sympathy, maybe something more, and I sought you out. I've no idea where this is going, and maybe we should think about that. But can we keep it simple? Take it slowly?"

She gave him a thoughtful look. "Jason, are you seeing anyone?"

"You mean am I going out with someone?"

"Yes."

He smiled. "No. I was. But that's long over."

She studied his face. "Was she important to you?"

"Yes, but maybe not the way you mean. She was easy to be with. And she was safe."

Safe. Can this man really need someone safe? Can he really be that vulnerable?

She sat back in her chair. "So where do we go with this?"

"Can't we just let it do what it wants to do?"

She looked away. Do what it wants to do? What did that mean? She decided to let it go. There were other things she needed to know, but not right now. In time. Maybe he's right. Don't press it. Keep it simple.

"Can we go back to where we started tonight? To Martin, the statue? A few minutes ago you told me that you didn't know how far this man Galante could reach, and then you said he could get to you if he wanted. Please stop trying to protect me. You don't need to do that. I've taken care of myself for a long time, but I can't do that if I don't know what's happening. You've told me enough about Martin, and I can deal with him. It's what I don't know that I can't handle. Can you understand that?"

He was silent for a few moments, not sure what to say. Perhaps the danger wasn't so real after all. Why bother her with it?

"Kate—"

"Don't try to protect me, Jason, and don't say you aren't trying to do that. I can see it in your face. You don't want to tell me about Galante. I can take bad news. For God's sake, just tell me what I need to know."

The waiter's interruption with the check spared him the need to reply.

When they were outside the restaurant, she turned to him again. "Come on, Jason, tell me about Galante. Should I be concerned? Is he about to turn up on my doorstep?" She had a look he could not read. Disquiet? Alarm?

"Not on yours, certainly. Maybe on mine. But can we talk about this later tomorrow? Outside the museum? At the moment, I'm just tired. I need sleep, and time to work on this."

He had grown silent on the drive to the Palisades, and his eyes had taken on the dark look she had seen before. He's gone inward, she thought, trying to solve some problem. But what? Martin? Galante? Her?

Jason's thoughts had nothing to do with Kate at all. They were all about Martin Pryce. And Cosimo Galante.

CHAPTER FORTY-FIVE

Martin Pryce. Cosimo Galante. Jason awoke thinking of the two men, two adversaries, one near and immediate, the other remote, almost an abstraction. He would have to move today. Galante will act very quickly. He could deal with Martin tomorrow.

He was beginning to think of a plan when the telephone rang. It was Kate. Her voice was urgent.

"Jason, have you seen the paper—the *Times*?"

"No, I put my service on hold when I left."

"For God's sake! I'll read it to you. It's just inside their foreign section. 'London Antiquities Dealer Dies.' That's the headline. Then there's this: 'Richard Maybank, proprietor of A. Richard Maybank Ancient Art, was found dead yesterday afternoon in his Jermyn Street gallery. The Metropolitan Police report the cause of death to have been a massive hemorrhage to Mr. Maybank's head, apparently caused by a fall. Mr. Maybank had been a prominent dealer in Greek and Roman antiquities for a number of years. He was a principal supplier of ancient art to museums and private collectors in Europe and the United States.'

"That's it. Nothing else. What the hell is going on, Jason? There's only one connection I can think of. You."

What other answer could there be? Pisano dead is one thing, but Pisano and Maybank dead, both probably murdered, is something else entirely.

"Kate, it's possible Maybank really did have an accident." It sounded hollow. He didn't believe it, and she wouldn't either.

"That's ridiculous. Obviously someone wanted to keep the two of them from talking. Permanently. It's got to be Galante. Because he thought Pisano and Maybank were a threat.

"And, Jason, if he wants to get rid of everyone who knows about it and who could get him into trouble, who's next on his list? You're the one he's after now."

His mind raced. It would have been no trouble for Galante to track him to Rome, to his meetings with Frescobaldi and Pisano. But getting to Maybank? Arranging for someone in London to kill Maybank meant an entirely different level of ability. He'd have had someone else do it. On contract, probably.

And if they got Maybank, it would be no trouble to go the next step. Galante would want them to come to Los Angeles to finish the job. That's what I'd do if I were him.

"Look, if Galante's behind this, if he's decided to send someone after me, they can't be here yet. Let's assume they killed Maybank. They must have done it yesterday. They couldn't get a flight out of London until today. And there's no London–Los Angeles flight, or Rome–Los Angeles flight that gets here before late afternoon. I took one of the earliest flights out of London I could, the one that arrived at four thirty yesterday.

"If you're right, and if he's sending someone, they'd want to hit me right away, before I talk to anyone. But they haven't, and that means they're not here yet. If they're coming."

"Damn it, Jason, you should assume the worst. Look, it's almost eight thirty. You've got time to do something. Go to the police.

Talk to them. Get them to protect you somehow. Now, please. Do it for me.

"And Jason, you said you weren't going into the museum today. Don't. It could be a trap. I know you think Martin's not involved with Galante. Maybe he's not. But if you go there today, you won't get to the police in time. And you certainly don't want them to come see you at the Gabriel. So, don't go there. Go to the police. And get out of your house. Now, Jason. Please don't take chances with this."

She was right. Assume the worst and act on it. He looked at his watch.

Three hours. Maybe three and a half.

"I'll be out of here by noon. What about you? If Martin connects you to me, he'll want you to tell him where I am."

"I'll go in. I have work to do, and I can't see any way Martin can connect us. I've got to leave in a few minutes—I'm already late. Use your cell phone and call me on mine, not on the museum's line. And Jason—if you're leaving your house, think about where you should stay. Somewhere in town, maybe. For a while. Somewhere," she added, "where we can still see each other."

She hung up.

I almost asked him to stay with me. And then what? Do I really want to get so close to him? This way? Images chased each other through passageways she had not opened for years and scattered into fragments like the pieces of a broken mirror.

Another thought struck her. What if they really *are* coming after him? And find him with me?

On her way up the coast she caught herself checking for a following car in her rear view mirror. There was nothing, of course.

CHAPTER FORTY-SIX

Above the North Atlantic, the flight attendants on Wednesday's late morning American Airlines Rome–Los Angeles flight had finished clearing the lunch trays. Giuliano Clemente, in business class, ignored the film that had started and began the process of mental preparation for his arrival in Los Angeles that afternoon. He had been told by his employer that he would be met by Antonio "Tony" Olivieri from Chicago, who would arrive before him, arrange for a car and hotel, and accompany him throughout the job.

Clemente had two paramount vanities. One concerned his dark suits, which were made by a very exclusive tailor who worked just off the Via Veneto, and his luxurious, Italian silk neckties. The other was the manner in which he worked, only with his bare hands. Clemente prided himself on needing just his hands to do his work. Anything else, a firearm for instance, was for those who had no idea how effective hands could be, were unwilling to use them, or who just didn't want to get that close.

Amateurs, he thought. Clemente knew how. He looked down at the instruments of his trade, took his left hand in his right, and cracked his knuckles and then did the same with the other hand. He took a squash ball out of his pocket and began to squeeze it, first in one hand, then in the other. The passenger in the seat next to him was so engrossed in the movie that he seemed not to notice. The young woman across the aisle with pretty features gave him a disapproving look and turned back to her book.

Interesting, he thought. Maybe, but not today. This trip was all about the job. His business training in San Diego had given him a keen appreciation for bottom-line results, and the attractive blond women he had met during his two years of study at San Diego grew on trees. They seemed particularly appreciative when he dropped cultivated English and lapsed into a heavy Italian accent. But there'd be no distractions until the job was done. The man in Rome had no tolerance for employees who broke the rules, and the most important rule was, always, business first.

Three and a half hours behind Clemente's flight, on the same jet route but at a slightly lower altitude, British Air flight 269 from London's Heathrow to Los Angeles was proceeding smoothly. A snack with a choice of wines or champagne was being served to the passengers in business class.

Michael Quinn, in a window seat on the left side of the aircraft, was also thinking of the business ahead. A man with the look of an aging athlete whose muscles had gone to fat, Quinn was, at forty-five, unusually old for the work he did for Bagger. But he had many years of service with the man, and he was efficient, loyal, and relentless and took the kind of special enjoyment in his trade that his employer admired. Quinn, who had for different jobs gone by the name of O'Sullivan or Gleeson, or sometimes Reilly—it was all the same, every name having been chosen from someone in his own family—was to be met in Los Angeles by a member of Bagger's Chicago affiliate who would take care of arrangements on the ground. The affiliate had an impeccable reputation for the efficient, just-in-time delivery of services and had been instructed to make someone with appropriate skills available to Quinn and ensure that the necessary tools would be at the right place when he arrived.

The Chicago affiliate had selected a certain Billy Rourke to assist Quinn in Los Angeles. The affiliate had informed Bagger and Quinn that Rourke would be picking up separate packages at the FedEx office nearest the airport, on West Century Boulevard. One package contained two Beretta Model 85FS Cheetahs. The other held two threaded silencers.

When lunch was finished and his tray removed, Quinn put his seat back two notches, scratched his nose, closed his eyes, and fell asleep, pleased to be getting out of London in December. He dismissed all thought of the business ahead. He knew from long experience that whatever plans might be made in advance of a job usually had to be torn up and rewritten once it had begun. He also knew he could make it all work after he had arrived. He had always been able to do a job properly.

Far ahead of both flights, Tony Olivieri and Billy Rourke were making their separate preparations to leave Chicago for Los Angeles. The two men had met each other in passing several years earlier at one of their employers' regular coordinating meetings, but the encounter was transient, and names were not exchanged. Such joint meetings had been recommended by a management consultant, a professor formerly on the faculty of the Wharton School who had been hired by Olivieri's uncle Raymond, CEO of the Olivieri enterprise, to help improve business operations and reduce inefficiencies. After some heated discussion among the members of the Olivieri management team, the consultant had been taken on and had done exceptional work in improving the enterprise's market share. The coordination meetings covered Chicago activities only, but not out-of-town contracts. Those were serviced on a first-come-first-served basis.

Olivieri, a handsome man in his late twenties, with a long, straight nose over full lips and dark hair and eyes, had been called by his uncle Raymond the previous afternoon. Both had been at a family dinner together only the week before and would see each other again at a wedding on Saturday. But Raymond never called him directly unless he wanted to discuss business. Olivieri waited for the explanation.

"So, Tony, are you very busy?"

Raymond knew he wasn't doing anything very much, certainly nothing that couldn't be broken off. Raymond wanted something, probably pretty quickly.

"Very busy, Raymond. Up to my ears."

"Now Tony, I hope you don't mind putting it all aside for a bit? I mean, how'd you like to take a little trip out of town?"

It was not a question.

"Where?"

"Los Angeles. Not so bad, huh?"

"When?"

"Tomorrow, Tony. Early flight."

Holy shit, Olivieri thought. This was really urgent.

"So, tell me, Raymond, what the hell is this?"

"Tina's place, Tony. In an hour. OK?" Raymond hung up.

"Tina's place" was a restaurant where they could talk details very privately, and so in the middle of the afternoon, Tony Olivieri met his uncle Raymond and took down the information he needed to know about the job.

Raymond, a meticulous and careful man, briefed Olivieri on the contract he had been given by his Rome associate. He told Olivieri that the principal on the job would be a man named Clemente, who would be flying into Los Angeles from London. Clemente would be executive officer for their two-man team and would give directions throughout the operation.

Raymond gave Olivieri the necessary backup cell phone numbers he would need and the names of the preferred hotel in Santa

Monica. He then handed Olivieri a file with the information that his highly professional backroom staff had developed on the objective, a certain curator at the Gabriel Museum of Art.

"And Tony, when you talk to people out there, pick some fucking name for the job that won't stand out this time, OK? I mean no more Pavarotti or Caruso, dumb-ass stuff like that. Try Santi this time, OK? Tony Santi. All right?"

"All right, Raymond, I get it."

"And memorize the fucking file and get rid of it, OK? This is a pretty simple job, Tony, but I don't want no loose ends I have to worry about. OK?"

"OK."

"And," Raymond added, "it's clean. No hardware. That's what we've been told. Just follow this guy Clemente and do what he says, and you'll be OK."

When Raymond told him it would be "clean," Olivieri sat up. The few clean jobs he had been on had always interested him. They entailed very close contact with the objective, and the practitioners of the procedure always seemed somewhat more interesting than the others, the shooters or car-wreck specialists. Olivieri had a special distaste for the latter, who he considered to be no better than apes. Doing a clean job well was an art he wanted to learn.

Olivieri had checked in at the American ticketing counter at O'Hare for a flight that would arrive at Los Angeles a few minutes after eleven. That would give him time to get a rental car that would fit the image he wanted and allow him to look over the local geography before Clemente arrived. There would be no trouble getting a vanity car in Los Angeles.

As Olivieri was moving through the security line, Billy Rourke, who sometimes called himself Bob La Tour, a family name on his mother's side that he fancifully and wrongly thought could be traced back to the French painter Georges de La Tour, was closing down his apartment in Chicago's North Side. A United flight would put him in Los Angeles a little before three, enough time to retrieve the two packages at the FedEx office and perhaps even allow him to relax a bit before the arrival of Michael Quinn from London at quarter past six.

In his mid-thirties, Billy Rourke was reaching the upper age limit for men in his line of work. At six feet two, he had the muscular build and demeanor of a pugilist and walked hunched slightly forward with the palms of his hands facing backward rather than to the side. He was good at firearms, the result of the two years of military service a Chicago court had ordered when he was nineteen, following a particularly brutal fight that had left his opponent with a broken right arm and multiple contusions around the head.

Rourke knew Berettas well. He particularly liked the Cheetah Model 85, which was compact and had the stopping power of a nine millimeter weapon. His ability with Berettas was so proficient that the "Man"—the person to whom he contracted his services and who had given him his instructions the night before about the job with Quinn—continued to find use for him. He dreaded the day when he'd be asked to use one of those fucking paper guns that the new 3D printers could spit out. Useless after two shots, big recoil, bad aim. But you could walk it through the TSA machines in a briefcase without a hiccup, and he'd seen the Man pricing one of the high-end printer models at Amazon. Bad idea, he thought. There was something deeply comforting about the feel of cold metal in the palm of one's hand.

Now he had a job to do and a new partner. Rourke had heard of Quinn but never worked with him. Still, whoever this guy Quinn was, he had to know what he was doing.

Three months had passed since Rourke's last job. He was looking forward to getting into play again.

CHAPTER FORTY-SEVEN

At exactly nine thirty that morning, Jason called the headquarters of the Los Angeles Police Department. The LAPD West Los Angeles office covered the Palisades, but he would have a better chance of explaining the situation to a headquarters office that dealt with international matters, not just local crime. The operator put him through to someone who answered, "International."

"Jason Connor. I'm a curator at the Gabriel Museum in northern Malibu."

A man who identified himself as Lieutenant James Folger of the LAPD international division came on the phone.

"Ah, Gabriel Museum? Ah, if you're calling to report an art crime, the theft detail would be the people to talk to. I can transfer you if you'd like."

Folger didn't seem very bright, and Jason wondered whether the "ahs" and pauses were a speech impediment or a mannerism.

"I'm not calling about an art crime. I'm calling about what I think is a murder in London, and probably another in Rome. And that the killers are probably coming to Los Angeles."

He waited impatiently for a response, thinking how absurd he must sound.

"Mr. Connor, what exactly *are* you calling about? Are you saying that you, ah, know of a murder in London? Or Rome?"

"Yes. Both. But what I'm really calling about is that I think the killers are coming here, to Los Angeles."

"And who are they coming to kill, Mr. Connor?"

"Me. They want to kill me."

Silence. Jason waited. Damn the man. He didn't have time for a lengthy explanation.

"Mr. Connor. Let me get this straight. You think there are killers loose in England. And Rome. And you think they're coming to get you. Is that right?" Folger had dropped his "ahs," and his words had an edge to them.

"Yes, that's what I just said."

"And do you have specific evidence of the murders in London. And Rome?" The question was pointed.

"No. The police in Rome think the one there is a suicide. The one in London looks like an accident, but it's not."

"I see. Ah, Mr. Connor, of course I believe what you're saying—"

Folger's tone was clear. He didn't believe a word of it. The conversation was going nowhere.

"—but I'm not sure the London Metropolitan guys or the Carabinieri will."

"What about the killers coming here?" Jason's voice turned sharper.

"Mr. Connor, do you know who the killers are, or how they're coming here? Or when?"

"No."

This time the silence was longer.

"Well then, here's what I suggest, Mr. Connor." Folger's voice had become solicitous, as if he were a parent talking to an upset child, and the "ahs" had returned. "Why don't you come into headquarters here, downtown, and, ah, give us a statement so we have all these things in writing, and we'll be glad to take it from there. We're on Los Angeles Street, just off the one oh one, second exit. Big concrete building. Third floor. You can't miss it."

Folger's professional voice had begun to irritate Jason. *The damned man just wants to end the conversation.*

Jason stilled his rising impatience. "Yes," he said, "I should do that. Thank you for your attention, Lieutenant."

He hung up and swore loud and long at his empty house.

The telephone rang. The caller ID window showed the call's origin as the Gabriel Museum.

It's not Kate. She'd call from her cell phone. Cynthia?

He was about to pick up the receiver but stopped.

Martin?

The telephone continued to ring, then fell silent.

He looked at his watch. 10:20 a.m. Six hours until the first London flight arrived. With a growing sense of futility, he tried to think what else he could do. Call the FBI? Would they believe his story any more than Folger?

Of course not. They'll just send me back to the Los Angeles police.

Talk to Jack Harmon in Washington? What could he do?

Probably refer me back to the FBI.

Could he talk to someone where it counted, make it go away? But who would listen? Who should *listen? Gabriel?*

Gabriel. The old man would want to know about this, wouldn't he? Call Gabriel, or go see him. He'll listen.

Jason found the number of Gabriel Assets and picked up the receiver. When he did, he heard the intermittent tone that told him he had voice-mail messages. There was only one call from that morning, and the caller had signed off immediately without leaving a message.

The operator at Gabriel Assets transferred him to Elspeth Clark. He had met the pleasant Mrs. Clark a number of times and was relieved to hear a friendly voice on the other end of the phone.

Mrs. Clark was short. "Dr. Connor, Mr. Gabriel is unavailable, but I'll let him know you called."

She would, he thought, but would Gabriel call back? Or would he call Martin and ask him what the curator wanted? He gave Mrs. Clark his cell phone number and hung up.

Ten forty-five.

Even if Gabriel wanted to help, what could he do? Stop Galante? Not a chance.

Robertson. Maybe Gerald can think of something.

He called Robertson's Pasadena number. Robertson's recording machine clicked on, the message he left saying he had gone to visit his children in Boston for the holidays but would be back in early January and asked callers to please leave a message.

Mancini. Mancini knows what's going on. He'll believe it.

He glanced at his watch again. Nearly eleven. Eight in the evening in Rome. Would he be in? He called and listened to the long, intermittent tone of the telephone ringing six thousand miles away. Mancini's recorded voice came on the line saying he was not available, and asked the caller to leave a message.

Jason identified himself and said he was calling from Los Angeles and then started to explain, before stopping. What good would it do?

He heard the telephone recorder shut off.

Jason felt as if he were caught in a chase dream from his childhood, pursued by demons that came ever closer while he struggled to flee with feet that were mired in glue. Or that he was Marshal Will Kane, trying to find someone, anyone, who would help him before the arrival of the noon train.

He shrugged off the melodramatic imagery and started to telephone Kate, but the caller ID window on his receiver lit up at the same moment. It was Kate.

"Jason, are you all right? What did the police say?"

"They weren't helpful. At all. I spoke to a lieutenant in their international division. He wants me to file a report. A report. Jesus. What's going on there?"

"Don't come to the museum Jason, whatever you do! *Do. Not. Come.*"

Her words were spaced out, emphatic.

"Martin is in high fury. He knows you are somewhere in Los Angeles. He's been questioning your staff to try to find out where you are. He's probably tried to call you."

"There was a call from the museum. I didn't take it."

"Don't. I really don't think you're safe at home either. You should leave, as soon as you can. Like right now."

"In a few minutes. I want to make one more call from here, and I'll throw some things in a bag."

"Then what? Where are you going? And for how long?"

"I don't know yet. I thought of staying with Gerald Robertson, but he's away."

There was a long pause at the other end.

"Kate? Are you there?"

"I'm here, Jason. Just let me think."

The line went silent again for another minute.

"Jason?" Kate's voice had strengthened. "You can stay with me. I have a guest room."

He did not respond immediately. He could only think of reasons to say no.

Too close. She doesn't know what she's getting into.

"Jason?"

"Look, Kate, I'm not sure this is a good idea. It brings you too close to me. If Galante sent someone to find me, and does, he'll find you too."

"But there's no one here yet, is there? No one would know where you are if you didn't show yourself. And you need a place to stay, and it doesn't have to be for long—only long enough for you to see Martin and get the matter into the open. That's what you said, didn't you? How long will that take? A couple of days?"

He thought for another long moment.

"OK, one night. No more than two. But it's too dangerous for you to have me there if it goes on longer. And—thank you." He was just not being polite. Kate had held out a hand to him, and he was grateful for it.

"Call me later, Jason, when you can. If you don't reach me, leave me a message. Let me know where to find you. We'll both go home from there."

Eleven thirty. He tried to call Gabriel again. Elspeth Clark said Mr. Gabriel was still unavailable. But he had the message that Jason had called. And, yes, she did have his cell phone number.

He was running out of choices and was almost out of time. His house was not the place for him to be.

Five hours. Until the first arrival. If they're coming.

He needed to make one more call, one that he'd never had to make before and had hoped he would never have to. The number was in the back of his address book, partially reversed, and disguised by other numbers, "underbrush" that he had written in around it. He keyed it into the telephone pad.

Jason had not spoken to Karel Benedict for two years, and it was never certain he would be at home, but his voice answered on the first ring.

"Yes?" Benedict never used more than one word if he could help it. And he never identified himself. If the caller didn't know his voice, he believed, they shouldn't be calling him.

"Karel, it's Jason. Have you had lunch?" The words were innocuous but the fact of the call itself underscored its importance.

"No. Let's. Pancho's at Manhattan Beach. Not lunch, just. Is one o'clock OK?"

"One's fine. See you."

It was time to move out. He emptied out the half-unpacked suitcase he had brought back from London and filled it again with clean shirts, pants, and underclothes and added his running shoes.

He glanced at his watch again. Twelve noon.

The next thought brought him up straight.

Four thirty? What if Galante, or an Italian connection, had gotten hold of someone in the United States? In New York. Or Atlanta. Or Los Angeles?

They could be here now. He was out of time.

Steady down, Jason. Stay cool. Think through the day. I'm about to run and I've got no idea who from, or what they look like, or how to evade them, or for how long. You've wasted time calling people, trying to get someone to listen. And except for Kate, no one wants to help.

Time to leave.

The telephone rang.

Twelve-fifteen! To hell with the telephone.

He picked up his bag and walked quickly to his Jaguar, threw the bag and laptop in the luggage compartment, pushed the garage door button, eased backward past the curb, and closed the garage door. He listened to the big V6 wind up to a high whine when he shifted into first gear, then went to second and third as he accelerated down the street.

Two blocks behind him a dark Lexus sedan turned the corner and drove slowly toward Jason's house. The occupant, Tony Olivieri, watched the green Jaguar disappear ahead of him.

"Nice car," he thought. "Wonder whose it is?"

CHAPTER FORTY-EIGHT

With the whine of the Jaguar's engine in his ears, Jason headed toward the Santa Monica Freeway and the southbound interstate.

He had not seen Benedict in two years. They had first met when Jason was at Camp Lejeune as intelligence liaison officer to the US Marines' Second Division.

Their differences were profound. In fact, few men could be more widely separated by upbringing, education, perception, and instinct.

In the spring of Jason's senior college year, he received a letter on heavy white paper that noted his interest in foreign languages and suggested that if he wanted to know more about how to serve his country, he should make an appointment with Constance Black at the Federal Building in Boston. At the top of the letter were the words *Central Intelligence Agency* and a seal showing an eagle's head above a shield with a compass rose. Beneath Black's signature were two lines that simply said Director of Recruitment. New England.

The salutation "Dear" was slightly displaced from "Mr. Connor," and Jason wondered how many others in the Boston area had received the same form letter that year, but he shrugged and went to meet "Mr. Black," whose name he thought must be some sort of an in-house CIA joke. He had nothing better to do, and the thought of being a spy was vaguely interesting.

The interview was brief. Black, a slight, serious-looking man in his forties with a short moustache, looked at a thin file, eyed Jason, asked him a few questions about his interest in foreign affairs, and then told him that he couldn't do much more, there, in Boston. Jason, he said, would have to go to CIA Headquarters in Langley, Virginia, for further interviews. He scheduled an appointment for the following week.

"How do I get there?" Jason asked. "Drive?"

"No one drives," Black replied. "Go to the USAir counter at the airport and they'll ticket you to Dulles. You'll get picked up by a limousine when you arrive."

"A special limousine?" This was classy treatment, he thought.

The comedown was immediate.

"Don't be funny. It's the regular limo that does the Dulles run every hour."

When he entered the CIA's main building a week later, he was escorted by a no-nonsense young woman to a suite of offices outside the security barrier, ensuring that he would see nothing of the building's interior.

He met two men in succession. One identified himself as Robert Brown. The other, an older man with thin features, a shock of white hair, and eyes a little too narrowly set, said he was Jonathan White and said he was the head of the CIA's junior officer program. Like Black in Boston, Brown and White seemed utterly humorless.

"What's the job?" he had asked Brown.

"I can't tell you. That's classified."

During the second interview, White told Jason that the work would be interesting, a challenge, and said something about the importance of "case officers" to the Agency.

"What does a case officer do?" he asked.

"I can't tell you," White replied. "That's classified. You'll learn more if we take you."

The same afternoon, Jason spent two hours checking boxes on a long questionnaire that asked, among other things, whether he preferred rainy days to sunny ones and whether he had a good relationship with his mother or "if not applicable, please answer the following question about your father." He endured a short medical interview. He assumed he had passed because he was taken back into White's office and offered a job on the spot if he agreed to serve in the Marine Corps for two years.

He accepted, and one afternoon at headquarters he met Karel Benedict.

Benedict, he found out, had been born in Prague and spent his first school years there. He was seven when the Prague Spring had broken the Soviet hold over the country, and barely eight when, seven months later, five thousand Soviet tanks rolled into the city to quash Czechoslovakia's new freedom. His parents fled the country with only the clothes on their backs, running and at times carrying the young Karel in their arms. They crossed into Germany, then went on to England, and finally arrived in the United States. Both had died in a car accident when he was ten, and he was passed into the hands of relatives. At the age of seventeen, just out of school, Benedict enlisted in the US Marine Corps.

He was an exceptional recruit. He graduated from boot camp at Parris Island with the highest possible marks in weapons handling and close combat. His skills led naturally to his assignment to one of the Marine Corps' elite units, the Second Reconnaissance Battalion at Lejeune. Seven years later he was selected for Officer's

Candidate School at Quantico, commissioned as a second lieutenant, and returned to Lejeune.

On an otherwise uneventful evening Benedict, then a captain at thirty-two years of age, was told by his commanding officer that two men from Washington wanted to speak to him. The men, both of whom were in civilian clothes, asked him if he would be interested in work that would use his particular skills.

"What work?" he asked.

"Work of importance to the country. Sensitive work."

He could think of no particular skills he possessed other than his ability with light weapons and his own very powerful hands, and he understood immediately that close-in, personal contact with mortal results was probably intended. In his inner heart, Benedict knew it was something that in all likelihood only someone like him could do, and that he was being given an opportunity to pay back his adopted country for everything it had given him.

It was no choice at all, he thought, and he agreed to temporarily resign his Marine Corps commission and enter the CIA's Operations Directorate. He was given an initial indoctrination, then four months of accelerated training on special techniques in an isolated corner of the Agency's training site just north of Williamsburg, Virginia. He was then assigned to a very small and highly specialized group of men—and one woman—who were tasked to use their new skills on the instructions of the Director of Central Intelligence, and sometimes only under the authority of a presidential order.

That was when Jason and Benedict met again. Both men were in Cairo. Jason had made a successful pitch to an individual of exceptional interest, a Russian, Dimitri Ochenko, who represented the TASS News Agency but who the CIA station knew was a colonel of Soviet Military Intelligence—the *Glavnoje Razvedyvatel'noje Upravlenije*, more generally known as the GRU.

Ochenko had agreed to defect but demanded that his wife and adolescent son be taken out before he would follow. The operation was complicated by the defection of a member of the Bulgarian embassy only a few months earlier, and Soviet Bloc personnel, including families, were being carefully watched for signs of disloyalty. Cairo Station was deeply worried that the disappearance of Ochenko's family would be noted and that he would be rushed back to the Soviet Union by his own people.

The plan Jason devised called for the colonel's wife and son to spend the weekend at one of the substandard hotels used by the Russians at Agami, a Mediterranean resort west of Alexandria. The Soviets would assume their security people at the hotel would be able to watch over the wife and son. But if their security could be diverted for a few hours or more, the colonel's wife and son could be bundled off on a fast boat and the GRU office in Cairo would not know about it until the following morning. By that time Ochenko would be gone.

That part of the plan needed help, and Benedict was sent to provide it. Benedict had the single job of ensuring that when Ochenko was met and taken off in a waiting car to a cruise ship scheduled to leave Alexandria, the security tail would be immobilized so that he couldn't follow or send up an alarm.

"Immobilized?" It was Benedict's first question.

"Stopped," Jason said. "Taken down if you have to. You've got to be close enough to the guy to get to him without his knowing you're there."

Benedict smiled thinly and his eyes had taken on a distant look. As Jason worked through the details of the operation he found in Benedict a man he could trust absolutely.

The extraction took place on one of Cairo's many dim back streets, at an hour of the morning so early there was no one else in sight. Ochenko exited his apartment onto the street; Jason drove up and stopped; a third man appeared from a side alley, opened the car's rear door, pushed the Russian inside, and followed, slamming the door shut as Jason accelerated into the center of the city before taking the main road to the Alexandria docks three hours away.

Jason had looked in his rearview mirror to see the Russian security guard outside Ochenko's building standing still in a state of shock, then beginning to run. Then something happened so quickly that it was impossible to follow. To Jason's view, the man just disappeared.

Two days later he read in the *Egyptian Gazette* that the body of an unidentified European had been found in an eddy of the Nile, some miles downstream from Cairo. The police were investigating, the report said. A separate item on a different page of the same paper reported the disappearance of one of the TASS bureau's Cairo reporters. The story was given an inch on an interior page of *al-Ahram*. By that time Ochenko was being debriefed on the outskirts of Washington and his wife and son were at a remote location in the Adirondacks.

Benedict returned to Washington for intensive counseling by the Agency's psychiatric unit to be sure that although they had created a killing machine, he was their very own killing machine and would not melt down on a job or go out of control in a crowded movie theater. He was then instructed to take three weeks leave, and he spent almost all of it snorkeling on the Pacific Coast of Costa Rica, having done in Egypt what he thought was simply a very good job. Better than that, his special talents had been used against a Russian. Karel Benedict hated Russians.

Pancho's was on the other side of Highland, just off Rosecrans. Jason drove the Jaguar into the parking lot and killed the engine. When he asked for Benedict, he was taken to an enclosed veranda and pointed toward a table at the rear. Benedict, slightly older than the man he had seen only a few years before, with salt-and-pepper hair cut close to the head and still very trim, rose and shook Jason's hand and then sat down.

"Good margaritas here. Have one."

No preliminaries. The same man, Jason thought.

"Karel, I can't. Busy afternoon."

"What?"

Meaning, Jason knew, let's get on with it and get out.

"I think I'm about to be hit."

The former Marine raised an eyebrow slightly.

"It's not certain. But there's enough to tell me that someone, at least one person, is coming after me. And I'm fantasizing."

"When?"

"Today at the earliest. If they can get here." Jason took ten minutes to summarize the events of the past two weeks.

"I need advice, Karel. You're the only person I know who can suggest what to do. But I want to be clear on one thing. I don't intend to run. At least not far. If the entire matter—the statue, Pryce's involvement, the killing of Pisano and Maybank—can be dragged into the open, there won't be any point in getting me. But I need breathing room to do that."

"Where are you staying?"

"With Kate Emerson. She works at the museum. For a day, maybe two."

"Who knows?"

"She does. No one else."

"This is new, then?" Jason shifted uneasily at Benedict's question, but knew it was essential.

"We're not an item."

"When are you going to see Pryce?"

"Perhaps tomorrow. No later than Friday."

"Do you have a plan? Or were you just going to go into the museum and knock on his door?" Benedict had a sardonic smile on his face.

"No. I need to find a way to corner him, then get him to admit that he set up the deal with Maybank. I haven't thought how to do that yet. I don't want to break cover until I'm ready."

"And you'd do that without protection?"

"What protection? No one gives a damn."

Benedict thought for a moment.

"Jason, are you as awkward as you always were? With weapons?"

The corridor talk at the Agency said Jason was brilliant about intelligence plans and collection and terrible at sidearms handling, explosives making, and a number of other technical matters the CIA thought every intelligence officer needed to know, no matter how useless they were in the real world of clandestine operations. Jason had almost failed this part of the indoctrination course at Williamsburg, but had so impressed his instructors with his mental agility—"subtle and devious" as one had described him in his efficiency report—that his scores still held to a high average.

"Probably. I don't have a weapon now anyway."

A few seconds passed before Benedict replied.

"It sounds as though you've got a problem."

"I know."

"I don't have advice. I don't know enough yet. If I knew more, I could think of something intelligent to say." Benedict paused before continuing.

"So, I'm going to find out more. I'll talk to you later. Maybe tomorrow."

"What does that mean?"

"Exactly what I said. Find out more. Talk to a few people. Follow you around a bit. If these fellows are really interested in you, they'll show themselves. And I'll pick them up." Benedict thought for a moment, then added, "Of course if they don't find you, we may have to bait them."

"With what?"

"You. You know the routine. You've done it before."

Jason knew exactly what Benedict meant. Break cover, go into the open, get the attention of his pursuers, lead them into a trap. Baiting the enemy was a game as old as war. Both of them had done it together, once, in Beirut, and he had been the bait that time too. It was risky work, and if anything went wrong—if one's support element got caught in traffic or was delayed for any reason—it could result in a disaster. But they had pulled it off, and Benedict's handiwork ensured that the two Army of the Prophet foot soldiers who had followed him became martyrs to their cause.

"Why would you do that? You'd be going far out of your way."

Benedict leaned over the table and looked straight at Jason.

"It's not far out of the way. And I'm not doing anything else now. I shouldn't tell you probably, but I'm asked to do some business for our friends back east from time to time." Benedict gave a slight smile. "But it's only for occasional work."

"They don't need me as much now. They've got a lot of younger people with special skills. And they want team players. I'm not so good at that, as you'll remember.

"But that's not the reason, Jason. You are. You were the only one at the Agency who really paid attention to me. I thought of you as a friend, someone in the same foxhole. In the Corps, we didn't fight for the country. We fought for the guy who was next to us. We fought for our friends. We took care of them. So, this is for you."

The former Marine came to the end of the longest speech he had made in years. His smile now reached to the eyes.

"And it sounds like fun. Right up my alley."

CHAPTER FORTY-NINE

Three men, none of whom knew each other, arrived at Los Angeles International Airport the same Wednesday afternoon.

Billy Rourke's American flight from Chicago landed a few minutes behind schedule at ten after three. By four, Rourke had picked up his bag and was at the Dollar car rental counter. Twenty minutes later, now driving a dark Chevy SUV, he found the FedEx office at West Century Boulevard and picked up the packages that held the Berettas and fitted silencers.

Rourke was pleased that he'd have almost two hours before his London visitor arrived. He wanted to find some entertainment near the airport before the pickup, have a drink, relax. He cruised slowly along Century, and when he saw a sign on a side street that said *Palm Skybar*, he turned and pulled into a gritty adjacent parking lot with an even grittier attendant in dreadlocks. A sign below the bar's name said it had sports TV, exotic dancers, and a "convivial atmosphere for world travelers."

He put the FedEx packages on the floor of the car, locked the doors, and walked in to order his first beer of the afternoon, a Beck's. The interior lights were low. The few people scattered around the room, businessmen like himself, a few younger men wearing sleeveless shirts, and half a dozen women in bikini swimsuits and heels, were little more than shadow figures. Two hours and three Becks later, he returned to the airport and began to slowly circle the inner loop road. Within minutes his cell phone chimed. Michael Quinn said he had cleared customs and would be at the terminal curb in five minutes.

By quarter to eight both men had checked into the Travelodge at the intersection of Ocean and Pico. Rourke had chosen the two-star, two-story motel because it allowed unnoticed arrivals and departures any time of day or night. The Travelodge office smelled slightly of stale cigarette smoke and something else that Rourke could not clearly identify.

They checked in and went to Quinn's room. Rourke gave Quinn a paper parcel with one of the two Berettas and a fitted silencer. Quinn locked both in his suitcase, lay down and propped his head on a pillow of one the room's two double beds, and folded his hands across his stomach. "Jesus, man, did you have to find a place that smells?"

Billy Rourke was not amused at the question. Who was this fat-assed guy to make a comment like that? He shouldn't be telling me what to do.

"Look, Quinn, we're supposed to be low to the ground on this job. Don't want a high-life hotel that'd ask for your passport. It's only for two days anyway. That's what I was told." He was supposed to give this Quinn guy backup, Rourke thought, not be his concierge. But it was only for a couple of days, and then he'd be back in Chicago.

The two men ended the evening at a diner on Pico. By the time they had returned to the motel, Rourke had decided Quinn was a slob. Not only was he fat and out of shape, but he had bad teeth and picked his nose. He also didn't have a plan about how to deal with the Connor guy. It was going to be a long two days, he thought.

By the time Rourke picked up Quinn, Giuliano Clemente had arrived from London on his own American flight. Clemente passed quickly through immigration and with his carry-on bag in hand, walked through the baggage lounge, passed customs, and headed for the exit. A quick call alerted Olivieri, who brought his Lexus to the curb as Clemente emerged onto the street.

Olivieri recognized Clemente by his dark suit and his smart Mediterranean look. Clemente threw his bag in back of the Lexus and settled into the front seat. They nodded to each other but did not speak for several minutes.

Clemente finally turned to Olivieri as they left the airport boundary. His English was almost perfect, but he used Italian.

"So, what should I know?"

"Nothing yet. Mr. C.—*Signor Ci*—is not at home. I went by his house today. He wasn't there. Maybe he's at his museum. We can go back tonight when there's no traffic. If it's quiet, we may be able to do business. But we'll have to see."

"And where are we staying?"

"Santa Monica, Casa del Mar. They're holding rooms for us."

The Casa del Mar, originally built as an ornate private club in the 1920s and converted in the 1970s to quarter the Pritikin Longevity Center, was now one of Los Angeles' newer grand hotels, with large rooms, a period art-deco entry hall, and a bar that had a commanding view of the beach. Olivieri had spent a week at Claridge's when he had business in London several years earlier, and there was no reason to go second class here either. The Casa del Mar fitted his image of where a respectable businessman should stay on a visit to Los Angeles. He also knew one might get lucky with the occasional lesser actress of a type who tended to visit high-end hotel bars in the later afternoon.

The two men continued to talk as the Lexus sped toward Santa Monica. Twilight had ended, and the sky was dark but for the sliver of a moon high above. Olivieri had a brief moment of uplift when they exited the interstate and drove along the Pacific shore. He was looking forward to talking to Clemente about the clean work that had made the man's reputation and his plans to use it with Connor.

Olivieri had carefully read the file his uncle Raymond's back room had put together on Connor. It mentioned the four years he had been at the Gabriel museum, his years of graduate study at Harvard and, before that, the fourteen years he had been a diplomat in the State Department.

A diplomat. Hell, Olivieri thought, this is going to be a piece of cake.

CHAPTER FIFTY

For the first time since Jason had bought the Jaguar it had become a liability. He needed another vehicle, something much
less noticeable.

The desk clerk at the Santa Monica Avis office, a young man
wearing a bright red blazer with the company's name on it, a pink
shirt, and light green bowtie, with an overly precise manner, said
he did not have a midsize car immediately available. He offered a
full-size Taurus for the same price.

Jason accepted immediately. The Taurus was an undistinguished dark blue, a perfect car that no one would take special
note of, one that could disappear among the others on the road.
Also, he was a Taurus. Jason did not believe in signs, but decided
that today he should not ignore this one. He asked the Avis agent
to hold his reservation for half an hour, garaged his Jaguar a block
away, and walked back to the Avis office. He left in the Taurus, feeling that he had at least accomplished something.

A little after three, he called Kate's cell phone. She answered
immediately.

She said she'd get back to him right away, when she was outside the museum. "Too many ears here," she explained. When she called him back, her first words were about Martin.

"I've never seen him in such a state. David and I saw him just an hour ago"—David Nalle was the Gabriel's paintings conservator—"and he was in a foul mood, just irate. He's not said anything to me yet, but I've been able to avoid him since then."

"If he asks you a direct question about whether you know where I am, what are you going to say? You ought to think about it."

"I've thought. I'll simply look him in the eye and tell him I've no idea. I don't like lying, but Jason, for God's sake, I'm *not* going to give you away, not to Martin and not with the Galante thing going on."

"When should I see you?"

"Seven. I'll be back by then and cleaned up, with something to eat. And Jason?"

"Yes?"

"We need another talk." She hung up.

The talk, as she called it, was everything he had not been able to put into words for himself.

He had arrived a little after seven with an overnight bag. She had met him at her door, reached upward and kissed his cheek, took his hand, and drew him inside, and pointed to the sofa.

"Put your bag in the guest room and come back and sit down. Wine?" She had already poured herself a glass of a Santa Barbara chardonnay.

"Scotch. Do you have any?"

"When did you start drinking scotch?" She found a half-filled bottle on her back shelf, poured dark liquid into a glass with ice, and handed it to him.

"Something I do once a month, maybe."

She sat on the sofa and fastened her eyes on him.

"You know, Jason, there's something about this that's a little nuts. Last night I told you I cared about you—missed you is what I said. That's not something I've done with anyone, not since Eric. Then, this morning, I had this fantasy about us. I won't describe it—let me just leave it like that—and it upset me.

"It brought me up short. It made me realize I may be in a little deeper than I'd thought. She looked away for a moment and then turned back to him.

"I'm not revealing much to tell you this. But, Jason, the more I thought about it, the more I felt it's too soon for me. Being attached to you that way, really caring about you. It would turn my life upside down.

"I have a really good life. I've got this wonderful job at the museum. I'm a recognized photographer with a following and with work people want me to do. I have friends, other women, good friends who I see every week. I go out with men sometimes, but mostly they're gay or very old, good company with no complications. Safe, Jason—you said it yourself. And I don't have to give up a thing. I'm as independent as I've ever been, as much as anyone could want. I don't have to *care* about anyone else. Caring for Eric when he was dying was the most painful thing I've ever gone through."

She searched his eyes.

"Can you understand what I'm saying? Am I making sense?"

He took her hand in both of his own. "We're lucky, I think."

"I'm serious, Jason—I'm not talking about luck!"

"I'm serious too. You said what we've both been thinking. It's the wrong time to get involved, for either of us. I have Martin to deal with and the damned statue. And the people I stirred up at Morgantina. And when—if—I can get through those, I'll still, also, have a perfectly good life. I don't need to have it turned upside down either."

"But?"

264

"But I haven't felt as glad to see anyone as I did last night. I hope it doesn't distress you for me to say that. Or that I've missed you."

She noticed for the first time that his eyes crinkled at the corners when he smiled.

She gave him a thoughtful look.

"No, Jason, no distress. I'm pleased. And you know—" There was a small smile on her face as she spoke. "You know, I didn't say this is forever. Just for now."

She got up and straightened her skirt.

"About the chicken, Jason, I hope you don't mind it spiced up. I've smeared this thing all over with garlic and rosemary, and it'll be ready in an hour. So, let's have another glass of wine, and you can talk to me about Morgantina. I got it up on the web when you were gone, but it's not like being there. I want you to tell me about it."

He did and found that the memory of his walk through the ruins of Morgantina and his meeting with the farmer was as sharp as if he had been there that morning.

He stood up.

"I almost forgot something with all this talk."

"What's that?"

"Give me a minute." He went to his room and returned.

"I thought of you in Rome, and this caught my eye." He handed her the small box with the scarab pin he had bought at the shop on the Via Margutta.

She opened the box and took out the scarab, held it in her left palm, then turned it over and looked at him.

"Jason, it's just beautiful." She was on the verge of saying something more but then stopped.

"But I won't."

"Won't what?"

"Won't tell you what I was about to." She laughed and wiped her eyes.

"Thank you, Jason. It's lovely. I'll wear it tomorrow. Now go to your room, damn it, and let me clean up."

Later that night, in the quiet of Kate's guest room, he composed a very detailed and explicit e-mail message to Angela that recounted the events of the last two weeks.

In case something happens to me. Angela can't do anything about Galante, but she can do a lot about Martin. And she won't rest until she has his head.

The talk he and Kate had came back to him for a moment, and a small wave of relief washed over him. He stripped, got under the bedclothes, and three minutes later was deep asleep.

Sometime in the early morning he awoke and sensed a presence. He lay still and waited for a sound but there was none, nor could his eyes see movement or any change of shapes or shadows in the room.

"Kate?" he asked softly, but there was no response. He knew he was speaking only to himself. He turned over and shut his eyes and slept again.

CHAPTER FIFTY-ONE

As Jason and Kate were finishing dinner, Karel Benedict exited Sunset in his dark BMW and drove slowly toward the end of Sumac Lane, past Jason's house, and onto Amalfi Drive. He then quartered back to make the same run from the opposite direction. He was looking for a vehicle with occupants, or just the glow of a cigarette or a radio light. He could see none. When he passed Jason's house a second time, he nosed into the curb a hundred feet away, on the opposite side of the street with a clear view of the entry. He killed his lights, lowered himself in his seat, and waited, his eyes half-closed.

Shortly after twelve thirty, he saw a vehicle turn onto Sumac, drive by, quarter back, and stop at the curbside some distance away. Two men inside the car, a Lexus, sat talking for a few minutes. Then one got out, walked quietly to Jason's house and circled it, opened a gate that led to the garden, and vanished toward the rear. In two minutes, he reappeared on the other side of the house and rejoined his companion.

Benedict watched the figure return to the car. More conversation followed. The two occupants then hunched down in their seats, waiting. The man in the passenger seat occasionally lifted a cigarette to his mouth, high enough for Benedict to see the glowing tip.

At a little after four, Benedict saw the Lexus move away with its headlights still off. When the driver turned on his lights a half block up the street, Benedict eased his BMW out into the roadway. He did not turn on his own lights until he had reached West Channel, which even at the early hour had traffic moving in both directions. Distancing himself a hundred yards behind the other vehicle, Benedict began to hum a few bars from his childhood, a tune that his grandmother had taught him when he lived in Prague.

Ten minutes later, the Lexus turned into one of the parking spaces outside the Casa del Mar. Benedict slowed to a stop where he could watch. When the occupants entered the hotel, he removed an airline bag from the trunk of his car, walked over to the Lexus, and slipped underneath. Five quick minutes later, with the device and its battery securely clamped to the Lexus's chassis and properly wired and taped, the installation was done.

Benedict drove to his small house in Manhattan Beach, scratched the back of the tawny Maine Coon with pistachio eyes that greeted him at the door, made certain the cat's water and food dishes were full, picked up a dog-eared copy of Ovid's *Metamorphoses*, and read himself to sleep.

CHAPTER FIFTY-TWO

There was a light knock, and Kate, in a pale-green bathrobe, came into his bedroom with two cups on a tray, sugar and milk on the side.

"I've no idea how you take it, so I brought everything."

She put the tray between them, sat on the end of the bed, and passed him a cup.

"About last night—are we OK?" Her eyes were thoughtful. "I'm just trying to find my way on a path I haven't taken in a long while. I just need a little distance. More time."

He smiled. "I think we can do that. Even without this other stuff that's going on."

"Me too. But it's seven thirty and I've got to get dressed. I have an early meeting, but there's time for breakfast. I'll see you in the kitchen in twenty minutes."

Over breakfast she came back to it again.

"Jason, I'm sure you're going to have a difficult day. Staying still would probably drive you crazy, and I don't think you're the type to wait around for me here. But you can't stay at your house, and you mustn't come into the museum until you see Martin. But today, you'll want to get out, do things, make things happen. That's what you want, isn't it?"

He nodded. "Yes, but don't ask, Kate. I've got to talk to Martin, but I need to set it up. And I don't want you involved."

"Come on, Jason. I *am* involved. I was involved the moment you told me about it."

"You don't understand. Martin doesn't know about you. No one does." He had a fleeting thought about Amelia Mumford and the shocked look on her face when she walked into his office as he was talking with Kate.

"You're not in Martin's sights. Stay clear. I don't want him to think you know about him and Maybank. Please listen to me on this."

"I can't imagine how he'd think that."

"Give me one more day to deal with this, then I'll be gone. It's safer that way."

Kate stood up, went to a small drawer, and took out a key on a chain. She handed it to Jason.

"This is your place, Jason. Come and go as you want. The only other person who's used this key is my mother, and she'd be furious if you lost it. I'll see you this evening. We can catch up then and you can tell me where this is all going."

As Kate was leaving her apartment, Quinn was finishing breakfast with Rourke. He turned on his cell phone and connected with the messaging service Bagger had instructed him to use in the United States. Bagger took great pains to keep his international calls to a minimum.

The man had called the night before. He wanted Quinn to call back as soon as he picked up the message.

"Quinn here. What?"

"Problem, maybe."

Must be a big problem, Quinn thought. The man never calls while a job's in progress.

"What?" he repeated.

"The client. The guy who wanted the service. 'E's been done."

"Bloody 'ell, you say. Done? Done 'ow?"

Bagger spoke at some length. He ended by telling Quinn to call back immediately once Quinn had carried out his instructions. He would then tell him how to proceed.

Quinn took down two numbers on a small pad of paper, said he understood, and ended the call. He turned to Rourke.

"Game's changed."

"Tell me."

"Our client's dead. Maybe we can pick up the contract on our subject again at this end. Got to talk with this Pryce guy. Friend of the client. Director at the same place what Connor works at."

Benedict woke up refreshed after four good hours of sleep. He booted up his laptop and tapped into the data fed by the transmitter that he had installed in the Lexus. The map that appeared on the screen showed the vehicle still parked at the Casa del Mar. He held the GPS display in place as he went through the small number of messages that had accumulated since the prior afternoon.

The device he had clamped under the Lexus had been made for Benedict by Nicky Koutoulakis, a brilliant technician he had met in Redondo Beach. Nicky had spent years disassembling and reassembling cell phones and computers and had responded enthusiastically to Benedict's interest in a device that would allow him to track a vehicle anywhere in the state of California, in any weather. By the end of the week, Nicky had his solution, and Benedict had exactly what he needed: an unobservable, real-time, transmission-on-demand, GPS-based tracking capability that could be attached quickly to any vehicle.

At nine thirty, Benedict was in his BMW heading north on Interstate 405 toward Santa Monica. His BlackBerry showed the Lexus still at the Casa del Mar, but the map display started to move almost immediately. The Lexus was on the road, heading to the coast road, or back to the Palisades. His guess was the Palisades.

He accelerated up the 405, took a left at Sunset and started the climb toward the Palisades, turning down toward Sumac. A single light burned in Jason's house. Further down the road, a dark Lexus with two occupants was parked on the opposite side.

Jesus. I hope Jason doesn't plan to go back.

That was exactly what Jason had in mind.

He had left for Kate's apartment the evening before without the copies of the Athena's files. Without the photocopied letters and the fax with Langlotz's real signature, who would believe him? He would go by his house to get them, a three or four minute stop, maybe less.

His cell phone chimed.

"Yes?"

"Jason, Karel. I don't know what your plans are, but don't return to your house. I repeat: *don't go back*. There are a couple of men in a car waiting for you there now."

There was a pause.

"Karel, I'm here now. You called just as I was getting out of the car."

"Jason, man, get back in your car and get out of there. *Right away.* They're on your street, very close!" Benedict's voice was almost a shout. He sped up Amalfi, then turned up Sumac.

At that moment, Benedict was conscious of only three things. The first was Jason, who he saw was just getting back into a car. The second was the Lexus, thirty yards away, with two men inside, both of whom were looking at Jason. The third was his own vehicle, which was halfway up Sumac.

He saw Jason pull away from the curb and in the next instant saw the Lexus start into the street. He gunned his engine, passed the Lexus, then slowed, blocking its forward movement. As Jason headed down Sumac, the Lexus kept trying to push itself around Benedict, the driver leaning on the horn and weaving back and forth to either side of the road. Benedict kept a measured pace to the end of Sumac, then made a turn and slowed again before he pulled over to the curb. The Lexus rocketed past him with a blare of noise. The rider on the passenger side leaned out the window and thrust out his arm with his other hand closed on it in an unmistakable gesture.

Benedict had given Jason precious minutes to get out of sight. He knew Jason would have cleared the area quickly.

He picked up his cell phone.

"That wasn't smart, Jason. Not like you."

"I thought I could get away with it. I won't need to do it again. But Karel, I need those files, the ones I came back for. If I don't have them, it's only my word against Pryce's.

"Where are you?"

"North of Sunset, heading east."

Benedict's BlackBerry showed the Lexus on the loop of Sunset approaching Palisades center, more than half a mile away and traveling in the opposite direction.

"OK, keep going. Tell me what files you want and exactly where they are. I'll get them."

"You need a key?"

"Have I ever needed one? But keep going. And for God's sake, man, *tell me* when you're moving, and where you're going to be. These are very bad people, Jason. You were right to talk to me yesterday. At least you changed cars."

"Yes."

"But now they know what you're driving."

CHAPTER FIFTY-THREE

The voice on the telephone sounded odd to Patricia Waller's ear. It was English, but peculiar, not very cultured. Almost all the English visitors she had met at the Gabriel had an educated accent, but not this caller. She asked who was speaking.

"Colin Gleeson." Quinn, on his cell phone, watched the gray Pacific out the window as the car sped up the coast highway.

"May I say what it's about, please?"

"'Scuse me, miss, please just let your boss know there's a Mr. Gleeson and a friend what wants to see 'im. From London. A business matter. 'E'll know what it's about."

Pryce was on the line in less than five seconds.

"Yes?"

"Colin Gleeson, Mr. Pryce. Ah, I think you've heard Mr. Maybank's sent us, but you've maybe heard 'e's had some, ah, recent difficulties? My manager wants me to talk to you about it. Today."

There was a pause as the director's mind raced.

"Where are you?"

"At the museum, Mr. Pryce. My partner and me're just coming into the entry now."

A moment of panic washed over the director. *Oh shit* was the only thought that ran through his mind. He buzzed his secretary.

"Patricia, there are a couple of visitors coming to see me in a few minutes. Send them in when they're here and then hold my calls until they're gone."

He turned and looked darkly out the window, wishing he were somewhere else.

Who the hell are these people Richard's sent?

He had tried to make sense out of Maybank's death since he had learned about it the previous day. The *Times* had given no further coverage of the matter since the AP report of the previous day. London's *Independent*, which Pryce had pulled up on the web, described in greater detail Maybank's burgeoning business, mentioned a number of his known clients, and carried a few laudatory comments and one quite nasty remark by a competitor about Maybank being willing to buy anything from anyone. The *Independent*'s article affirmed that the dealer's death had been an accident.

Richard? An accident? Pryce shook his head. Unbelievable. First Pisano, then Richard the next day? That's too much of a coincidence. And now the people Richard had sent to take care of Jason are here, inside the museum.

Take care of Jason? Kill him. Richard had twisted his arm to agree!

The intercom buzzed and Pryce stood up from his desk as Patricia Howard held the door open for the two men. The larger one, who looked like a wrestler, held out a massive hand, gave a smile that showed bad teeth, and said he was Colin Gleeson. He introduced his partner without giving a name.

"Would you like coffee, or a soft drink?" Patricia's tone was flat, but as she closed the door her look and the arch of a brow behind the visitors' backs were clear. *Who the hell are they?*

When the two men were seated, Quinn spoke first.

"Too bad about Mr. Maybank."

"Yes. What happened?" Pryce struggled to stem the panic he had begun to feel.

"Papers say 'e hit 'is 'ead."

"Isn't that a bit odd?" It was lame, but what else could he say? All he wanted to do was to get the two men out of his office.

"Yes. But Mr. Pryce, that's not why we wanted to see you. We've come 'ere to see if you want us to finish up, Mr. Pryce. You know, us not having Mr. Maybank's say-so an' all."

Pryce had known the question was coming. "What do you mean?"

"The job, Mr. Pryce. The job what Mr. Maybank asked for. We do it clean an' we get out."

"What else?"

"An' you complete the payment when it's done."

"Complete payment?"

"You see, Mr. Maybank made the deposit to our office, but there's the payment of the rest. That won't be coming from Mr. Maybank now, will it?"

Quinn paused and watched the director in silence.

"The rest?"

"We'll be wanting a quarter of a million dollars from you on completion."

Pryce felt his knees go weak.

"But not all now, me manager says. Over three months would be OK, paid monthly. 'E's a businessman. Doesn't expect the whole lot right away but wants regular payments, 'e says. Very reasonable man, 'e is."

The noose Pryce had felt around his neck Tuesday seemed to tighten another notch. He sat in his chair, unable to move.

If I say no, these awful men will walk away. Jason will appear and lay out the evidence against me, and Maybank's estate attorney will substantiate it. And I'll be out of my job. Maybe arrested. And if I say yes, then I have to find a quarter of a million dollars to pay whoever sent them. But they'll have taken care of Jason.

But Jesus, I can't have Jason killed! That's crazy. That's what Richard wanted, not me! I don't like the man, but killing him?

I can end it here, right now. Tell them to keep Richard's money, just leave. Forget the money. It's not worth it. He turned back to the two men and was about to speak but then stopped.

But Jason won't give up, will he? He's—what did Barovsky say?— he's unforgiving. Stubborn and unforgiving. He'll do whatever he can to make the wrong right and bring me down at the same time. If he's dead, that would give me breathing room, wouldn't it? And then I could have a talk with Richard's attorney. Cut him in. Why wouldn't that work?

Pryce felt his stomach churning. He turned and shook his head.

"Does that mean no, Mr. Pryce? You don't want us to go ahead?"

Pryce looked around his office for some means of escape. There was none.

"It means yes." His voice was faint, and Quinn had to ask him to repeat what he said.

"Yes." One word, he thought. It seemed so simple.

"OK, done." Quinn smiled slightly, only a parting of the lips. "Now then, where's our bloke?"

"I don't know. Somewhere in Los Angeles. I tried to call him yesterday, no answer. I don't think he's at his house."

"If you do find out where 'e is, you'll let us know, won't you, Mr. Pryce? And you'll do that right away, Mr. Pryce? We don't want to be around too long."

Quinn's voice had taken on a hard edge. The other man had remained silent throughout the exchange.

The two men rose. Quinn handed Pryce a small slip of paper with his cell phone number. As he reached the door, he turned back to the director.

"An' Mr. Pryce, me manager 'opes there won't be no payment problem, right? See, 'e wants me to tell you, you don't want to have us back 'ere."

Pryce stared at the backs of the two men as they left. Holding his hand to his stomach, he went to the small washroom next to his office, convulsed, and vomited as quietly as he could.

As Quinn and Rourke walked back through the central courtyard toward the museum entrance, they passed two dark-haired, well-dressed younger men who were heading along the portico toward one of the museum's offices. Quinn made brief eye contact with one of them.

Who the fuck are they? Olivieri thought. Don't look like they're here for the art, I'd say.

He turned to Clemente when they were out of the other men's earshot.

"That's strange," he said.

"What's strange?"

"The two guys we just passed. They're both carrying."

"Cops?"

"Maybe. Can't tell. Can't imagine who else. One looked a little familiar, but that doesn't make sense."

When Clemente told Olivieri that he wanted to meet Jason, Olivieri was incredulous.

"Like, why do you want to do that?"

Clemente carefully explained that he wanted to know who the subject was, unless there had been some previous contact.

"This isn't a shooter's game, Tony. You can't stand off at a distance and take down someone and not know who he is. You got to have some personal contact. You just gotta look into a guy's eyes before you do him. Then he'll know something's wrong, you know, and you can see the fear light up inside. *Then* you do him."

Jeez, Olivieri thought, that sounds nuts. And he's a pro? Sounds like he's got something else on his mind. I've met assholes like that before.

Olivieri had run into a lot of different types in his short career with his uncle Raymond. People who didn't want to do jobs unless they could see the suffering, hear the last desperate pleadings of a doomed man. Clemente sounded like one of them. But Olivieri stilled his thoughts. How the guy gets his rocks off wasn't any concern of his. And it wouldn't do for him to complain and have it get back to Raymond.

Clemente pulled his cell phone from an inner pocket, punched in the museum's number, and asked for the antiquities department. A woman answered and rather stiffly asked what he wanted.

"To talk to the curator. A Mr. Connor, is that his name? About some antiquities we have."

He heard a muffled conversation in the background, and a woman who said she was Cynthia Greenwalt came on the line.

"Dr. Connor's not in the building. I'm his assistant. I have a few minutes, and if you'd come into the department, perhaps I can help you."

Clemente said that would be fine. He rang off and turned to Olivieri.

"The Connor guy's not here. We're seeing his assistant. Maybe she'll tell us where he is. I'll do the talking."

Olivieri was only slightly assuaged. The new plan sounded better than the original one. At least he wouldn't have to look in this Connor guy's eyes. That would be just too weird.

Clemente and Olivieri had just made their introductions to Cynthia Greenwalt when a man walked in. The new arrival, clearly someone with authority in the museum, gave them a brief look and turned to Greenwalt.

"Cynthia, where's Jason? I know he's in Los Angeles, but he doesn't answer the phone."

"I've no idea, Martin. He hasn't called me. I don't understand it." She looked puzzled.

Pryce turned and fastened his eyes on the older woman who had been sitting stiff-backed in her chair, fingers fidgeting at her desk but doing nothing, listening quietly.

"Amelia, I'm sure you have no idea either where Dr. Connor is, but if he calls please let me know immediately."

Amelia Mumford peered at the director over her reading glasses. She sat up even straighter.

"Dr. Pryce, I will certainly let you know if Dr. Connor calls. And I don't know where he could possibly be."

She turned back to her desk. In an undertone she knew would carry, and uncaring about who else in the room might hear her, added, "Unless he's seeing Kate Emerson."

CHAPTER FIFTY-FOUR

So Jason was seeing Kate? Pryce walked into the museum's central court and went down the stairs to the conservation department. He found her at her desk.

"Kate, I understand Jason's in Los Angeles but hasn't come into the museum. He's not answering my calls. I want to get hold of him. Do you know where he is?"

Kate's eyes wavered slightly and then looked straight at the director.

"Why no, Martin. I haven't heard from him." Her voice was steady.

"If you do, you'll let me know, won't you?"

"Of course."

Pryce had what he needed. He shut the door to his office and picked up the telephone. He would have to handle this call very carefully.

"Andrew, Jason Connor's back."

"Back? From where?"

"Europe. Italy. Apparently, also Sicily."

"Why would he go there?"

"I think he wants to discredit the statue and embarrass us. He may think he's found something over there that'd help him do that."

"That's interesting. He tried to call me this morning."

"He did?"

"I didn't take the call, Martin. Too busy. I also wanted to talk to you first. But why would he want to talk to me?"

"Andrew, you'll remember our chat at dinner? About Jason seeing the statue as a mistake or even a setup? It has to be about that. And since he knows he can't convince me, he wants to see you."

"Where's he now, in the museum?"

"Not yet. But he's going to have to come in at some point."

The silence lasted for several seconds.

"Martin, I don't want to talk to him. You do it. Now, what's your plan to handle him?"

Pryce was stunned. My plan? What's the old man up to?

"Andrew, I need to hear what he has to say first. I'll let you know then."

"I hope there's no problem. Do you understand, Martin? No problems."

The line went dead.

Pryce threw the receiver down on its cradle in disgust.

For God's sake! My plan, he says. No problems, he says. He wants me to fix it so he can wash his hands of the whole thing! Will this awful day never end?

He paced to the window, came back to his desk, then made a second call. Quinn came on the line immediately.

"Gleeson? I believe I know where you can find Connor. He may be with a girlfriend. A woman who works at the museum."

"Who's that, Mr. Pryce? What's she do there?" The question was pointed.

"Conservation. She runs the conservation department here."

There was no response.

"They take care of the art."

Still no response.

"You know, Gleeson, preserve it?

"And where's she live, Mr. Pryce?"

"Palisades." Pryce read Kate's address over the telephone.

"But Connor. You want Connor. Not the woman. I don't want the woman hurt; do you understand?"

There was another silence. When Quinn replied, his voice was level, without inflection.

"Of course not, Mr. Pryce. Of course not."

Quinn rang off and immediately called a New York number that connected with a London exchange. He spoke softly into the cell phone when a man's voice came on.

"Bagger, the bloke says OK to the new contract."

"No problem?"

"Squirmed a bit, 'e did. 'E isn't too happy about the money, but 'e'll pay up all right."

In the garage, Quinn turned to Rourke.

"We're going to the Emerson's woman's place. I've got the directions. Maybe the Connor guy's there now. She's 'is girlfriend."

"And what do we do if he's there?"

"Fix him. Maybe both of them."

"Like that? In the woman's apartment?"

"We'll figure it out when we get there."

Jesus, thought Rourke. This is getting really bad. How did this guy get the job anyway? He hasn't got a clue.

As they drove down the coast highway, Quinn wondered why his companion seemed so irritated, but he shrugged and adjusted the holster under his left arm. The silencer rested by itself deep in his trouser pocket, digging slightly into his thigh. The sensation comforted him.

Clemente had heard enough of the exchange between Greenwalt and the man who had just entered—the museum's director?—and the comment by the older woman with the eyes like thumbtacks and hair up in a bun. He had to change plans quickly. Someone would think it very odd for two visitors to the museum to appear so interested in Connor now.

Greenwalt asked how she could help. Clemente took on a heavy Italian accent, sprinkling vowels at the end of his words and hesitating as if he didn't know the exact word.

"The Gabriel—it buys many, how you say, antiquities, no? *Antichità*. We've got friends in Rome who want to know if you'd like to buy nice Italian antiquities, *Antichità romane*," he said, with the skewed, boyish grin that said to American women he was a charming Italian fraud. "You know, things that have been with my friends' families—uh, for many years!"

He knew the woman's answer would have to be no.

"No," she said. "No. I'm afraid we can't be interested. Italy forbids the export of anything but registered material. Didn't you know that? So we just don't buy from Italy. I'm sorry. I hope you're not too disappointed. Any museum in the country would tell you the same thing, I think."

Clemente looked at the curator. He said it was not a problem. They had other business to do and it was nice to be in California anyway. He smiled his lopsided smile again, apologized for taking her time, and left with Olivieri following him.

When they reached the courtyard, Olivieri came up beside him.

"What was that all about? Why did we get out so fast? I thought you wanted to find out where Connor is."

"I know where Connor is. At least I know how to get to him. We just need to find his girlfriend. He'll be with her. Or she'll lead us to him. If that doesn't get us to Connor, we'll have a talk with her, work on her a little bit."

Benedict called Jason mid-morning. He told Jason to go have lunch somewhere, go to a movie, take a tour of Universal Studios, do something, anything that would keep him occupied and away from his own house through the afternoon. He said he had tracked the Italians' Lexus to the coast highway west of Los Angeles.

"But I've lost the signal. It's probably in a garage somewhere. I'll pick it up when they go back into the open. But Jason," he added, "I want to keep my eyes on them and not you. And I need some rest first. It might be another long night. So go some other place where I don't have to worry about you."

With that, Benedict drove to his Manhattan Beach home and slept into the middle of the afternoon. His large pistachio-eyed cat crawled up on the bed beside him, turned on its back, stretched, and lay silent, eyes shut, mouth parted enough to show a row of small, very sharp teeth.

Kate had difficulty focusing on her work. Had Martin believed her? And what if he didn't? Maybe a cup of tea would help. She ran into Cynthia at the cafeteria and sat with her at a corner table.

"So, I had this funny visit this morning. These two Italian guys, from the countryside probably—they were barely able to speak English—wanted to know if we'd buy antiquities from their 'friends' in Rome. I sent them away. They must have known I'd have to say no. And Martin came in while they were there."

"Oh?" Kate sat up a bit. Two Italians? Martin? "What did Martin want?"

"Jason. He's been looking for Jason and can't find him."

"When was this?"

"A little after ten, maybe ten fifteen."

So Martin asks Cynthia about Jason, then he immediately comes to see me. That's not a coincidence. "What else did he say?"

Cynthia hesitated and then looked directly at Kate. "Look, this is none of my business. You're my friend, Jason's my boss, and one

285

of the best I've known. I should probably just have shut up. But Amelia Mumford let a cat out of the bag, kind of. She said to herself, but loud enough so that everyone could hear, that she thinks Jason is with you."

Cynthia stopped, embarrassed, then continued.

"Kate, I really don't care if you and Jason are involved. I mean," she went on, now more quickly, "it's your business. But if Amelia mentioned it to us, she'll do that with others too. And I'm not asking a question either. You know I wouldn't do that."

Kate felt a small ripple of apprehension rise inside her.

"So, who was there when Amelia made this remark?"

"Me. Martin. The two Italians."

A cold hand closed over Kate's heart. She excused herself, pushed herself away from the table, stepped out into the gardens, and opened her phone. It was answered on the first ring.

"Jason, I think we've got a problem. A big one."

CHAPTER FIFTY-FIVE

Karel Benedict came out of a deep sleep refreshed and ravenous. He showered and had his first full meal of the day. When he turned on his laptop, he saw the Lexus back in Santa Monica at the Casa del Mar. Good enough. His voice mail had a message from Jason. It was brief.

"Call me."

Jason's voice was tense. "They know where I'm staying."

"How?"

"My secretary. She seems to have let loose that I may be staying with Kate. Martin was in the room. That's not a big deal. I can handle Martin. But there were two other men who probably overheard her. At least one is Italian. From the description Kate gave me, they're almost certainly the same ones who were looking for me earlier today, the ones you cut off this morning. If they're interested in her it'll take no time to find out where she lives."

"Jason, you know I can't keep following these people. I need to get ahead of them, or get rid of them. They're in Santa Monica now. But whenever they go I have to follow. You're going to have to go somewhere else."

"Of course, but they've got Kate in their sights now. You know what they'll do. They'll wait until she leaves the Gabriel and follow her home. Then they'll use her to flush me out."

There was a silence as both men thought through the possibilities.

"Karel, I don't think we have a choice anymore. These guys won't leave until they've finished what they came to do. We've got to go on the offensive."

"What do *you* want to do? It's really your call. But if you want my advice, I'd say we've got to stop reacting. Go after them. Hurt them."

Jason was silent for another minute.

"OK, let's do it. Hit one of them, hard. And let them know it's not an accident and that there's someone else working against them. The other one probably won't continue. These are professionals, and they work as a team. Break up the team, you break up the plan.

"Hit hard?"

"Seriously injure. Make him a hospital case."

"And if that doesn't do it? How far do you want to go?"

"Karel, I know you want me to tell you we should take them out. I can't do that. I want to get rid of them. That's all."

"And if there isn't a choice, if they're really on top of you, then what?"

"Then do what you have to. I don't see any other way."

"That's what I thought. I don't either. I just wanted to be sure we understood each other."

Jason ended the call. "And to answer the question you haven't asked, yes, I'll be the bait again."

He called Kate, again on her cell phone.

"Don't say anything right now. Just listen for a minute, please. The two men Cynthia mentioned. Stay away from them no matter what. They'll want to see you. They know who you are and where you live. They're likely to go after you to get to me. Unless they get to me first. So you can't go home. They'll either be there or they'll be going there to wait for you."

"These men are coming after me now?" There was an edge to her voice.

"They've left the museum now and are somewhere on the coast highway. They may come back. If I find out where they are, I'll call you. But you've got to stay somewhere else tonight. We need to decide where. I'll let you know where we can meet. And Kate?"

"Yes?"

"I'm sorry this has caught up with you. I shouldn't have let you take me in."

"Jason?"

"What?"

"Don't be an idiot."

Jason called Benedict and then Kate again. He asked them to meet him at a small *cucina* a short distance from the Marina, at seven. Kate would be coming directly from the museum, and he wanted her and Benedict to be able to identify each other.

He tried to still his impatience. Dealing with the statue and Martin Pryce had meant improvising, but it was working. Galante had thrown him a curve ball, and since the death of Pisano, he'd been reacting to events, forced to decisions. Now, with Karel at his back, he could turn on his pursuers. But it meant patience. He could do that.

Kate found the two men seated, each nursing a beer and talking about something they had done together in the past. She could only make out a few words before they saw her and stopped, rose from the table, and greeted her.

Dinner was short. Jason explained what he wanted done the following day. It would involve risks. The greatest risk, the worst thing they could do, he said, was to do nothing. Kate remained silent throughout the meal.

They found a hotel near the beach south of the Marina, a place with little distinction but with clean rooms and the smell of the Pacific. They bought small things they needed that would carry them into the next day. By ten o'clock, they were sitting in Jason's room, he on his bed, Kate in the only chair.

"You're angry with me, aren't you?" It was Jason's question.

She looked away for a moment, then focused her eyes directly on his.

"Oh, Jesus, Jason, don't you understand? Yes, goddamn it, I'm angry! Yesterday—only yesterday!—we had dinner and talked, and these guys weren't more than a bad dream. And today they're real, no dream, and we're running for our lives, both of us.

"When I learned they were actually in the Gabriel today, I had a moment of pure panic. And denial. This *thing* that's going on can't be possible, I said to myself. But of course it *is* possible. And it's happening now! These men have come to find me, and then kill you. Or more likely, to kill us both.

"Angry, Jason? Yesterday I had choices. Today I don't have any. Do you understand? I can't go home; you can't go home. My choices have disappeared, just gone. I'm not just angry; I'm also a little terrified."

He wanted to say something, anything that would give reassurance, but found nothing that would do.

"Look, I can't tell you how this will work out. But it has to end. It will, soon. And running from it won't work."

She regarded him quietly, her eyes expressionless.

"Let's call it a night." She left for her room.

Benedict was puzzled about what he was seeing. He had tracked the Lexus to the Chautauqua Palms. When he knew exactly where the car had stopped, he drove to the same street and parked on the opposite side, half a block away with his lights out, facing Kate's apartment. Twenty minutes later a dark SUV with two men inside passed by Benedict very slowly, then went on to the next block, turned, drove back, and stopped further down the street facing in his direction. The driver turned off his headlights, but neither of the two occupants got out.

Benedict slid a little lower in his seat.

Now who the hell are these people?

CHAPTER FIFTY-SIX

The fog returned on Friday, covering the southern California coast from Ventura south to Oceanside. In the immediate Los Angeles region, Pasadena and other highland areas were clear, but from central Los Angeles to Long Beach, Santa Monica and the roadways leading up to Malibu and beyond, it hung, a heavy dark curtain enfolding cities, suburbs, roads, and the lower hillsides of the coastal mountains.

Jason had woken long before the sun was up. He was barely rested, having spent the night with a recurring dream that had dissipated into fragments, a dream about fleeing in a dark forest from unknown pursuers. Everywhere he turned there was another behind him, then another.

He remained amid the tossed sheets, eyes open. The pieces of the puzzle didn't come together. The statue. Martin's arrangement with Maybank. Galante, a third piece. But Galante wasn't connected to Martin or Maybank. Galante couldn't care less about them. Maybank had threatened his business, and he'd killed the man. Now he's sent people to get me.

He ran his fingers through his hair. Had he missed something? About Martin, perhaps? Martin would be desperate to stop me, but how far would he go? Murder? Could Martin do that?

He tried to get into the director's head. Martin would do a lot to protect himself, but deciding to go after him, deciding to have him killed, and then making it happen—each step involved a leap beyond the earlier one. It was beyond imagination. Could Martin really want kill a member of his own museum? It was ludicrous.

Maybank was another story. Maybank was ruthless, close to some of the roughest people in the business, runners who also carried drugs or guns, and if it suited them wouldn't hesitate to slit someone's throat. Or his own throat. Could Maybank do that? With Martin?

Maybank and Martin together? Maybe. But Maybank's dead. Galante did that. So that leaves Martin by himself, no Maybank to prop him up. And Martin's not a serious threat.

So, pay attention to Galante's men. Take away their reason for pursuing him. Let them know they can be attacked. And hurt. If Karel injured one badly enough, the other would pull out. That would end it, wouldn't it?

It was too simple. There was a piece missing from the puzzle, but every time he reached out to grasp it, it disappeared.

"Jason, get up." Kate was outside his door. She knocked again. "Get up! It's almost seven. We need to talk. Let's get breakfast. I'll see you at the hotel desk."

He showered and pulled on his clothes. They drove to a nearby diner and ordered.

A cool reserve had taken the place of her alarm of the day before. It may have been a trick of the light, but her eyes seemed darker, harder.

"Now tell me exactly what you want me to do. And what you're planning."

"*You're* not supposed to do anything. I've got to take care of this, get Martin into the open, and tear the covers off his plan for the statue. And I need to get the story of the acquisition out and visible, the one that leads back to Sicily and that's put Galante on my case. If I can do that, it won't make any sense for him to keep coming after me. He'd call off his men. These people are professionals. They operate on instructions. If they're told to end it, they'll end it. I want to get them into the open, flush them out and stop them from coming after us."

"How are you going to do that?"

"Karel. He'll tell me where they are. I'll run my car past their noses and lead them to the Gabriel. Get them inside the gates—into the garage or on the grounds, somewhere where they can be peeled off and Karel can get to them."

"He can do that?"

"He can. I've seen him at work."

His next words were spoken almost to himself. "That may be the best solution."

"What solution?"

"An accident—maybe something more, something really bloody like a killing on the museum grounds." He smiled to himself for a moment. "Now *that* would bring the police in pretty quick. Martin would have a hell of a job explaining it."

"You'd have these people killed? Like that? Are you serious?"

"No, I wasn't serious. I don't want them dead. I just want them out, gone."

A thoughtful look crossed Jason's face. "But Kate, these guys aren't innocents. They are very bad men. They've killed people before and they'll do it again. It's their job. It's what they do. They're here now, looking for us, and they'll get us unless they're pulled off somehow. If they can't be pulled off, or if they get too close to one of us, I'd have no hesitation in taking them down."

"And how are you going to do that?

"I'm not. Karel will. He'll need to mess with one of them, badly. Let them know they've been blown, force them to stop and pull out."

Her eyes had fastened on her hands for a moment, and then she looked up at him. "And you want me to go to work, is that it? You don't see a problem with my being in the museum?"

"I see problems everywhere, but once you're in the museum, you should be safe. These men aren't going to walk in and kidnap you at gunpoint. And when you leave at the end of the day, I'll be with you, or Karel will be directly behind you. So, go in. Have a normal day. Appear as though nothing's wrong. Martin won't bother you. I'll call him this morning and tell him it's time for us to meet. There'll be no need for him to ask you about me after that."

She fixed her eyes on his.

"Jason, do you have anything to protect yourself with? A gun, any kind of weapon?"

"No. I haven't carried one for more than ten years."

She thought for a moment.

"I don't like it. You're setting yourself up. If any damn thing goes wrong—"

"Look, I intend to be careful. But I have to do this. Today. It won't wait. We can't go on ducking and weaving around Los Angeles and not be able to go home and lead normal lives. Or go to work and do what we're supposed to do." A small smile appeared, no more than an upturn at the corners of his mouth. "Like bring the damned Athena matter to an end. And nail Martin."

"Do you have a plan for that?"

"I do." He took ten minutes to explain it to her and then watched her drive away toward the coast.

She's worried about Martin, he thought. She doesn't know him as well as she thought. But she can handle him. And in the museum, she'll be safe from the others, Galante's people.

The missing piece of the puzzle passed like a shadow across his consciousness, then disappeared.

Quinn and Rourke had had a bad night on hard beds and were short tempered. Quinn was particularly frustrated. The disappearance first of Connor, then Emerson, meant they'd have to stay through the weekend, maybe longer. Unless Connor went to see Emerson at her apartment. But the guy was running, so that was unlikely. Or unless she went back to the museum. Then they could have a friendly chat with her about Connor.

They'd be persuasive. The chats that Quinn had with people who didn't want to tell him things were always persuasive. And successful. Screw that Pryce guy, not wanting her hurt. How'd he think they'd find her boyfriend?

Rourke, for his part, now knew beyond any shadow of a doubt that Quinn was an asshole. He was not only a fat slob with crooked teeth who picked his nose, but he'd no idea about how to take out Connor. Or even find him. And now he was talking about going to the museum. To do what? Bounce the Emerson woman? Tear her ear off, get her to tell them where her boyfriend was? That fat idiot just made that up. Unfuckingbelievable.

Rourke hated confusion. Quinn was confused about what to do, and the more Rourke knew about the man, the less he liked. His company manager would not like it at all. He wondered whether he should call his manager but decided against it. The manager didn't like complainers. But maybe he should start thinking of an exit plan.

At ten o'clock, as the Gabriel's doors swung open, Rourke parked the SUV in the museum's garage. The two men went to the desk just inside the main door marked Information and Memberships.

"'Scuse me," Quinn said to the young man who stood behind the desk, "we're interested in what you do to take care of your things. You people must have, like, a big conservation department, don't you?"

"Oh, not too large, eight or nine people, I'd say."

"Here every day, are they?"

"Almost. Unless someone's sick or traveling."

"Today too?"

The young man examined them more closely. Strange question, he thought, particularly from someone who looked like a wrestler and spoke with an odd English accent. But then the Gabriel had visitors of every type.

"Yes, I'd imagine so. Do you work in conservation yourself? If so, I could call them and ask someone to talk to you." He tried to put a helpful look on his face.

"Nah, thanks, it's OK."

Quinn turned and was about to walk away, but Rourke lingered for a moment.

"D'you know the painter de La Tour? George, his name was. George de La Tour. French guy."

The young man brightened and gave an optimistic smile. "Yes, of course."

"D'you have anything he did? I mean, I think 'e was a relative. Way back, it was."

"No, I'm afraid not. But we've got some other Caravaggists on the third floor."

Rourke looked blank.

The young man blinked. "Uh, here, take this. It's a short guide to the museum. I'm sure you'll find a lot of things you'll like. I'm sorry we don't have any de La Tours though."

Quinn and Rourke went over to the museum's bookstore and started to browse through the shelves. It was going to be a long day.

The young woman behind the counter looked at the two men just as one of them, the bigger one with the unbelievably large hands, glanced at her.

She averted her glance and fastened it on the receipts she was holding, anything to avoid his eyes. She could feel the hair rise on the back of her neck. She shivered slightly, ran her hands over her arms to settle the goose bumps that had suddenly appeared, and pulled her sweater more tightly around her shoulders.

Who the hell are these people? Not the usual visitors. Looking, not buying. Idling.

She glanced at the register to make sure the drawer was closed.

Maybe they're waiting for a friend, she thought.

CHAPTER FIFTY-SEVEN

He picked up his cell phone, punched in the Gabriel museum's number, then added the extension for the director's office. Patricia answered.

"Jason! Where have you been? Martin's been looking for you everywhere."

"I'm sure. Could you put him on?"

"Of course, just a minute. I know he'll be glad to hear from you."

The curator felt his shoulder begin to itch again.

"Jason?" Pryce's voice had an undercurrent Jason could not identify. "Where are you? I understand you've been traveling. In Europe." Pryce's tone was without inflection.

"Yes. In Europe."

"You're back in town, then. But why haven't you come in to the museum? I'd like to hear about your trip."

"I had to clean up and put a few things in order. And get myself ready for our talk."

"Our talk?" Pryce repeated.

"Yes, the one we need to have. About the statue."

Pryce was still for a moment before he spoke again. "Well then, come see me."

But not right now, he thought. It's too early, too many people around. And I need to talk to this fellow Gleeson. Where the hell is he?

"Jason, I've got time in the later afternoon. Say, five thirty?"

The visitors would be gone. Most of the staff will have left. We can meet, and Jason would leave, and then Gleeson could take care of him, somewhere away from the Gabriel.

"Five thirty."

It was also exactly what Jason wanted. The museum would be almost emptied out at the end of the day. He'd be there a few minutes earlier to give Karel the time he needed.

He felt a small jolt of adrenaline. He'd be both bait and bait-setter. Bait for Galante's men. Bait-setter for Martin.

Pryce called Quinn seconds after the end of Jason's call,

"Gleeson, Connor's coming to the museum at five thirty. You'd better get out here."

"Ah, well, Mr. Pryce, we're already 'ere, in the building. See, we thought we'd wait for the woman to go home, or wherever she's staying. Have 'er lead us to our boy."

The ache in the director's stomach seemed to get worse. "You don't need to do that now. He'll be here at five thirty."

"We'll stick around then, OK, Mr. Pryce? Have ourselves a nice bit to eat. Take a stroll. Very pleasant it is, your museum, Mr. Pryce. Nice looking young figgers here, Mr. Pryce. And I'm not talking about them statues, am I?"

Pryce could hear a snicker on the telephone. He tried not to sound disgusted.

"Stay around and wait for him if you want, but I don't want anything happening in the museum. Or to Emerson. Not a thing! You can pick him up outside, wherever you want. But outside—just not here, inside my museum!" He started to put down the receiver, then put it back to his ear again.

"And an accident! Make it look like an accident!" But he was talking to a dead line.

Holy Christ! These men are about to kill Jason here? That's just nuts! That jackass Maybank sent these—these assholes—to kill Jason. What the hell have I done?

At that moment another wave of nausea washed over Pryce. He stumbled into the washroom and vomited again.

CHAPTER FIFTY-EIGHT

S ix hours.

He wanted to take his mind off his coming confrontation with Pryce and Galante's men. Disengage, step off the planet, he thought. A year earlier he would have called Rosa and suggested lunch somewhere in the hills or the new restaurant at MOCA. Not now. He drove slowly east on Sunset, then dropped down to Santa Monica until he reached Melrose and found a place to park.

Jason had not been to Melrose in more than a year. He had been taken there first by Rosa, the aging but still devastatingly attractive French-born actress he had been escorting at the time, a woman who had played female lead in numerous lesser thrillers of the sixties.

Rosa was full of upbeat charm and endlessly entertaining. For Rosa, Jason not only shared her bed but could also be dressed up—"tricked out" as she called it—in jacket and tie, and sometimes black tie, in a city whose residents seemed to pride themselves on the difference in the cut of their designer jeans.

Rosa was high return and low maintenance. She wanted to be amused—"Come on, Jhay-son, you know what women want—make me laugh!" She never asked for more than his company and occasional overnight attentions. She did not intrude. She did not ask to know his inner soul, and said she was not interested in that at all. She said she knew him well enough and did not demand more than he could give.

They had seen each other exclusively for the better part of two years. They had gone to dinner with each other and with others and enjoyed exploring the kitschier parts of Los Angeles, which meant a few areas around Santa Monica and Beverly Hills, and a lot of Melrose.

One evening at dinner, Rosa had taken him by the hand and told him that she adored him, but she'd met a man she wanted to pay more attention to, someone Jason knew was a film-industry titan whose wife had died a few years before. The man had occasionally appeared in Los Angeles' heated celebrity press, each time with another smiling young woman on his arm. He never seemed to be happy with any of them.

Rosa said she didn't know whether her new relationship would work out but wanted to give it a try. She really couldn't continue with Jason and her new friend at the same time, could she?

"I know you'll understand," she had said, "but can't we be friends? I mean, Jhay-son, real friends. And," she had gone on, "darling, I hope you won't mind coming home with me again tonight, you know, a last wonderful night together. You wouldn't mind that, would you?" He said he would not mind.

The memory of his two-year relationship with Rosa still resonated. It had been good for him and had left no wounds. It took him some time to realize that Rosa had done more. She had healed him.

Like Rosa, Melrose was different. It catered to a contemporary audience of younger people who were into left-of-center art, tattoos, clothes, and jewelry, including men's ear-wear. The streets were filled with boutiques and small shops sandwiched between more orthodox chain-store outlets, many of which opened for a few years then moved on in discouragement as the smaller privately owned businesses that could operate on a shoestring prospered.

He wandered through the smaller galleries with a sense of mild astonishment at some of the more bizarre art works that were being offered. From one, there was a faint scent of an incense he did not recognize, from another, the distant strain of an instrument that sounded like a sitar.

He looked at his watch. Three hours. His short diversion in Melrose had done exactly what he wanted.

On the way to his car, his cell phone rang.

"Jason." Benedict had probably just gotten up.

"Yes, what?"

"Your new best friends from Italy are in Santa Monica, but they're moving. Either to your place or Kate's or up to the museum. My guess is the museum. But I can't tell yet. I'll let you know before you get close to them."

"If they're going to the museum, they've got to take the coast road. They should pick me up there, somewhere."

"We'll work it out. But Jason, there's something I don't get."

"What's that?"

"Is there someone else who's interested in you? Not the Italians? Two other guys?"

CHAPTER FIFTY-NINE

Clemente and Olivieri were in a state of near rage. They had waited through the night for Kate Emerson to come home or for Jason to come to her apartment. Neither had appeared. At dawn, they had returned to Jason's house to find it as empty as they had the day before. They returned to the Casa del Mar, grim-faced, not speaking to each other, and went to their separate rooms.

Both men had awakened in an irritable mood. At breakfast, Clemente uttered the thought that had been bothering him since the previous night.

"What the fuck's going on here? This Connor guy is here somewhere, but he's running. So's his girlfriend. What're they running from? Us? How's he know we're here?"

Olivieri did not answer for a minute. He was still angry about having had to sit in the Lexus for the entire night with nothing to show for it. Finally he spoke.

"Screw up somewhere?" His tone was accusatory. This was supposed to be a simple job, something quick. Raymond had been clear about that, but the chicken was running, and Clemente didn't seem to have any good ideas. Olivieri had a few doubts about him, but Clemente was the job boss, and Olivieri knew he'd have to be careful. It wouldn't do to get Raymond upset.

"Maybe he heard about this Pisano guy you did in Rome, and about Maybank, and like, they've added up two and two?"

"It's not just that," Clemente shot back. "He's running, his girlfriend is running, and they're both ahead of us. It's almost as if they know where we are. I don't know what's going on, but I don't like it."

Olivieri sat, his mind going over the possibilities. He shrugged. Stupid idiot, he thought. He's the fucking boss. He looks good but doesn't have a clue what's going on.

"Why don't we find his girlfriend's car, you know, like, at the museum, then we follow her when she's leaving? Or pick her up on the road? She'll take us to the Connor guy. Just like you wanted." Olivieri made the suggestion sound tentative, wanting Clemente to take it rather than come up with some other idiot idea.

It was Clemente's turn to fall silent. The plan was too simple. It wasn't even a plan, he thought, but it had a dopey elegance. He kicked himself mentally for not thinking about it first, then looked at Olivieri and summoned up his false half-smile.

"OK, bright boy, we go to the museum. Then we find the car. And we pick her up outside, on the road. But I'll call the shots here. And you drive."

Olivieri shook his head. Fucking idiot. Not a clue.

At noon the two men went back to the museum for the second time. They located the staff section of the Gabriel's garage and found Kate Emerson's space, which held a very old maroon Volvo. Jason's space was vacant, but to make sure he hadn't come in, each man took one of the two garage floors and walked slowly along the aisles of parked cars trying to find his Taurus. They decided not to go into the main building again. Someone, the security guards

or maybe the woman they had spoken to in the antiquities department, would mark their second visit in two days, and they didn't
want to draw that kind of attention.

Still angry and speaking to each other in terse voices and only
when necessary, Clemente and Olivieri drove south along the coast
highway until they found what they wanted, a small restaurant next
to a stoplight that had a clear view of the road and easy egress
from the parking lot. They parked facing outward, took a window
table, ordered a late lunch, and waited, pointedly avoiding each
other's eyes and peering through the mist that swirled around the
road. Clemente put enough money on the table to pay their bill in
case they needed to leave quickly. They would wait for Emerson's
Volvo to appear and then get out fast and follow her to Connor, he
explained.

Olivieri's mood had turned foul.

"There's a fuckup going on, Clemente. You said it yourself. I
don't know what it is, but you're the bright guy here. If he's running and not from us, then from someone else, maybe. You said
you're calling the shots. So you figure it out."

Clemente looked darkly out the restaurant window, angry with
Olivieri for throwing the problem at him. He didn't have any better idea what to do than the one he'd come up with. Find the girlfriend and squeeze her. She'll let us know.

He had squeezed people before. They always let him know what
he wanted. Sometimes he let them go, afterward. Not this time, he
thought. When we do Connor, we'll do the woman too.

CHAPTER SIXTY

At two thirty, Jason called Benedict.
"Where are they now? The Italians?"

"They're stationary just east of Malibu. They may have decided to take a break. Or changed plans."

"What's your guess?"

"My guess is that they're a little crazy that they can't put their hands on you, they don't know why, and they've probably decided to work on Kate to force her to tell them where to find you. If they can get to her."

"Jesus, Karel, can we stop them right now?" Jason's voice was urgent.

"Yeah. But we're going to have to move fast."

"Jason, you know it means we have to get you in direct sight of these guys? Pretty close?"

"Yes. We've done this before."

"This is different. It's a damned made-up, improvised plan, and we don't have any intel on them at all, except what their car looks like and where they are. We've got no backup. In Cairo we had backup."

"Karel, we don't have a lot of choices. And we've got to move *now!*"

His call to Kate was short.

"Kate, don't leave the museum at all. For any reason. There are two men down the road waiting for you. If they can't get to me, they want you. They'll do anything to you to get at me. Stay there. I'm meeting Martin at five thirty. We can drive out together, at the same time. Karel will be with me, or close behind me when I come."

"Jesus, is this *thing* really going to end today?"

"It has to. I've got to get it all out of Martin, let him know he's finished, and make enough noise so that everyone can see what he's done. And Karel has to go to work on Galante's friends so they're blown. And hurt. They have to be stopped."

"Five thirty. That's hours from now."

"Yes, but I need to start sooner, get the attention of the men on the road, bring them into the museum. Or at least the museum grounds, where Karel can do his work."

On one of them at least. The other will want to get out of there as fast as he can.

He went up to Sunset quickly, then turned west, slowed to clear traffic on the curves, then added gas on the straightaway. Once he saw a distant blinking red-blue light in his mirror, but it had disappeared by the time he had reached Westwood and the loop around UCLA.

Two other men? Not the Italians? Who the hell are they? He worried at the problem but found no answer. Then it hit him then like a hammer.

Oh Christ. Maybank!

Maybank's dead. But he set something loose before he was killed. The men Karel saw last night must have been sent by Maybank.

The next thought made him sit up straight. Maybank wouldn't have done it unless Martin agreed.

He tried to call Kate again. There was no response.

She's in a meeting, he thought. The message he left was short.

"Stay away from Martin. He's decided to come after me. You too, if he can get to me through you. Do whatever you can to keep away from him. Whatever it takes."

At five o'clock the light, diffused by the fog that lay along the roadway, was beginning to fade. Clemente jumped up and grabbed Olivieri by the arm.

"Look! Connor's car! At the gas station. The other side of the road!"

The two men ran out the door and got in the Lexus. Olivieri turned on the engine and sat still, eyes riveted on the man on the other side of the road who seemed oblivious to their presence.

Jason finished at the pump, went to the station office, bought a Mars bar, walked back to his car, got in, and drove slowly away to the west.

"He's going to the museum," Clemente said. At last. Connor had come right into their arms.

Olivieri gunned the Lexus's engine and made a fast exit from the parking lot, skidding onto the coast highway between traffic and turning onto the westbound lane. He swerved around two other cars and a pickup. When he had positioned the Lexus three cars behind Jason, he slowed to pace the other traffic in his lane.

Half a mile behind the Lexus, the occupant of a dark maroon BMW watched the frantic departure of the two men from the restaurant. Karel Benedict quietly observed the play unfold in front of him and nudged a disk into the car player.

I've been around for a long, long year
Stole many a man's soul and faith
As heads is tails
Just call me Lucifer
Cause I'm in need of some restraint

The Stones, "Sympathy for the Devil." He put on the Stones when he wanted to get psyched up. It always worked.

When Benedict was certain the Lexus was on Jason's tail, he moved in behind it, lagging slightly to let traffic pass. He called Jason again.

"OK, man. You have what you want. It's showtime."

He turned up the volume and started to sing, accompanying Jagger at the top of his lungs.

So if you meet me
Have some courtesy
Have some sympathy and taste
Use all your well-learned politesse
Or I'll lay your soul to waste!

CHAPTER SIXTY-ONE

At twenty minutes to five the Gabriel slowly began to close. Beginning with the galleries on the third floor, the guards shepherded the last of the day's visitors downstairs, toward the museum's entrance doors. The information booth and bookstore next to the museum entrance were shuttered, the restaurant and coffee shop doors closed and locked. When the last visitor had exited, the museum's great bronze front doors were swung shut. The circuit breakers that controlled the main lights in the galleries and courtyard were turned off.

With the front doors closed, there were only two remaining entries to the museum. One was on the main building's western side, which could be used by departing staff and by the museum's four housekeepers who cleaned the washrooms and swept the floors in the early morning. The other was a rear entry that gave staff working late in the Gabriel's outer buildings access to the main building. Both doors were locked but could be opened with a security card until six. After six, entry to the building was only permitted with the assistance of a security guard.

The last visitor exited the building at two minutes to five. The underground parking area had nearly emptied out. Dark began to settle over the museum grounds.

Patricia Waller was preparing to leave. Jason was expected in half an hour, but Martin never asked the Gabriel's support staff to stay late. The director would normally stay in his office half an hour or more after the museum had closed to visitors, finishing up paperwork or making end-of-day telephone calls.

She had just turned off her desktop computer when Pryce buzzed from inside his office.

"Patricia, tell whoever's at the front gate I'm expecting Jason. I'd like them to let me know the moment he arrives."

Odd, she thought, no "please." He always says please. Something's bothering him. And he's looked awful since he saw those two men. She wondered for a moment whether she should wait until Jason appeared but decided against it. Martin didn't need her assistance at meetings with staff. She put her head inside his office.

"Dr. Pryce, Valdez is at the gate this evening. He'll call you as soon as Jason's arrived."

"Good, thank you. That will be all, Patricia."

That's quite a dismissal, she thought. Wants me to clear out. Wonder what he's so anxious about? Jason. No, that couldn't be it. Those two men. But they've gone.

With a mounting sense of anticipation, Jason turned into the Gabriel's entry drive. Instead of waving to the gate guard and driving in as he usually did, he stopped and rolled down his window.

"Hugo, there are a couple of people who want to see me—one or maybe two cars behind me. Please just let them through."

"Sure, Dr. Connor, no problem." It was unusual for anyone to come into the museum so late in the day, but curators ran by their own rules. And if Dr. Connor wanted him to let other visitors in also, that was fine with him.

As Jason headed up the main drive, Valdez carefully noted in his log that Jason had passed through the gate at five-twenty. He looked up to see the headlights of another vehicle coming into the Gabriel's driveway.

Quinn's cell phone rang. It was Pryce.

"He's here. Just coming up the driveway. Remember, I don't want this inside the museum. Outside. You have to do it outside!"

Stupid prick, Quinn thought. He turned to Rourke.

"He's here. You drive. And move it, Rourke. Just swipe the fuck-er. Then stop. I'll fix him."

Rourke started the engine and drove out of the garage, the wheels throwing gravel as he turned away from the museum. He pointed the nose of the big SUV down the driveway.

Rourke knew what he had to do. Block Connor's car, force it to the side of the driveway. Quinn would get out and shoot him through his window, twice, maybe three times, make certain of him. Then they'd drive quietly to the coast road and disappear into the traffic. They'd get their tickets at the airport and be on their way home that evening.

Rocking slightly, the SUV accelerated downhill.

Jason rounded the first bend in the drive toward the museum en-trance and saw the headlights of a car coming directly toward him, fast. He pulled toward the right side of the roadway to allow the ve-hicle to pass, but the other car fishtailed in front of him, following his move. He turned further to the right, then pulled the wheel sharply to the left.

What the fuck are they doing?

In the instant before the collision, he saw two occupants in the other vehicle.

Jesus God, he thought. The others. Maybank's men. Martin's brought them right into the museum!

He swerved hard to the left, no longer trying to avoid a collision, only trying to put his passenger side toward the other car.

The impact was hard. It threw his upper body to the right and snapped his head to the left side. A sharp ear-splitting sound filled his senses. The Taurus came to a jarring stop, shuddered, and the engine died.

Jason sat in his seat, stunned. Through a haze, he watched the occupants of the other car reaching for their doors to get out. He turned and saw the collision had torn his right door off its hinges and bent the right side deeply inward.

The front end of the other car was crushed, its hood crumpled, front window broken, and side mirrors bent. The two men inside had begun throwing themselves violently against their doors in an effort to open them. The one in the passenger seat seemed to be shouting at the driver.

There was a drumming inside his head. *Out, get out, get out, now, Jason, get out!*

He came to full consciousness, pushed open the driver's door, forced one leg, then the other, out of the Taurus and staggered onto the roadway. He turned and saw the headlights of a second car coming up the drive. In the distance, behind the trees, the lights of a third vehicle were approaching.

He crossed the driveway and ran for his life.

CHAPTER SIXTY-TWO

Clemente downshifted and gunned the Lexus up the Gabriel's driveway, braking abruptly as he came to the smoking wreck in the middle of the road. He saw Jason's Taurus slewed to the left with its far side shattered, headlights shining into the fog toward a line of royal palms. Just beyond was a shattered SUV, its front end crushed, raining fluid down onto the pavement. Inside, two men were hammering on the doors. The lights of the two vehicles illuminated the scene with a bright, suffused radiance.

Olivieri saw a figure disappearing into the tree line to his right. "Stop the damn car, Clemente! That's Connor!"

Clemente reversed and spun the Lexus to his left, bringing it to a halt at the side of the road, facing downhill. Olivieri grabbed his door handle and pushed himself out the passenger side, came to his feet and started toward the trees. Behind him the lights of another car appeared, coming up the drive.

Fast, this has to be fast, he thought. Five minutes, ten, no more, then get out of here. He turned and shouted.

"*Come on! Go, Clemente!* That's Connor! At the trees!"

"Rourke, you're going to hit the goddamned car!"

Quinn thrust his hands out to brace himself but was catapulted forward when the SUV came to a sudden stop. The car's airbag deployed, bouncing his forehead onto the side door. Dazed by the impact and blinded by the headlights of the other car, he pushed at the airbag and brought his head up slowly, turning it to either side. His upper lip and chin felt wet, and blood was spilling from his nose. He wiped his jacket sleeve across his face and looked up to see Jason throw his door open and run toward the ravine wall.

"Shit, Rourke, Connor's getting away!"

Dimly, Quinn heard the sound of another vehicle but ignored it. His only thought was to get out of the SUV. He reached for the handle and tried to push his door open, but it gave way only an inch and then stuck. Desperate, he leaned back on Rourke, lifted his right leg and kicked. The door gave way entirely, spilling him onto the roadway. As he came to his knees, blood dripping from his face, the smell of gasoline filled his nose and he saw a small pool of liquid widening rapidly beneath the car.

Rourke stumbled out of the driver's side, rounded the rear of the vehicle and pulled Quinn to his feet. "Move it, Quinn. Over there!"

Quinn staggered up, wiped his hand across his face again, and began to run in the direction Rourke had pointed. He caught up with Rourke, grabbing the younger man by the arm.

"What's back there?"

"Another car. Not our business."

Quinn uttered an obscenity under his breath and ran on into the mist. Rourke tried to follow, but Quinn had already disappeared behind the first row of palms.

Fast, thought Rourke. Big, old, and stupid, but fast. He followed up the hillside, stumbled once, and moved forward again, cursing.

This is wrong, too complicated, he thought. Too many people, too much chance of a screw-up. And this fucking Quinn slob. How the hell do I get out of this thing?

Jason sprang toward the tree line and the slope behind. He was fleeing for his life from four attackers. Not just Galante's men but now also the two others Maybank and Martin had set on him. Neat trick, he thought. Just stay ahead of four killers. How the hell am I going to do that?

He was on familiar ground and in good physical condition. And Karel was somewhere back there in the fog and dark, behind the men who were after him. He just needed to stay away from them long enough to allow Karel to make his move.

Steady down, Jason. Stay cool. Think. You know this place a lot better than they do.

He ran. He ran behind the line of palms, then between two large agave bushes, avoiding the spines, and then through more vegetation and began to climb the lower slope of the ravine. The scrape of his feet on dirt and his breathing seemed very loud.

Where are they? Stop, now. Use your ears. Use your head. This isn't one of the training games they gave you at the Farm. This is for real.

He paused to listen. He thought he could hear voices behind him, but when he halted, there was only silence. He started to climb again, toward the pathway that circuited the Gabriel's south garden. From there he would try to lose himself along one of the side paths that branched off the main pathway.

Come on, go, get ahead of these people. But go where?

In the dark behind him, shadows moved up the slope. Olivieri, a trained hunter, ran with the easy long-legged gait of a distance runner, Clemente close behind, held back by his flared pants, which caught occasionally in the underbrush. They stopped and listened and then ran again. Their quarry had gone somewhere upward. There was a faint noise in the darkness ahead, then another, and then the sound of movement on the hillside behind them.

Shit, thought Clemente. Who's that? Museum guards? Do we have to deal with them too? He hated guards of any kind. Six years earlier, he had come out of a cold prison north of Cremona with a visceral hatred of prison guards, a loathing that gripped his stomach whenever he saw a security person anywhere.

The slope increased and the two men slowed, avoiding the fronds of a thicket of palmettos. Clemente came up to Olivieri and put his mouth close to the younger man's ear.

"Ten minutes. You go left up the hill. I'll go right. Be back at the car in ten minutes. No more. Let's get this done and go!"

The two men separated.

Idiot, Olivieri thought. It's gone bad. Time to end the job and get out.

Quinn staggered and swore silently. His nose was still bleeding. He was winded, and the Beretta dug into his side. He had stumbled into one of the garden pools, his feet sinking into the deep muck at the bottom, and now his pants were wet above the knee and smelled of rotting vegetation. Rourke had passed him in the darkness and was now running on, somewhere ahead.

I'm not supposed to do the goddamn chasing, he thought. I'm supposed to shoot the guy in his car, not run around in this fucking dark. If we don't get Connor in five minutes we're out of here!

Quinn's shout was a sound of sheer agony. The needle end of an agave plant had sliced his pants and driven deeply into his right leg. He felt his ankle give way as he fell.

Rourke came out of the mist, looked at Quinn, and gave a disgusted snort.

"Quinn, shut the fuck up. You're making too much *fucking noise*! And Jesus, man, do you stink. You're a fucking disaster."

Quinn's breath was rasping, coming in short gasps. The Beretta made a sharp ache against his side, his pants were torn and wet, and he could feel blood running down his face and leg. The pain in his ankle was excruciating. They were on a pathway at the top of the lower ravine wall. It forked, one branch running uphill to the left, the other to the right and down.

It was Quinn's turn to tell Rourke to shut up. He put his finger on his watch, then held up his right hand, palm out with his fingers outspread, then pointed down the hill they had come up and pushed his outstretched palms together then apart, as a gate might close and open.

The gesture was unmistakable. Five minutes. Be at the gatehouse in five minutes.

He motioned Rourke to go left, then pointed to himself and toward his right. He watched Rourke disappear in the mist, wiped his hand against his face, then wiped it against his jacket, and hobbled down the pathway that circled the gardens to the south, grunting slightly with each painful step. He was out of breath, and the Beretta dug further into his side as he half-ran, half-walked along the barely visible track. He took the pistol out of his belt and clutched it in his right hand. He was tired and wet and smelled like rotting garbage. The image of Connor, somewhere nearby, laughing, taunted him.

Shit, he thought. This whole fucking thing's going to hell.

The SUV caught fire at that moment. There was a loud thump as gasoline fumes mixed with air beneath the hood and were ignited by the hot engine. The hood flew off in a high arc as flames engulfed the car and lit up the night.

Jason stopped and looked back from the pathway. All he could see was a bright, pulsing glow that permeated the fog and illuminated the bushes around him. He retreated into the deep vegetation at the side of the garden and began to run again.

He came to a clearing and sprinted across it, then stopped, sucking air into his lungs. He probed his memory of the garden to find some exit that would not take him directly into the hands of his pursuers. He saw the vague outline of a bench and knew he was close to the garden's high overlook.

He hesitated, turned toward the underbrush, stopping against the great Montezuma cypress that had marked the place for more than thirty years. Behind him the glow from the burning cars cast an unearthly light through the mist.

Shadows flickered. A figure appeared, staggering slightly, his left hand wiping his face, head turning from side to side as he moved in Jason's direction.

The man held a pistol with a long silencer in his left hand, pointing it ahead of him as he moved forward. Jason wanted to run again but instead drew back against the trunk of the tree. If the fog and night made it difficult for him to see a backlit figure, it would be even more difficult for him to be seen. Stay still, don't move. He leaned further back into the protecting darkness of the tree's lower branches.

The figure slowed and stood for a moment, peering over the precipice and into the night. Suddenly it turned toward the cypress and pointed the weapon in Jason's direction.

A shadow emerged from the dark. It stepped forward, reached up with both hands, clamped them on the standing man's head, and then twisted sharply. There was a noise that sounded like the muffled snapping of a branch, and the larger figure collapsed on the ground.

"Fucking guard," the second man said, then turned his head to face Jason directly.

There was a whisper of noise, like a loud puff of air and the muted thump of a hollow-point bullet striking flesh. The standing figure jerked once, then collapsed to his knees and fell face forward to the earth.

The unmistakable shape of Karel Benedict emerged from the mist. He stood for a moment looking at the two bodies that lay before him, then moved the muzzle of his pistol and finished off the second with a shot to the head. He turned to the pool of dark beneath the tree where Jason stood.

"Jason, go to the museum. There are two others still out here somewhere. I'll take care of them. But you get out of the way."

"We should do this together, Karel."

"No. This is my game, not yours. You'd screw me up. Now go." Benedict turned and disappeared up the pathway, a shadow that melted into the dark.

Rourke had just ended his search along the pathway that circled the northern ridge but had found nothing. When he heard the explosion and saw the yellow light of the car fires through the mist, he turned back and picked his way down the hillside toward the burning vehicles and the gatehouse.

Fucking idiot Quinn! The Man will go stark staring nuts when he hears what we've got ourselves into. Time for me to go. Asshole Quinn can take care of himself.

Rourke tried to still his rage at his partner and his disgust at the botched job. He came to the high palms that lined the drive and turned downward toward the museum's gate when he saw the Lexus, nose pointed in the direction of the exit. A man, barely visible, stood by the car.

Not Connor. Who's this one?

He pulled the Beretta out of his belt and felt the silencer with his other hand to be sure it was fastened securely. He slowed and then moved forward.

Olivieri had returned to the car moments before. His thoughts about Clemente were exactly the same as those Rourke had about Quinn. Nice clean job, he said to himself. What a fucking idiot. Not a clue. If he doesn't appear in three minutes, I'm gone. Raymond will shit when I tell him about it.

Olivieri heard the scrape of a shoe and spun around to see the muzzle of a silencer pointed at his nose.

Rourke's question was a whisper. "Who the fuck are you?"

"Doesn't matter. Who are you?"

The question went unanswered.

"*Who are you?*" Rourke repeated, now insistently.

"Doesn't matter." Helpless, hands by his side, Olivieri waited for the shot that would end his life.

A long five seconds went by. Rourke spoke again.

"I've seen you before."

"Not likely.

"Chicago? You from Chicago?"

"Yes."

"We've met. Four years ago." Rourke looked at the Lexus and then at Olivieri.

"You got the keys?"

"In the car."

"You drive then. Lets get the hell out of here."

Karel Benedict emerged from the tree line and watched the Lexus disappear down the roadway, walked to his BMW, turned it, and started toward the Gabriel's gate. When he reached the coast highway he began humming to himself, a small smile on his face.

I'm finished here, he thought. There's no one else to deal with. Jason should be all right now.

CHAPTER SIXTY-THREE

The shriek of tearing metal in the entrance driveway caused Pryce to jump in his chair. He went to his window but could see nothing through the darkening fog that swirled outside.

Jason. It must be Jason coming up the drive! And those two men—could they have hit Jason's car? Could they all be dead? The thought that at a single instant all his tormentors might be done away with at a single stroke filled him with an unreasoning sense of relief.

He started out of his office toward the museum's rear entry when his telephone rang.

"Dr. Pryce. It's Hugo—Hugo Valdez, at the front gate. There's been an accident. In the driveway. About halfway up. I can't see it from here."

"I heard it. Call the security office. Get someone there. And tell them to report to me right away."

There's been a screw-up! If those men were involved, would they kill Jason? But if their car was wrecked, how would they do that and then get out? And if Jason wasn't hurt, what would he do?

He'd come here, to see me. But the others would want to get out, wouldn't they? *Christ*, he thought, his mind tumbling in confusion.

Pryce went to his doorway and peered out into the courtyard. Two museum guards had come crashing down the stairs from one of the upper floors and were running along the portico toward the rear entry. The safety lights high in the corners of the courtyard illuminated the building's interior, but the galleries were dark.

He turned back into his office, unlocked a bottom drawer of his desk, his hand groping, finally finding the Smith & Wesson .38 that he'd bought years ago with the thought of joining a gun club for recreation. But he had never followed up with the club, and when Frances had made a scene and declared she would have no firearms in her house, at all, he took the weapon into the museum and locked it away. It was cold weight in his hand, heavier than he remembered.

I can protect myself against a thief, can't I? I can shoot an intruder in the dark, when the guards aren't here. That would work, wouldn't it? How could I have known who it was?

The idea was barely credible, but he could think of nothing else. It had to serve, and serve right now. The museum guards were outside in the driveway but would be back in moments.

He reached deeper into the drawer and found the small box of ammunition. His hand trembled as he held the pistol and opened the cylinder and fed the cartridges one at a time into the chambers. He shut the loaded cylinder and went out into the darkened portico and stood, holding the gun to his side.

I don't have to look for him. He'll come to me.

And then what? Then what?

Chest heaving, Jason reached the museum's rear entry. He passed his badge across the door's magnetic reader and heard the bolt withdraw. The only other sound was that of voices yelling outside the museum, somewhere on the upper driveway. He could see no one.

Where are the guards? There should be at least two guards in the building. But where are they?

He walked slowly into the court and started past the fountain toward Pryce's office on the other side. He stopped when he saw a figure outside the director's door, standing still, hands low by his side.

Martin. No one else. No guards.

A memory struck him, of another time and place when he had been sent to pick up a man who had documents the station badly wanted. They had been told the man had been vetted, and he appeared where he had agreed, late at night on an empty street. He had circled, then saw a second figure in deep shadow at the corner with something held low in his hand, and he had driven past without stopping. The contact had been bait. The trap had not sprung. It was the closest moment Jason had ever come to death, until now.

He stepped backward and spun, looking for something, anything, to put between himself and Pryce. He turned into the rear vestibule and reached for the door.

It was locked. He reached for his badge again, heard a noise behind him and turned again. Martin Pryce stood ten feet away, the muzzle of the .38 leveled directly at the bridge of Jason's nose.

Afterward, Jason would say that he had frozen in his steps and that his mind had gone blank. But it was his own voice that spoke, as if from a great distance.

"Can you really do it, Martin? Can you really just shoot me?"

"Why shouldn't I? What choice do I have?"

It was unearthly still inside the courtyard. Outside, far away, voices called to each other.

Jason saw someone he had never seen before. Not the museum director. An uncertain, utterly frightened man. Terrified about where he is, terrified of what he's about to do.

His heart thumped in his chest. Is there a way out for him? Can I find it in time? Talk to him. Get him talking to you.

"I don't think you want to kill me, Martin. That's someone else's idea, not yours."

Far inside the building there was a dull thud and the hum of an elevator. Pryce's eyes flickered but held steady on Jason. The muzzle of the pistol remained pointed at his face.

"Who's then, if not mine?"

He doesn't want absolution. He wants—what does he want?

"Martin, this isn't you. This is Maybank. Maybank has pushed you into this. I don't think you wanted to go here at all."

"And if you were me, Jason, what would you do? Now? Why wouldn't you want to end it? Which of us should be left?" The words came out almost as a whisper.

End it? He's that deep? If he doesn't kill me, he kills himself? Or both of us? Is that what he's saying?

Keep him talking. Show him a way out.

"Martin, think about it. You can still walk away from it."

"Walk away." It was the only response, two repeated words that said nothing. Pryce's face was expressionless.

"For God's sake, Martin, *think about it*. Who the hell is going to know but us? Maybank's dead. He's sent people to get rid of me, but one of them was killed in the gardens and the other's gone. And whatever it was you thought you wanted to do, you haven't done it yet. Who's to know?"

Across the courtyard an elevator door opened. Footsteps echoed.

"Walk away, Jason? Can I really do that? Can you give it up? Can *you* let go?"

Searching. He's searching for a way out of this mess. Pleading.

He let out a slow breath of air. When he drew it in again, the pungent, sweet smell of eucalyptus flooded his senses.

Give it up, Jason. Let him go. Just let him go.

"I can. I will. And you can walk away. Go somewhere else, do something else. Live somewhere else."

On the far side of the courtyard a figure materialized and came toward them.

"Who's to know about it? Everyone's gone. Except you and me. We both can walk away from it."

He breathed in again. "You can. I can."

The pistol slowly fell to Pryce's side.

Kate stopped when she saw them.

"Jason," she said, the words a hoarse whisper. "Jesus, Jason. The gun. Martin's got a gun."

He turned.

"Everything's fine, Kate. It's OK. The guards were gone. Martin thought there might be an intruder.

"It's all right now. Isn't it, Martin?"

CHAPTER SIXTY-FOUR

I n time, the echoes of the event quieted, and the many intrusions
of the police and the FBI came to an end. Giuliano Clemente's
fingerprints were on file with the Italian police, so the FBI was
able to identify his body, but they'd had no success whatever in
identifying the second.

The Bureau and the Justice Department's narcotics people
asked themselves if the killings had taken place over drugs, but
they could find nothing on the two bodies or in the SUV, and it
was not clear why an Italian, even someone with Clemente's record,
should be involved in what was normally an exclusively Mexican
business. They wondered whether they were seeing the emergence
of a new distribution network. In time, a junior agent was instructed to open a new file.

No one could explain why the killings had taken place inside
the museum grounds. After a round of interviews, the police
concluded there was no connection to the museum itself. When
she was shown photographs of the two men who had been killed,
Cynthia Greenwalt said the one they identified as Clemente had

asked about the museum's interest in Roman antiquities and that there was someone with him, but she really didn't remember what he looked like.

The police and FBI thought it very strange that the young man who had been on duty at the information booth the day of the killings and a still very upset female bookstore clerk said they recalled the big, ugly man whose neck had been broken. He had a funny accent, they said, Cockney or something else. Martin Pryce provided a clue when he helpfully came forward and said the same man and his companion had demanded to see him that very day.

"Called himself Gleeson, I think. Brutish type. He wanted to know about some Italians who might be in the museum. Had an odd English accent. Maybe he was an Italian who grew up in London? Anyway, I had no idea what he was talking about and of course I threw him out of my office, along with the other one."

As for Jason, he had seen almost nothing. His car had been hit, and he had been in a daze, he said. He saw two men trying to get out of the dark SUV, but they had bolted into the darkness. He said there was a car behind him, and it might have been a friend, Karel Benedict, who was to visit him that evening. But Benedict was a somewhat timid person, Jason said, and tended to get rattled easily. He must have turned around and left when he saw the fire. He wished he had further details that could help, he said, but it had been hard enough for him to struggle into the museum, and he was fortunate that Martin Pryce had taken such good care of him. A fourth car? Yes, he had seen the lights of another car further back but didn't have a clear recollection of what it was or how many people may have been in it. He was shocked that a shooting had taken place in the museum gardens, just outside his own galleries.

It was a puzzle no one could solve. Eventually the police visits stopped and the museum's staff went back to the business of museum staffs everywhere, thinking more of the work that needed to be done and less of a drama that faded into memory with every day that passed.

Martin Pryce quietly told Andrew Gabriel that he intended to resign as director, effective at the end of the month. It seemed sudden, he said, but his doctor had expressed the deepest concern about his reaction to an unceasing accumulation of stress. In any case, he said, he wanted to spend more time with his family.

It was regrettable, but everyone seemed to understand.

"Poor Martin," a distraught Patricia Waller said. "I never realized he was so stressed out."

"Poor Martin," Gabriel said, in the privacy of a second-floor room at Café Torino one evening, a week after the board meeting. "I've come to depend on you for your advice. We'll miss you." Gabriel had given the director an odd smile and said he would get a generous severance package, one that would allow him to live almost anywhere.

"But what will I do for a director now? Who could I possibly get who has the initiative and vision to guide it in the future?"

Pryce looked at the old man and said simply, "Jason."

"Jason? I thought you wanted to get rid of him."

"I was wrong. Jason recognized the Athena as a problem long before I did. He was suspicious of the documents, and he was right. I was going to send him to Morgantina and London to find out more, but he anticipated me, and he did everything he could to protect the museum. He understands the place thoroughly, Andrew. He's a lot better than I thought, and I shouldn't have doubted him."

"Martin, I've never heard you say such nice things about anyone."

"I can this time. And, I'd add, Andrew, he has something you can't just go out and hire. He's not intimidated easily. Maybe not at all."

The old man remembered the moment when, over dinner, Jason had interviewed *him*, and nodded his head.

331

CHAPTER SIXTY-FIVE

Jason celebrated Christmas weekend in New York with Angela and Harry, who had succumbed long before to his wife's insistence on exchanging presents as long as he didn't have to attend a church service and listen to songs he'd never learned as a child. It was a riotous, noisy time that refreshed and exhausted him. He was glad to return to his house in the Palisades and put himself in order again, and the long flight home had given him time to reflect on the suddenness of events of the past month. The sense of Kate was still with him, and it would not let go. A few days before New Year's, a Monday, he went looking for her in the galleries and found her by herself.

"Ojai," he said.

Her reply was immediate. "Innsbruck."

"Ojai."

"No, Jason, you mean something with a K."

"I meant Ojai. What are you doing this weekend?"

She gave him a long, measuring look.

"Something. Not much. What are you talking about?"

"I thought we could go up to Ojai and stay, you know, at some nice place, ride horses. Talk a bit. Separate rooms," he added needlessly, but he had to say it.

"Ride horses. I did that once. I don't know if I can do it again. I may not be ready for it."

He caught her meaning and gave a slow smile, watching her eyes. "You could try. You won't know unless you do."

"Ah. I don't know. I may not be ready."

Who was the barrier for? Him? Her? "I'm patient."

"Oh, come on, Jason, you've never been patient. But you are persuasive."

So they drove up the coast to Ventura and then beyond to Ojai and took separate rooms at a small lodge niched into a side valley and visited a nearby vineyard and rode horses and talked, about friends and travel and books. They avoided speaking about the events at the Gabriel until they were resting their horses in a meadow. It was Kate, of course, who brought it up.

"So, why did you really do it, Jason? Requital? Payback with Martin? Something else?"

He turned in his saddle and looked back at her. "Not knowing, I think. I hate not knowing. The pieces didn't fit. I had to find out." Then, almost under his breath, "For lust of knowing."

"Flecker. That's James Flecker."

Again he was surprised. "You know him?"

"I do," she said, and drew the words from memory.

We travel not for trafficking alone;
By hotter winds our fiery hearts are fanned;
For lust of knowing what should not be known
We take the Golden Road to Samarkand.

Her dark eyes shone. "It's you, Jason."

On their last evening they had risen from the dinner table and gone out into the dark, their warm breath condensing as it mixed with the winter air. She turned to him, a shadow in her eyes.

"So, it's done, then? It's over, isn't it? There's no unraveled end to this, is there? There's nothing else?"

"You want more of it?

"Jesus, no. No more of that. But you know, I've never felt so— alive. When we were running."

"The chase?"

"Yes, that." But she seemed to be saying something else.

His eyes turned away and came back to her. The breath caught in her throat when he touched her hand lightly. "You know, we don't have to go back."

"Back? Back where?"

"Where we were. Sleepwalking. I think I've just woken up. That is, I've just woken up about you."

His touch was a caress that she did not want to stop. His glance dropped to her mouth for a moment and then went back to her eyes. She said nothing, searching his face.

"When I came back from Rome, I told you I missed you. But there's more. I mean—"

She raised her hand and put her finger to his mouth. "Jason, enough. You don't need to explain. Not now. I know what you mean. Be quiet, please, and kiss me."

He did, and held her, his hands high on her back, then at her waist, bold and gentle as he pulled her toward him, feeling her lips open slightly to let the tip of his tongue caress hers, the gentle thrust of her breasts against his chest.

"My room," he said softly. "It's nearer."

When the door was closed behind them, they kissed again in the dark, this time with an unexpected urgency, their hands tugging at each other's clothing until the buttons and zippers were undone and their clothes fell in chaos on the floor and the bed-clothes were pulled away and they were in each other's arms.

Much later, hours later, when they were quiet again and she had her head on his chest, she reached up and held his earlobe for a moment and smiled, then ran the fingers of her hand across the small scar that ran across his eyebrow.

"Is that really from an accident, Jason? I mean you can tell me now, you know."

"Um. I could tell you, but—"

"Oh, for God's sake, don't say it—don't say it!" And quite suddenly they both started laughing and kept on until they could no longer laugh at all, and slept, she on her side with his arm around her and his hand in hers.

CHAPTER SIXTY-SIX

Tuesday morning as they were leaving, she turned to him and said she would like to drive.

"May I?"

"Well, yes," he said, hesitating. "She's a little temperamental, but she holds the road nicely. See if you can take her to thirty-three hundred on the straight run when you get to the coast. You'll like the sound." And with his head back and eyes closed and with the satisfying roar of the Jaguar's engine in his ears, she drove him back, downshifting as the traffic built up around Malibu, then accelerating beyond until they reached Sunset. He opened his eyes once to glance in the mirror, but there was nothing, no blinking lights. And no surreptitious tail. That was all in the past.

At the entrance to her driveway, they got out of the car and held each other for a moment.

"Do we need to talk?" It was his question.

"I don't think so. Not yet. Let's let this go where it wants to go." She gave him an impish grin. "And have fun. You know, this is going to be fun, Jason. I can't wait. Give me a call when you'd like dinner."

"What makes you think I'd like dinner?"

She laughed. "Oh, go away. I'll see you at the museum."

She went inside, unpacked and changed into her museum clothes. At her bedroom dressing table, she picked up the photograph she had placed there years before. Hesitating, she slowly ran the fingers of her hand across the face of the man who looked out at her. She smiled and held it to her chest for a moment and then took it and placed it gently in the bottom drawer. She was at the Gabriel half an hour later.

When Jason opened the door to his house, the telephone was ringing. A writer for the *Times* was on the line, wanting to know if he could say something about his new appointment.

"New what?"

"Appointment. As director of the Gabriel. Can you say something?"

He put the receiver down and called Cynthia. "What the hell's this director stuff?"

"Jason, I don't know, no one tells me anything. I've been getting a lot of calls too. I'm sort of alone out here. Perhaps you'd better come in."

The next call was from Elspeth Clark.

"Dr. Connor, Mr. Gabriel wants you to meet him at the museum."

And so on the late afternoon of an early January day, Jason mounted the museum's front steps, walked rapidly past the Gabriel's bronze doors, and found himself confronted by a sea of faces.

Every member of the Gabriel's staff—curators, security guards, preparators, conservators in their white coats, bookstore attendants, docents—stood in the central courtyard, museum visitors mingling among them. As he stepped inside, voices stopped, heads turned, and for a brief moment a deafening silence descended in the afternoon air. Then there was a noise from behind, a clap, then others, and the applause swelled and echoed and continued on and on.

In time, the tumult subsided. The crowd parted and a short figure with white hair and startlingly blue eyes, wearing his signature bowtie, emerged and walked haltingly toward him.

Andrew Gabriel stood and folded both hands on his cane. He looked up at the curator.

"Jason," he said. "Jason, I hope you'll say yes."

It was pure Gabriel. Simple, theatrical, and, Jason knew, from the heart.

Later, after he had shaken a hundred hands and the crowd had dispersed, the old man gave him a long look and asked the question he knew was coming.

"We have to send it back, don't we?"

"Yes."

"Damn." It was a surprise. Gabriel rarely swore. "And what will they do with it?"

"Put it in the local museum, I'd guess."

"And can the local museum handle it? Show it? Take care of it?" Gabriel was asking the same questions Jason had asked himself.

"The museum's small, Andrew. I drove past it when I left Aidone in December. It's not built for something as large as the Athena."

The old man thought for a moment, then turned back to his new director with a smile on his face.

"Well then. Let's do something for them. And let's go to Morgantina. After all this, I want to see the place!"

CHAPTER SIXTY-SEVEN

Now, on a late summer morning, Jason found himself once again at the ancient site on the hill. This time there was no fog. The *Serra* was bathed in sunlight. The wheat fields to the side of the Aidone road had turned a golden yellow, and the orchards were filled with ripening olive trees that would be ready to harvest in a few months. The pomegranate trees between the fields had grown lush that year, and their fruit had already been picked. The rain of the night before gave the earth a fresh smell. High over the *Citadella*, a lone hawk circled lazily.

An expectant crowd filled the entrance to the excavations. Men in white shirts and dark trousers spoke in small groups, women in black dresses stood separately in conversation, children chased each other in a nearby field, dogs barked. Just inside the fence, there was a row of chairs in front a small podium. To the side a large block of stone, dark stone from Morgantina's hillside, rested on the earth. A short distance away a new shed, fenced and locked, covered the great statue that lay within.

The chairs were filled. On one side sat Aidone's mayor, next to him the governor of Enna and an official from Rome, then the senior priests from the town churches, and the director of the town's small museum, a small, wan man with glasses and the demeanor of an undertaker. The foreign visitors were there too. Andrew Gabriel sat with a wide smile, with Jason and Kate on one side and Gerhard Ettinger on the other. A young woman from the American consulate in Palermo fidgeted nervously in her seat at the end of the row, striving to understand the local dialect. A band played Sicilian themes, mostly on key.

At the rear of the assembled crowd, the family and friends of Cosimo Galante looked on—Galante, once *capo* for all of Morgantina, now dead, killed in an exchange of gunfire with the Carabinieri, who wanted to talk to him after they had discovered a decomposing corpse deep in the earth. A short man with strong, dark features, a younger version of Galante, stood silent and watchful on the outside of the crowd.

There were speeches. The mayor stood and introduced the governor, whose welcoming remarks lasted for many minutes. Finally he returned and extended his hand to the small figure seated in the front row.

"Thank you, *Signor* Gabriel," he said. It was all that was needed. The applause lasted for minutes.

The band started to play again. The mayor beckoned the assembled people to a nearby tent where large tables were laden with dishes piled high with pastas, artichokes and cheese, salads with olives and wild fennel, lamb in lemon sauce, pastries with almonds and chocolate and bottles of new wine, last year's vintage from the surrounding vineyards. Aidonesi and visitors, men, women, and children, filled their plates and ate with gusto as they talked excitedly about the return of the ancient goddess and the new museum that would hold her. It was one of the most genuinely joyous events Jason had ever seen.

Toward the end of lunch, Gabriel came up to him and nodded toward the shed where the statue lay.

"She'd have been a hell of an addition to the museum. I really wanted to see her there."

Jason voiced the thought that had been with him for the past six months. "Be glad you didn't get her, Andrew. This is where she belongs."

"You don't understand. She was going to belong to *me*. I wanted her the moment I saw her in London."

Jason went still. "What are you talking about? When was that?"

Gabriel hesitated. A small, wry smile that said nothing and everything came across his face. "Last year. Before Martin was there."

Jason's thoughts tumbled. The missing pieces of the puzzle, the ones that had swirled at the edge of his consciousness and that he had never seemed able to pull together, fell into place.

"You! Not Martin. Not even Maybank. Andrew, you've been behind this all along."

The crinkles at the corner of Gabriel's eyes deepened. "Oh? Tell me more."

"If you saw the Athena in London, then Maybank must have told you about it. Before he told Martin."

"Go on."

"And if Maybank did that, then the two of you were working together. But Martin had no idea about that, did he?"

Gabriel's eyes sparkled slightly. "Good, Jason. Please go on." The smile broadened.

"You and Maybank? How would that have happened? Was Maybank working for you?"

"Ah. I was wondering when you'd figure that out. What do you think I've been doing for the past few years, Jason? Creating museums, buying art, buying art galleries. I bought Maybank's two years ago."

"And you set up Martin? You told Maybank to offer him the deal? Why would you do that?"

"Trust, Jason."

"Trust?"

"Exactly that. In my world, it's the most precious thing one can have. I need to trust everyone I do business with, everyone around me. I had to know if I could trust Martin. Would he go for the deal or would he play it straight? He went for the deal. He failed my test."

"Would you really have allowed Maybank to pay him? To buy the statue?" He tried to keep the irony out of his voice.

"Of course not. The museum would have got it, though. But for you."

Jason thought for a moment. "Can I ask a blunt question?"

"How blunt?"

"Very blunt. Are you really that mistrustful?" *Are you really that paranoid?* The question came unbidden.

"If you were me, Jason, you'd be the same way. In my world, trust is everything. It's the glue that holds us together. There can be no meaningful relationship without it." A shadow crossed the old man's face.

"I need to trust the people I depend on. If I can't do that, I don't want them around. There are people everywhere who'd like to take advantage of me. Some of them are trying to do that now. I just haven't dealt with them yet."

The crazy old coot. Crazy like a fox. But a *murderer*? He had to ask. "And the killers, Andrew? The ones Maybank sent after me? You told him to do that?"

"Never, Jason. I'd never do that. Maybank tried to call me after you'd seen him, but we never connected. I was on a flight coming back from Tokyo. He panicked and brought them in himself. I tried to return his call the next day, but he was already dead."

Gabriel paused and looked away again. A long minute passed before he spoke. "You may not think so, but Maybank did me a favor when he tried to cut you in on the deal. But you didn't take it. Martin failed the test. You passed. I shouldn't have been surprised, should I?"

The old man shook his head slightly, a rueful smile on his face. His eyes turned to the shed that held the statue. "Damn it, Jason, I really wanted her. But you just wouldn't give up. You had to keep going."

He paused for a moment, his sharp blue eyes focused on Jason's. "I can see we're going to have a few good fights about what the museum should and shouldn't buy. But Jason," he said, pointing to the shed, "we're building a museum, aren't we? So you're going to have to find something that's as good as she is. Aren't you?"

And with that, Andrew Gabriel took hold of his cane and disappeared into the crowd.

66416939R00195

Made in the USA
Charleston, SC
19 January 2017